The
Graduates

The Graduates

Edward Whitley

HAMISH HAMILTON

LONDON

For Araminta

First published in Great Britain 1986
by Hamish Hamilton Ltd
Garden House 57–59 Long Acre London WC2E 9JZ

Copyright © 1986 by Edward Whitley

British Library Cataloguing in Publication Data

Whitley, Edward
    The graduates.
    1. University of Oxford—Alumni—Interviews
    I. Title
    378.425'74   LF525

    ISBN 0–241–11788–7

Photoset and printed in Great Britain by
Redwood Burn Limited, Trowbridge, Wiltshire

Contents

Acknowledgements

Although *The Graduates* is narrated through me, at some of the interviews either Araminta, Marcia, or Rebecca, or David, Harry or John came along with me. Without them the questions would never have been so successful, and the book would never have got off the ground—nor would doing it have been such fun.

I would also like to thank John Murray Publishers for permission to quote from Sir John Betjeman's poetry.

E.W.
January, 1986

Introduction

In my second year at Oxford I moved into a large farmhouse with seven friends. We were all sitting in the kitchen one day wondering what to do when someone mentioned a magazine. It was quickly imagined that it would be eight issues, edited by each of us in turn, comprising short stories by Guy and Araminta, poems by Tracey, drawings by Harry and Marcia, David's photographs of Oxford, feature articles by John and interviews by Edward. What it would actually be about was never resolved, apart from something to do with Oxford and rather more to do with us.

The magazine never took off because nobody would buy advertising space. Impatient restaurant owners shook their heads and shooed us away as we fumbled to explain what it would be. So by the time Finals came and swept everything away, all we were left with was a drawer of unfinished stories, a folder of Oxford photographs and a handful of interviews.

Interviews had been my quota, and I started off by visiting local Oxford figures such as Mr Carter of Hall Brothers, various butchers and fishmongers from the Covered Market, and Fred Elkins, the landlord of the Victoria Arms. It then struck me that people who had left Oxford might also be interesting, so I began finding out who were the household names who had been to the University and writing to them asking if they could spare an hour or so to reminisce about Oxford.

One of the first things I found out about interviewing people is that they don't like it. Without exception, all the people who make up this book refused my first letter, and most of them refused my second and third. A typical reply to my sixth or seventh letter came from Philip Larkin:

Dear Mr Whitley,

The Graduates

Professor Larkin has asked me to say that he finds your communications on this subject tiresome, and that he hopes that there will be no more of them.

Yours sincerely,

M. Elliott
Secretary to Professor Larkin

or from Margaret Thatcher:

Dear Mr Whitley,

Thank you for your letter of 2nd May. I understand that you have been in touch with my office on a large number of occasions.

You will appreciate that the Prime Minister receives literally hundreds of requests of this kind, and there are simply not enough hours in the day to accommodate them. I regret having to disappoint you yet again, but there is, I fear, no point in your pursuing the matter.

I am sorry. But you surely will understand the pressures upon the British Prime Minister's time.

Yours sincerely,

B. Ingham

The first breakthrough came when, just two weeks before my Finals, Iris Murdoch finally agreed to see me. This was to change the direction of the book completely. As normal, we started off talking about her Oxford days, but then gradually found ourselves straying towards subjects far beyond—the world of her philosophy, her ideas about language, art-forms, people, dreams, monsters. As I was drawn in by her imaginative power, it seemed a waste to confine questions to her memories of Oxford. So likewise for the rest of the interviews, whilst Oxford was always something which the subjects shared and which became more absorbing as it was re-defined, its real significance was to act as the frame for the opening questions which would then break up and uncover the patterns of conversation and feelings of whoever I was talking to. Dudley Moore noticed this—when we said goodbye, he looked at me with surprise and said: 'Was any of that of any use? We've come a long way from Oxford.'

But I did not interview Dudley Moore until over a year after I left Oxford, and in the meantime I had started a job and the book was still just a handful of cassettes. With Iris Murdoch as a cornerstone, I began to transcribe them and see what sort of articles they would make, plugging away for others at the same time and slowly adding more and more scalps to the list.

Something which had struck me about most published interviews is that the writer generally gives the interviewee very little to say. He hogs the limelight with his own observations and heavily edits the text to bring out a few headlines. I decided always to quote verbatim and in full context to keep the feeling of conversation present, intact with all the non-sequiturs and contradictions of speech. This I hoped would keep alive the immediacy of two people talking.

In parallel with this, I began to learn not to be afraid of asking direct personal questions. I realised that there was no point in going to see someone without trying to find out what sort of values they held closest to their lives. And if there is only an hour to do this, there is no time to be squeamish of asking the sort of questions which made Michael Palin run out of his house or Cardinal Hume tell me to go away.

Looking back on that period, I remember it like a photograph album; there is me asking international directory enquiries for Mrs Gandhi's number: 'Yes—*the* Mrs Gandhi'; my stomach turning in embarrassment as Michael Palin ran away; lunch at 'Strawberry Hole'; photographing Dudley Moore on Long Island in the evening sun; Cardinal Hume turning off the tape recorder; playing croquet with Auberon Waugh at Combe Florey; shivering in the frost outside Sir Robin Day's house; laughing with Bob Hawke as he warned me about 'going arse over tip into the harbour'; leaving Sir John Betjeman in his wheelchair in the dim Chelsea room and knowing he would shortly die.

I suppose the book has grown a long way from the original magazine, but it still has the basic theme of being something to do with Oxford and rather more to do with me. Instead of being a series of autobiographical reminiscences, it has developed into a collection of conversations which, although still linked by the sequence of Oxford changing through this century, are more importantly linked by the sequence of my reactions to these people. Perhaps that is all in the context of Oxford. It is still about education, and in many ways writing the book became my education at the hands of these different people in their different worlds.

Sir Harold Acton

CHRIST CHURCH, 1922–26

'The Railway Club was founded by John Sutro, who was omniscient about railways from their earliest days; every historical fact and he knows it—the Orient Express, the Flying Scotsman, their timetables, he has everything in his mind. And he thought how fine it would be to have dinner somewhere en route!

'So we would engage a whole train going to Reading or some place and dine. On the journey, we would stop at various stations for toasts, where we would be met by the station master and pose for group photographs, and there would be speeches—chiefly in honour of railway trains and the pleasure of feeling rolled off into the distance with the views ... how the early trains had inspired Turner—*Rain, Steam and Speed*, an early painting of a railway train advancing, rapidly; poems on speed by Henley. It was all rather a lark, but well organised.

'Once we stayed at the Royal Albion Hotel in Brighton, which was owned by a charming old man who had been a boxing expert, Sir Harry Preston. He had been much favoured and knighted by King Edward VII. He was very jolly and entertained us freely with the most wonderful meals and brandy—always with mineral water. He didn't believe in drinking brandy neat.

'We had excellent dinners, very good wines. In those days, England was full of excellent wines—burgundy, claret. We would drink copiously on the journey, and arrive back in a rather sad condition. Really! Some of them ... Evelyn Waugh was very fond of the bottle!'

As though polishing an old lamp, Sir Harold Acton rubbed one hand over the other and with a genie's grin conjured more spells from the past: 'I must say, after public school it was marvellous to be able to

'There has never to my knowledge, and I have lived in or near Oxford for much of my life, been a more famous or prominent figure as an undergraduate.'

Lord Longford

entertain in one's own rooms. I once had (which I've never had since) oyster, cooked oyster—rather rich. And they provided mulled claret in the winter and delicious cups in the summer—all very lavish after school fare. School was very austere; Oxford was anything but that. You could have had cold mutton, but mostly if you gave a lunch you ordered what you imagined people were going to enjoy, something a little out of the ordinary. I suppose people who entered only for athletics and were thinking of their form and athletic ability starved themselves, but I'm afraid none of my friends thought of that.

'Several smart, slightly older, Americans came to Oxford in my time and introduced us to cocktails, which before then didn't exist—it would be just madeira or sherry. This was viewed as the beginning of decay and decadence—everyone had "cocktail" parties from that moment on. These Americans imposed American ways of living, rather smart ways of living, which involved beautiful cars, beautiful girls. They were well to do, not to say rich, and they also introduced us to modern dancing. The Black Bottom and the Boogie Woogie replaced the Charleston and we had a bohemian club dancing to all this called The Hypocrites, where we had tremendous goings-on. Robert Byron painted the walls with amusing pictures of Queen Victoria and Disraeli and Gladstone, and girls came to dance from London. It really was most amusing.'

'Whereabout was it?'

'It was a ramshackle old tumbledown Elizabethan building in St Aldates', with two ramshackle old tumbledown servants who prepared sausages and cakes—simple food, but in the summer, of course, asparagus: the most marvellous asparagus! But as we had to wee-wee into a pail in the kitchen, the smell of these asparagus was, to put it mildly, really rather offensive! Most of the people there went in much more for swilling beer than drinking wine. Living here, I confess I never took to beer.

'The club was eventually closed by the Proctors because it became too noisy, too riotous and balls were given which were not allowed, and the girls from London were discovered, who were not allowed either.'

The phosphorescent reputation of 1920's Oxford was largely shaped by Sir Harold, who introduced his contemporaries to the world of modernism, to 'the intoxication of the new'. His taste for the exotic and the contemporary dispersed the post-war gloom:

'I believe very much in colour, so when I went up to Oxford after the First World War, everything seemed very drab. There were many people who had come from the Army, like the poet Robert Graves who lived at Islip, who had been gassed or shell-shocked and who were keeping Oxford under the shadow of war. One had to revolt against that and bring a little colour into the scene with bright shirts, bright waistcoats and so forth. One could express oneself in beautiful clothes. There was a good deal of showy dressing by under-graduates—one had Hall Brothers at one's disposal to broaden or limit one's trousers (in my case they broadened them). Even Evelyn Waugh wore rather bright checks and Robert Byron wore deer-stalker hats. There was a certain extravagance in costume, with people even wearing velveteens, which I never went for—it was too 1890-ish for me, but a man called Prendergast at Balliol wore very strange costumes—long velvets, silken jackets—the sort of things one might wear for smoking in the evening.

'Nothing outrageous by modern standards. You walk down the King's Road—I haven't been down there for many years, but when I was last there, I was told it was well worth it, so I did—and everybody seemed extremely exaggerated in their costume. Girls like witches with extraordinary hats and blacking around their eyes, young men equally strange in their clothes and make-up—at Oxford we were pale in comparison.'

We were sitting in the pink shell-covered grotto in the garden of La Pietra, 'an amusing place for a pow-wow', and as the endymion language whispered on, it seemed to weave us further into the web of this rose-tinted past as though into a cloud of candy floss.

Sir Harold's turn of phrase has been much mimicked: 'Real G-g-green Chartreuse, made before the expulsion of the monks. There are five distinct tastes as it trickles over the tongue. It is like swallowing a sp-spectrum,' but few of the subsequent Anthony Blanches have shared his intellectual acumen, which I realised, as he recalled an episode later adopted by Evelyn Waugh, is the core of his flamboyance:

'One of my early books had been published in my first term, *Aquarium*, which had an unexpected success for a book of verse. I couldn't, wouldn't want to see it now, it would horrify me, but then I was very proud of it and very pleased with it and I used to recite the poems at public meetings. One was full of oneself; one thought one-self a genius. I think all young people should think themselves geniuses.

'I consciously belonged to a rather vociferous minority. I remember they asked me to recite a poem for the League of Nations party in Worcester Gardens. I recited through a microphone what had then fairly recently appeared, T. S. Eliot's *The Waste Land*. This caused a terrific sensation! People got up and hissed and walked out saying it was "outrageous", the *Oxford Magazine* said it was "absolutely insult-ing people to read such nonsense", and now it's a classic. One of my Chinese pupils at Peking University translated it into Chinese.'

'Successfully?'

'That I doubt, because how can all those references to Wagner, to Shakespeare be understood? It is like a Latin canto—it brings in quotations from all sorts of people, a line from Verlaine: "*Et O ces voix d'enfants, chantant dans la coupole!*" It ends with Indian, with Sanskrit: "*Shantih shantih shantih.*" How could the Chinese, without knowledge of this, without knowledge of Shakespeare: "Good night, sweet ladies, good night, good night"—they wouldn't know what it means. You have to be familiar with English literature and with a certain amount of music and foreign literature too. There's a line from Dante in it, and there's Gérard de Nerval: "*Le Prince d'Aquitaine à la tour abolie*" which is not generally known, you know. I don't think that that's very well known even in England. So *The Waste Land* is full of that; Eliot is full of that. He is a bookish poet, and at the same time, by fitting these together, he produces marvellous,' he paused, 'cinerama. Ha, ha! Well, wonderful but rather despairing.'

The delight Sir Harold takes in artistic licence makes his persuasion for the controversial so infectious, and it was easy to imagine him as an undergraduate enjoying the highly conspicuous task of redefining the critical expectations of his contemporaries: 'It is true that I was being very precocious, but I think Oxford had been a little on the bleak side before I came up. There was still a fog of war over the city. The poetry which was admired at that time was all Georgian under the influence of J. C. Squire, who ran the long-defunct *London Mercury*. The poems in the *London Mercury* and in the Georgian anthology under the editorship of Sir Edward Marsh were of a uniform banality. There are, I suppose, some exceptions—W. J. Turner occasionally, Edward Shanks, but most of these poets are rather forgotten now. The tone of this poetry was very much cricket-playing, ale-drinking, Shropshire-laddishness under the influence of A. E. Housman. And, you know, it was all so dull.

'We wanted the funfair, the columbines, the harlequins, the Commedia dell'Arte which we have here in Italy—we wanted to have colour! And modern music—Stravinsky and Willy Walton, who now lives at Istia (poor man, he's almost blind), but then he produced the music for Edith Sitwell's *Façade*, which was highly coloured verse, and he wrote very amusing, witty music. I don't know if you have ever heard it, but it really is delightful and it still wears well. Funnily enough, they occasionally do it on Italian radio.

'And the Sitwells were bringing in a taste for Baroque art; Sacheverell's book *Southern Baroque Art* was sensational when it appeared, and people started to look at buildings which they had been taught by Ruskin to despise. Everybody had been fond of Gothic architecture (which we have now returned to through John Betjeman), but the Sitwells were devoted to Italian, Portuguese and Spanish architecture. And then Sacheverell Sitwell wrote poems—*Dr Donne and Gargantua*—which seemed perhaps better than they actually were, but they were very stimulating after the endless poems about ash and cedar and ale—cedar and cider!

'Once the Oxford Union invited me to speak on "Modern Art", and I remember it was full of highly antagonistic people against me. I was much more for modern art than I am now, but I also liked Betjeman, and we organised an exhibition of early Victorian art, which was banned by the Proctors—the pretext was that it took people away from their work, their lectures, their tutorials! So we wrote a violent letter to the *Daily Mail*, and journalists came to interview us and see what we had gathered, which was a number of things all very much in the Betjeman taste—fruit under glass domes, amusing objects made of shells, paintings by early Victorians (who are now coming back to fashion) like Augustus Egg. We pretended, even if we didn't admire her very much, that we were Victorian sympathists!'

Sir Harold leant back in the wicker chair and laughed. Dressed in a dove-grey suit, he still has the crystal-cut elegance for which he was remembered at Oxford. Lord Longford had described him: 'There has never to my knowledge, and I have lived in or near Oxford for much of my life, been a more famous or prominent figure as an undergraduate. He was the most glamorous figure, wearing a bowler hat, artificial whiskers and Oxford bags, his own invented style of trouser. He used to nance about like this....'

Sir Harold leant forward and I noticed how large his head was, rounded and smooth as the head of a Victorian sailor doll:

'In England, all people who are artists or fond of the arts tend to seem rebels, because the majority are totally indifferent. Consequently one is fighting against a mass of people who are only interested in football, cricket and that sort of thing, and not in what is being built or painted.

'As far as I was concerned, I was invariably up against the philistines. The rather extreme athletes used to throw us into Mercury, sack our rooms, throw out our books. There was a good deal of rough antagonism. Once I knocked one down (one must protect oneself).'

In defiance of these philistines, Sir Harold founded a literary club, 'The Ordinary'. The friends he invited to speak, however, were rather more than ordinary in literary influence:

'I used to invite Walter de la Mare and T. S. Eliot down to lecture us, Robert Graves, Edith Sitwell certainly. For Edith Sitwell we gave a huge party with a tremendous cake, a long Swiss roll with *Edith*

Sitwell inscribed in icing, and she was superb. But the most extraordinary, the most sensational, was Gertrude Stein—ah! She was an old friend of mine from Florentine days, who occasionally came here to visit her brother, Leo Stein, with whom she eventually quarrelled. He was the first collector of Picasso and Matisse—it wasn't really Gertrude, but she followed him and they quarrelled over that, because they were both very proud and each thought that they had been the first to spot these geniuses. Well, I invited her to speak, and everybody expected some young, beautiful or striking or strange bohemian figure, instead of which a little elderly woman, extremely dowdy with a strong American accent, appeared. She read out *Composition and Explanation* which sounded absolute nonsense to the ordinary ear, but when you read it there were certain things she was trying to get out— she was trying to produce a thing called "the continuous present", and, to exemplify this, she recited a series of portraits of people she knew, people like Edith Sitwell and Jean Cocteau among them. These were pen portraits put together with words anyhow, with repetitions. It really was something which had not happened at Oxford before.'

'And what about Evelyn Waugh?' We turned to that familiar question with reluctance:

'Everybody asks me that. We were very great friends, but he was a character rather apart. He had been at Lancing, which was a small school which he rather despised, and was at Hertford, which he also rather despised. He loathed the Dean of Balliol, whose name he brings into his novel—Crogue, Cran, Craw—I'm afraid my memory is going. Towards eighty, one's memory is not so fresh. It is so long since I've given a thought to this—I live in the moment, for the present, for tomorrow, and I don't think of the past. I really don't and I'm distressed by it.

'*Brideshead Revisited* is the book I like least of Evelyn's—his best books are the war books: *Sword of Honour* is classic, better than any book I've ever read about the last war—the most vivid, the very atmosphere, temper of the war. But I regard *Brideshead* as a bit of nostalgia, rather false—I dislike the prolonged death scene. The Oxford part certainly borrowed a good deal from one's own experience. It is my rooms which are described as the hero's with the teddy bear, and as for the teddy bear—of course, John Betjeman was always photographed with a teddy bear as a small boy.

'Evelyn always used, like all writers, experiences and friends; he picked a little here, a little there, to describe the figures in *Brideshead*.

'... The name of that Don he hated was it Crotchwell? Crutwell! And Evelyn used to shout insults outside his window: "The Dean of Balliol sleeps with men! Sleeps with men!" Poor Crutwell was slightly dotty anyway. In the end he had to go to a sort of asylum, I heard. That may be true, although I may be libelling the poor man! But he was thoroughly hated, and he was full of violent likes and dislikes. He was a small man, physically, and, like many of those people, was more pugnacious than larger, taller people. Urquhart, his real name—and "Sligger", his nickname. And Sligger used to have these reading parties in a Swiss chalet. And Cyril Connolly was always among them—yes, I seem to remember he chose some people more for their looks than for their brains.

'As far as I was concerned, I was invariably up against the philistines.'
Sir Harold Acton, Florence

'Those philosophers!' Sir Harold laughed. 'Kant is the best name for a philosopher. I had one living next door to me in Christ Church. My scout told me that he once found him lying naked in two hip baths saying: "Go away—I'm an oyster!" Well, I suppose Oxford hasn't changed all that much!'

We left the grotto to catch the last view of Florence before the sun went down. As we walked to the edge of the garden, he looked at me mischievously:

'Do you have female scouts now? It must be embarrassing—those eager female eyes, and there may be golden hairs on the sheets....'

Before I had time to answer, through a gap in the yew hedge was the view of Florence with the burnt orange rooftops spread out beneath us like so much gingerbread. We stared as the sunlight slanted darker, until only the Duomo was left in the light.

'Do you know what they once wanted to build here?'

I shook my head. He looked back to the orange and blue skyline, and pronounced the words with curiosity as though trying out a foreign limerick:

'A Hilton hotel!'

The Marquess of Bath

CHRIST CHURCH, 1924–26

'During my time, Oxford was beginning to move, by Jove. The war had ended in 1919, and the Bright Young Things had just started doing the Charleston and carrying on like hell. Women were beginning to get rather drunk, which they never used to, and smoked with cigarette holders.'

Lord Bath practically smacked his lips at the memory. It was going to be a rip-roaring spin into Twenties nostalgia. He had met me at the door of Longleat House and, a curious blend of host and visitor, guided me around the crimson ropes to his library. Here, safely out of bounds of tourist inspection, he sat back in his leather armchair and gathered his assorted dogs to heel.

'Oxford was so different in those days from what it is now: one didn't go up there to learn anything, one went up to make friends and have a good time. We aimed to get away with as little work as possible.'

Lord Bath is nonplussed by the trappings of academia: 'I'm not sure that being academic really helps you. All these "A"-levels needed to get a job are ridiculous, and what is all this fuss about the "Eleven Plus"—does it really show if you are an intellectual or not? All you need to get you round in life is common sense—look at Churchill!

'I was never very clever. I was always bottom of the class at Harrow, and only at Harrow because I failed the exam to Eton. My family had always been to Eton, so people went to the Headmaster there and said: "Look here, you really ought to take Weymouth—his family has been here for ever and ever." "I cannot take him," he replied, "he is a moron beyond reach. Completely uneducated and could not be educated!"

'He is a moron beyond reach. Completely uneducated and could not be educated.'

The Headmaster of Eton describing Viscount Weymouth (*top right*)

'So I went to Harrow, which was very bad then. We had two black boys, which was unheard of in those days—a Jamaican and an Iraqian. The Headmaster welcomed a "Viscount Weymouth" to elevate the social class—I was the only Lord there. At Oxford we were all called "Harrow Cads", because Harrovians never went there, so all my friends were Etonians.'

'And what did you read?'

'Well, if you read any subject apart from Agriculture, you were not allowed to run a car, so I chose Agriculture like a shot! It would also help us as we were all going to be landlords, but I never did any work and three weeks before the exams, I had to be tutored by a chap—a very nice whatever-you-call-'em,' he pondered, 'don; he taught me in less than three weeks what it would have taken three years to learn. I passed the exam, but because I was fed up with not working and only spending money, I left after my first year and went to America— couldn't do anything else: I hadn't got the brain!

'At Oxford, you see, I was just a playboy! At Harrow, my father had given me pocket money of £3 a term and an extra £3 at Christmas, which made £12 a year. On going up to Oxford, he gave me £600 a year. I thought I was a millionaire! I used to spend it like water: I bought endless gramophones, and started to collect saxophones. I never played the saxophone—I didn't want to sweat to learn how to. In one year, I got into debt to the tune of £2,000. That was for the first and last time in my life. Never been a penny overdrawn since then. You see, it didn't please my father very much; my mother came to see me (she had to do all those sorts of things) and said: "Your Father doesn't like you to be overdrawn. He thinks it is very bad, but he will pay up as long as you haven't spent it on wine or women." I hadn't spent it on either wine or women—just saxophones! He paid up.

'As a matter of fact, I didn't know any women at Oxford. I cannot even remember whether there were any. My company was completely male ... and Brian Howard!'

'Who was he?'

'He was the chief man there, and a roaring queer. He had a great influence on us, and we all did whatever he suggested—I don't know why, because none of us were queer, but we did mad things, were constantly seen to be tight in the afternoon and were despised by the rowing people!'

Blood ran strong and blue in those Twenties days: 'We were supposedly "Aesthetes", but that was a lot of twaffle. We were all members of the Bullingdon Club, where one was to learn how to get drunk. We went to such expense, that we were vomiting outside between courses'—he seemed to be giving advice—'but at least it taught you

13

'Even now, people come up and want to talk to me because I'm a Marquess. That's all bosh.'

The Marquess of Bath

how to behave in public! Everybody has to go through that stage, and we did it at Oxford. All I remember about those dinners is being roaring drunk and going outside to be sick.

'If there was any prank to be got up to, Brian Howard would lead it. After one breakfast, we all drove hell for leather up to London. In those days, you could park anywhere, and we parked outside Selfridges. In his very queerish way, Brian Howard decided to play "Follow my Leader", so we followed him as he jumped over all the counters and clothes racks and beds! If you did that nowadays, you would be thrown out, but then people were pretty good-humoured. Old Brian Howard! He was absolutely as gay as you could make anybody, but, as these people sometimes are, he was a very forceful personality and had us all completely under his thumb.'

Lord Bath was by now well into his stride. 'Another queer was Harry Acton's brother Woolly. He wasn't of any influence at all. He used to hunt with the Drag; that was for respectability. Old Woolly was once rather keen on a chap in Christ Church, who is now a respectable politician, who lived in the top of Canterbury Quad, and so he visited him, but had all his advances resisted. As the boy turned round to put on the gramophone, Woolly threw himself out of the window! Drunk as a lord, he fell sixty feet to the ground and got straight up again. All the matter with him was that his monocle had broken. He then went for a swim in Mercury Pond and swam around to sober up. The dons gave him stick for the swim, but never remarked upon the jump! Always full of liquor, Woolly....'

His train of reminiscence was interrupted by the sounds of cars' horns through the window. A small traffic jam of tourists was sorting itself out on the way to the Safari Park. I asked Lord Bath how he reacted to the changes in the class structure, which had meant that stately homes like Longleat had become commercial leisure centres.

'Up to the Great War, it was the good old days. The lord of the manor was lord of the manor and had forty servants. The working people were working people and kept to their place. Whenever you wanted anything, you rang the bell. You would never dream of getting it yourself. Those were the good old days for my class of person! Not for anybody else, though.

'After the War, things began to move. People began to dress differently and have different, new ideas. Trade unionism, which never existed in my time, began to expand, the middle classes began to grow richer, and now, yes, you find houses like this open to the public. I don't resent it—it was my idea, as one way of keeping the place going.

'If you were to ask me whether I would prefer to live in the old society or the new, I would answer that from my personal point of view of comfort—I would sooner live as I was—but from a practical point of view, it is far better today, because everybody should have an equal chance. This is how it should be. Take Oxford, for example: in my day it was simply not open to the comprehensive type of person. There was class distinction to keep them out; that is the great trouble with this country—class distinction. Even now, people come up and want to talk to me because I'm a Marquess. That's all bosh.

'You cannot get away from there being poor people—everybody will complain about money, you do, I do, there will always be poor people, so I hope fascism wins out. It's communism in reverse, if you like, but as I see it, it allows the individual to go on ahead, whereas communism levels everybody down.

'The future is going to be Communism. Look at Wedgie Benn. People say he isn't, but he is. When you say Communism, you always think of Russia, but old Wedgie is introducing a form of Communism.

'There is no doubt that the Left will get to dominate this family, for instance. I don't mind that—I live in the present and work in the present.'

'But as a Marquess you do have a seat in the House of Lords, so you could campaign against it,' I suggested. He brushed this idea aside.

'I am all for abolishing the House of Lords. I think it's scandalous that just because I was born a peer, I can go and sit in the Lords. I've got no idea whatsoever how to govern a country! The House of Lords as such should be abolished, and peers elected on the basis of merit. If you had done something of worth, then you should be elected a life peer, and it should be those people who run the country. They would vote whichever way they thought, and the electorate's influence could be damned. If that was the case, it would stop the politician being terrified of failing to be elected. This is today's mistake in politics—in a modern democracy, the politician is always looking back over his shoulder to impress his constituency, and not concentrating on the job. Look at the Americans! Always having to kowtow to some wretched sector in their State where they need the vote. It's an absolute racket—they're campaigning for votes so hard that they never get the chance to govern!

'Now, look here, I have to go off for a meeting with the Estate Manager. I suppose you'd like to look around the house, wouldn't you?'

As I was introduced to the guide, and he prepared to go, he fired his parting shot.

'You're at Oxford, aren't you? What's all this about an "Oxford Myth"? Evelyn Waugh was at Cambridge, wasn't he?'

Well pleased, he went off to look at his accounts. Judging by Longleat's success, I imagined they would please him as well.

Lord Longford

NEW COLLEGE, 1924–27

Lord Longford shares with traffic wardens that phenomenon of being someone for whom everybody has indignant loathing: 'I'd love to meet him', my grandmother told me, 'I'd ask him what he bloody well thinks he's playing at.' Henry Root wrote: 'What a foolish old man! He'd ban the *Sun* and the *News of the World*, but would set child rapists and killers free ... If he succeeds, I only hope they all go and live with him.'

He has become such a bogey man that, as I walked along Museum Road to meet him, I imagined him in a pantomime: 'Sssssssss! ... He's behind you.... Oh yes he is!'

Whilst I stood by some dustbins and hesitated at Number 42, a tramp crept through the rubbish towards the door. He bent down towards the keyhole, and I recognised the back of the humpty-dumpty head of Lord Longford. I said hello and shook the squashy jumble of knuckles of his right hand. We went upstairs and into his office where he shrugged his jacket off onto the floor and tucked his maroon sweat-shirt into greying underpants (a habit which John Carey had once told me implied a pre-First World War nanny).

'On the one hand, I led the ordinary college life and played games. You see this scar here,' he pulled his trouser up over one knee to show a long scar across the bone, 'this is from playing soccer for New College. I played hockey and rugby which was the average honest-to-God college life with plenty of work. In my last year I shared digs with Hugh Gaitskell, and we became something more than average when we both got Firsts. So I was a respectable if not very exciting college figure, except in my last year I met Lord Birkenhead and joined the Bulling-

'It is awfully irritating when people go around saying, "Widmerpool is meant to be Lord Longford." It never crossed my mind, if one may so put it, he doesn't greatly interest me as a character.'

Anthony Powell

don Club. They regarded themselves as the lords of creation.'

Lord Longford seemed oddly dislocated from what he was describing. He sat in a careless lump on the chair, his crooked hair and glasses giving me the impression of a Dickensian effigy—a sort of cross between Pickwick and Fagin, and his voice had the texture of slurry with his words getting all muddled between carrion teeth, but the past he was describing was the very stuff of Bright Young Things.

'In the Twenties, people were desperate for fun—I remember I started a society called The Athanasians, where we would all dine in clerical dress. We looked rather comic all dressed up as clergymen! We would have the annual dinner in some pub up in Headington, then there would be a race down the hill into Oxford and up along the High Street to Carfax with all these clerical robes flying behind us!

'I came from a large family, so I was accustomed to fun, but I hadn't been accustomed to smart society either from school or home until I found myself in the Bullingdon. Even Evelyn Waugh would have conceded that that was glamorous.'

At his own mention of Evelyn Waugh, Lord Longford sat bolt upright and straightened out his turkey neck as though in response to a challenge: 'Evelyn Waugh wouldn't have moved in smart circles whilst he was an undergraduate. He was a beer drinker, and would have been in beer-swilling circles. He only moved into society in London, so he came to know Oxford in a grander way later.

'And after Oxford, before I was married, I did see a lot of him in London. We went to a lot of parties and did a good deal of social climbing together—we were both at the Savile Club. Later, of course, Evelyn left the Savile Club, and joined White's. I joined the Athenaeum and then the Garrick, but in 1930 we were both very close and when Auberon was born Evelyn asked me to be his godfather.'

'And there was Harold Acton too,' I said.

'Harold Acton was a great man in the Oxford of his day. He was called an "aesthete".'

'What would be a definition of an "aesthete"?'

'They would have liked to define themselves as "lovers of the beautiful", but the "beautiful" included loving people and there were very few girls. A lot of the aesthetes were homosexual, a lot of them were not, but pretended to be. Everybody would address each other, "Oh, my dear..." in the manner of what would now be called "pansies". There used to be rather indecent songs at the Drama Society's Smoker. I remember one sung by a boy with effeminate gestures wearing a roll-neck sweater:

I'm just a jumper boy,
A high-necked jumper boy,
My mother's only joy
(I swear it's true).
But when I do my tricks,
I'm in an awful fix,
Because I only know the way...
... To jump a boy!

I would now regard that as pornographic.'

'Didn't you then?'

'I wasn't in that world particularly—I only went to that show as an escort.'

I waited for the answer.

'Well, I suppose as there weren't any girls, homosexualism was very much more natural—like the Army. I'll tell you a little story about homosexuals. I was coming back from lunch the other day, and I stopped to buy an evening paper at this stall in Tottenham Court Road. Next to the paper was the *Gay News*. The man saw me looking at it, and said: "Do you want to buy it?" So I said: "Are you a homosexual?" "No governor," he said, "I'm sorry—the missus wouldn't let me do it for you!"

'Quite ridiculous, as I have six children!'

Lord Longford didn't enjoy the joke as much as I did. He returned to the heterosexual fold.

'Do you know, I never met an undergraduette (are they still called that?) during my whole time at Oxford! It wasn't that I was a woman-hater (I had four sisters and I used to go up to London for rather mild deb dances), but I never met a girl until my last day and then I met my wife.'

With his pebble glasses blinking silver in the sun and the head above domed like Tintin's Professor Calculus, Lord Longford incongruously told one of those love stories which seem to happen in the world of Oxford summers.

'Finals were over, and I was at the New College Ball. It was the middle of the night, and my partner had left me. I remember I was lying fast asleep in the Garden Quad, and this girl came up and leant over me and kissed me. I was wearing Bullingdon coat-tails, so I was probably looking my best. I woke up and realised that this was my last day at Oxford. She was very beautiful—everyone compared her to Zuleika Dobson—but it was the end of my time there. She was then Hugh Gaitskell's girlfriend. So I went down, she stayed at Oxford and I didn't see her again for three years.

'And three years later, I went to see her at Oxford on impulse—really as a result of a dream I had had in which I visited her. So I called on her at her rooms, and then she came to stay with me in Ireland. We finally got engaged in the waiting room of the railway station at Stoke-on-Trent. Have you ever been there?'

Once married, Lord Longford left London and went back to teach at Oxford. It was now the 1930s: 'People associate the Thirties with Auden and Spender and the Spanish Civil War—well, poetically that might have been true.

'Of course, in 1933 there was the King and Country resolution passed at the Union. That was a protest against the patriotic appeals which had led to the First War. The books which were being read were Robert Graves' *Goodbye to all That*, Hemingway's *A Farewell to Arms* and Remarque's *All Quiet on the Western Front*; there was a great feeling that young men had been led to slaughter by horrible old people. There was great interest in left-wing politics—I joined the Labour Party in 1936.

'By the approach of the war, this convulsive political interest in the Left died down, and Churchill wrote: "Little did the foolish boys who passed this resolution realise that they were soon to conquer or die gloriously and prove themselves the finest generation ever bred in Britain."

'I was so upset when the Labour Party voted against conscription that I felt I must do something. Although I was unqualified, I could ride (rather badly) so I joined the Territorial Cavalry. We had a lovely time galloping around Port Meadow before breakfast.

'By 1937, 1938, the war was a great shadow—it was hanging over us, if I may say so, much more definitely than is hanging over you. Since the war, I have never felt that young people have ever been in danger of being killed. Then I was teaching undergraduates and I felt most of them would be killed.'

After the war, Lord Longford moved into the world of politics and social reform. Taking his political career first, which has been confined to the seat in the House of Lords which he inherited from his elder brother, I asked why his belief in socialism had not involved, as with Tony Benn, giving up his inherited peerage. He immediately sensed the change in pace and was on guard with a straight bat:

'I did try to give up my title—I tried to renounce it—but I was unable to due to the technicality that I had originally accepted it. So I am in the clear.'

This answer seemed inadequate, and when I said so, he was quickly provoked by my cynicism.

'It is patronising and silly to say that they seemed "extenuating circumstances"—that's a silly remark, the first silly remark you've made. You asked why hadn't I given up my title, and I answered that I tried to. I think an apology from you would be in order.'

A deeper reason surfaced after he had accepted my apology: 'If I wasn't able to go to the Commons, if it had meant just giving up the Lords, then I would have been giving up public life, and that would have been an absurdity from the point of view of my ambition.'

'Was it fair on other politicians to use your birthright like this?'

'It is an interesting point of discussion as to whether Christ felt contempt. Certainly not for Judas.'

Lord Longford

'To short-circuit this discussion—I am not a rich socialist. I go second-class on the train, if you want to know. It is true that I have just had lunch at The Gay Hussar, and so you could say that my level of expenditure is not that of a good socialist, and you could catch me out in various similar ways—if you wanted to pursue it, you could say that I shouldn't belong to the Garrick Club. But the fact remains that when I succeeded from my brother, I handed over all my inheritance to my eldest son, so I am not vulnerable in the way you think.

'My record is like the title of that Iris Murdoch book, *A Fairly Honourable Defeat*. Questions which try to catch me out bore me—I'm only telling you this so that we don't waste any time, they bore me. Questions about my war record are more embarrassing as it was rather inglorious—I collapsed in ill-health. Looking back on my life, I really regret that, but this thing about socialism does not get far—you must understand that it has been the most important thing in my life.'

He waved a friendly carroty finger at me.

'You must not assume that all politicians are disreputable. All journalists assume that, but then all politicians assume journalists are disreputable and they will both assume that all businessmen are crooks! There can be idealism. When you meet an elderly person who has been labouring away for years, you mustn't assume that it is your job to catch them out. Bulow said, "Real politicians are governed by two motives: love of country and love of power"—that's not true. Do remember: there can be idealism.'

One of the primary areas into which Lord Longford's idealism has led him followed hard on the heels of his last comment.

'My prison reform has been made to seem more controversial than it is because I have taken on Myra Hindley. But you must not be led astray by the *News of the World*.'

'How do you react to their criticism?' I wondered.

'The difficulty about my reaction to their outcries is that contempt is not regarded as a Christian quality. If you ask me, "What do I think of the *News of the World*?" My real attitude is one of absolute contempt, but then I tell myself that this is not a true Christian attitude, that this is the wrong feeling, so then I must confess it and ask for the *News of the World* to be forgiven.

'It is an interesting point of discussion as to whether Christ felt contempt. Certainly not for Judas. Contempt for any fellow Christians should be confessed.'

'A lot of people felt contempt for Myra Hindley,' I volunteered.

'The majority of the British public know nothing about Myra Hindley. The press know there is a lot of feeling so they play to it. I hope you share my contempt for the *News of the World*. You cannot share their attitude. When the poor girl was taken for a walk, they made a foul outcry against it, which was thoroughly disgusting—most unchristian.'

'But weren't they only reflecting the widespread concern about re-leasing child killers?'

'Please don't put yourself in the position of defending them. I think such an attitude is wicked. If we talk about anti-fascism or anti-semitism or feeling against the blacks, we say it is wicked. You must understand my feelings, and I think this attitude of stirring up hatred against a person, a murderer, is wicked and revolting.

'When considering these criminals—let's consider one I don't know, like Jack the Ripper—who of course is revolting—but if you consider him, you have to say to yourself, "What is the right attitude to take? He has a father, a mother like me—what is the right thing for me to do?"

'If you cannot even begin to feel compassion, then you are not start-ing to be any sort of Christian. What is the conclusion from that? The conclusion cannot be to lock people away for ever.'

As I gathered my things together to leave, he reverted back to our argument. I apologised for my unnecessary provocation, but he answered:

'No, forgive me. It's just that we may not meet again.'

And as he stood there, a sort of shabby puppet, my image of him was transfigured and I suddenly felt enormous affection for this funny old man who tries so hard to shape his life around the teaching of Christ, and I remembered the way his moth-eaten voice had anxiously re-peated, 'There can be idealism.'

He showed me down the stairs, and I mentioned I was off to visit Anthony Powell, his brother-in-law, next week.

'I shall go on claiming that I am Widmerpool,' he said. 'Although everybody denies it, I like to think it is based on me—he is the sort of comic villain of Anthony Powell.'

'Are you a comic villain?'

'That's for you to judge.'

And then of course, when I returned to my car, there was a parking ticket sellotaped to the windscreen.

Sir John Betjeman

MAGDALEN, 1925–28

The Last Laugh

I made hay while the sun shone.
  My work sold.
Now, if the harvest is over
  And the world cold
Give me the bonus of laughter
  As I lose hold.

Chelsea stood motionless in thick heatwave as I drove along the King's Road to Radnor Walk. Despite the heat, no sun was visible and the Sunday morning lay stunted beneath a yellow shroud of what felt like sulphur.

I picked out Sir John Betjeman's house by the ramp sloping from the front door to the pavement, and when I stopped outside, the door was open and a chromium hand rail followed the corridor waist-high around the corner.

Sir John's secretary, Elizabeth More, showed me into the heavily curtained front room, where, mollusc-like in his wheelchair, Sir John sat by himself. There was a pile of brown and white photographs and postcards on the desk in front of him, which his left hand turned over and over.

'There he is—Sir Horace Jones. A very nice man.'

He pushed it across for me to see.

'There he is. He was the architect of Tower Bridge. A very good architect and a very good building, and he is obviously right for the

25

'Failed in Divinity! O, towers and spires!
Could no one help? Was nothing to be done?
No. No one. Nothing.'

Sir John Betjeman, sent down in 1928

City, which is why he is wearing knee breeches and City things. And that, I think, is Sir Horace's daughter.'

'Do you like the City?'

'I love the City. I think it will be always an inspiration to us. People will go back there—I think I will like it more and more—it isn't planned, it is just a gradual growth. I like Eliot's, T. S. Eliot's, City poem: "Unreal City, The something fog" ... what is it? ... "that lingers and falls...."'

And then he gave up and we both got confused when I added 'rubs its back upon the window' and then thought it was different. His head fell back to his chest: 'So be it.'

'Which other poets do you like?'

'I don't dislike any poet. I find envy an afflicting thing. I don't like it.'

'I find some of your poetry rather like Thomas Hardy—'

'Oh, Thomas Hardy is very good. I am very honoured to find myself spoken of in the same bracket. Hardy is wonderful—I know a lot of Hardy by heart,' he ended sadly, 'but I am finding it hard to remember.'

'You are both able to evoke so much power through simple language.'

'Thank you.'

'Are you aware of this power?'

'One doesn't know what one is doing. Everything is by courtesy of the management.'

I asked about some of his word compounds: 'Bees-winged eyes', 'schoolboy-sure', and 'ginger-beery sweet'. Sir John was silent for a long time, then he lifted his head:

> How pleasant to know Mr Lear!
> Who has written such volumes of stuff!
> Some think him ill-tempered and queer,
> But a few think him pleasant enough.
>
> He reads but he cannot speak Spanish,
> Cannot abide ginger-beer
> Ere the days of his pilgrimage vanish,
> How pleasant to know Mr Lear!

He looked at me, happy: 'Isn't that marvellous! I have thought of writing like that, but you know—it is so very difficult to do.'

He found another postcard and pushed it towards me.

'Conan Doyle, I think. I have always been influenced by Sherlock

Holmes—he makes me like him—his language, and I think his plots are lovely, and I think he has got great narrative power.'

'Would you have liked to have been a novelist?'

'I couldn't have been a novelist—I am not ingenious enough. I don't know when to stop. I would have liked to have written more narratives. I think I am best supported in narrative.'

He broke off and gave an astonishing high-pitched yawn, like a jammed radio tuner.

'Oh! Excuse my yawning. Shall we have a little drink?'

I noticed behind him a large Victorian edition of the Bible, and as I had been arguing with our parish vicar the evening before, I asked whether he preferred the older versions of the Bible to the New English edition.

'Yes, I think that really I prefer the mistranslations and the sound of things of the older version. I like nothing new.'

I explained that my sister was to be married later in the month—

'Oh—whereabouts?'

'St Edith's Church at Pulverbatch, south of Shrewsbury.'

'I think I have been there.'

'This vicar wants me to read from the New English, but I would rather read from the old.'

'So would I.'

'He says the Bible should be in easy language.'

'Yes, yes, I daresay.'

'Perhaps he'll give in.'

Sir John said with concern: 'I hope he will. I would want to read from the old Bible because of the sound of it.'

Then there was a pop from the kitchen, and a bottle of champagne was brought in.

'It is nice to see you here and sampling champagne. It is much the best drink in the morning. It goes with . . . it goes with not working!'

We drank. He looked at me over his glass.

'You are very nice. You, I think, will do well—so far as anyone does well.'

And then at my tape-recorder:

'It is very bold of you to bring this thing along with you.'

'It doesn't bother you?'

'No, it is lovely, this instrument. I am not at all awe-inspired by it—I think we are using it to its fullest capacity! And which publisher do you have?'

'Hamish Hamilton,' I hoped.

'They are Scotch. Have you noticed how most publishers are Scottish? I think that publishing must be a Scottish thing—"Whiskered

Hal" was what we used to call Harold Macmillan.'

'And about Oxford—what do you remember?'

'When I was younger I was very much struck by Oxford. I think that I first loved the things in architecture, and also I loved my prep school, the Dragon School, because at the Dragon School I met friends who have stayed with me. I love it still. In fact, it was my mother who insisted on my going to Oxford. I found her position more sympathetic as I got older, and I found my father most sympathetic. He didn't mind me going to Oxford, and I don't think he minded me leaving Oxford, and I think he was sympathetic to me becoming a poet.

'It was a mixture of Oxford architecture and the friends—if you ask me ... yes.'

I told him how Sir Harold Acton had spoken of his influence in his love for Victorian things.

'Did he? I didn't know my taste had been influential. I used to hope that it would be—I was always longing to get my words heard. I liked Harold Acton, but he was senior to me, and that made a difference. Sir Harold is a very good writer. Has *Aquarium* been reprinted? That's a pity. Robert Byron was a friend of Harold's, but I don't think he ever particularly liked me. Lucy Byron, his sister, was an influence on me....'

And then he fell silent: 'I am not a scholar ... not even in this hot weather do I want to go to Oxford to see it, or....'

And again he fell through the middle of the sentence like some huge beetle falling over onto its back and lying there tired of getting up.

'Do you hope to go to Cornwall this summer?'

'Yes. Cornwall is very pleasing to me, it is home to me ... the sea and the vegetation.

'St Enodoc is where I lived in my childhood, and it was a very impressionable time. Do you know, I always have imagined that I am Cornish—I am actually Cockney, and I don't hold with people saying they are Cornish unless they are. Rowse is Cornish—he is a very good Cornishman. I ought not to say that I was Cornish.'

'What do you like so much about Cornishmen?'

'They are given to hear the sound of things, and they are influenced by that. That's quite good on them.'

St Enodoc Church, I knew, was one of Sir John's favourites.

> Oh lichened slate in walls, they knew your worth
> Who raised you up to make this House of God
> What faith was his, that dim, that Cornish saint,
> Small rushlight of a long-forgotten church,
> Who lived with God on this unfriendly shore,

Who knew He made the Atlantic and the stones
And destined seamen here to end their lives
Dashed on a rock, rolled over in the surf,
And not one hair forgotten. Now they lie
In centuries of sand beside the church.
Less pitiable are they than the corpse
Of a large golfer, only four weeks dead,
This sunlit and sea-distant afternoon.*

'How important are churches to you?'

'They are always homes to me. They are nice—I would be very sad without Church. I don't see any point of life without Church.'

'Are you sad that they are so uninhabited now?'

'No. I think that always they will never be popular. I think that they have just got to be there. I see them, if you like, as homely and also as an inspiration in fact.'

And in fact Sir John preferred churches to be uninhabited rather than have their clarity spoiled by people tampering with them and re-storing them—seen by him rather as do-gooders on the make than selfless Christians: 'I resent all their modernisations of churches—I daresay that is naughty of me, but I don't know why people do it. I think, you know, that people are really nice and that we would be powerless without them, but why that happens or has to happen I don't know. They ruin everything.'

When he said that, I remembered how violent his poetry could be, like *Sun and Fun*:

> But I'm dying now and done for,
> What on earth was all the fun for?
> For I'm old and ill and terrified and tight.

and *Mortality*:

> The first-class brains of a senior civil servant
> Are sweetbread on the road today.

'Oh yes, that civil servant was based on Lord Bridges, who was a nice man, but not endowed with imagination like mine. He had a dif-ferent imagination—he liked possessions and he always saw the other person's point of view. I never have done that.'

'Did he deserve such a violent poem?'

* St Enodoc church is now where Sir John Betjeman is buried.

'I suppose it is quite violent.'

'Did you mean it?'

'I did when I wrote it.'

He was quiet. Outside a dog barked.

'That dog again. I think now, on a hot day in Chelsea, that I am not so violent.'

I wondered what changes he had felt in his writing:

'I traced my development in *West Hill Highgate* as I was a child. Peggy Purey-Cust was very important to me then ... her gold hair. I can see her now ... and I believe she is still alive. We were both of an age, I was eight—that is my earliest recollection of her,' his voice cracked and whispered, 'beautiful blue eyes, gold hair and she walked with springy steps.'

In *Summoned by Bells*, he had written:

> O Peggy Purey-Cust, how pure you were:
> My first and purest love, Miss Purey-Cust!

And now, old and ill, he knew he would never see either her or himself like that again.

'But you think she is still alive?'

He looked up, gollom eyes large with hope.

'Yes, yes I believe she is. I hope so.'

And then he smiled over a later love, Myfanwy: 'Myfanwy was Welsh, but I only realised that later!'

In *Youth and Age on Beaulieu River* Sir John compares Clemency with Mrs Fairclough and, when I mentioned it, he recited it to me carefully, like a blind man feeling someone's face:

> To her boat on Beaulieu water
> Clemency the General's daughter
> Pulls across with even strokes.
>
> Schoolboy-sure she is this morning;
> Soon her sharpie's rigged and free.
> Cool beneath the garden awning
> Mrs Fairclough....

He stopped—'that was actually somebody called Lady Dent'—and puzzled over something: 'Schoolboy-sure she is this morning—I think that was your idea, Elizabeth.'

'No, it was nothing to do with me. I didn't know you in those days.'

'Is Mrs Fairclough a sad figure?' I asked.

31

'Yes. I think Mrs Fairclough did feel sad.'

'Has your point of view changed towards hers?'

'Yes, I think it has changed to Mrs Fairclough's.'

His eyes, large and black, strained across the dimness like those of some creature brought up from the bottom of the ocean:

'I think envy and resignation are things we shall all suffer. We are always frustrated.'

A long silence fell. I awkwardly changed the subject and asked what he felt about the British class system, something his poetry is careful to protect:

'I think that we are class-conscious, all of us. Which do you think you are?'

I thought upper middle-class.

'Yes, I think I am that too. I think that we would be sad to find ourselves somebody different.'

'But isn't it a bad thing if people aspire to different classes?' For a while, I thought he hadn't heard, but then he began searching in the pictures.

'Here is a symbol of working class lifted into middle class: Giles Wilson, Sir Harold Wilson's son, by a railway. It is a very nice photograph of him.'

And then his answer: 'Well, we are all in these islands.'

He held the photograph for me to see. 'He is a very good man. I admire him because he speaks his mind and he likes a four-centred arch (and there is one). That one is on the Great Western.'

'Why do you like it?'

'It is a nearly flat arch, which Brunel designed. It is a sort of Tudor arch, almost flat, which is to me the perfect arch.'

Sir John's voice was now a whisper, and it was time for his medicine. After I had photographed him, I asked him something I had been trying to articulate all along.

'How do you manage to affect so many people?'

His eyes turned up towards me, lost and bewildered.

'I never knew—luck.'

'I think now, on a hot day in Chelsea, that I am not so violent.'
Sir John Betjeman, shortly before his death

Anthony Powell

BALLIOL, 1923–26

'If you are absolutely determined to see me, ring up and come to tea.'

Over the telephone, Mr Powell was less than enthusiastic. 'Some people are frightfully good on their life stories, but I can never think of anything to say at all. If you ask questions, I might be able to produce something.'

And after tea and shortcake, when I tried out my first question, Mr Powell threw something of a wobbly. 'This is awfully difficult! Life is an enormously complicated business, you know. In interviews one really talks absolute rubbish because one cannot explain life. The whole idea of interviews is in itself absurd—one cannot answer deep questions about what one's life was like, one writes novels about it. You have got to realise that any answers you get to these supposedly profound questions will be quite absurd.'

This is going to be difficult, I thought, as Mr Powell settled defensively behind his jawbone. I desperately turned to my notes, and read: 'Canker galls the infants of spring (Laertes/Powell's memoirs)—does he mean it?' I looked up to catch Mr Powell glancing at his watch. The dialogue which followed had me wildly lunging out with questions whilst Mr Powell steadily backed off behind the teapot like a prodded lobster, wincing from each question as though from a shrimping net.

'Do you think that Laertes was right that "the infants of spring" are going to be "galled"?'

'Yes, always I would have thought. That's what Shakespeare thought anyway.'

'Why do you think so?'

'Well, that's the sort of question I just can't answer.'

35

Anthony Powell (*front row*) as a fag at school

'Why should they necessarily be "galled"? You're not galled, are you?'

'One can't answer these questions. "Are you galled?" It's like asking, "Are you happy"?'

'But you said that Cyril Connolly was "galled".'

'Well, I'm talking about somebody else. To talk about somebody else and to talk about yourself are very different things.'

'Why did you say that "he was galled by a canker"?'

'You're talking in extraordinary sort of clichés.'

'I'm quoting you!'

'Well, all I can say is that that is what I wrote. When I make a remark like that, clearly it's in some relation to what I've thought—otherwise I wouldn't have said it.

'All young people learn things: I mean—"the canker galls the infants of spring" means, presumably, that young people coming on like spring buds and so on, are, you know, galled by life.'

'And this happened to you at Oxford?'

'Well, it was all the beginning of finding out what life is really about—it was an age of innocence which gradually became more worldly. One gradually became aware of various things—aware, for example, of people who would have cut absolutely no ice at school, but who were run after at Oxford—it would eventually turn out that they were extremely rich.'

'Is that a "worldly" thing?'

'I think that the world is a "worldly" place—the word "worldly" comes from "being like the world"—if it's not one kind of snobbery and one kind of money, it's another kind. You have got to learn that, and Oxford lets you down fairly lightly.'

'So what affected you most at Oxford?'

'Well, that is another absurd question which I just can't answer. One just can't say: "At Oxford I was so and so, or I liked so and so"—one writes novels about it. One cannot give it a one-word answer.'

I rather ran out of steam at this point, and asked if he minded my smoking a cigarette. Completely unexpectedly, the rock-pool tension vanished.

'It doesn't bother me in the least. I regret that I don't smoke—it is so tiresome of people to object to smoking. I am entirely in favour of it.'

I gave up the idea of Oxford as a bad job, and moved to his writing. 'Did you always want to be a writer?'

'No, I didn't plan to be a writer at all; I think I thought I should just be a publisher. The thing was that practically everybody who was at all literary was trying to write a novel, and it would have been quite extraordinary for me not to have been writing one too!

37

'After I had written one, I thought it would be nice to write three.'

A Question of Upbringing, published in 1951, was the first of what became a twelve-volume novel sequence, *A Dance to the Music of Time*, which was completed in 1975. Mr Powell concludes the final volume, *Hearing Secret Harmonies*, with a quotation from Robert Burton's *Anatomy of Melancholy*:

> I hear new news every day, and those ordinary rumours of war, plagues, fires, inundations, thefts, murders, massacres, meteors, comets.... Now come tidings of weddings, maskings, mummeries, entertainments, jubilees, embassies, tilts and tournaments, trophies, triumphs, revels, sports, plays: then again, as in a new shifted scene, treasons, cheating tricks, robberies, enormous villainies of all kinds, funerals, burials, deaths of princes, new discoveries, expeditions; now comical then tragical matters....

'Did *A Dance to the Music of Time* eventually resolve itself into a tragedy or a comedy?'

'Well, you see tragedy and comedy are very close. It's a cliché to say it, but they are always on knife edge.

'Burton has some very funny stuff in him, I don't know whether you've read him—he takes a bit of reading, and he also has some very sad stuff. At that date, you see, a humorous man was not what we now mean by humour, i.e. making jokes and being funny; it meant somebody who was very jumpy and rather tragic. That is the whole Burton idea—that if you know what is funny and what is tragic, they are very close indeed.

'*Dance* might be tragic or might be comic. That is the whole point of the long quotation from Burton at the end. He says: "I now talk of sometimes tragical, sometimes comical matters and so on." He does cover all those things, and that is the whole point of it—to try to indicate what the whole novel is about.

'The interesting thing is that I did actually make this note from Burton when I was about twenty-two, and I didn't in fact use it until *Dance* was finished, when I was coming up to seventy.'

'Would you say such a mixture of comic and tragic is a sort of realism?'

'Realism is a very difficult word to define—you see, so many things are fantastic in the world, that many things which appear in writing as so-called Romantic are, in fact, the way the world actually exists, realism if you like.'

The twelve volumes of fiction were followed by four volumes of memoirs which tell much the same story but from the autobiographer's point of view. In *Hearing Secret Harmonies*, the narrator, Nick Jenkins, remembers something Trapnel said:

'People think because a novel is invented, it isn't true. Exactly the reverse is the case. Because a novel is invented, it is true. Biography and memoirs can never be wholly true.... In a sense, you know more about Balzac and Dickens from their novels than Rousseau and Casanova from their confessions.'

It seemed an appropriate comment to quote to Mr Powell, who has written about a million words of each.

'I do, in fact, agree with Trapnel. Trapnel is, of course, put up to say that, but I do think that there are certain things that you can only say in a novel.

'That is one of the objections to—' He chose an equally appropriate example. 'If you ask somebody what happened to them at Oxford, they will only be able to present a kind of scrappy, quite unreal, possibly totally stylised picture of what happened to them. If they were to write a novel about it, they would present a far more coherent and truer picture of how it appeared to them. 'If you employ the relative, it is a way of telling the truth.

'So, in a funny sort of way, you do get a better idea of what Dickens or Balzac were like than Rousseau or Casanova. With Dickens you have innumerable examples of what he thought in a thousand different ways and what he thought of a thousand different people. But Rousseau or Casanova try to *tell* you what sort of people they are, and other people who saw them would give you quite a different picture of them, so you wouldn't know which was true.'

'Is this true of you?'

'I am sure that it is—if it is true for one writer, it is true for another.

'That is why when people say, "Well, Jenkins is a very dim figure"—mind you, I don't say that the most intelligent people say that, but it is a popular thing to say, I disagree because in point of fact there are so many examples of how Jenkins behaves in all sorts of different circumstances that, if you checked up on him, you should get quite a good picture of him.'

'And of you too?'

Mr Powell instinctively reverted to the lobster. 'No, not necessarily of me. All I set out to do with Jenkins is write about someone who has lived roughly the same sort of life as me, but who does quite a lot of things I have never done and so he becomes quite different and quite different rules apply.

'You cannot define in any simple way what is enormously undefinable.'

He reverted to the perception of truth: 'An awful lot of things happen in a book which the author doesn't know about—he merely presents what is within his compass, if I can put it like that. The author only knows certain things, he doesn't necessarily know everything. The whole point about life anyway is that you don't know everything, and the reality of the novel must reflect that. To some extent, you go through life not knowing what is happening, and that is all part of the reality.

'If I may say so, I think that some of the reality of *Dance* is due to that being recognised. In a great many novels, certainly in the nineteenth-century novels, you lose much of this reality by every "t" being crossed and "i" dotted. My natural instincts are that whatever you say in a novel should be implicit rather than explicit.

'The next thing I've got to review is the *Oxford Book of Death*'.
Anthony Powell at The Chantry, Frome

'The less you interfere the better—if you look at Proust, you see how he always keeps Marcel fairly low. Proust is a supreme master, and I wouldn't presume to compare myself with him, but he does do this same thing of always being very careful about what he says about Marcel.

'I'll tell you what I think.' Mr Powell was by now beginning to warm to me rather as a highly enthusiastic master might warm to a bovine schoolboy. 'People often say with Proust, they often say: "Proust is the one person in *A la Recherche du Temps Perdu* who is not represented as being queer—every bloody person except Proust is a homosexual. Why, as Proust was a homosexual, doesn't he say so? And also Proust was half-Jewish, why, when he talks quite a lot about Jews, is that never mentioned?" And why isn't it?'

I didn't have an answer.

'The point seems to me, as a novelist, to be perfectly clear.' Now he was beginning to bray like a rather tipsy schoolmaster, perhaps the one who buttonholes some parent on Speech Day, making them the last out of the marquee. 'If he had written from the point of view of a homosexual, it would have been a queer novel, and had he written from the point of view of a Jew, it would have been a Jewish novel. Now Proust, being an exceedingly clever chap, realised this, *and that's why he didn't do it!*'

His point proved, Mr Powell collapsed back on the sofa.

'You always have this objectivity about both the main subjects he deals with. Technically, there is an enormous amount to be learnt from that.'

And, as with tipsy schoolmasters, the conversation somehow turned to sex.

'After the Chatterley trial, you really could say virtually what you liked in novels. This has never worried me much—my own feeling about frank descriptions of people going to bed with each other is that it is practically always undesirable. I think a total misunderstanding is, in fact, the way to describe what sexual emotion is like and, indeed, as far as I am concerned, can be beautifully erotic. I had much rather not have enormously detailed descriptions—it doesn't excite me erotically at all, although I think it does some people.

'I remember one year we were in Sundsvall in Sweden, going down the equivalent of Bond Street, and there would be a great picture of a lady's whatnot facing you. I don't think anyone wants it any more than one wants to leave the door open on a mortuary. But quite how to put the lid on that without preventing people saying that you cannot publish *Ulysses* or *Lady Chatterley's Lover*, I don't know. Actually, I think *Lady Chatterley* is a frightfully bad book, but if Lawrence wanted to publish it, he should have been allowed to.'

Mr Powell was one of the literary witnesses called in for the Chatterley trial. 'I remember one rather interesting thing at that trial—there was a clergyman who was called on to give evidence. He told the court that he didn't think the various acts were obscene, provided that you identified with them. If you regarded yourself as a sort of third party behind a tree, then it would be indecent. I thought this was an interesting point of view.'

'Why?'

'Well, if you are a novelist and reading a novel, one of the troubles is that you are always thinking: "How would I have done this?" So I don't think I identify at all with the characters—it never occurs to me. This does, in a way, spoil the whole thing of reading. It is almost impossible not to think how I would have written it.'

Mr Powell comforted himself with a literary reference. 'Oddly enough, I came across something which Henry James wrote saying exactly the same thing.'

'What about when you're reading Shakespeare?'

'I must say, it does take on rather extraordinary dimensions when I read Shakespeare. I am actually a great Shakespeare reader. In later life, I am very devoted to him, and indeed every night now I read a few pages of some Shakespeare play.'

'But do you really think how you would have written it?' The irresistible idea of Mr Powell as an Elizabethan master marking Shakespeare's plays crossed my mind.

'It is true that I do often, to some extent, think how I would have put this. But, on the other hand, it was written three hundred years ago, and the English language is rather different.'

I was about to move on to something else; he harked back. 'But when I am reading about Falstaff, I do very much think: Well, I know him so well, how would I have dealt with him? Or with Hamlet, I think: If I had to deal with a chap like this, how would I have tackled it? Or Shallow! Shallow so totally lives as a person, as a comic! I really did toy with the idea—got as far as noting down all the things we are told about Shallow to write a piece about him, but it was impossible. Shallow's age is a bit difficult to work out. . . .'

I didn't really know what to say to all this. 'Does this make you feel envious?' I asked at last.

Mr Powell waved a benevolent hand in the face of Shakespeare. 'No, I honestly don't think I am envious. I would say that that is one of my better qualities, that I am not envious of other writers.

'In fact, it's rather like pretty girls—'

I must have looked rather askance, because he patiently explained:

'You know—it is a perfectly wrong principle for a girl who is very pretty to have a lot of ugly girls in the same room. I think that they drag the standard down. If there were a lot of other pretty girls in the room, they would give you the idea that she is the absolute star among the others. I think it is the same with writers—if there are a lot of bad writers, it is not socially good for writing. I am always delighted when somebody writes a good book, although one may not necessarily like what contemporary writers are producing.'

'Do you read many contemporary writers?'

The question amused him. 'No, I don't know anything about contemporary writing. It is absolutely impossible for me to be in touch with it. One thing you don't realise is that after the age of forty (even if you're a publisher) it is frightfully difficult to keep in touch!'

'How would you classify your work?'

'I suppose I belong to the classical tradition of the English novel, but it so happens that most of my favourite novelists are French or Russian—the Russians have made the chief impact on me.'

I was halfway through a further question about the nature of his writing, but he saw it coming and stopped me: 'I never tire of saying that the less you examine yourself in this way, the better. It is fatal if you are perpetually asking yourself: "Did I write like Hemingway this morning? Am I writing like Dostoevsky this afternoon?" The less you think about it, the better. One of my great things about writing is that I maintain that whilst I present my novels, it is really up to other people to analyse them.'

The full stop at the end of that sentence seemed fairly conclusive. Remembering Lord Longford, I asked if Widmerpool had indeed been based on him.

'It is awfully irritating when people go around saying, "Widmerpool is meant to be Lord Longford." It never crossed my mind. If one may so put it, he doesn't greatly interest me as a character. He is just my brother-in-law.

'What happens about Frank is that he does produce these endless volumes of autobiography which, it is perfectly true, do sound awfully like Widmerpool.'

Mr Powell glanced at the door, possibly to check if it was shut. 'Some absolute imbecile of an American read some of Frank's books, and did a most extraordinary thing—he wrote some incredible drivel, two volumes of it, and sent them to me. It was meant to be a kind of life of myself, but he hadn't the faintest idea of what an English life was like because he had based it on one of Frank's autobiographies! Which are, when you come to look at them, pretty incredible, and are written in this peculiar language.'

'And going back to Widmerpool, do you think he is a failure? I could never understand why he joined that hippy commune.'

'Do you know John Bayley, Iris Murdoch's husband? Well, he reviewed the last volume, and he made this point—he said that one of the objections to the book was that, if Widmerpool was keen on power, why should he be drawn into this commune? Otherwise, everybody who is keen on power should do the same.

'My answer to that was that I remembered, when I was at school, somebody saying of the then Captain of the House that he would much rather boss Watkin-Williams around in the Rifle Range for an hour than have the most beautiful woman in the world.

'Now that seems to me to be a terrific sort of true saying about certain people. Watkin-Williams was this rather unattractive boy, who subsequently became an Eton master oddly enough, and for all I know is still going. The point was that this Captain of the House would prefer to have the power to boss around in this frightfully minor way than have some great romantic thing happen to him. It seems to me to be a frightfully good image of what some people are like.

'This is what I meant with Widmerpool. It is really in the hope of getting more worldly power that he joins this commune (in which matter he subsequently failed as Scorpio Murtlock sat above him), because in the long run he felt that there was more power there than, so to speak, in being Prime Minister.

'People who practise the occult think there is a lot of power there. It was slightly one of the things I was brought up with, fortune-telling, and this business of all the chaps running past in Greek tunics actually happened where we lived just before the First War. And I have played planchette.'

'How much of it do you believe?'

The lobster's smile: 'It has all helped me write.'

'And what are you looking forward to now?'

'Oh, I think I shall probably be carried away in a long box before long.'

It was time to go. We got up and moved to the window. There was a lone cock pheasant preening itself outside.

'That pheasant is well known. He's a local character who never seems to get shot.'

'Does the thought of dying frighten you?'

'The thought of dying doesn't frighten me in the least.' He corrected himself. 'The thought of dying is not very pleasant because one doesn't know what sort of form it will take, but the thought of being dead couldn't worry me less.

'People often die rather unpleasantly and I don't wish that, but the thought of just being removed couldn't worry me less. We have all got to do it sooner or later.'

'Has your writing helped you to come to terms with it?'

'I don't know what "coming to terms with it" means. There are two quite separate things. I am afraid of dying as much as anybody else is, but what doesn't worry me is death itself. I don't know whether you've read that poem of Philip Larkin's about dying, in which he describes his absolute horror of thinking that he will just cease to exist—I don't think that that worries me at all—"ceasing to exist" doesn't worry me, but all the circumstances of dying do.'

He indicated a book on his desk. 'The next thing I've got to review is the *Oxford Book of Death*!'

Having tucked up generations of fictional characters, Mr Powell is quite well placed to do it himself.

Indira Gandhi

SOMERVILLE, 1937–38

The Sikh guard moved to open the door. As it swung open, I remembered in a rush, as a drowning man is said to, all the details of the story so far.

The telephone calls:

'Hello? Can you hear me?'

'Velly bad line, sir—try tomorrow.'

On one day, a clear line:

'You like see Prime Minister? No problem.'

And then the letter, heavy with the red wax insignia of three Bengal tigers:

Dear Mr Whitley,

I have your letter of May 30th.

I should like to help you for your book on Oxford. However, I was at Somerville for only a year and I am afraid even then my thoughts were far from education. That was the period of the struggle for Independence in India, the civil war in Spain, trouble in China, and rising fascism and Hitler's expansionism in Europe.

Most of my family was in prison, and because of my travels, friendships and the historical perspective given by my father, I felt involved in and deeply anxious about these events.

Yours sincerely,
Indira Gandhi

And I remembered Iris Murdoch's description of her: 'I first met

'She was very shy and frail, and I think very unhappy.'

Iris Murdoch

her at school when we were both fourteen. She was very much a 'titch', poor girl! One could never have dreamt that she was going to be the most powerful woman in the world.

'And later at Oxford she was thinking more about her country, and there was a lot of activity among Indians about what was happening in India. Her father was probably in prison at the time.'

'She was very shy and frail, and I think very unhappy. You can still see, of course, that she is a frail and slim person; very fine face, and almost invisible with that particular kind of North Indian pallor. Extremely beautiful and a frightfully nice person—I was very fond of her.

And then Rebecca and I had landed in Delhi and walked outside the airport slap into the middle of a commotion of white smiles, turbans and pyjamas and long brown arms reaching towards us.

'Sir! Sir! You want cheap hotel?'

'Go to Kashmir, sahib? You like houseboat?'

'You buy sari, sir, silk sari for madam.'

'You have dollars maybe? Cheap price!'

'Madam, you like gems—no money just look.'

'You want taxi?'

Then followed the long argument between the taxi driver and the rest of the commotion as to who deserved baksheesh for hooking the tourists.

Later, there was our visit to Varanasi, where the holy River Ganges flows by. The mud streets, the traffic teeming with rickshaws and bicycles, water buffalo, magic buses, women with wicker baskets on their heads, men squatting to piss, holy men in orange, beggars on boxes and, of course, the funerals.

We saw the bodies, wrapped in bloodstained saris, decorated with orange flowers and tinsel and buzzing with flies, being carried on bamboo stretchers to the riverside ghats; we got up at dawn to watch the ritual bathing in the River Ganges as hot ashes from the ghats blew in our faces; we drank char amongst old men who spat betel juice which stained the street with its blood-red blotches; and a madman with an ear cut off chased us into the Durga Temple, where Rebecca was bitten by a holy monkey.

Having no idea how all these jigsaw pieces could add up to one woman, I followed Rebecca through the door, heard, 'How do you do, Mrs Gandhi,' and then saw them standing together. Iris Murdoch was right—in the grey shadowed room, Mrs Gandhi stood no taller than Rebecca's shoulder. Slight and pale as a candle, she had a sort of Jane Austen grace of movement. She shook hands with soft formality, adjusted her sari across her shoulder and we sat down.

'Was it your idea to go to Oxford?'

'I don't really know; I think perhaps it was.'

'What did you hope to get from it?'

'I don't know; I don't think I hoped to get anything—I mean I had to go somewhere to college, and I just thought that it would be a good idea to have experience of university life in England.'

'And what did you feel you got from that experience?'

'Well, here, you know, we were in the midst of the freedom struggle, so I don't think I could have really studied at all. Not that I did much at Oxford, but at least there was some discipline which meant I did do my tutorials and lectures and so on! I just thought it was a good experience to have, and to get to know the British.'

There were politics too: 'Most of my friends supported Indian Independence, so we all naturally drifted into the Labour Party. We met and had discussions, and I took brief part in one of the Oxford Students' Union elections, but our candidate lost,' she smiled, 'of course.'

'How much do you think academic instruction can prepare one for government?'

'That must depend on the individual,' whom she pronounced as though he had six or seven syllables; 'you see, my own life, as I wrote in my letter to you, was involved in politics, but not politics as it is understood today—not politics as a career, or being somebody, or occupying a particular post—but in the trends of our political movement, which at that time was an anti-imperialist one. The stress always was on the idea—that this was not against one party or another, it was not against the Britishers, it was against a system, the way of thinking of imperialism.'

'Can academic ideals be kept intact when put into practice? The ideal of non-violence for example?'

'Well, even at the height of the Thirty One Movement, any Britisher could walk on the street without having any harm done to him. There were only a few terrorists (one Governor was assassinated), because Mr Gandhi was very particular about non-violence and using only peaceful means.

'And the ideal of non-violence was put into practice with the exception of one incident in 1922, when the police were harassing farmers in an area called the United Provinces, and the villagers came and surrounded the police station and set fire to it—those people inside died. But Mahatma Gandhi said, "I am not going to tolerate this sort of thing, this is not meant to happen and we can't have our movement like this," so he suspended them.'

'Is this ideal of non-violence still as important to you?'

'You try to—obviously, if we're invaded or if there is aggression against us, we have to fight back, but we do our best to try to avoid such a situation in so far as it's in our hands.

'You see, Mahatma Gandhi and the whole Freedom Movement stressed *means*. He said that if you take the wrong means, then you are liable to get diverted from your objective. For instance, if you are going to war, you forget why you are in the war, and the main point becomes only the winning.'

'How much do you look to Mahatma Gandhi as an ideal?' There was a classic Indian wobble of the head. I don't think I realised how close we were treading to the political myths of India:

'I don't have any ideals as such. I think you have to work out your own ideas and ideals and so on. As a man, he was a very great man, and nobody else could have done what he did for India. The ideas he had, his whole concept of non-violence for example, is very relevant to the whole world. Even if you cannot be totally non-violent, you should try to be. You should have an ideal towards which you're trying to work— I accept that. But I didn't accept many of his other ideas, social ideas and others.

'He made a very big impact on my family. He was the one who really brought my father into politics and influenced me. Although my grandfather had been in Congress even earlier, he had no rapport with, say, the peasantry of India—mind you, the Congress then was very much an upper-class party wanting more rights for Indians, they were not even thinking of Independence. It was only when Mahatma Gandhi came and converted it into a mass movement that the first split in the Congress took place and the people who didn't want the peasants and all those people in the party (they thought it was letting the mob in and how could anything serious be done?), those people left the party. Initially my grandfather did have doubts whether he or indeed my father should go the whole hog with Mahatma Gandhi, but because my father was so strongly influenced, he urged my grandfather to go along with him.

'So I looked upon him in childhood, you know, one doesn't think of a person as great or small, I just looked upon him as a family elder, and he was consulted by the family as such—much as one would consult one's grandfather for instance; even in my grandfather's lifetime and, after him, even more so by my father.'

There was a silence whilst she waited for the next question. Both Rebeccca and I were fumbling for something to say. I caught her eye for help, but we were interrupted by Mrs Gandhi who seemed to have decided that we were young enough and helpless enough to be confided in. She leant forward with the happy smile of a young girl.

'For instance, when I wanted to, when I decided to get married—

because my husband belonged to another religion, there was a certain amount of commotion in the family and the general public. My father said I should talk it over with Mahatma Gandhi.'

'What did he advise?'

'Well, I don't think it was so much advice, because I had made up my mind, and he knew that I wasn't easy to divert once that had happened. He said if I'd made up my mind, and if I was sure it was the right thing to do, then I should go ahead. Otherwise, you see, he was generally advising people not to marry at all, he was advocating celibacy and so on.'

The whole interview began to turn inside out and focus on what was private beneath the celluloid images of India's political dynasty. I pointed out that it must have been quite a divergence to marry someone who wasn't politically . . .

'No, he was very political.'

'Politically supportive of your father, I meant.'

'No, no, no—he was actually most supportive. I couldn't have married him if he hadn't been.'

She looked at me, and I saw what Mahatma Gandhi would have seen in the determined eyes of Jawaharlal Nehru's only daughter. 'I mean,' she said. 'I wouldn't have.'

'Couldn't you have?'

'No, I couldn't, no. At that time, you see, the question was just of Independence and of everybody being willing to sacrifice everything and to put everything else aside for Independence. So initially I decided that I wouldn't marry at all, because it would mean I couldn't give up myself so wholeheartedly to the Movement.'

'But you changed your mind?'

And there were the eyes too of the frightened lonely girl who wanted to marry, whom Mahatma Gandhi had also recognised and cared for.

'Lots of things came in, you see, when my mother died. It leaves a big void.

'And of course my husband proposed to me when I was quite small, when I was sixteen. We didn't actually get married until I was, I don't know—twenty-four or twenty-five.'

She laughed and the retainer in the room looked at us, astonished.

'The story he actually told me was this. We used to have flag-hoisting ceremonies on various days for the Thirty One Movement, and there was going to be a flag-hoisting nearby to where he lived. I went along with some of my friends to participate, we were just part of the crowd, and Feroze was sitting on the wall watching what was happening. When they started hoisting the flag, the police suddenly came and began to beat up everybody. They tried to snatch the flag away, which was being passed around, and the police kept on arresting each person to whom this flag was given.

'So ultimately the flag somehow landed up in my hands. I was terribly afraid that I would let it fall because it was so heavy and I thought I couldn't manage it. But somehow I did, and passed it on, but of course I fell down myself and was beaten up by the police and so on.

'Feroze told me that that was the day he decided he would marry me. I didn't know about this until many years later.'

'What a lovely story!'

'Whether it's true or not, I don't know, but that's what he told me.'

'And what about motherhood?' I asked. 'Did you enjoy having children?'

'Very much, yes. In fact, that is really why I did get married, because I wanted to have children.'

'Did you ever feel tied down by your marriage?'

'No, I didn't consider myself tied down at all—not even by the children, except when they were very small and I was mostly with them. When they were old enough to go to school, I organised my life so that I did other work while they were at school, but was available when they came home. You see, the more you do, the better organised you are!'

'It must be lonely without your husband.'

'That is a very difficult question ... I mean obviously you do miss them, people to whom you were very close. When he died, I was in a sort of trauma for quite a while, because although he had been ill, somehow death is so final—and whenever it comes, it is unexpected.

'But loneliness is something quite different—lonely is something that you can be even when you're with people, but you need not necessarily be lonely when you're alone.'

'Do you feel that you might see him in another life?'

'No.'

'Without him, who do you trust?'

'I trust my senior colleagues.'

'That's not quite the same as loving someone—'

'Well, what do you mean by 'trust' exactly?'

'Deriving strength from, I suppose.'

'I think your strength you have to derive from yourself. I don't think you derive strength from anybody else, because that's really like a crutch, isn't it?'

'But don't you feel that you define your emotional edges in some way against other people?'

'I don't know ... I speak for myself naturally and, as I said, from quite early childhood I had to stand on my own feet. There were periods when there was nobody at home at all—everybody was in prison. Of course, you know, children do tend to identify themselves with their parents, and I felt very protective towards mine and I used to get very angry sometimes about what the police were doing to them, but I never looked to them for protection. I felt that they were doing a very difficult thing, and (this was the feeling I had even as a small child), that I shouldn't ask for protection.

'And in our household, it was not just my parents who were involved—it was the whole family on both sides—grandparents, all my mother's family and my father's family, my uncles, aunts, cousins and so on. Everybody was getting beaten up and taken to prison, which meant I was left by myself. I did have an old lady, my grandmother's sister, who had been living with us, but I didn't see much of her. She lived her own life in prayer and what not, and she didn't have anything to do with the house. So, when I was still quite small, I was looking after responsibilities like which school I should go to, what do I have to do, looking after the servants and that sort of thing, and so I grew to depend on myself, and that way I have always depended on myself.'

'Are you entirely self-reliant, then?'

'I don't think anyone is entirely self-reliant, but I think to a very large extent, yes.'

'You don't believe in any sort of God?'

'Well, it depends on what you mean by "God". I mean if it's a "father figure", or something like that, then no. But I do believe that there is *something* that gives you inner strength. Now exactly what that is, whether it is a set of values or a philosophy, I don't exactly know. Fortunately, you see, in our religion, the Hindu religion, there is no dogma. It leaves the field wide open to you to choose to do exactly what you like.

'Mahatma Gandhi always said: "Well, God is Truth." Now everybody else can interpret that in his or her own way.'

'What is your way?'

Mrs Gandhi was silent for a while before answering. She was sitting with her back to a high window which overlooked the garden. I looked past her, through the glass, towards the midday light outside.

I could hear the clinks of the gardeners' hoes as they worked on the flowerbeds below, and I began to wonder whereabouts in Delhi they lived, and then imagined the streets where their family might live; I remembered all the scores of tuck-box-sized wooden shops propped up any old how, which line every Indian street with their red-brown awnings stretched out and forming patchwork ribbons above the pavement; I thought of the men sitting among the sacks of rice, the sandalwood tea chests, the bowls of blood-red curry powder, the bicycle seats or whatever they're selling; and the children, perched cross-legged on the counters, selling red betel wrapped in leaves, samosas, sugared fudge, blackened-green vegetables, single cigarettes.

Bathing at dawn in the River Ganges, Varanasi

I took the sacks of rice and followed them back along the mud roads to the country, back to the villages which stand, mud and wattle, among a clutter of trees with the straw-woven bedsteads outside the huts; where, near the well, there will be a white plaster shrine to Ganesh with a mirror and flowers; where the fields around are ploughed by oxen and water buffalo, and the women stand knee-deep in the paddy fields and a single man will be walking along a dyke and nothing moves.

The intimate vastness of Indian life stretched in every possible direction beyond the quiet garden outside the Prime Minister's office. It all lay beneath the same sunshine which I could see flecking the top branches of the margosa trees outside, and this whole spectrum of life streamed in with the midday light through her window where, like an infinitely coloured rainbow passing through a glass prism, it was absorbed and transformed, emerging as a single vision of white light.

The small figure, sitting upright at her desk, finally answered.

'My way is the way of no conflict.

'Our religion says that there are many paths to God, or whatever you like to call it, and different people have their own paths and they have a right to their own paths. And where the minorities are so large in numbers as they are in India, it is also a political fact that unless everybody learns to co-exist peacefully, you cannot have a peaceful country or any type of peaceful development and you can't even hold it all together.

'So this is why we as Government in India (this started long before Independence) have always had our politics consisting of all people of all religions. We adopted the word "secularism" which is not exactly the same as the dictionary meaning because in the dictionary it says "non-religious", whereas here we take it to mean "equal respect for all religions". Not that it always works, but usually when it doesn't work, there is some other reason—there's an economic or political reason.

'To me all people really are equal. In our household there was never any distinction between the different castes, the different religions or different nationalities. It is part of my being—I just don't see a person as, "he is a Christian, he a Muslim, he a Sikh," I see him as a human being. He may differ with me on other things—certain beliefs perhaps, but the basic belief of most religions is love and brotherhood and so on: in fact all religions are the same.'

'What about when the "love and brotherhood" start breaking up?'

'Well, you have to try and bring back and cool the passions.'

'So you have to keep your own passion out of it?'

'No—I don't have any passion. I mean I only have a passion against the violence, or the killing or the destruction or whatever it is. But certainly not—I don't take sides. It has never occurred to me: this is the very first time that such a question has been put to me, and otherwise I have never even thought of it.'

'But religion causes so many deaths....'

'Well it did in earlier times, but is it now? Not really....'

'Particularly in India, religion and politics seem very interconnected.'

'Well, I don't think it has to do with religion as such. People say it's religion, and even caste comes in there, but I don't think it's religion as such. Lots of people try to make it religion, and now we have these chauvinistic sort of parties who dwell on this aspect and try to arouse the instinct. And of course it's become much worse since this Fundamentalism has come up in what we call West Asia and the Middle East.'

'So isn't your idea of a "secular" India rather an illusion?'

'No, no—I am sure it's going to win out.'

'It isn't there yet—'

'Well, it's largely there. When you see that we are nearly 700 million people, the number of people who are affected by this is a very small proportion. These tension spots are a very small area.'

'It strikes me that in many ways the Gandhi name is practically the only thing which holds the country together.'

'Actually,' she corrected, 'it's really the Nehru family, you know. That's from where it has come.'

'How important to you is it to have some sort of family continuity of leadership?'

'Not at all important.'

'Is your son Rajiv on his own?'

'He has to be. How else can he be? I mean if he is elected, he has to be elected on his own work, so it's for the people to decide.'

'But won't they just vote for his surname?'

'No, I don't think it's just the family, because there have been other people in my family who would have liked to have been more in politics, people who played a very big role in the Independence struggle, but they didn't succeed.

'So it's what you are doing, not what you have done. I mean the family name may influence people initially, but I think after that you are absolutely on your own.'

'How much do you groom Rajiv?'

'Not at all—I hardly see him! He's always busy touring.'

'You must be very proud of him—'

'Well, you know, I am close to my family, but from the beginning we have had a different type of perspective. I mean, it's a much bigger family—what I mean is that I have to consider the Indian family and so it's no use to think exclusively of him, although naturally I want him to do well.

'I didn't want him to go into politics, neither did he or his family, but he felt that he had to help me and this is what he's doing. He's not trying to get to be Prime Minister or a Minister or anything like that, he is just trying now to help me out in Party affairs.

'But it is true that he does attract a bigger audience when he goes anywhere than most other people—this happened with my younger son too—but that kind of audience won't come twice. If you're not doing anything, it will come the first time out of curiosity, but it won't continue to come if you're just somebody's son or daughter.'

I picked up the mention of 'daughter', and asked if it felt strange to be a lady in power. She was amused:

'Not at all—and no Indian would ever think of asking that question!'

'Why not?'

'Because they accept this. Although I won't say that woman has equality here, because in many cases she doesn't and she is a second-class citizen, but she does have equality under the Constitution, and it was Mahatma Gandhi who first brought the masses of Indian women into public life. He said: "We cannot succeed in a non-violent movement unless the family as a whole is involved—especially the women who form half the population."

'And the women did come out in very large numbers, and as more men were arrested, the women automatically occupied their positions. My mother was President of our City Congress Committee, and other women were office bearers and various things. We had three women Presidents before Independence, and nobody then or later ever said, "Well, this is a woman, and she can't be in this or that job, and he would be a better person to do it!"'

'Do you think it may be to do with the fact that Hinduism isn't such a patriarchal religion as Christianity?'

'It may do—you see, mythology-wise the symbol of energy is the female. But I don't know whether that's it or not, because there have been Queens in most countries.'

She put her head to one side, and the white streak of hair turned silver in the light.

'I don't know whether such a large proportion of them went to war as they have done in India—even against the Britishers. We had at least two Queens who were very highly praised by the British generals who opposed them.'

'Who were they?'

'One was killed in battle. She of course was betrayed by her own people—the other princes! And the other was captured and died in prison. You can find lots of her statues. She died in 1857, and the other one was earlier, 1830. She is the best known here.

'Actually, I'm reading a book right now by a Frenchman called *Women in Power in History*.' She tried to keep a resolute face, but couldn't stop a giggle. 'Actually I'm still stuck at the Roman period! But this man does show how, when they removed the original Mother Goddess and broke this link with Nature, the Empire began to break down—the men thought they were the creators, and that the women had no part.'

I wasn't surprised that this Frenchman failed to interest a grandmother in sucking eggs.

'I don't think a society can be whole if you think that only one section of it is able to do things or give leadership. Especially now, when we need other skills—we don't want war-like skills, we don't necessarily want muscle or power or that sort of thing, so it seems a waste if half the talents of a society are left unused.

'You see, most people are mixed—I mean nobody is wholly male or wholly female: your genes are always mixed so everybody has both qualities anyway.'

'What do you hope your leadership will attain?'

'Well, a different kind of world—not just India, but I can't go to the world until India itself has achieved something! Although technology has brought about more revolution in people's lives, they are basically still thinking in the old terms. Whether it's economics or politics, they are still using the same phraseology of either "Capitalism" or "Marxism" which are both completely outdated. I don't think either can solve any problems today.

'For instance the whole thing is based on "What is wealth?" and "Labour is wealth" and this was the concept. But now in affluent countries, and to some extent in India too, the machine plays a very big part and whereas earlier a small factory could be a unit by itself, now they are all linked to each other and there is nothing which is by itself. Unless you can see the total picture, you will never get the results you want.

'This is happening in the political sphere as well—people tend to say, "Well, this is a Palestinian problem, or a Sahara or a South African problem," instead of seeing that they really are all linked, and until this basic attitude and policies are tackled we won't be able to solve any problems. You may solve one problem, but you will have another in its place.'

'Let us imagine that you have left politics,' I changed the subject. 'What would you do?'

'Well, I actually was out of power for three years, and if the Opposition had left me alone, I would not have wanted to come back. I remember when I heard I was defeated in the election, I honestly felt as if a tremendous boulder had gone off my shoulders. I was not feeling the weight before, and I had never felt that being Prime Minister was a burden, but suddenly I felt much lighter. I began planning to get a small house up in the mountains somewhere.

'But then they had all these cases against me, none of which they could prove, although they moved heaven and earth to pin something on me or my son. I became the focus of their attack; everyday I was the headline, when all I was doing was sitting quietly. But because I had to keep defending myself, that is how I came back into politics—they wouldn't leave me alone.'

'And would you have lived in the mountains?'

'If I ever have to live in retirement, I will go up there somewhere. I am very much a "mountain" person. Actually we call them hills, but they're pretty high by European standards!'

I was sceptical that she would be able to live in hibernation: 'truthfully, how would you actually live? I can't imagine you playing patience all day!'

'Well, I really don't know—I *am* one of those people who get involved...'

'Do you like getting involved?'

'No I don't—' she held out her hands in confusion: 'I don't know whether I do or not! I don't know what it is. That's why I can't really have a holiday. Wherever I go, no matter how far away it is, there are problems and somehow they just come and land up in my lap! People laugh when I say that basically I am a lazy person, but I never had time to be lazy!

'I remember a very long time ago, before I was anything at all, when the children were not so small—I think they were already at boarding school ... we were doing a trek to one of the glaciers. Well, it wasn't a real trek because we were going by ponies, and the children wanted to race ahead and I said, "Look, we are here only for a short time together in your holidays, now what is the point of you being away from me up there?" And they said, "Well, you're bound to be surrounded by people with some problems and we don't want to get mixed up in all that." I said, "Don't be silly! We are up here on a glacier, who on earth is going to come near us?" And then lo and behold, suddenly, out of nowhere, people came and blocked our way up this mountain pass. I got off my pony and asked what the matter was. They told me they had some problems and besides which somebody was ill, and they wanted me to cure him. I kept on saying, "Look, I'm not a doctor, I won't know what his illness is, take him to the nearest hospital." But they insisted and said, "No, we're not going to let you go unless you give him medicine."'

She paused. 'Did you cure him?'

'Well, as it happened I did! I think he didn't have much wrong with him, but at that moment he was looking very ill, and he was quite old also. And I said, "Look," I told them honestly, "The only thing I have with me is aspirin, which is for a headache and it does not cure anything else at all, but if you insist, well all right, here it is." I gave him two, and told him to take them with hot milk. They let me go then, and we went to camp in our tents. The next day, my sons said that there were all these people coming to see me. I wasn't sure whether I dared see them and I thought: "Oh no! Now these people are coming to murder me, because if that man has died (and he looked pretty near dying when I saw him), they will lynch me." And I didn't want to go, but they were all shouting, so I went out thinking: "All right, here I go to the gallows!" But they were all cheering, saying he's better, and we want more of your medicine!

'So you see wherever I go, even if I go abroad, these problems which have nothing to do with me or with India somehow turn up, and I get involved!'

We got up to leave, and gave her as a thank-you present a copy of the new Kit Williams book.

'Oh, you don't have to give me anything—you mustn't think that when you visit a Prime Minister, you have to give a gift.' She opened it up. 'Oh, this is by the same fellow who did *Masquerade*. Did you manage to solve that? I am hopeless at this sort of thing! My grandchildren are always asking me riddles which I can never answer!'

She looked at my camera and said, 'We can go outside in the sunshine if you prefer, although there may be monkeys!'

Rebecca stopped her in her tracks. 'I was bitten by a monkey yesterday.'

Mrs Gandhi spun round with concern. 'That's very serious—did you take anti-tetanus?' and she stooped to look at the wound. 'Oh that's lucky—it didn't break the skin.'

We stood on the balcony and I photographed her whilst she told Rebecca this story.

'A long time ago, when my father was Prime Minister, there was a German woman who came to interview him. At that time we had three little tiger cubs, very very small—I mean as big as kittens. They were walking up and down the lawn because my father was fed up with sitting all day in the office, and I was sitting to one side. I looked up and noticed one of the cubs beginning to stalk her.' She gave a wonderfully feline impersonation of the cub. 'I called out and said, "Look, move out of his way—or, if he does something, you just stand still." But she didn't, and so when he jumped on her, she started waving her leg around, and the more she waved, the tighter he held on and so naturally he dug in deeper ... the next thing we saw was this article: "How I Was Bitten By Nehru's Tiger"!'

As we thanked her, Mrs Gandhi said gently that she hoped not too many questions had been left out, and I realised what a different sort of interview it would have been if she hadn't seen us as helpless and shy as she herself had been when Iris Murdoch knew her—two titches in the Prime Minister's office—and leant forward and smiled at us with her story of her husband.

'If I ever have to live in retirement, I will go up there somewhere. I am very much a "mountain person".'

Indira Gandhi, New Delhi

As the door swung open, I turned and looked back. In the middle of the room, lost in thought, she stood with the dignity of a pre-Raphaelite. When she realised I was still at the door, she waved goodbye and I saw the last glimpse of her camomile-pale face, framed by that black and white hair.

The same Sikh guard showed us down the stairs and into the garden outside. We walked away and did not know that a month later he or one of his kin would shoot his Prime Minister dead, and her body would fall and her blood would stain the pathway with betel-red blotches.

Iris Murdoch

SOMERVILLE, 1938–42

We had arranged to meet in her husband's rooms at St Catherine's College. It was the end of May, a few weeks before my Finals. I left the Bodleian Library, walked down Holywell Street, up Longwall Street and then turned off towards St Catz where a military red and white pole was across the road to keep cars out of the college grounds. St Catz itself has the sterilised air of a military or chemical research centre, built as it is of concrete, yellow brick and plate glass.

The porter pointed me across the main quad, or rather zone, where, along a series of antiseptic corridors, I found Professor Bayley's rooms and Iris Murdoch.

'I came up in 1938. It was that strange year before the war, full of anxiety and fear.'

'That must have been frightening.'

'Yes, our state of mind was pretty troubled. We were worrying about Hitler and the concentration camps, the Spanish Civil War was still on, there was a feeling that Europe was falling apart, and that the only thing which could save us was some kind of left-wing movement. There was a great deal of this sort of idealism in Oxford at that time, which led people into left-wing politics. . . . Are you left-wing?'

'No, I'd say not.'

'You're right-wing? Well, I have moved towards the right. I started on the very far left, I joined the Communist Party in my second term, but I now think a lot of time can be wasted during one's education on left-wing politics.

'I had been to a progressive, left-wingish, rather Quakerish school. It was very concerned with international understanding, and also full

'I remember my joy when I came up, having been called "Iris" at school, when they said, "Miss Murdoch". I was delighted to be called "Miss Murdoch"!'

Iris Murdoch

of Jewish refugees (there were scholarships for Jewish girls), who gave us a pretty horrific insight into what was happening in Europe.

'So it was an alarming time; but on the other hand it was very exciting and marvellous to be in Oxford.'

Suddenly and radiantly she smiled. It was easy to picture her as an undergraduate, and a beautiful one. What kind of social life had she led?

'Well, a lot of it was connected with meetings, gatherings, demonstrations—not just left-wing politics, but all sorts of other high-minded groups one belonged to, peace groups and so on. And then just a lot of fun and dancing. There was plenty of perfectly ordinary frivolity. Many undergraduates weren't thinking about politics at all, they were just happy creatures enjoying the *dolce vita* and the Commem. Balls and so forth. Of course, we were so high-minded that we didn't go—we thought it was a terrible waste of money to spend £5 on a ticket for a dance! I rather wish I'd been a bit more frivolous, but we were immensely idealistic and we thought all this money could be spent on better causes.'

'And now what is it about Oxford which has kept you here for most of your life?'

'Well, I married somebody who works here, and I enjoyed teaching very much. I like the particular kind of teaching, the tutorial system and the college system. It's also a pleasant and interesting place to be, and it's a very free place—nobody tells you what to do, what to teach or how to teach.'

'What sort of teaching relationship did you have with your pupils?'

'To begin with, I think a certain formality is proper, but one can then become a friend. I felt affection for my pupils, I was interested in them, and I liked to know about their lives in so far as they wanted to tell me.

'Philosophy is a rewarding subject to teach, because no one tutorial is like another, and it is very much a matter of argument and discussion. This sort of give and take is important, and I think the atmosphere should be relaxed. But, as I said, a little formality at the beginning is helpful—in fact I remember my joy when I came up, having been called "Iris" at school, when they said, "Miss Murdoch". I was delighted to be called "Miss Murdoch"!

'During the student revolution this formal politeness was regarded as wrong: there should be no "Mr" or "Miss", and one should call the dons too by their Christian names at once. I think, as in ordinary social life, people should be formal and polite until there's a good reason to become more familiar.'

As I knew nothing about the student revolution, and could imagine nothing more absurd than students taking themselves seriously enough to want to act like trade unions, I asked Miss Murdoch to tell me something about it.

'Well, Oxford was quieter than many other universities, but some of the students were really quite extreme. It's an aspect of what is happening now in the Labour Party, a warning signal that a small number of people can disrupt an institution—that a few bloody-minded people can have a great deal of power. There was a lot of nonsense about not taking exams and how students should be allowed to dictate all their own courses.'

I tried to pooh-pooh the idea that this was important, but she disagreed with me.

'It's a warning. You see, chaps like you aren't interested. An eternal rule of human life is that those who want to be on committees will be on them, and many well-intentioned and intelligent, right-thinking people who don't bother may find that the power in their institution has gone to those they disapprove of.

'It got out of hand, students would come from the LSE in London, people who weren't Oxford undergraduates at all, and spend their time organising sit-ins. There was a sit-in at the Clarendon building; John and I were coming back from a dinner party, and we asked whether we could go in. We found them all sitting round watching propaganda films on Cuba. It was such an unnecessary protest in a free place like Oxford. Of course no one interfered with them. The saddest thing of all was that the "revolution" damaged relations between students and teachers, some distinguished dons who couldn't possibly be called "fascist" were sent to Coventry by their students.

'I was talking to a German academic the other day during some rather picturesque ceremony, and he was saying how, since the student revolution in Germany, they don't have any regalia or ceremonies of this sort any more. The students won't have anything to do with them. I think that's sad. I think that tradition in Oxford, respect and love for this place which has gone on for such a long time, is all part of what one gets from being here, an expression of one's love of learning.'

I so entirely agreed with her, and had found her descriptions of Oxford life so true, that I asked why she had never written about Oxford in her novels.

'Oh, it's an impossible subject. It's already a novel! I've never felt any urge to write about it in a historical sense, and I've never wanted to put it into my novels—I know it too well. Stories about Oxford have a certain familiarity, the dramas of college life, how dons fight with each other, what it's like to be a student. Somehow it's too close.'

Moving the subject more towards her novels, I asked how she would label herself as a writer. She shifted in the upright chair and turned so she could look out of the window.

'Labels can be so misleading.'

I realised I was making an 'A'-Level mistake. 'But if you had to . . .' I lamely added.

'I suppose I'm in the tradition of the English/Russian nineteenth-century novel. To say that one's a "Realist" now might suggest that one is a documentary writer. It's not very helpful to put these simple labels on. People from behind the Iron Curtain are fond of labels, and always ask "Are you an Existentialist or a Social Realist?"'

'But the novel is a complex form, it's a great free form, and it's very hard to describe a novelist.'

'I read something you wrote about the novel form being under threat by the present-day habits of living and technology. Do you really believe this?'

'Yes, I think books could be beginning to disappear because of all the other means of communication people now have, ways of storing information and ways of thinking about the world in terms of computers and computer languages. The word processor menaces prose style.

'I think this is a deep meaning of structuralism and the pseudo-philosophies which are now appearing in modern literary criticism. It is a warning sign about the nature of language. In the past we have had a faith in language which was in some ways philosophically naïve—a feeling that language and the world correspond to each other, which is what the man on the street would say but which is actually only a half-truth. It is very difficult to say in detail what the relation between language and the world is, because words are not simply names of things (labels if you like) in a pre-determined world. But this itself does not entail that language is *unable* to refer to the world— "reference" is made in many ways, and our use of language in relation to an independent world is a prime aspect of our experience. One's faith in truth can be shaken by being too impressed by computer languages and the ways in which linguistic signs are internally related. The idea of reference to an extra-linguistic reality is essential. Meaning and truth must not be separated.'

I began to see what she was getting at, as well as wishing that I could have been taught by her. 'So it is a breakdown in our faith in language's ability to describe the world?'

'Yes, and a faith in truth.' Miss Murdoch leant forward and I felt that she really cared that I understood. 'I think that the idea of truth is at stake here.'

'What do you mean?'

'Well, the simple conception of truth suggests that if you say, "That's a green lamp-shade there," then it is true if there is a green lamp-shade there. This conception of truth as correspondence is too simple but cannot be just set aside. Mathematical languages are true by reference to themselves, in terms of the other symbols of the system. If this is thought to be a model for ordinary language, then the commonsense idea of language being able to reach out and touch the world is undermined.

'This affects literature quite deeply. The notion of the realistic novel and the story begins to be under attack. Young writers lose faith in the traditional novel, and in language's capacity to tell the truth. They begin to feel that language should be playing about within itself, and that is indeed all it can do. It is as if everything had become rather obscure poetry.'

'How does this affect your writing?'

'Oh, my writing will look after itself, but I think that some young novelists are frightened by critics who suggest that there is something fallacious or insincere about writing a story. This is the sort of thing which academics too can get into their heads—you must have come across it.'

'Do you find a tension between telling a story, which you do as a traditional novelist, and expressing your philosophy of the world?' I asked. Because I was rather out of my depth, it was a long-shot question which Miss Murdoch, I think, recognised as such and was kind enough to straighten out for me.

'I don't express my philosophy in my books. It's quite a different matter. But any artist has a tension between looking at the world which interests him and delights him—after all, the world is the thing—and creating something of his own which is out of the world, which isn't a copy of the world, but yet is related to it. A good painting is not a copy of what the painter sees—even if he's trying to make it so, it isn't. It is something else. It's a special kind of image—it's a work of art. We know what that is, though it is difficult to define.

'Obviously "telling a story" is not just reproducing things that have happened, it's doing something remarkable to them. So art is quite "arty" enough (if I can put it this way) without the artist being driven into some kind of ghetto where he can only play about with language and not make ordinary observations about the world, because even ordinary observations of the world involve this subjective transformation into art. So the artist need not therefore feel obliged to indulge in "self-referential" work in which he stops "telling a story" or "painting a picture" and produces more of a puzzle picture which the reader has to decipher, and which is partly mystifying and partly perhaps about your own method of telling stories—a story about telling a story. This leads to a kind of obscurantist art which does not feel it has to make any clear statement because the audience can do it all for themselves.'

'And you don't do this kind of thing?'

'No, I'm a traditional novelist. I'm writing a story with characters; obviously a traditional novelist now is at a different stage in history from thirty or forty years ago. My work is in a deep sense traditional, but the atmosphere and the tensions and the mode of the art can be rather different from those of older traditional novelists.'

Feeling rather like Prufrock approaching the overwhelming question, I asked, 'What are your novels about?'

Miss Murdoch looked surprised, and when she answered she was looking away out of the window again and her voice sounded far-off.

'... People, life, thought, morality and so forth. Imagination, invention. One can only write from one's own mind, within the limit of one's own understanding of human life. This will be marked by your history, where you've been. What's interesting about the novel is that all kinds of things that you know and feel and think, a great variety of things, are elicited by the art form, so in a way writing a novel is a process of self-discovery—you know much more than you think.

'It's rather like going into exams! One was always told: "Don't worry, you'll find you know much more than you think and you'll find yourself writing much faster!"

'The novel is a mode of reflection upon all kinds of details. One is reflecting on the art form and reflecting in terms of making a work of art. The unconscious mind is the great source of the power of art, and all these things will emerge if you wait for them and summon them.'

Her wide blue eyes followed somebody walking outside, then she turned back towards me with that prioress's smile.

'I plan very carefully, but none of this would be of any value without imagination and invention which give *life* to the book. The novel is a work of imagination. Novelists are individuals and novels are tremendously individual works of art, which is why I resent modern critics who try to tell novelists how to write.

'You can do all sorts of things with the novel, it is a very versatile form—you can write dialogue, rhetorical prose, poetic prose, plain denuded descriptions, drama, every sort of device you can use. And you're trying to portray characters, *free* people, who are unpredictable and at the same time you're trying to fit them into a pattern, perhaps a mythological pattern for instance, which the novel has generated for itself.'

'Which of your novels do you like most?'

'And human beings are so extraordinary and so mysterious, so various and so full of power. And characters in novels, in the sort of novel I try to write, should be like that. They should be mysterious and alive, opaque to each other, surprising.'

Iris Murdoch

'I think my later novels are better than the early ones. *Under The Net* was under the spell of Beckett and Queneau, and there is something artificial in a limiting sense about the early novels. I quite like the middle ones, but I think the later ones are best.'

She shrugged her shoulders. 'But the work is never good enough.'

'Why not?'

'It's not as good as Tolstoy or Shakespeare! The imagination isn't high enough, the people are too constricted, the characters aren't liberated from the forms.'

There was a quotation of hers which I had noticed in the 1982 English Finals paper, and I read it out to her: 'Against the consolations of form, the clear crystalline work, the simplified fantasy-myth, we must pit the destructive power of that now so unfashionable naturalistic idea of character.'

'What sort of thing did you want the examinees to discuss?' She asked me to read it out again, which I did, whilst she thoughtfully twisted a knot of hair.

'The difficulty is to produce really live characters who are different from each other, and who are individual centres of reflection. I think the word "destructive" is quite in place, the individual is destructive of his environment. I don't mean in a bad way, but he modifies it. If somebody comes into the room, he's not like a piece of furniture, the whole place is modified—you are confronted by this extraordinary mysterious object.

'And human beings are so extraordinary and so mysterious, so various and so full of power. And characters in novels, in the sort of novel I try to write, should be like that. They should be mysterious and live, opaque to each other, surprising.

'A work of art should promote thought and be disturbing. It should make you see more of the world. This would be one way of describing what I want a work of art to do.

'The good artist makes you see the world more vividly, because he has understood a part of the individuality of the world, whether it's the individuality of objects or of people. So there is a kind of explosion coming from inside the work of art, if it's good, because something unusual and powerful has been seen and portrayed. And of course, the human individual is the most potent thing of all.

'You have to explore and extend your limits. This is why reading is so important, learning languages and reading literature—another world is pulling you out of yourself, and to get out of yourself is the great thing, to realise that there is another larger world and that other people are different from you.'

One of her images which I had found deeply disturbing was the appearance of the monster in *The Sea, The Sea*. The narrator, Charles Arrowby, is sitting on the cliff near his house, looking out over the sea, when an immense black and coiled creature rises some thirty feet out of the water in front of him. 'What was that monster?'

'I think you have to decide that yourself from the book. There are various ways of looking at it—it might be just a hallucination.'

'But he describes it so clearly.'

'Well that's what he's "seeing", but would anybody else have seen it?'

'Is it symbolic then?'

'The word "symbolic" suggests that there is some exact meaning, but in the context of the work of art there is a great deal of careful ambiguity about any symbol.

'But to pursue your monster, and whether he's real or not (whatever that means), I think one should take quite seriously the idea that James, the narrator's cousin, actually has had rather strange experiences in Tibet and has certain paranormal powers.'

'Do you believe in these?'

'That, for example, people can raise their bodily temperatures to survive in the snow, I do believe. I don't believe in the raising of the dead or anything like that, but just that the human mind is a mysterious thing, and if you train yourself in certain ways, you may be able to develop certain unusual powers.

'Later in the story, it is conceivable that James uses some paranormal power to rescue Charles—very much against his own wishes because he had come to say goodbye to him; but that James is really in love with Charles is part of the story.

'Anyway, the monster: Tibetan Buddhism is very much concerned with demons, attendant monsters which go with you, so the monster could be a kind of attendant demon of James, an image of James, which has just got separated from him.

'Monsters—one's mind is full of monsters. I'm very interested in dreams. We are accompanied by a dream world, the unconscious mind teems with strange things.

'And a work of art is a place where you can formalise and present some of these strange things which are just outside the focus of your ordinary consciousness.'

'So monsters inhabit another region?'

Miss Murdoch was anxious that it should not be so easily labelled. 'This is putting it all too precisely. Obviously, a monster must be connected with something and have some role. Monsters in one's dreams play roles—they're menacing or they're friendly. I don't know if you know the paintings of a man called Carel Weight?'

I shook my head.

'He has a series of paintings which have ghosts in them. You see an ordinary scene, and then there's a ghost crossing it. I mean, you can put such things into art, and they then become public property but they will still retain a kind of ambiguity. If you did it all the time, it might be a bad idea, but I think you can do it sometimes—like the monster in the book.'

And thinking of Charles Arrowby and his monster, I asked whether her characters surprised her as she wrote their stories.

'The surprises for me would happen early on, when I'm inventing the characters. I go through a period of not knowing what they're like, and then I discover.'

'How do you invent someone's character?'

'To begin with, the story is part of the character, so one knows roughly what he's going to do, but I also think about people in a general way—I think: "What was his childhood like?" and other things which won't necessarily come into the book, but which give the person *life*, so that you feel that he is *there*. He may have mysteries of his own—one doesn't always know what he may do later.'

'And are the characters not drawn from your own life?'

'No. I couldn't do it anyway, because, in my case, the imagination would prevent it. Drawing from life tends to inhibit imagination. If you can invent people why copy? Copying is dull.'

Miss Murdoch's characters often experience moments of surprise when they recognise something passing between them which takes them half out of their own lives and half into each other's. In *The Sandcastle*, Mor is aware of this sort of feeling as he follows Rain Carter into the garden to pick roses:

Mor took her hand in his and let her guide him up the steps. Her grip was firm. They passed between the black holly bushes, and released each other. Mor felt a strong shock within him, as if very distantly something had subsided or given way. He had a confused feeling of surprise. The moon came out of the clouds for a moment and suddenly the sky was seen in motion.

'Do you think such epiphanies are actually possible?' I asked. 'Especially amongst older middle-aged people?'

'Yes, of course, people retain this capacity. I think that these "epiphanies" are happening all the time. If people have any strong relationships at all, and most people do (the family is very important), then these discoveries and these dramas happen all the way through life. Having friends and knowing a certain number of other human beings well is a very important thing! Of course Edward, for you, this is a time in your life when you will be acquiring friends for ever.

'And, you know, relationships change and you make discoveries about other people. People are very secretive—even your best friends are secretive. This is why when people sometimes say to me, "Nobody is as odd as that," about people I've put in a book, I say, "But they *are*, and odder still!" People are terribly odd, but they conceal the fact. You're not going to tell other people how odd you are.'

We realised that it was late, and I stood up to go. As she gathered her things together, I asked if she regretted not having children.

'Well ... yes and no ... it wasn't in my stars. Some women have strong feelings about this, but I don't think I have very strong feelings. It wasn't one of my aims in life.'

I poked my head back out into the antiseptic college. 'Don't you hate living in this concrete breeze block?'

It seemed an important question to Miss Murdoch, and she put me right, 'No. This college has its own beauty. And there are people here.'

Kingsley Amis

ST JOHN'S, 1941/5–47

'Sorry about that egg on the window.'

We had bumped into each other as he returned from posting a letter, and he was leading me through the back door.

'Somebody threw it, and it's been there for weeks. It's very difficult to get off. Better than having it on your face!'

Kingsley Amis lives high up on a hill in Kentish Town, where the sky spreads low and wide over the curved lines of chimney pots, and the brown and grey houses seem only remotely inhabited. Inside, his house is shabby. Two green corduroy armchairs faced each other across the grate, which was littered with empty cigar boxes.

'I had four terms from April 1941 to June 1942, and then was called up. Luckily I returned in October 1945, when I took an incredible amount of money from the Government and stayed another couple of years.'

'What was Oxford like before the war?'

'Well, it meant that, although friendships happened, it was all very short-lived. One minute friends were there, the next minute they were in the Navy. There were no lunch parties, no coal to be got, food was rationed, liquor was hard to get, beer was short—everything was cut back. Everybody was spending hours in trains waiting for things to happen, or hours queueing for food—not essential food, but for any luxury. If you liked cakes, you had to queue for them, and for cigarettes, and there was enforced pub-crawling because one pub would sell beer early in the evening, and another later on, so there would be groups of us just drifting around. It was just a question of getting through the next bit. And that's what Army life was like later.'

75

'I was once helpless with laughter in a taxi reading one of Martin's books. The driver was alarmed and said to me, "You can't laugh like that over a *book*." But you can. You ought to.'

Kingsley Amis

'So you were living for the moment?'

'That's right, although "living for the moment" sounds much too much like Horatio—"Drink and be merry, because tomorrow you die" sort of stuff. You couldn't drink very much, you couldn't be merry very much, and it was term time with an exam at the end. In 1941, everybody thought that we would very likely lose the war, and we were wondering how soon the Germans might arrive.'

'But you did have this friendship with Philip Larkin when you were both at St John's College—how did that start?'

'Jazz mainly, and beer and a bit of culture, though not very much. People say to me earnestly and piously: "I expect you had some very interesting conversations about literature with Philip Larkin" . . . .'

Mr Amis's pumice-stone face retched. '"What?!" I say, "Oh yes, we had some interesting conversations about Louis Armstrong, but not about *poetry*!"'

'Did reading English help your writing at all?'

'Not at all, I should say. I've thought about this a lot over the years. I think it's a bad thing for writers. I should have read History.'

'Why do you say that?'

'You know, all the enquiries you're supposed to make of yourself and into the text as to what literature is about, what makes a good poem, what makes a good page of prose and all that. I think that's good for readers—having read English at Oxford, I'm a better reader and I see more in what I read, but I don't think it does any good to writing.'

'Why not?'

Mr Amis itched away with his fingernail at a stain on his sleeve. 'It's bad to say to yourself: "This poem that I'm writing, is this good poetry? Am I forging a personal diction in the way we're told Hopkins or Wilfred Owen or Wordsworth did? Should I be developing an original voice?"'

He pulled his lemon-sucking face. 'That's terrible! You can't *decide* to develop—a poet with any chance can only hope to write the next poem.'

'Who are your favourite writers?'

'John Betjeman, Philip Larkin, Robert Graves as was, bits of Roy Fuller.'

I remarked that they were all from Oxford.

'Yes, isn't that sinister! Well, I could go back to Tennyson to find a Cambridge poet for you, but Oxford has produced more poets.'

'Is that just coincidence?'

'Not altogether. It's interesting to compare those two places, and one can draw up a short list of differences. Cambridge is more parochial. Although they're almost exactly the same distance from

London, Oxford feels itself much closer to London. You can tell just by looking at the town plans that they are different sorts of cities. Oxford has always been on several main roads, it's what they call a "communication centre", and you're much more likely to find it's an Oxford don who edits a London literary periodical.

'I remember asking somebody a terrible question once. I said: "What have you learnt at Oxford? What has Oxford taught you that Cambridge couldn't?" He'd probably been asked the question before and got the answer ready, because he said, "Not to be afraid of the obvious." I laughed—it's quite a funny answer.

'But when you think about it, it's important not to be afraid of the obvious. A good example of the obvious is Lord David Cecil. He'll tell you that Swift writes with savage indignation or that Wordsworth turned his back on the poetic diction of the eighteenth century, and you've got to go through those stages of thinking before you get anywhere else. Cambridge tries to avoid that sort of stuff. I think there are great strengths to be derived from not being afraid of the obvious.

'I came across this when I was reviewing the new *Oxford Book of Christian Verse* (I was the obvious person to do it) which was originated by Lord David Cecil, and a new edition with a completely new selection had been done by Donald Davie. Lord David had put all the obvious ones in, so he had given us *Rugby Chapel* and a lot of Christina Rossetti, but Donald Davie left them out—he didn't even give us *In the Bleak Midwinter*. The reason why the "obvious" is obvious is because it's better.'

'Why were you the "obvious" person to do the review?'

His puff-pastry cheeks dimpled. 'That was ironical—I'm not much of a Christian!'

I kicked myself for falling into the trap and then asked, 'Would you say both John Betjeman and Philip Larkin concern themselves with the obvious?'

'Yes, they're obvious in the sense that you can make head and tail of what they mean—the poetical feelings that they go in for and the subjects they pursue.

'Housman, by the way, who is older than most (older anyway than both of those), he's my favourite poet of all. It took me quite a long time to disentangle that notion about not being the greatest poet, but he is my favourite poet.

'I very much like Robert Graves' definition of poetry: "Heart-rending sense." Very short. Or: "Enchanted commonsense," which is my description of the music of Handel. I think it would do for a lot of things I like, too. In a way, Betjeman concerns himself with the obvious, with the things you see, but with the unexpected parts of it, or where it leads you. Or with Larkin—the wonderful thing about Larkin's work is that it starts off, like Betjeman's, with something very commonplace, something like a photograph album, like a glass of gin and tonic, like an agricultural fair, like looking out of a train window. Starting in this unobtrusive, commonplace way, he begins to dig down. And he digs deep.'

'Is this true of your writing?'

'I don't know. That's another thing—I am the very one who can't say that. I'd like to think that it did, that it did go towards something more universal, but one can't tell.'

'Why do you choose these same commonplace beginnings for your work?'

'I don't think it matters where you start—what matters is where you get to. It's like thinking, it's like living: it starts from small things and reflections on those things. I don't know. I can't talk about myself in that way.'

'What do you aim to write about?' His eyes met mine, rather watery and remote as though both of them might have been glass.

'Human nature. In fact, human nature as it has always been—as far as possible, as far as I am capable of doing: love, ambition, loss, grief, fear, friendship, sex, money, religion—all these things which have always been there.'

'Your books often don't seem very romantic.'

'Well, I don't know whether you've read *I Want It Now?*'

'No, I haven't.'

'That, to my mind, is a love story, although it takes place very much in our world.

'I like reading romantic fiction—if I know that it's not much to do with me. I've just finished *Greenmantle* by John Buchan. Marvellous! And that's never been much to do with anybody. It's not much like life, and I bet it's not much like Central Europe in 1916, if only because he had never been there when he wrote it.

'What I wanted then with *I Want It Now* was a love story. I had to work to keep my emotions hidden. It's about this thrusting, pushy, not-very-nice television engineer who meets a rich girl. She is really neurotic and dreads and dislikes men, although she's very promiscuous. She also has a terrible mother to whom she is subjected. He decides that he is going to get those dollars by marrying this girl, but then, of course, he actually falls in love with her and finally marries her without the money. In fact, he has the choice: he could take the money or, if he is going to get her away from the mother (which he thinks is important), he has to pass up the money.

'It is so arranged that he insults the mother on television in a very big way, and so sees to it that he never gets the money, but they get away from the mother.

'Now, that is as much of a love story as you can stomach, or ought to have to these days. Oh yes, it starts off with unpromising beginnings with this nasty little fellow who does a nasty little chat show and puts people down and is left-wing because he thinks it's fashionable and doesn't care at all, but that's where a lot of people start.'

'Having started off like this, how far into idealism does your writing stray?'

'Oh, idealism is very suspect. Any idealist would have to be an unsympathetic character, wouldn't he?'

'I don't see why.'

'Well, look at the great idealists of our time. Number one: Adolf Hitler. Now he didn't do any good to anybody. Idealism is dangerous.'

'Surely there are idealists who have done great things?'

'No, I don't like it. I think there has got to be a little idealism, but it should be heftily tempered by pessimism.'

'What would that achieve?'

'Pessimism is the great virtue. It prevents us from making so many mistakes. By "pessimism", I mean taking a pessimistic view of human nature, not a hostile one. It would be pessimistic to say, for example, that if you give one man as much power as Lenin or Stalin were given, the chances are (human nature being what it is) that you'll end up with ruthless authoritarianism. That's pessimism, and it's very justified.

'So we're getting political now, but I think as soon as we mention idealism, then politics are evoked. I don't think you can have private idealism. When my friend Ronnie says, "Come what may, I must get her away from her mother!" Now—is that idealism? No, I'd call it "generosity of spirit" or "an ability to put someone else first", I wouldn't call it idealism.'

'What about Jenny Bunn's idealism in *Take A Girl Like You*? Why couldn't she remain an idealist? The ending is one of the most unconsoling I have ever read.'

'Yes, pretty bleak, isn't it?' Mr Amis looked pleased. 'There's a sympathetic idealist for you, Jenny Bunn. And why couldn't she stay that way? Because the world isn't like that—as Patrick points out to her (from very base motives, but he's quite right). If Jenny had kept her illusions, she would have been a very peculiar person. To have led the kind of life she wanted to lead, and seen those people she wanted to see, would have made her virginity difficult if not impossible.'

'So do you consciously avoid heroic characters?'

'People accuse me of that, but I can't think of any heroic characters in other people's books. There's Richard Hannay in *Greenmantle*, he's jolly heroic, but . . . .'

I interrupted. 'When I say "heroic", I mean characters who are not necessarily terribly virtuous or courageous, but who are in some way larger than life'—I groped for examples—'you know, Hamlet, Othello, Brutus.'

'Brutus is a very good example.'

'Why?'

'Because if anyone ruins the Roman Republic, it's Brutus—that's what the play's all about, isn't it? That scene has always puzzled me when the conspirators bathe their arms in Caesar's blood. Isn't it strange? I want to say, "What are you *doing*? Civilised men like you? Scholars?" Brutus is so nice to his little page boy: "Look, here is the book I sought. I found it in the pocket of my gown." A nice fellow. But it's his suggestion: "Stoop then and wash." Because that's what you get when intellectuals and high-minded chaps decide to act. They kill the dictator and wash in his blood.

'And the terrible mess that Brutus makes of his speech to the mob, and the frightful success Antony has with his. That's what you get with idealism, you see—it's dangerous.

'I don't know what the state of play is at the moment on Shakespeare's Roman plays, but surely it is also to do with government; how under Caesar you had stability, and when you pull that apart, well, you get the devil you don't know.'

'Going back to *your* characters, how much do you sympathise with them?'

'I have to like them all. They're so much a part of me, that however unsympathetic they are to the reader, they're sympathetic to me. That isn't to say I defend everything they do: look at Roger Micheldene! A terrible man! Really frightful! You can't like him for anything he does, but you can feel sorry for him because he loves Helena as much as he'll ever love anybody.'

'What's the basis of your sympathy?'

'To begin with, they're all human beings in a sense. Human life is so unpleasant that I think people can be forgiven quite a lot if they have any redeeming features—there's something to be said for them, even if it's only an excuse.'

'And in your writing, do you portray human life as you see it or as something else, some sort of fiction?'

'It's very hard to disentangle those things. If you say, for example, "Would Lucky Jim have got the girl in real life?" I say: "I don't care— all I know is he's got to get the girl in this book." I'm fed up with novels where the hero doesn't get the girl. Of course he gets the girl! It would be wholly inappropriate if he didn't. It would leave the reader feeling'—he switched on his constipated-waste-disposal voice—'"Oh, trying to give it profundity, is he?"

'It's also important that he shouldn't sympathise with the people on the other side. I did a first draft of *Lucky Jim* and showed it to Philip Larkin, who said, "Oh, you've got Dixon developing a soft spot for Bertrand. He shouldn't do that. When he sees him the first time, he hates him; when he sees him the second time, he should hate him more!" I said, "You're right!"

'By the way, that's how writers discuss literature—it's always about specific points. You would never say to a writer'—he cleared his throat for an 'and-is-Virginia-Woolf-coming-to-tea?' voice—'"Don't you think that a certain consistency in tone is important?"' And answered himself with a Laurie McMenemy: '"Yer what?!"'

Mr Amis's poetry is an aspect of his writing which has been largely neglected. 'And what about poetry? Why do you no longer write it?' I asked.

'I know it sounds cynical, but be it noted that Anthony Powell said, knowing me and Roy Fuller quite well, "Yes, Roy's poetry gets in the way of his novels. People take him seriously as a poet. Your novels get in the way of your poetry, people don't take you seriously enough as a poet."

'It could also be that the poetry isn't all that good, but we needn't go into that! I think it's all right. But the reason I'm not a poet any more is the same reason that Larkin will say that he's not a poet any more, and Betjeman will say the same about himself. I last wrote poetry in 1979, I've got two or three bits lying around in some drawer which I'll probably finish, but otherwise I won't write any more—it dies away. The words stop coming. I don't know whether that's a natural way of putting it, but it will do.

'When the muse or the unconscious has got something to communicate, however small, if you don't listen or pay attention, you deserve to be shot. You cannot forge a message from here', he tapped his forehead, 'it has to come.

'I always stress that the part played by the unconscious is immense. Do you do crossword puzzles? I think you might enjoy them. I can tell you, I like doing them. You write in the ones you know in the morning and you look at the ones you can't do. Then you put the paper aside. Later, in the evening, you pick it up and, hey presto! The ones you couldn't do in the morning are easy.

'I can give you innumerable instances of the unconscious: if you sleep on it, that's the unconscious, if you go for a walk, that can do it. Once I spent two days like a fool staring at the typewriter not knowing how to get off the ground. I knew what I wanted to write, but every possible start seemed blocked. So the third morning, I decided to leave it, and I went off to buy some cigars—things happened. You notice things that start you off, you see people. The girl in *I Want It Now* was the problem—I knew a lot about her, but I didn't know what she looked like until I was walking to buy those cigars and a car went past and my subconscious said, "That's her!" You were nearly there already, you just didn't know you were—sallow complexion, very dark fair hair, lots of moles.

'It's no use saying, "I'll write up this character today," they appear of their own accord. People often ask me, perhaps not a bright young chap like you, but it's a favourite question of people like mother-in-laws: "Do you find the characters taking charge?" And I say, "Well, not exactly, no." I can't say, "Fuck off!" That wouldn't be right.

'Actually they may be right. I suppose there are two things here: you've got what you think you've got in store for a character, and you've got what he's actually got in store for you. In *I Want It Now*, one of the characters was just supposed to be one of the horrible rich people hanging around the heroine. Then after about a hundred pages, I thought that there should be somebody who the mother wants her to marry—somebody really horrible. And there he was, waiting. Then I knew why I had brought him in with just a little bit more detail than the others. I didn't have to go back and make him more important, he was just right as he was.

'So it's as if there was somewhere, up in Plato's cave perhaps, an ideal copy of every novel, and you can be fed with bits of it. The bits you don't get, you have to somehow fill in. I can believe what Mozart said about himself that he conceived the whole of the finale of the Jupiter Symphony simultaneously. He didn't say whether he salvaged it all, but with a mind like his, I should think he probably did.'

I remembered what Iris Murdoch had told me about planning her novels, and the background she explored for her characters. 'Are you saying that your writing is all spontaneous combustion? That you don't trace the characters before or beyond the book?' I repeated what Iris Murdoch had said about their childhood and schooldays.

'I don't work like that. I might sometimes think to myself: Now look, I don't know anything about this chap's childhood ... but then I usually think: "Bloody berk—why should I?" or again I could think: "If this chap has always been as much of a shit as this, how did he get on at school?" and I might put a hint in.

'It seems Iris Murdoch does it with work beforehand—I'm probably doing it simultaneously and putting it in later. When I'm writing a novel, I don't know what I'm doing half the time. I don't know why the story might take that particular course. I have vague objectives which

83

are the story and the plot, so I know I've got to arrange it sooner or later that those two quarrel and she goes off with the other chap, but that's about as much as I know when I start.'

I told him that I was finding it difficult to swallow the idea of him just hijacking a complete novel from Plato's cave and forwarding it to the publishers. Mr Amis laughed. 'But you must be *looking* for particular subject matter?' I said.

He didn't seem to be pulling my leg. 'No, it's something which finds you more. It chooses me; a lot of it is not consciously chosen—it marks you down, or it strikes a chord in you. That's actually not a bad way of putting it.

'Take remarks, for example. You can suddenly say, "Ah! That's my kind of remark," and you make a note of it. Joyce was always doing that. "Epiphanies" he pompously called them, instead of "good ideas" or "funny bits", and he would always rush around and make a hoo-ha and send all his guests out of the room whilst he wrote them down. But you do have your own sort of remarks.

'Once I said to my son, who's had his marital problems (I wasn't very sober at the time), I said, '"Look, it's no use saying anything to a woman", and I was going on to say, "Unless..." but he said, "Hold it there. Don't add anything, don't spoil it, it's fine as it is—*it's no use saying anything to a woman.*"

'That's my kind of stuff, so it's going into my current novel, slightly souped up: "Well, you know Stan, it's no use saying anything to a woman!"'

'When what?'

'When nothing. Just that.' Mr Amis grinned.

'Does that express the whole of what you want to say?' I asked with some sarcasm.

'Nothing expresses the whole of what I want to say—otherwise I would have said it, wouldn't I?'

'Well, that comment strikes me as completely unimpressive and meaningless.'

He squashed me firmly. 'It won't be meaningless when it comes in, don't you worry. On page two hundred it wouldn't be unimpressive at all.'

'Let's talk about your son's writing—how do you feel about Martin's work?'

'I love his success' (he winked) 'I think we've had about as much of it as we need. But I don't really cotton on to what he writes. I shouldn't really say much about this, but it's too sort of self-conscious for me.'

He suddenly shouted with unexpected fury, 'NABOKOV IS A FRIGHT-FUL INFLUENCE! His books should be banned for the good of literature!'

'Look, it's no use saying anything to a woman.'
Kingsley Amis, Kentish Town

'Why?'

Mr Amis screwed his face up like a squeezed sponge: 'I want to *kill* him! He's so *juvenile*! Martin gave me *Lolita* to read which I thought was going to be a wonderful pornographic daydream, but it wasn't that at all: "I saw a man in the street today." Exciting stuff. "He was about thirty-five years old, short and dark-haired. Actually, he wasn't—he was twenty-five years old and tall and fair-haired. I just told you a lie. I just misled you, didn't I?"

'Ho, ho, ho, ha, ha, ha, I hate it! It's pathetic! We were writing that sort of thing aged *fourteen*.

'Actually, Martin's new novel is very much more "accessible" as we now call it. The galling thing is that he can be incredibly funny in a straightforward way. I was once helpless with laughter in a taxi reading his book. The driver was quite alarmed and said to me, "You can't laugh like that over a *book*." But you can. You ought to.'

'Do you like people to laugh over your books?'

'Yes.'

'I mean *really* laugh?'

'Yes.'

'Do you laugh yourself as you write them?'

'Yes; and cry. Dickens used to do that. He laughed and cried as he wrote.'

'He was a Victorian.'

'Yes, but that's all right. One of my favourite men, one of my heroes—C. P. E. Bach (born 1716) said, "The artist who is not moved by his own material cannot expect anybody else to be moved by it." Good that, isn't it?'

Mr Amis showed me out down the steps, back past the egg. He asked which college I was at, and snorted when I told him St Anne's, an ex-ladies' college. What did he think of mixed colleges?

'I couldn't think of anything more wonderful if I was twenty-one. It wouldn't appeal to me so much now. Do you know, I am the kind of person that I could have never believed I'd become when I was twenty-one. When I was your age, there was never a time when I didn't want to be in the company of a girl, except perhaps very briefly in the pub. Nowadays, I see the virtues of not being with them!

'I'm a member of the Garrick, and there is part of the club where no females are ever allowed, so I sit there. If any woman pokes her head around the corner, I go ...' he slowly grew the face of a hippopotamus inflated to bursting point, 'and if she doesn't retreat from that, I'll start shouting, "Take her *away*!"'

I left Mr Amis wheezing with laughter and fading to a normal colour.

John Mortimer

BRASENOSE, 1940–43

As always when starting off an interview, I felt completely tongue-tied. The tape recorder whirred on for a while whilst Mr Mortimer sipped at his mug of tea and glanced across the desk towards me. It was as though we were both waiting for a prompter at the beginning of some piece by Samuel Beckett.

'At the end of *Clinging to the Wreckage*,' I began, 'you spoke of Henry Winter who killed his mistress and committed suicide. You wrote: "I think about these things often, but I cannot explain them. I can only suggest that Henry Winter suffered terribly and unusually from having rejected the violence which was made available to us all at the age when we went to Oxford." What did you mean by that?'

'I meant the violence of the war really, but then I wasn't afforded that either, and I haven't murdered anyone! Henry was a pacifist, a dedicated pacifist, so really what I was saying, I suppose, was perhaps he was suppressing all those instincts and aggressions he had which were then bottled up until that day.'

'So it wasn't Oxford which could have released those instincts?'

'No, no; I didn't mean that. I meant that he was denied the opportunity of a violence which the world was having during the time we were at Oxford.'

'Do you think Oxford does provide any form of release?'

'I think probably less so now. In my time, your life was very sheltered up to the time you went to Oxford, then suddenly you found yourself released into the world of grown-ups. I don't know if public schools are still like that. I actually hate the idea of them so much that I

'Now, by the time you're twelve, you've practically had all the adult experiences you'll ever have.'

John Mortimer

try to avoid thinking about them, but I can't believe that people's lives are nearly so sheltered now.

'Now, by the time you're twelve, you've practically had all the adult experiences you'll ever have. I would say my daughter, who is twelve, is as grown up as anybody else I know.'

When he said this, I lost interest in asking any more questions about Oxford. I did not think they would somehow fit someone who sees education and growing up so much through the context of his family. The tape-recorder whirred on by itself once more as I rethought the interview.

We were sitting in the study of his father's old house at Turville Heath in the middle of the Chilterns. The house is tucked away off an avenue of beech trees, and was almost overgrown by the scramble of surrounding hedgerows and garden. From reading *Clinging to the Wreckage*, I felt I already knew the house quite well, and as I had walked around the outside to find the front-door, it had been easy to imagine Mr Mortimer's father being guided to pick the weeds or catch earwigs.

I decided to bring the interview closer to this home life. 'You seem to have led a life very much as a user of words, being an advocate and a writer—how did it start, this way of seeing words as your exclusive medium?'

'I think it happened because I was an only child. My father was blind, so I had to read aloud to him a great deal, which meant I heard words and I got very used to their sound. Because I was alone much of the time, and because at school I was totally unattracted to any kind of sport and couldn't sing in tune, I used to read most of my spare time.

'I always knew that what I was was a writer. It didn't particularly matter what I wrote—plays, books, fiction, autobiographies or whatever, it was all writing to me. It was the one thing I wanted to do. I sort of fell into being a barrister as a money-making thing until I could support myself by writing, but then the whole thing got slightly out of control, and I became too involved in the law for my own good.

'But I was never the least degree interested in the law—I never knew very much law. I grew up in the law doing divorce cases, and everybody knows that that law is ridiculous. It is just a maze of absurdities, so all I had to do was steer people through it and get them out in some sort of recognisable and sane situation at the end; that's how I grew up looking at the law—I never thought it was anything but absurd. Criminal law is a bit more sensible. What I was was an advocate, which is using words again, trying to persuade people things. So, in a way, that was a literary life too.'

'Words are strange things, aren't they? They're such a slippery medium.'

'Yes, they are.'

'Something which has always puzzled me about barristers is that you plead for your clients without ever knowing whether they're innocent or guilty.'

'No, you'd never quite know that. You'd asssume that they're telling the truth.'

'You'd never ask if they had actually "dunnit"?'

'No. That's the last thing you want to know.'

'So the core of it is missing.'

'The core of it may be missing, but you do feel very protective about your clients, however ghastly they are.'

'Without any core of truth, without knowing your client's sincerity, how can you get the jury to come to any real judgment?'

'Well, they're not sincere. But then nobody is sincere—I don't think sincerity is a very predominant quality around the Old Bailey.

'They're in trouble really, that's the appealing thing about them—people in trouble. They're lying, of course, but people don't have to be criminals to lie or make up fantasies about themselves, which is not really lying. Most of the people you defend have convinced themselves that what they're saying is true. People who aren't professional criminals but who have done something terrible or ridiculous or made great mistakes, they don't stand there thinking they're lying. What they do is convince themselves after a long process of self-persuasion that what they're saying is true. And that's true of everybody.'

He had once described it as 'suspended disbelief', which I had thought made it sound theatrical. I said so.

'I thought it sounded religious.'

'Why religious?'

'Isn't that what Catholics do? They suspend their disbelief. If they are to have religious faith, they have to suspend their doubts to accept things.'

'I've always thought of "suspending my disbelief" as being at the theatre—pretending it's all real.'

'Well, there you are. It's the same thing. On the whole, I think that's how people live, that's how everybody lives. We all live in our own world of fantasy (Mrs Thatcher or the Archbishop of Canterbury are just the same), which only bears some sort of occasional or accidental relation to the truth of the world about us. Living in fantasy isn't something confined to criminals, it is the essence of life—and of art too. The whole business of writing is to explore the contrast between the real world and the world which people believe they're in, both of which are constantly in collision.

'So everybody is acting. The whole thing about the Court is that everybody is acting, the Judge puts on his wig, the barristers prevaricate, the criminals might be cheerful Cockney characters—it all proceeds by people playing roles.'

'But then at the end you get a decision.'

'No, you don't get a decision. The decision is not necessarily truthful, it may be founded on the truth, the decision can be just as much the product of people's fantasies as anything else.'

'Isn't it a real decision?'

'Oh yes, they're real factors: the death of the victim, the crime, prison—all those things are reality, but it's the way people look at them.' Mr Mortimer looked amused. 'I say, this is a really philosophical conversation!'

I turned the question over for the last time: 'How could you justify persuading a jury to come to a verdict, when the medium through which you led them was so theatrical, so much to do with slippery words?'

'I don't know whether a verdict is absolute. I don't quite know what that means.'

'A twelve-year prison sentence is absolute.'

'Yes, a twelve-year prison sentence is a twelve-year prison sentence. That's right. And it's an awful thing. Yes, if you write a bad play you don't get sent to prison for twelve years! And the verdict is not necessarily right. That is what finally put me off it. I couldn't take the responsibility any longer. By the time I was finishing, there were these enormous stakes—a person's whole life, vast sums of money, vast terms of imprisonment; it all became too much. It's a terrific relief not to have to do it any more.'

'I remember you saying something which interested me about murderers—you said that actually they were very nice clients. Why is that?'

'Because murder is the sort of crime that anybody, any non-criminal person, could do. The sort of murder which I liked doing would be the sort of murder which any ordinary person had stumbled into—like quarrels between husbands and wives, between friends in pubs. The vast majority of murders happen between husbands and wives, lovers, landlords and tenants when a momentary quarrel goes out of control. I liked helping those murderers, because actually you're only dealing with ordinary people to whom something dreadful has happened.'

'You don't think there's an underlying trace of violence in that particular person?'

'No, I think there's an underlying trace of violence in everybody. If you become a murderer, you've been unlucky enough to find the one person in the world who brings it out. Murderers mostly only murder the one person they needed to murder—they weren't going to murder anyone else.'

'And now you no longer do it?'

'No, I've done enough. It's a great feeling of relief. Funnily enough, I don't feel responsible for the law any more. Every time I heard some awful decision, I used to cringe and think it was all my fault because I was a lawyer, part of the organisation. Nowadays they can behave as stupidly as they like, and I don't have to worry about them.'

During his life as a writer and a barrister, Mr Mortimer had used words both to entertain and to advocate judgment. The area where those fields overlap or diverge was somewhere I was interested to examine: so which of the two worlds works closer to the truth?

'In art you do discover the truth or some truth about life—I don't think the whole truth is discoverable anyway, but you are on the path of the truth much more than you are in a legal case. That's why writing is more important to me than being a barrister—because you have much more concern about the truth. If you're a barrister, facts are something which you fit together to form a theory, a tenable theory, which isn't what you do as a writer. If you're writing, you're trying to present a truthful picture of the world as you see it. Writing can give you some insight into yourself, into the human situation. If it's good, you recognise that you've learnt a little bit more about what life is about; I would say these experiences are rare in law courts.'

Mr Mortimer leant back in his chair and cupped his mug to his chest. Above the striped mug, his face fascinated my attention: behind his glasses, the eyes are deeply slit and tilted as if Siamese, the forehead above is high and broad, but the rest of the face collapses into a mongoloid pudding—the cheeks fall into suet jowls and, stuck in the middle, a catfish mouth opens with broken teeth. This pursed itself into a chubby round hole when I asked, 'What's it like to write a book about yourself?'

'It's quite hard. The first thing you have to decide is how to deal with your own character. I decided to be quite quiet about myself, and put all the colouring in the surrounding characters. So I'm a sort of camera to all this life as it goes around me. I didn't decide to write a book because I was trying to probe down into the great innermost secrets of my life.'

'Though you do let slip a few secrets. At one point you discuss the breakdown of your marriage to Penelope, and you write: "I don't know if the 'marriage ending' cards were dealt when we first stood on the beach in Ireland and Penelope was overcome with thoughts of death." Why did you want to confide that?'

'Maybe I shouldn't have included that. I don't know. It's very difficult to make those judgments. I've always found with characters that
they do what they think they'll do, they don't do what you think they'll
do.

'I'm not trying to get out of saying whether that was a right thing to
do or a wrong thing to do, maybe it was a wrong thing to do, but when I
found myself writing that page, somehow it seemed the right thing to
say. Certainly that was an artistic rather than a moral judgment. I
wouldn't mind what I said from a moral point of view.'

'You don't seem to make much distinction between your own life—
I thought *Clinging to the Wreckage* began to move beyond autobiography into something approaching fiction.'

'No, I don't regard fiction and autobiography as different—I think
of the whole thing as fiction. I regard myself as a character in fiction
really, and so everybody I know becomes a fictional character to some
extent. I mean, I can't distinguish if I'm writing about Rumpole or my
father. My father has become a fictional character because he's
become a character in a play, and Rumpole has become in a way a real
character.

'Everything I write is pretty close to me. I don't regard *Clinging to the
Wreckage* as really very different from the Rumpole stories. I don't
know whether you'd call *Voyage Around My Father* a play or an autobiography or whatever. Everything in writing seems to me to be
experiencing life and then trying to translate it back into words, into
some sort of entertainment. I can't distinguish between fact and fiction.'

Giving him an acid test on this, I asked whether he had, in fact,
made love with Angela Bedwell during his marriage to Penelope. His
instinctive response was to resort to that well documented trick of his,
removing his glasses. I knew he would now be seeing me, and by impli-
cation the question, as a distant blur.

'I just wanted that story to end like that. Now, whether that happened or whether that didn't happen, that's how I wanted to end that
story. Because it's an unexpected ending, it's better than just ending it
where it was. Now, that's an entirely artistic answer to that question.'

No kidding, I thought, and I pushed a little harder.

'No, whether that's true or whether that wasn't true doesn't seem to
me to matter really. It wasn't what I was thinking about. In fact, I think
it probably was true, but what I was thinking about was the way of
writing, the shaping of the book. I wasn't really thinking about what
the readers would think of me as a person, I was thinking of making
the character of "me" into a character who would be interesting to
read about.

'What I can't believe in is God as a "Spirit of Goodness." I find that difficult in view of his record.'

John Mortimer, Turville Heath

'My chief thing in writing my autobiography was not to say, "This is the sort of person I am," because I'm not sure that you can derive that. What I wanted to do was to say how life appeared to the narrator, and I hope you'll enjoy it, find it funny or touching, or whatever.'
'Did you feel it was like a confessional at all?'
'No, it's not a confessional.'
'Would you want to confess to anybody?'
'I don't do much confessing. I'm very religious, except that I'm an atheist.'
'Wouldn't you like to?'

'No. I'm not terribly conscious of guilt really. I'm not filled with guilt.'

'You're religious, but you're an atheist—so where do you turn?'

'I think about religion a lot—I like writing about religion, and I love interviewing bishops. I always ask people about God.

'But the only God I can think of is a God I wouldn't like. He would seem to allow some really terrible things to happen which he would obviously be able to prevent. So, if he exists, I haven't got any great sympathy with him. I don't know how people reconcile their idea of God with the idea of concentration camps.'

'That's something you always ask, isn't it?'

'Yes. It's a terribly simple question, but I've never found an answer to it. Nobody, including Cardinal Hume and the Archbishop of Canterbury, has ever given me an answer which I've found in the least bit satisfactory. It's such a childish question too, but they none of them will answer it. They say they don't know, or that you've got to be agnostic about it. Well, you know, if you're cross-examining someone in Court before a jury, you ask very simple questions—so I'd like to know the answer to that. And I don't know what the answer could be; I cannot believe that there is an all-powerful God who is testing us out to see whether we're good enough for some other purpose.'

'What sort of God can you believe in?'

'The sort of God I can believe in, the nearest I could come to, is a sort of pantheistic, Wordsworthian "Spirit of Nature". As far as religion is concerned, I feel Wordsworth is the most religious writer. I could also believe in the Greek gods, who had no morality. I can believe in gods with no moral sense who weren't interested in the problems of good or evil—the Greek gods were quite prepared to fornicate and thieve like everyone else, which makes them quite credible to me.

'What I can't believe in is God as a "Spirit of Goodness". I find that difficult in view of his record. But I certainly wouldn't like an unreligious world. I would hate an England without churches, but I still don't believe that they're particularly inhabitable. No, I would go back to Wordsworth's idea of "all-pervading Nature" as perhaps the most powerful force one could think of to have around.

'I'm not actually very worried about religion—I mean, I don't want to be immortal, I don't wish to live for ever, hanging around for all eternity.'

I had read Mr Mortimer sounding off like this before, but when I mentioned a God of Music and pointed to the row of records on his shelf, he fell through a trap-door in his atheism and seemed to reach for the escapism of music.

'Yes, you can forget all about your troubles. You can forget all about the world.' He went on, 'Someone said that what you need to find is the religion which is implicit in the moment of time that you are in. The significance of that individual moment. I think that that is as far as I could go—looking for something which has a significance above itself. You've got to find out how very important that is, that moment in time, every moment in time.

'Anything can contribute to such a moment—it could be music, eating, making love, working, anything. There should be some feeling of magic about it which you shouldn't lose.'

I said that I supposed the alternative was absurdity—farce.

'Oh, farce! That's terribly interesting to me. I've just translated another Feydeau play which is coming on at the National. It's wonderfully theatrical—if you take any tragedy and play it at fifty revolutions a minute, it becomes a farce.'

'But anyone can play a record at the wrong speed and it sounds ludicrous—so what?'

'Because Feydeau is so expert. Nothing is wasted, every tiny little thing pays off in the last act. You know, there is always someone with a deformity in each Feydeau play because they have to stop the story being told, so the moment when they have to tell, they can't do it because they've got a stutter or they've got a cleft palate or terrible breath so nobody comes near them. In *A Little Hotel on the Side* there is a character who has a terrible stutter, but only when it rains. When it isn't raining, he is a barrister who can speak endlessly. So just when he's about to tell the important part of the plot, it starts raining! It's so absurd! And you see, I think life is absurd—I think that the truth about our existence is its absurdity. A lot of things which happen in life happen just by some ludicrous accident.'

'But you never get three sets of couples leaping into each other's bedrooms in real life—what's so true to life about that?'

'Well, you see, little things you do which you might think nothing of at the time do lead into an incredible whirlwind of disasters—this is quite true of life, I think. In criminal cases, some tiny thing will lead to a huge catalogue of catastrophes. But apart from that, Feydeau's plays are so wonderful. The mechanism is so perfect and so beautiful—it's like a watch. Also, I love those characters. They're sort of bourgeois, middle-class, uninteresting people who are projected into this wild, wild world. Lost their braces and all that! Terribly hard work for the actors—they have to run a mile. And they haven't got anything to fall back on. You can't worry about your inner motives or anything like that when you're rushing around. You haven't got time to worry whether you were dropped on your head when young!

'It's very refreshing to get into that sort of world where all that matters are the actual events. If you take the story of *Othello* and the lost handkerchief, it is exactly the same as *A Flea in Her Ear* and the lost pair of braces. One of them's a tragedy, one of them's a farce—it just depends how you look at these events.'

'Would you like to write tragedy?'

'No, I wouldn't want to write anything that wasn't funny. It's much harder to write, and I think it's much more true to life. I think life is funny, basically it's a funny thing. I need to be funny. Whatever I write needs to be funny. I wouldn't like to write anything that was unrelievedly tragic.'

Mr Mortimer grinned. Rather like the Cheshire Cat's grin which so perplexed Alice, it opened wider and wider whilst the rest of him seemed to dwindle away, until I had the impression of nothing but pure grin swinging from side to side above his face. There it hung like a hammock, but with broken teeth, which I did not think could have been chipped on the edges of farce alone.

'But unrelievedly tragic things do happen,' I countered. 'I mean, you must have felt sad sometimes.'

'Well, the best way of expressing that is always a joke. I don't think I've ever taken anything totally seriously. I was born without too much reverence.'

The grin became something more determined, defensive perhaps. 'I suppose that's a way of surviving.'

There was the sound of a car crunching on the gravel of the drive outside. Mr Mortimer's daughter had come home from school. He struggled round in his chair to wave to her, and I caught a momentary look past his head through his glasses. Seen through those thick lenses, the room and the window blurred, drunkenly distorted as though everything was under water, or reflected in one of those circus mirrors. I supposed that when he took them off, this would be how he would see the world—it seemed an appropriate image for someone for whom the worlds of home and fiction have run into each other; for someone who insists on seeing the world in his terms of making it funny—for a man who is, after all, perhaps only trying to make the most of what he sees outside, beyond his family home at Turville Heath, as a godless world.

Cardinal Hume

ST BENET'S HALL, 1944–47

The room was tall and stately, with a splendid fireplace, white cornices and everything else marmoreal in white and cream. I stood near the fireplace and waited for the Cardinal, aware that something was very wrong. I looked around again, noticing the curved Victorian furniture, sash windows, a Benson and Hedges bar of sunlight spreading across the carpet, then finally the icons. I realised what it was: *icons*. The lame Irish priest with his black suit and dandruff hadn't told me about this. He had let me into the room and just left me in its sunlit silence. He hadn't mentioned that, by the way, you should know that this is a place which takes God entirely for granted. This was something I knew I was unable to share, and it was this which gave me the feeling of a trespasser. So there I waited, completely out of my depth, conscious of a sinking feeling deepening in my stomach. Still the Cardinal didn't arrive, and now I was imagining myself waiting there as vulnerable as fishbait, as vulnerable, as it would later turn out, as the naked girl on the cover of *Jaws* with that shark nosing up towards her.

And in came the Cardinal. Not much of a shark at first sight—tall, stooping slightly and with his long out-of-joint nose and flop of hair, he has rather more something of the hunched and peaky look of a kiwi. He did not shake hands so much as hold mine with both of his and look at me with the concern of a doctor.

'You became a monk,' my first question began, 'at the age of eighteen. That must have been quite a decision.'

'I became a monk at the age of eighteen,' repeated the Cardinal. 'Yes.' He may have decided then and there that this interview was

99

'Oh—so you've got all the answ

going to be a non-starter. 'But there is an awful lot about me you can read all over the place.'

'Yes,' I said, 'I have read some of it—I've read *Searching for God*.'

'Oh—so you've got all the answers!'

'Not at all,' I rejoined, feeling my own nose being tweaked out of joint, 'I wanted to ask what made you become a monk rather than a priest.'

'I must have said that one hundred and one times.'

The Cardinal wasn't going to let himself be accused of playing ball. I looked around the room hoping for inspiration, and found myself looking straight at the Cardinal's ears. The bar of sunlight had shifted and now shone brilliant pink through their scallop spread. In between these two bubbles of strip-lighting, the Cardinal's face was full of polite impatience. Perhaps he was waiting for me to go.

'In some of your addresses to the Ampleforth monks, you stressed how important it is to share the mechanics of living with each other. What I don't understand is how you can share the idea of God with each other.'

'I'm sorry, I don't get what the problem is,' the Cardinal replied. 'I mean, people have been writing about prayer ever since New Testament times, and before that the ancient apostolic writers. There is a whole science about prayer—it's part of the subject, being written about as much as anything else.'

'Which doesn't make it any easier—'

'Oh no, everybody's got to learn how to do it themselves.'

'So how can you share it with anybody else?' A long pause widened between us.

'People have written books about prayer,' he said eventually. 'There is a whole art of how you pray, different ways of praying and different traditions of prayer. This is the whole world of the life as a religious person. The Buddhists have prayer, the Hindus have prayer.'

'Right,' I pounced, 'how much can you sympathise with and understand other people's forms of prayer?'

'Just as much as I can understand, or as much and as little as one person can understand another person.'

'Which always strikes me as not much.'

'Well, you will know some people better than others, won't you? But there is always an inner sanctum which nobody else can penetrate.'

'And wouldn't prayer be in that inner sanctum? After all it's the person's most precious belief.'

'No, you would sit down with somebody else and ask them, "What happens when you pray?" I did it with a hundred young people last week. We were sitting on the floor of the room next door, and I asked,

"What does prayer mean to you?" And they were marvellous. They can explain how it is they can sit silently for ten minutes and just dwell in the presence of God. Their experience will often be described in images, some of them use their imagination, but they have a sense of the presence of God. They might take scenes from the Gospels and think about those, or they might take words and savour those, or take the Psalms: the Psalms have thoughts, and the thoughts are about God and you share those thoughts.

'But if you want to know my views on prayer, you want to get that other book I wrote called *To be a Pilgrim.*'

'Yes,' I said, 'I couldn't find that.' I approached the question of sharing God from another angle. 'I remember you writing in *Searching for God* that often a monk is asked to leave the monastery by the abbot—is that right?'

'Well, there are always two things.' The Cardinal turned his head slightly, so instead of being transparent and ballooned by sunlight, the nearside ear now glistened pink and opaque like an ox tongue. He continued. 'One is the desire of the individual who says, "I want to be a monk," and the other is somebody else who decides whether you are suitable or not. It is the coincidence of these two things. The person may want to be suitable, but may not be.'

'But how do you know that? Isn't that as if one of the young people from next door tried to describe their idea of prayer and you said, "No that's not right"?'

'You may be able to suspect that person is unsuitable from the way they behave. They may be escaping from reality, may be escaping from the world. You can't go into a monastery because you are frightened of things. Some people just think they are coming in for a cosy life—that's no good. You have got to come in for the right reasons and stay for the right reasons. There may be somebody who simply isn't capable of living well in a community, simply doesn't learn not to be arrogant, doesn't learn how to live in a team. Those people are unsuitable.'

'Presumably it is generally agreed—otherwise you would be like a judge.'

'You may be sometimes, but normally it is agreed. Sometimes, it is rare, you get people who really think they ought to be monks, and in fact are unsuitable. You may say, "Look, you'd be better off married." That is one of the factors, whether you should be celibate or not.'

I decided to leave the predictable question of celibacy which the Cardinal provoked, knowing that his answer would be, as it had with John Mortimer: 'Journalists always ask that.' Instead, I launched into something I had never understood about religion. 'How literally do you take the Testaments?'

'How do you mean?' said the Cardinal.

'Do you take them literally, or do you see them as parables and metaphors?'

'You are asking enormous questions! I accept them as the word of God. The word of God expresses itself in different ways—there are stories, there are revealed truths and different literary forms within the Bible itself. Just as prayer is a whole science, the Bible is an enormous science.'

'It seems to me,' I went on, 'that the Bible has gradually materialised, that each generation has added to it and each society changes it to make it more local to their particular needs. So when we read the Bible, we are inheriting a lot of different inputs.'

'How do you mean?' rose the Cardinal's eyebrows.

'Just that everybody has added to it.'

'When do you think the last bit was added?'

'The James the First edition, the Modern Version . . . .'

'No, no—when do you think the last book of the Bible was actually written?'

'That's not the point I'm making.'

'The last bit of the Bible was probably St John's Gospel, which was written about AD 90. No one has added to the Bible since then.'

'But they are adding to it all the time.'

'No. These were the sacred books. After the Resurrection of the Lord, the Church said: "These are the canonical books, these are the official books of the Christian religion." An awful lot of books were rejected as not the official word of God.'

'The point I'm trying to make,' I struggled in the implacable face of the Cardinal, 'is that I see various religions which are all locally based, and they seem to be just locally appropriate to whoever lives there— that to me makes them seem like contrived metaphors.'

'I don't understand,' answered the Cardinal, stubborn as a stone-fish, 'I . . . I just don't begin to understand your thinking.'

'My thinking is that you have a number of different religions, the major ones being Hindu, Buddhist, Church of Rome—and even taking the Church of England. . . .'

'The Church of England and the Church of Rome are both Christian churches—Christian, Christian,' the Cardinal enunciated as though asking for crispy crackling. '*Christian.* Religion and churches are not the same thing.'

'All right—taking those three, then, wouldn't you say that they must all share the same thing?'

'They share what is instinctive, at least what I believe is instinctive in human beings, namely the instinct for God, the instinct for the absolute.'

'So you would say that they are all just different ways of looking at the same thing?'

'No, I wouldn't. They are different ways, but I believe that the Judeo-Christian tradition is the authentic tradition.'

'So what if you were born . . .?'

The Cardinal stopped me: 'But these are enormous questions. I mean I hope you're not going to write about me on the basis of this.'

This interrupted my crucial question. The Cardinal moved into the pause with:

'What is the purpose of this interview?'

'To talk with you about your life in religion.'

'You are writing a book?'

'Yes.'

'On graduates?'

'Yes.'

'Okay, well, what are you going to write about this interview?'

'I don't know.'

'Because I would be slightly alarmed if you were to write about me on the basis of this. I mean, you have obviously never read a book on prayer.'

'No, I haven't read an academic book on prayer.'

'You've never read a book on the Bible?'

'No.'

'Well, we are passing like ships at night.'

'Well,' I tried to salvage the interview. 'Can I take one thing: your idea of prayer?' But the Cardinal stood up.

'Let me give you in about ten pages a book I produced on prayer. You'll find it all there. I would much rather you read that. I'll give you a free copy.'

And he was off across the room. He came leaning back, holding out a book.

'Here you are—page 126.' And he rattled off the chapter headings: 'Ways to Pray; Planning to Pray; Effects of Prayer; Alone with God.'

'When you pray,' I tried to interrupt, 'you are looking. . . .'

The Cardinal smiled down. 'You'll find it all in here.'

I went on: '. . . towards some sort of vision. If you're a pilgrim, you want to find the end of the road.'

'Yes, yes—but human life is walking through the darkness, isn't it?'

The Cardinal relaxed in the comfort of the homily.

'That's what I believe, but if you're a Christian, aren't you by definition looking for something more?' The Cardinal turned to me and smiled. I saw his teeth spreading wide as, dove-grey and sleek, he cruised up.

'Are you a Christian?'

'No.'

'Ah! Because I can't get the hang of this. I can't get the hang of what you're interviewing me for.'

'I just want to talk about what you understand,' I said as I was buffeted about.

'Well, an engineer can write about another engineer, but if you yourself don't profess to be a Christian, it's not possible for me to tell you in half an hour things that I think are important. We're talking at cross-purposes the whole time. All I can say is go away, read this book and come back, because then we have something to chew on.'

Leaving me well-mutilated, the Cardinal lost interest and turned to nose away back into the deep.

'But I see there is a chapter called "Chinks in the Cloud of Unknowing". What do you mean by that?'

The Cardinal's reply came pat and off-hand: 'Little rays of light which from time to time one sees and understands.'

'Are they enough to sustain your belief?'

'I think so.'

'Don't you ever get impatient?'

The Cardinal came back, looking at me with those shark's eyes—black, incurious, empty:

'We're miles off beam, we're miles off beam.'

'No,' I fought back, 'I don't feel miles off beam. I'm just trying to ascertain how happy you are and what you're looking forward to.'

He circled further away. 'These are terrific questions.'

'I'm not expecting answers.'

'I really don't understand your questions—they're not my questions. They're not coming from anything I understand.'

He nipped in to pick a last shred of flesh off me.

'It needs maturing, I would have thought. Your thoughts need maturing.'

'They're just the curious thoughts of someone who hasn't shared your sort of life.'

'But at eleven in the morning, it's difficult to talk in half an hour about things which I see are problematic for you. When you are talking at this level on things of this kind, you need leisure and time to be able to meet another person's mind.'

I tried to pull together another question, but it was no good—the Cardinal had stood up and switched off the tape recorder.

'Come back,' he said.

John Schlesinger

BALLIOL, 1947–50

'Next right, then go along until you see a grocery shop on the left. Take that left-hand turn and follow the road for half a mile. The drive is off to the left just before a small bridge. The house is called "Strawberry Hole". Yes: "Hole." That's what everybody says! It's actually an old oast-house.'

The deliciously named oast-house stood with two kilns whose tops curved up like helmets of Egyptian statues in clear profile from the woods behind. When I turned off the engine, I could hear their chimneys creaking as they turned with the wind.

Mr Schlesinger came round the side of the house to greet me. In contrast with the kilns above, Mr Schlesinger could be described as Roman. His head, round, bald and trimmed with a white beard, was easy to picture poised sagely above a toga and sandals. As it was, he was actually wearing a sort of Mexican army shirt with *The Falcon and the Snowman* badged on one side. He had invited me to lunch to discuss the article I had written after our first meeting.

I had first seen him on a warm Kensington evening when everything was in bloom along Victoria Road. He had let me in and led the way straight through the house to the balcony. I had the impression of high ceilings, mirrors, and a widespread arrangement of sculpture and pottery. From the balcony, a wrought-iron staircase dropped to the garden below. Mr Schlesinger poured glasses of ginger beer. I said something about the pottery upstairs, and he looked up with his china-doll blue eyes.

'Do you know, if I ever gave up making films, or if I had the energy and the application, I'd like to learn to be a potter: it's quick, it's sensual and it's unexpected. You never quite know how something will

John Schlesinger as Trinculo in *The Tempest*, 1948.

turn out—like glaze. I adore pottery and I collect all sorts of things from student pottery to Picasso. I have a Picasso jug, and there is a plate made by a student in Dundee which I found when we were doing *An Englishman Abroad.*'

'You filmed it in Dundee?' I asked, taken aback.

'Yes, I knew I had a very limited budget to create Moscow, so we looked for places in Britain before we started thinking of going abroad. We went north to Scotland, which doesn't look like England, and with very skilful work from the art department and the location manager, we found things which measured up to the photographs we had seen of the period in Russia.

'So physically we were able to find the place, but orally, of course, what set the tone and the atmosphere so much was hearing people speak Russian—just odd words all around the periphery of the story. I chose very carefully not only actors who spoke Russian, but extras as well. I went to all these working men's clubs and found little groups of Lithuanians and Ukrainians and so on (whom you can find all over the place if you look) and used local talent, made them improvise. By *hearing* Russian, you are more than halfway there in atmosphere.

'Exactly the same happened in *The Falcon and the Snowman.* We chose Russian actors and limited what David Suchet (the one British actor playing a Russian in the film) had to say in Russian. By making the others around him speak Russian more volubly, it looked as if they all spoke Russian. At one time the company backing the film wanted us to put subtitles in, but I said no, we wouldn't need it. People will understand what's going on. And the question never arose again.'

Mr Schlesinger paused to drink. I noticed I hadn't touched mine.

'You know, the need for literalness in films has changed. It is not so far off that when there was a change of scene, there would be a long shot of Big Ben and a subtitle: "London, 1940." That isn't necessary now. People, through television I think, have travelled more widely. By watching commercials, they're quicker to catch on, they can accept something that's told in a very encapsulated way. It's amazing what you can say in thirty seconds. I've never had any professional lessons in my life, but that's one thing the experience of making films has taught me.'

'You've had no formal training at all?'

'No, never. Not for films or theatre.'

'What about Oxford, didn't you join any film society there?'

'There was a film society at Oxford, but it seemed to me to be run by slow-coaches. There was no energy behind it. They just seemed to want to teach everybody how to take long shots or medium shots. Well, you don't have to learn that! They were making a slightly ponderous'—he leant on the word—'documentary about one of the colleges, and they seemed not to be enterprising or very welcoming, so I formed a breakaway group. I made my first film called *Black Legend* during my first year, which was about a local gibbet near my parents' house. It was a landmark on the Berkshire Downs where I lived as a child. We decided to retrace the history of this gibbet, and we made a movie around it in 16mm film with music and special effects and then we toured village halls with it. It had a big success.'

Such rejection of comfortable institutions has been a recurrent theme in Mr Schlesinger's life as a film director. He is seen as something of a maverick in the British film industry, with nobody quite sure whether he makes British or American films. What I was to find was that beneath his imperturbable and emmental smile, he is the most courageous risk-taker. The films he has made cover a spectrum which no other film director can match for variety: *Far from the Madding Crowd, Midnight Cowboy, Marathon Man, Sunday Bloody Sunday, The Day of the Locust, An Englishman Abroad* and *The Falcon and the Snowman*, to name a sample.

Mr Schlesinger told me about his childhood and upbringing which was to influence this prolific adult imagination.

'I am conscious that in my life I was a late starter at most things. When I was young, I felt terribly inadequate. Our family was very happily brought up in a comfortable middle-class background. My father was educated at public school and went to Cambridge; I followed in his footsteps to the same public school and then went to Oxford, but I always felt that I was in the shadow of the reputation which had gone before me. I was never any good at the things they expected me to be good at—I was hopeless at games, didn't get a commission in the Army (I was only a lance-corporal). I suppose at that age I very much wanted to prove myself in the eyes of my family, and felt rather as if I'd let them down. They never made me feel that, but I *did*, I felt inadequate. Then my brother, who's younger than me, did all those things: he was good at games, got a commission in the Army. Bit by bit, I became something of a rebel.

'So I suppose it was Oxford that solved my problems....'

He stopped himself with a laugh. 'None of my deep-seated problems will ever be solved or dealt with—one's simply become adjusted to them!

'When I went up to Oxford, it was the first time I felt civilised. I had hated my school days because I was so hopeless at physical things, but when I got to Oxford and was able to do all the acting and directing that I wanted, which was how I started making films, I first had an inkling that I might be good at something.

'I started as an actor in rep, when my parents certainly gave me every encouragement all along the line. My father, who was a busy doctor, would take a night train up after he'd finished at hospital to see me in some appalling performance! He would say encouraging things, stay the night and go back the next day.'

'Do you still get that support from your parents? Is it still important for you?'

'My father died a year ago. I get support from my close friends and my mother, who is a rather infirm lady now. I don't think she's still interested in films, but she's interested in anything I do at the theatre or the opera house. She made an enormous effort to try to come to *Rosenkavalier*, but she couldn't make it, she couldn't sit in a theatre for that long. But only last week, the first time she'd been out of the house for a long, long time, she came up to see the videotape of *Rosenkavalier*. She sat wide awake through it although she can barely hear, and it was touching to see her attentiveness and be able to share in something that I'd done.

'But in the end, you know, one does something for oneself. I choose my subjects (hopefully with an eye which is not going to empty the cinema), but they all have to have something which appeals to me. It's personal choice.'

'What is it which generally appeals to you?' I asked. 'Is there a consistent theme in the sort of characters you make films around?'

'I am fascinated by human behaviour—by characters who are pushed to the edge.' His wide blue stare met mine. 'By characters who have to compensate for their lives by taking refuge in fantasy. People who are not the norm, who are living on the fringe—if you look at the films I've made, they might not seem to be that stream of choice but I have a feeling that, underneath, they usually are.'

Dustin Hoffman in *Midnight Cowboy* struck me as being the most immediate example of this sort of person. Following a train of thought back from the character to the actor, I asked what it was about Dustin Hoffman which had made Schlesinger choose him for the part.

'The very clever way in which he deliberately dressed for our first meeting so that he'd blend in with the society of 42nd Street.'

'Why, what did he do?'

'He's a chameleon-like actor,' answered Mr Schlesinger, 'and a very perceptive man. He took me to a restaurant in an Italian quarter, Hell's Kitchen as it's known, butting on the end of 42nd Street and 8th Avenue. He said he was going to take me to this restaurant (he was wearing a dirty old raincoat) where I would find that if Ratso had been a success, he might have ended up as head waiter. So we went, and over dinner he kept pointing at this head waiter who was always pocketing his tips and not putting them in the kitty! He's very perceptive. In

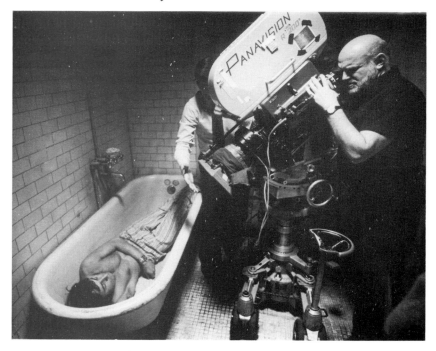

John Schlesinger filming Dustin Hoffman in *Marathon Man*, 1976.

the small hours of the morning we ended up roaming the bars and pool halls of 42nd Street and talking to someone who had a beautiful angelic face, yet the eyes of a killer. We were talking about violence, which does interest me (and interests Dustin I think) and how not everybody who's violent necessarily looks it.'

'Do you think violence interests Dustin Hoffman? I've seen him in various films, and he seems soft.'

'No, not soft, no—he's passionate. He's got a terribly aggressive, insecure, questing personality; never pleased personality. He's an unusual guy. Very difficult to work with, but enormous talent and a great sense of humour which is his saving grace.'

'What is this violence which interests you?' The light in the garden had darkened. Instead of green, the ivy behind him clung black and streaked silver to the wall. The lamplight from inside ran out golden through the balustrade above us into the evening.

'How, in somewhere like Los Angeles, underneath all that indolence and apparent gratification or possibility of gratification of every kind, there lurks the most appalling violence and frustration.

'I have a house in a street which leads off Sunset Boulevard, and all the residents in the street have meetings as a result of all the robbery, rape and murder which happen in the area. It's very interesting to contrast the equivalent meetings of residents around Victoria Road, where we might discuss: "Look, would you mind awfully if you didn't have a roof garden? It rather ruins the view...." In Los Angeles, the meeting is all about violence: "How do we protect each other, should we have each other's phone numbers, should we report strange cars coming down the street?" It's very frightening. I could very easily come in and find someone behind the door with a gun. My gardener has just been murdered—he disappeared, his car was found abandoned and the police eventually identified him by dental records. My next door neighbour was found stabbed to death.'

In one of Mr Schlesinger's lesser known films, *The Day of the Locust*, violence is suppressed all along, until the final scene. It then explodes in an overwhelming vision of raw destruction as Donald Sutherland stamps on the blond boy's head and is in turn torn to pieces by a hysterical crowd.

'How did you come to that scene?' I asked.

'What happened was that Donald Sutherland had an accident— fortunately for us, because the script was incomplete and we desperately needed time to finish it, he crashed through a plate-glass door in his hotel and injured his forehead and so couldn't work. We had about ten days' grace in which to regroup ourselves before we shot the scene and to collect Donald's insurance money. In order to get finance for the film in the first place, we had rather short-changed the script in our presentation to the distributors, so it had almost just been "and here a riot ensues...". We didn't know that we would actually take a week to film it and spend $1 million—which is what happened!'

'An expensive line...'

'It was an expensive line! And nobody had worked it out—the writer had flunked it, and none of the rest of us had attempted it. I got a bout of 'flu with a high temperature and someone said this was the moment to jot down images. So with this high fever, I wrote down some ideas and we discussed them with the designer and the producer and the writer around my bed. We then had the run of the Paramount Studios, as nothing else was being shot, so we went in and turned it upside down!'

'Did you want that violence to shock?'

'Yes—and I think West shocked. What I think West was writing about in that novella was about a time of terrible destruction which was about to burst upon us; he was also writing about the destructive nature of Los Angeles iself which I think is as true now as it was then. I think it is absolutely the most accurate piece ever written about Los Angeles.'

'And what happens right at the end? I've forgotten how the film finishes after the stampede.'

'Well, the stampede at the film première is partly real, partly imagined. West foresaw an apocalypse happening, but it was written as an hallucination. What then happens is that a phoenix rises from the ashes of this experience—the girl who's been rejecting him all along comes back to try and find him as if to say she's sorry, and just finds a plastic rose in a crack in the wall: she finds it's too late.

'So you get the whole collapse of this great fantasy. You see all the apparent promise of a place like Hollywood, and the anger when all the hopes and the dreams are unfulfilled.'

I stared into the bottom of my drink, feeling rather glum in the face of this massive collapse. Mr Schlesinger on the other hand was grinning like a rather jolly Shakespearean character—not quite Falstaff but perhaps Autolycus.

'It's the same in *Far from the Madding Crowd* of course,' he added as an afterthought.

'Why?' I tried to reconcile the crowd hysteria of Hollywood with the timeless countryside of Wessex but found them too far removed. Mr Schlesinger showed me how.

'The great blows of Fate: that idea of collapse of dreams which is forever present for all of us. I think I enjoy sardonic comments on those sort of situations—on disappointed hopes.

'What I tried to do in *Far from the Madding Crowd* was to take the essence of the book, of Hardy, which is always there in his writing, which is how Man is dwarfed by Nature, and that terrible blows of Fate will strike him down so that he must somehow pick up the pieces, and get up and carry on. It is a philosophy I totally adhere to myself, though perhaps not quite as finger-wagging as Hardy sometimes is. Hardy is actually a bit sentimental—he sometimes goes over the top: "You haven't got away with it this time, and you won't get away with it next time either!"

'I used to call it *Far from the Madding Pisspot!*'

Just as I was about to get stuck in with some of my own Hardy jokes, Mr Schlesinger was serious again and told me more about Hardy than I had learnt from years of studying him for school exams and degree put together.

'You see, I think that if Hardy had lived now, I'm sure he would have written for the cinema. He was such an extraordinarily *visual* writer. We just took dollops of prose and put it on to the screen—we just had to visualise them: like the way he described the weeping of the lime trees with the morning dew on the coffin as it stayed outside whilst the driver of the cart got pissed in the pub. There are whole things I remember—that beautiful scene of the boy who is trying to remember his Collect which was such an effort, and Bathsheba who is sitting having stayed the night under the tree. And she sees, god! This poor little guy who has this terrible problem (for him a terrible problem) and she realises: "What are my problems!" It's all there for her to contrast. It is an ironic contrast, and beautiful.

'Or that other contrast when Troy plants the flowers on Fanny's grave, and that grinning gargoyle spews all over them and washes them away—wonderful ironic quirks of Fate!'

'You said that Hardy was visual—how do you manage to make something like *Far from the Madding Crowd* so sensual as well?'

'Isn't something visual partly sensual?' asked Mr Schlesinger.

'But isn't it difficult to keep intact a sense of sensuality through the camera?'

'Well, the lens is a funny animal. It sucks out different personalities. The camera loves Julie Christie—I think that's partly the whole secret of what makes something work in the cinema. I can't define it because there are lots of well-known actresses that the camera doesn't like and won't photograph well.'

'So you didn't have to work at making her particularly more sensual?'

'No—she has it, enormously so: the camera loves her. She is an extraordinary-looking woman—not traditionally pretty at all, but with that wonderful sensual mouth.'

Thinking about Julie Christie's mouth made me think of *Sunday Bloody Sunday* and that extraordinary male kiss. When I asked Mr Schlesinger about that kiss, he was careful to explain that it was not just an outrageous moment in a sensationalist film, which I suppose I had been hoping he was going to talk about, but part of a delicate exploration of the theme of the film.

'*Sunday Bloody Sunday* is probably the most personal film I've made, and I made it at a time when I was full of confidence. I'd had enormous success with *Midnight Cowboy*, and it seemed the moment to get anything difficult off the ground. You know that old cliché about "filming the telephone book"? Well, I felt this was the moment in my life when I could. I wanted to do a film about a relationship which dealt with varying forms of sexuality. I wanted to do a story about somebody who was having an affair with two people at the same time, with an older woman and an older man—both of whom knew of the existence of the other, and tolerated it. Eventually, the woman decides that half a loaf isn't better than no bread.

'The film deals with the nature of love, the nature of relationships

which may seem odd to the outside world, but which are actually perfectly normal to those who are going through them.'

'How could anyone be able to compromise a relationship so much?'

'But I think the nature of relationships is a compromise anyway.
Marriages or people of the same sex living together or parent/children
relationships are complicated and complex things which need a good
deal of tolerance and an enormous amount of compromise.'

'Isn't it possible to be close enough to someone that you don't have
to compromise so much?'

'No, I don't think so. I think it's a rather romantic notion that you
can "have" someone totally. It occasionally exists—my parents were
blissfully happily married for sixty years, and perhaps because we are
in the shadow of that example, the rest of their children have not been
able to find it so easy. But I think that any marriage must go through its
problems. It has to. It's silly to think that romantic love is just roses and
walking into the sunset all the time—it just isn't.

'*Sunday Bloody Sunday* attempted to analyse albeit a more compromised relationship—but one which I believe is near the norm. What I
wanted to do was take a perfectly ordinary group of people who are to
all intents and purposes "the norm". So there is a busy, caring successful Jewish doctor who just happens to be gay. When the boy, the
bisexual boy, comes to visit his older lover, they kiss quite fully and
enormously affectionately and immediately. The reason why people
were so shocked, was that they always expect someone who's gay to be
a stereotype. People are more comfortable with stereotypes, so they
expect a gay to be witty and charming and outrageous. *La Cage aux
Folles* was such a success because it dealt with characters behaving in a
stereotypical, outrageous way which made it palatable to everyone.

'The kiss which you asked me about, I remember arguing about for
a long time with Penelope Gilliatt, the writer. She said, "Must they
kiss and go to bed? Can't we do it in long shot or silhouette?" And I
said, "No, that would immediately constitute an apology, and there's
nothing to apologise about. They should just come in quite naturally,
and kiss, and get on with the scene. There should be no special pho-
tography about it, or keeping away from it as if we were ashamed of
something." I was determined not to make a big deal about it.'

'Yet people were very shocked by it, weren't they?'

'Well, that's their problem, not the writer's or anybody else's—not
mine. I remember the camera operator looking away whilst he was
filming going: "Yuugh!"'

Mr Schlesinger's mouth twitched once or twice in the corners, then
a wide grin broadened sideways into his beard.

'I don't believe that homosexual love ends with "I am the love that dare not tell its name" or whatever that quote is! I don't believe it has to end with people walking into the sea and drowning themselves any more. That's all ludicrous. People's sexuality is their own affair and they can do what they like, but if you're going to deal with it, the best way to do it is not to make some big deal of it. I don't want to do something that's ridden with guilt—guilt is such a terrible waste of time! I also think that *Sunday Bloody Sunday* did a lot for people who were scared shitless of admitting to themselves or their parents what the nature of their sexuality was.'

Mr Schlesinger seemed to add the last bit in italics. 'I think for me, at that moment, it was a highly personal film. It was quite considerably autobiographical, and I felt secure enough in my life to make that film and make that statement.'

'When making a film, even a highly personal one like that one, are you conscious of trying to make an impact on your audience?'

'I think that anything to jolt an audience out of their general state of self-satisfaction and, you know, *timid* suburban security. I want to make them think a bit, look at something differently or even just accept that other characters can live as the film shows. Just to shake them all up a bit. I don't set out to do something outrageous for its own sake, but at the same time I think certain things need saying, and that it's just as well to say them as clearly and as unsentimentally as possible. If that's going to shock people....' He clucked his tongue in his cheek like the crack of two conkers: 'Tough.'

Mr Schlesinger seemed to enjoy this machete analysis of his audience. Earlier in the interview the telephone had rung, with a mildly hysterical woman making herself heard across the room for some minutes. Mr Schlesinger had listened in absolute silence, then interrupted by saying: 'Now, listen. There are three words you should use in a situation like this which I find very useful and use a lot.' There was a pause in which she must have asked what the three words were, to which Mr Schlesinger's answer came back: 'Fuck off, cunt!'

He finished what he was saying about why he made films.

'I think I would like to think that I am giving someone a special experience. That means making them laugh, making them afraid, making them angry, making them worry—giving them something to think about. Shocking them out of their apathy: so a special experience.' He held his hands wide. 'Otherwise, why go to the terrible length of trouble and personal agony that one goes to every time one goes out there to make a film? Take years off your life!'

And we had left it at that. Down at Strawberry Hole, Mr Schlesinger had marked the article up, and then we had gone for a walk around some woodlands. I gave him a lift back to London, and he told

'If that's going to shock people ... tough.'

John Schlesinger, Strawberry Hole

me about his life when he first moved to Hollywood as a young director. One of the most memorable stories was how he met Ruth Gordon
(getting on for seventy, in her pink mini skirt). She eyed him up, with
the single comment: 'So, you did *Far from the Madding Crowd*, huh?
Well, that'll teach you to do the fuckin' classics!' Advice, it seems, that
this highly original and unpredictable man has stuck to ever since.

Sir Roger Bannister

EXETER, 1946–50

It was an apt coincidence that the inventor of *The Guinness Book of Records*, Norris McWhirter, should have been holding the stop-watch on 6th May, 1954: 'I overheard his first words after breaking the tape: "Did I do it?" He had to wait for my announcement: "Ladies and Gentlemen. Here is the result of Event Number Nine, the One Mile. First, number 41, R. G. Bannister, Amateur Athletic Association and formerly of Exeter and Merton Colleges, with a time which is a new meeting and track record and which, subject to ratification, will be a new English native, British national, British all-comers, European, British Empire and World record: the time *three* minutes . . . (lost in the roar of the crowd were the words) . . . fifty-nine point four seconds."'

The legend of that story begins just after the war, when Roger Bannister, a gangling seventeen-year-old, followed the steps of Lovelock to Exeter College.

'I came up as a schoolboy in 1946, when some 80 percent of the places were filled by ex-servicemen. Many of them were twenty-five, a few had even been brigadiers in the Army and they had won the war. There was immense contrast between these two groups, the schoolboys and the ex-servicemen, which meant that we felt very young and immature; in a sense we compensated for this by doing things which we could do as well or better than those ex-servicemen—we certainly couldn't drink as well! We couldn't play rugby as well either, but I knew I had an interest and some ability as a runner. . . .'

Sir Roger grinned, fumbled at the cuff of his interview suit and

'There is nothing else which is sharp and artificial like running that four-minute mile. In a way, its very appeal was its absurdity. It is just chance that four laps of one minute each happened to add up to a four-minute mile, and that it hadn't been done before.'

Sir Roger Bannister

unrecrossed his legs again. Not at ease in front of a camera and recorder, he stiffened under his collar and plunged into his interview story.

'... So I took up running. I remember my great impatience when I went down to the Iffley Road track on my second day, and there was nobody around. I couldn't believe it! Actually I had gone along to the College ground first, because I didn't dare show up at the real Iffley Road track, and I began chugging up and down in my gym shoes. After about half an hour, the groundsman came up to me: "I've seen you running up and down here," he said. "You're not thinking of becoming a runner, are you?" "Well, I did have this vague notion that I might. . . ." "Well," he said, "we had Lovelock at Exeter College. I used to watch him, so I know quite a bit about running. I can tell you, you'll never make a runner. You haven't got the style for it—you haven't got the shape for it, you see."

'I was a bit crestfallen, but eventually some nice people turned up, ex-servicemen, who said, "Yes, we do a bit of training, then we go back for a drink at the Turf and chat. At the moment, we're plotting how to beat Cambridge in the relays and, oh yes, the Freshmen's Sports—you'd better run in that."

'I had never run a mile before, and although I was beaten, I did just break five minutes. There was also a cross-country practice run. I was astonished at the speed at which they ran. Well to the back, I can remember saying to someone, "They don't actually go as fast as this all the way, do they?" He turned to me: "Well, *they* do, but you needn't. We could walk for a bit." So we walked on for a bit and made friends. Charles Wenden, now Bursar of All Souls College, is a friend of mine still.

'So there was this curious contrast in attitude. We learnt to realise how impatience, youthful impatience to get something done, was not the way things happened. We learnt I wouldn't say to "disguise" enthusiasm and aggression, but to temper it.

'The next stage was the coach.'

His wife on the sofa smiled expectantly. This was an old family chestnut.

'This coach stood by the side of the track; he had a black bowler hat and a formal suit with a waistcoat and gold watch chain. He was the coach who had coached Lovelock. You may not know, but Lovelock was the Olympic Mile Champion, Gold Medal winner in the 1936 Berlin Olympics, a New Zealand Rhodes scholar, and, as it happened, he had read medicine at Exeter College. So he was the criterion. Anyway, this coach, Bert Thomas, felt that, just by having known Lovelock, he could make didactic statements.

'"Run round, run round!" So I ran. "You're bouncing, you're bouncing!"

'"What do you mean?" I panted.

'"Shorter strides, do it again." So I ran again. "Now I'll give you a time trial. Run three laps. . . ."'

Sir Roger looked back with his mind's eye.

'He may have said two laps, because then it was a three lap to the mile track. It went around behind an elm tree, the roots of the elm came up through the cinders. We had to be careful not to trip up over there—a few Cambridge people did trip. It was rather tactical. In relays, one suspected that the older runners would be having a good jostle as they disappeared behind the tree!

'So I ran round, and when I came back, this coach had forgotten to time me! I realised that if I was to be interested, then I would have to do my own training.'

1947 dawned on one of the bitterest winters of the century, and the Iffley Road track was frostbound. Norris McWhirter remembered how 'this unknown, rather loping, aspirant athlete from Exeter College was selected as third string for the Mile in reward for his indefatigable work day after day shovelling snow. Not yet eighteen, he must have been one of the youngest undergraduates in the University.'

Sir Roger described that Blues race. 'During the race, I was lying well back as third string because I was supposed to keep out of the way and let the first and second strings do their stuff. I was still fairly far back on the back straight, when I suddenly felt that this was where I ought to see what I could do. I found that I could, in fact, accelerate, although I was tired, and so I overtook the others for a time of four minutes thirty seconds, which for those days was quite reasonable.'

That first triumph reshaped Sir Roger's Oxford career by taking him into administration, where he found a talent to organise. As President of the University Athletics Club, he decided to rebuild the obsolete Iffley Road track.

'We couldn't really do modern athletics on that old track, and I can remember looking through the telephone directory for building contractors. We found one called Fiddler & Son of Reading, which eventually turned out to be a warning which we didn't heed. Fiddler & Son, of course, went bankrupt, and it looked as though all the curled-up turves of grass in the middle of the track which the football club were going to play on were getting browner and blacker by the day. It was all very embarrassing, but eventually another contractor built it. When I went back in 1954 to run the four-minute mile, that was the track.'

Sir Roger also organised two tours, the first of which was to Germany. 'Late in 1947 we went to Germany and we were the first team who had any contact with the defeated Germans. We hired a diesel bus and we drove down to Hamburg, Cologne and Düsseldorf. We saw the effects of war at first hand, which were incredible, and we competed with the German Universities.'

'So the tour had a political role too?'

'Yes. The Germans did make some political points—for instance, the runners in the distances over a mile suddenly dropped out, saying that they couldn't do it on their rations; and on one dramatic day they produced a one-legged high jumper—he'd had his leg blown off. There were these undertones, but nevertheless it was a success.'

The implications of this tour reached well beyond the record books of the University's Sports Club. 'The British public has never particularly wished to be vindictive after a war is over, and the whole policy was to be more understanding than we had been after the First World War, which had led to the Second World War. I think it really meant something that somebody was trying to heal the wound.'

The other tour was to America, where less love was lost in the tactics to win. Sir Roger was just nineteen years old.

'I was Captain of the Oxford and Cambridge team which toured Harvard, Yale, Princeton and Cornell. There were all kinds of celebrations and parades, and the Americans were overwhelmingly hospitable. As the matches drew nearer, I noticed that they would have the English team ordering anything. My team saw food that they had never seen before, hadn't seen for seven years—I watched them start off their breakfast with a pint of milk, then steaks and ham and eggs followed by lashings of toast and marmalade. All at once it struck me that my team's chances of winning anything were disappearing with every meal they had. They were unable to cope with all that food, and soon they would be unable to walk, let alone run! So I intervened and organised a special table so that we couldn't get mixed up with all that food. I introduced a system of rationing, which made me very unpopular, and stopped our team from drinking milk!'

How did ex-Army majors respond to such treatment from a nineteen-year-old?

'I just had to point out that they were being silly. In a way, I was able to get away with it because I was a good runner. The formula is that if you can do something better than other people, then they will listen to what you have to say.'

As he prepared to disembark from this story, his wife could contain herself no longer. She had been making impatient noises and prompting him with the odd word, but now she put her foot down. 'I must say that my husband is being too modest about this particular tour, because it was a very great triumph. England had had a very hard time after the War. We were more severely rationed than during the fighting, and that cold winter had been no joke. For a team from England to come and meet the finest athletes of Harvard and Cornell, and jolly well beat them to it, was a real boost for English morale. It made people sit up and think that the Empire wasn't going down the drain after all.'

Having put her husband's modesty to rights, her hackles relaxed, and we turned our attention back to Sir Roger, who was describing the changes of attitude which took place regarding training and athletic discipline.

'It was ridiculous to have this 1930s coach with his bowler hat making didactic comments about what was right and wrong in running on the basis of nothing he was prepared to discuss. Everyone realised that it must change.

'Sport was in a state of transition, and certainly for reasons which were then all-important or seemed all-important, beating Cambridge was important. Thus, working backwards, anyone who would or could help the team to beat Cambridge was listened to, if he talked sense. It was not quite *Chariots of Fire* stuff, it was a little beyond that, but it was still very primitive compared with today. Although people were prepared to submit to some discipline and train hard, the concept of being in training all the time, as is true now with Ovett and Coe, was not recognised. Ovett and Coe are really never out of training. At one stage they may not be capable of beating world records, but they would never do anything which would not aid their overall fitness. Our concept then was simply of ups and downs—you shouldn't peak too soon; you shouldn't be stale, so you did some cross-country running during the winter; you would build up to the event by running on the track for four or five weeks. That was thought to be working quite hard. We had no concept of how hard people could train, which was the reason why times and performances thirty years ago were so low. We had really no idea how much the body could stand.'

Sir Roger stands as the last milestone of true amateurs. The world records of today now come from an élite of professional athletes, and whilst Sir Roger admires their prowess, he has stayed true to a wider ideal—that of the all-rounder. His skill as an administrator has laid roots far and wide throughout British sport, from which the specialists may evolve, but which are primarily aimed to support the sport of the nation.

'Let me quickly explain.... After Oxford, I eventually qualified as a neurologist and settled in London. I was invited to become a member of the first Sports Council, set up in 1964, and then became

Chairman of its Research Committee. We wanted to make the sporting opportunities which had been available to us at University available to everybody. At that time, there were probably only a dozen tracks in the country, so if you didn't live near one, you could not be a runner. Swimming pools were rare, and the ones which were around had been built by the Victorians to aid cleanliness. There was no thought for them fulfilling a recreational need. It became clear that, unless there was an organised national programme to remedy these needs, people would be denied sporting opportunities. We produced a paper called "Sport in the Seventies", in which we argued that the country needed four hundred multi-purpose indoor sports centres, and asked the Government to do something about it.

'The relationship between Government and sport is a complex one: the Government is interested not only in the health and welfare of the nation, but also in being seen in a good light for what they do. This means that they are concerned with the performance of the country at a high level—in the Olympic Games and other international events. So there is this rather complex pyramid in which at the pinnacle there are Olympic performances. But in order to be able to produce these Olympic performances, you need an infrastructure of clubs and facilities and coaches, all of which cost a lot of money. Unless the Government and local authorities agree to spend this money, you will not achieve the results.

'What has happened since our paper is the commercialisation of sport. It is mainly the advent of television, which means that top-level sport gets wide coverage—and anything which appears on television is the legitimate subject for advertising. There is even a back door for tobacco and cigarettes through the use of brand names. So the financial support for this full-time dedication is now readily forthcoming from the world of advertising. This is why there is now a quasi-professional basis, and why the amateur all-rounder is disappearing. Amateur athletes are now in the second division.'

'What about Sebastian Coe?'

'Well, he is exceptional. He is a full-time student in the sense that he's studying economics of sport at Loughborough, which is the sports university, but I think he would be quite candid in saying that his work is organised around his sporting life rather than the other way round.

'There is no doubt that if I were starting as a student now, there would be no world records that I would run. I couldn't be a doctor and break world records.'

'Would you say that sport was an important aspect of education?' Sir Roger was emphatic. 'Vital. When I say "sport", I really mean some other non-academic area of interest. It might be political clubs, acting, poetry, it might be anything you choose to name, but some activity which is set apart from work and which has to be organised in co-operation with other people is vital.'

'Going back to the political aspects of sport, what did you feel about the boycotting of sports events? The East and the West over the Olympic Games, for example?'

'Well, I wouldn't like to comment on boycotts. All I would say is that the objective should be for all parts of the world to have a reasonable opportunity to enjoy the expression of their leisure and recreation activities with whatever facilities are available.

'I'm much more concerned with what we call "Sport for All" than I am with the more élite levels of sport.'

'Do you mean the Olympic Games?'

'Yes, I am more concerned with recreation provision than with the Olympic Games. The Olympic Games are more important for politicians than they are for me, and I think the politicisation of sport at that level has to be reduced.'

'How would you do it?' Sir Roger's answer again showed how shrewd administration can percolate through community activity.

'What we did in the Sports Council was give grants of between 10 percent and 20 percent to local authorities to build sports facilities. They, of course, would be heavily biased towards recreational pursuits for the community and they would be able to persuade their finance departments to raise the rest of the money, which would have been far in excess of what we could have offered. The country now has those four hundred multi-purpose indoor sports centres. In other words, the programme has happened, and there are many people to be very much praised for this.

'For example, take running: recreational running is now far more important than top-level running. There has been a revolution in people's attitudes towards recreational running. Next month there is the biggest marathon in the world taking place in London: 18,000 are running, whilst 100,000 people tried to get in to run it, and there are eighty other marathons around the country because not enough people can get into the London one. As far as I am concerned, this is a more important change than how many world records or gold medals a country can win.'

'So you get all these runners. But don't you need results?' Sir Roger's answer struck me as unexpectedly Christian.

'Every participant in the London marathon is a winner, if I can put this concept to you. Each of them who takes part has a result. He has done something which he wanted to do—perhaps he's done it faster than before. My son has just run in the New York marathon; he hadn't run one before, and he was thrilled to come in the top 10 percent.'

Sir Roger fears that that honesty and exhilaration could be lost from some top-level events, as international politics begin to surface.

'Politicised sport could reach a point when other countries will decide they want none of it. If a country decides to use every method including drugs to win, then the point of sport has been lost. I have been involved in schemes to try to detect the use of drugs, anabolic steroids for instance, but it becomes difficult if not impossible to detect drugs. Some runners are able to make fantastic special preparations which are altogether abnormal in order to reach world levels and I think this has gone too far. Too high a price is being paid, both individually by the athlete and collectively by the country, for such prize performances.

'I am very worried about drugs. They probably pose the biggest single threat to top-level performers. I see, for instance, that the officials for a recent modern pentathlon decided that some competitors had been taking drugs to steady their nerves to stop the pistol wobbling. Because they could not find ways of detecting that drug, they decided to put them into the cross-country event immediately after they had shot, with the intention that those who had given themselves sedatives to steady their nerves would do badly in the 5,000-metre run. I mean, it's becoming almost farcical, and this is the aspect of modern sport which I abhor.'

'So what do you say to the Soviet bloc's derision of the thousands of English joggers running, but being unable to win Olympic medals?'

'The Russians have devastating social problems, which you probably know a little about. If the Russians could achieve voluntarily what we are achieving in a recreational sense, I think they would be absolutely delighted.'

'The last thing I wanted to ask you about is the four-minute mile—although you are more committed to "Sport for All" than world records, your status as a household name is none the less built around four minutes. Do you think your fame is just coincidental with that time tag, or with the ideal you have since maintained?'

The most famous of mile runners gave a shy, lopsided smile. 'Fame is a funny thing . . . what I can say is that seizing the opportunity to run this race made life more difficult for me, in that it made it less likely that I would be taken seriously as a doctor for the next ten years. I had to do more work in my medical career, for example writing more papers, so that people didn't just think of me as a runner.

'It also meant that I worked through a lot of different aspects of what you call "fame" rather early. Due to the individual activity of running,

I was catapulted onto the national scene, even as an undergraduate.'

'Have there been no other four-minute barriers for you to break?'

'No, there is nothing else which is sharp and artificial like running that four-minute mile. In a way, its very appeal was its absurdity. It is just chance that four laps of one minute each happened to add up to a four-minute mile, and that it hadn't been done before. That is so artificial that obviously there are no other things like it.'

'Were you amused by it?'

'Yes, I was amused, but it didn't make my desire to do it any the less—nor my realisation that it wouldn't be done by chance, and that it was something which had to be attacked as a problem.'

'The point occurs to me that until somebody breaks the three-minute mile, you're always going to be the most famous mile runner.'

'No, that's not true. I mean, obviously Coe and Ovett are far better runners. Coe has broken thirteen world records and thinks he might stop when he's done twenty. He is more ahead of other runners of the world than I was. It just so happens that Ovett is almost as good, and maybe he will beat him again, but in terms of systematic achievement over the last four years, Coe must be singled out in the field of middle-distance running—I would say he's a phenomenon.'

We went outside into the middle of Edwardes Square to take photographs. High clouds sped overhead, constantly changing the light to and fro between dull grey and bouncing sunshine. I asked Sir Roger what he considered the role of the athlete to be; he stopped and considered whilst the breeze swirled and rose around us.

'What is the role of the athlete in society? . . . Well, I'd say that the role is to continue to be an individual.'

'What do you mean by that?'

'I mean that he should regard his running as something like a pianist would regard his music or an artist would regard his art. My daughter is a painter—she is trying to express something through her paintings which is a comment, if you like, on what she believes is inside her. I would say that that is the role of the athlete.'

'What did you want to express in your running?'

He lifted his head, and his eyes followed a cloud disappearing high over the horizon. 'It is an attitude of freedom, of excitement—a harnessing of mental and physical capacities. It is also about communion with external events and surroundings; it is also a communion with others who are runners and it is a communion with those who watch you run. It's a very complex affair. There is also some psychological tie with the other runners in the race.

'But it is also simple—the simplicity of running which has an appeal. You don't need anything else—no apparatus—and you do it,

SIR ROGER BANNISTER

'The formula is that if you can do something better than other people, then they will listen to what you have to say.'

Sir Roger Bannister, Edwardes Square

as I have tried to say, not because anybody tells you to do it, you do it because you want to do it. It is something inside you that you want to express. I think that is as much as I can say about it.'

Sir Robin Day

ST EDMUND HALL, 1947–50

Sir Robin described one of those timeless Oxford days.

'I used to drift on during the day doing nothing. I would finish reading the morning papers after breakfast, and then say that, well, there's not much time to do more than a quick nip into the library before eleven. But by eleven o'clock I wanted a coffee, and coffee would go on with a rather good argument over that morning's *Manchester Guardian* or the *Economist*. Of course, there was no television to talk about in those days. By then it was almost lunch. Lunch and pubs went on rather longer than you meant, and then we had to go somewhere for tea. And then after tea you would bump into someone, and they would say there's this party, so I would go and put on a clean shirt and—well, the day had gone!'

'You make it sound very extravagant.'

'No, not at all extravagant. The amount of money you spent in the course of such a day only amounted to about half a crown. Coffee, talking, a pint of beer—just lazy. Very interesting and very lively. That went on for weeks and weeks.'

'Well, eight weeks at a time, wasn't it?'

'No—I stayed up in Oxford during vacations because both my mother and father had died by then. My home was Oxford.'

'Were they killed during the war?'

'No. My mother died shortly after the end of the war, and my father died soon after that.'

Thinking how desperately lonely it must have been for Sir Robin at the end of term, I forgot my question. Sir Robin interrupted the silence.

'Why is St Anne's taking rubbish like you then?'
Sir Robin Day to EW

'We seemed to live on porridge and kippers and South African sherry! It was really quite austere in 1947. One or two undergraduates had cars—they were thought to be very grand people, and their cars were usually things like clapped-out Austin Sevens. I used to take my girlfriends out to Woodstock by bus and walk around Blenheim Park. I rarely had enough money to take them to an eating house in Woodstock, but one never thought about things like that because it was such fun and excitement.

'It was the most marvellous period of my whole life, and it was undoubtedly the most wonderful period in Oxford, the golden age which has never since been surpassed. I remember my first breakfast in Hall in October 1947. There was a twenty-eight-year-old lieutenant-colonel on my right, who had fought and been wounded at El Alamein, and on my left was a young boy, a scholar of seventeen straight up from school. I myself had spent nearly five years in the Army and was twenty-four. So there were several generations of people, which meant there was a great range of talent, and this put everybody very much on their mettle.'

Sir Robin was elected as President of the Oxford Union in his final year.

'It was an enormous honour, and something I knew I would be proud of for the rest of my life.'

'What did it teach you?'

'You learnt how to speak properly in public, how not to lose your temper in front of an angry debate, and how to debate on reasonably equal terms with eminent public figures. This was all good training.'

Ex-presidents of the Oxford Union had trodden a well-worn path to Westminster, but not Sir Robin. I had read an article in which Sir Robin, interviewed by Bernard Levin, had said that he would rather have become a politician—'Having said this, do you feel your career has failed to live up to your expectations?'

'Yes, I would rather have become a Member of Parliament early on in my career. That doesn't mean to say that I think I necessarily failed, but if you would like to say "failed", yes, I'll accept that. I don't mind you saying that.'

'No', I backpedalled, 'one could only judge by one's own standards, and I just meant to ask what your standards were.'

'Yes, I agree. One can think of politicians who probably think they have failed. I'm sure in his heart of hearts, Quintin Hogg, Lord Hailsham, thinks he is a failure although he has been Lord Chancellor and a very distinguished figure in public life. But he would have liked to have been Prime Minister.

'In the same sense that my interest in politics has led me to the media rather than to Parliament, I would accept that as a failure. As a young man, I always wanted to be a parliamentarian.'

'Do you regret this?'

'Only the sort of passing regret that one expresses in a conversation like this. I don't live my life feeling deeply embittered or anything like that.'

His use of the word 'parliamentarian' interested me. When I mentioned it, Sir Robin nodded his head vigorously—suddenly looking exactly like Mike Yarwood. 'You've put your finger on a very key point, because I deliberately used the word "parliamentarian" to indicate that my hope when I was an undergraduate was not for power in the sense of being Chancellor of the Exchequer or anything of that nature. I just wanted to be a parliamentarian and I hoped that in due course I would become a good one. Never, even in my wildest drunken dreams, did I visualise myself as becoming some great Cabinet Minister!

'I suppose, had I got into Parliament, I would have then acquired the dreams and aspirations of every M.P. One is surprised to learn of various Members of Parliament who have seriously considered themselves as future Prime Ministers!'

All his talk of parliamentarians made me think of the English Civil War, and I wondered if he was interested in it. In return I got a quick dose of a Robin Day interview myself.

'It's not an essential interest of mine. Why? What do you want to ask me about it, then? Are you a Roundhead or a Cavalier?'

'A great Cavalier,' I laughed.

'Would you think of Margaret Thatcher as a Cavalier or a Roundhead?'

'Probably a Roundhead.'

'Well,' said Sir Robin accusingly. 'I wonder if Michael Foot would agree with that. He's a great Roundhead, of course.'

I half-expected the camera to swing to Michael Foot and see him bursting with rage behind a microphone and beaker of water. 'What I was driving at, Sir Robin, was really how perfect a form of democracy do you think Parliament now is?' Sir Robin recognised an eighteenth-century question when he saw it, and knocked this one soundly on the nose.

'Well, I don't revere Parliament as being a perfect institution, but what I do say is that it is the central forum of our democracy and, whatever its shortcomings in the past, it is the basis of our democratic liberties. In answer to your question—what sort of a country would we have if we didn't have Parliament? What could we have instead of it? Can you point to any other democratic institution in any other country which you would prefer to have?'

I nodded vigorously back with what I hoped gave the impression that these were purely rhetorical questions. 'But what about you,' I said, turning the spotlight back again, 'what are your political views?'

'I don't belong to any political party. I was a Liberal twenty-four years ago, but since 1959 I've concentrated on television as a career. My views are genuinely independent and run across the grain of political parties.'

'It seems to me that the price you have paid for this is that people only want to listen to your questions, not your point of view—does this make you feel impotent?'

'If you are saying: "Do I think that a job in which one's main work is interrogative is a lesser job than that of providing answers?" Well, yes—certainly. I regard the job of asking a Cabinet Minister why he hasn't done this, or why he is doing that, as a lesser function than being that Cabinet Minister and being responsible for those things.

'On the other hand, I don't think one must spend one's life in trying to provide the answers, because, as we all know, there are all sorts of problems which have never been solved. I don't know the correct answer to inflation (if there is one), I don't know how to get the Russians out of Afghanistan, I still don't know how to solve the problems of Northern Ireland, I don't know how to eliminate unemployment without creating worse inflation. Nobody seems to me to be able to solve these problems, but I know what questions to ask in those areas, and that helps other people make up their mind.'

'So although you've been asking these questions for over twenty years, you're still no closer to finding any answers?' Sir Robin's rabbit-eared eyebrows shot up:

'I've been asking questions about inflation and unemployment and nuclear weapons, all these things—I've been listening to all the debates and rest assured I understand all the arguments, but no, I don't necessarily have the answers. Even if I did feel I had the answers, I don't see why that would be interesting because lots of people have lots of answers, and my answers wouldn't be any better than anybody else's. In fact, they may change from year to year—I went through various stages of opinion on the Common Market: strongly in favour, then very very doubtful, then on the whole feeling it was probably the best thing.'

'What's the use of just being so mentally agile?'

I could tell Sir Robin was beginning to enjoy himself. His eyes gleamed behind those black glasses like two minnows. 'I think that people who don't have the job of interrogative journalism, and who don't have the job of reporting and analysing politics impartially, probably find it easier to have an opinion. But if your job for a good many years has been to interrogate and summarise and describe politics in a reasonably impartial way, then this in itself tends to inject a certain objectivity in one's views.

'If you're a politician going down to his constituency every weekend, you have to have a view on everything. But as I'm not, I don't—I don't have to get up and say what I'm going to do about Northern Ireland tomorrow.

'I'll say to you what I've said to Bernard Levin, when he said, "I've spent my life being paid for the expression of my opinions—you're paid not to express them." The answer I gave was this: "If I had to choose between two liberties, the liberty to ask questions and the liberty to express opinions, I would choose the right to ask questions".'

'Isn't that somewhat irrelevant?'

'Well, it is a somewhat artificial choice because one is not going to be faced with those extremes. But I put it that way simply to say that I think the function of asking questions has a useful place in a democracy. "Educative" is a patronising word, but asking questions can help other people, who don't know very much about the issues, understand what they are. It's an educational influence rather than a partisan influence.'

'Someone described you as "the man in the studio for the man in the street". Is that a helpful way of looking at you?'

'What did he mean by that? He must have meant that I was the person in the studio on whom the man in the street was relying to put the questions he wanted. Well, I hope that is so, but of course I do more than that, because the man in the street only knows the first question which should be asked. I found this on the telephone-in programme. The first question is jolly good: "Mr Minister, I run a corner shop and I can tell you that your policies have made an absolute mess of my business. Why the hell aren't you doing something about it?"

'Then he gets a smooth answer, and I say, "What do you say to that, Mr X?" And Mr X says, "Oh yes, I see. But it's still made a mess of my business." All he can do is repeat his point. So then it's up to me to ask the second question which the shopkeeper would ask if he knew more about it, but which he trusts me to ask.

'The reason why so many interviewers fall down in their job is because they just sling aggressive questions at somebody and don't remember that their job should be to help the viewer.'

'What about your contemporaries who interview—what do you think of Brian Walden for example?'

'I admire Brian Walden very much. I was sorry when he left Parliament to go into television (the reverse of my own aims if you like), because he was a brilliant parliamentarian. I think he's tending now, as shown in a recent interview with the Prime Minister, to become just a little too conversational in his interviews. I'm not saying that he should be aggressive, but I think if you do become too conversational, the viewer isn't clear what point you're making.'

'Sir Robin,' I practically had to hold my hand up for attention, 'do you ever have just a conversation?'

'Well, I'm having an extremely enjoyable one now.'

'I meant, as opposed to an argument.'

'Certainly, I've done interviews of a conversational kind, but the trouble is that people then say: "What's wrong with Robin Day?"'

'Most of my so-called "tough" political interviews have been done within the space of ten minutes at a particular point of political history, and there's no time for conversation. There's no room for me to say, "How's your wife?" or "How did you like the opera last night?" I have to get on and ask about the mass unemployment.'

'What about conversations in your family life?'

'What about my family life? If my two little boys were here, we could have a conversation with them, but they're not. They're at school.'

'Do you quiz them over breakfast?' Sir Robin's huff-and-gruff voice barked back as though he suspected me of pulling his leg. 'Well, there isn't much time at breakfast. I do quiz them, yes, we quizzed them yesterday. What was I explaining to them? Oh yes, all about this chap David Martin and how he was caught and what it was all about.'

'Do they watch you on television?'

'They have done, but rarely because it's generally too late. They hear *World at One* when they're on holiday and they mimic me a bit!'

Sir Robin's wife came in at this point with some tea. It had been thirsty work. He introduced Lady Day with 'This is my wife, who was a don at your present college.'

We discussed colleges going mixed, and Sir Robin concluded, 'What I think is wrong is that you necessarily have men and women at the same college. There should be some colleges left which are single-sex.'

I contradicted him, saying that I had only got into Oxford because St Anne's was going mixed and welcomed any men applying.

'Why, which school did you go to?'

'Shrewsbury.'

'Shrewsbury! What, along with Ingrams and those other drop-outs? What "A"-levels did you get?'

I admitted to an A and two Ds. Sir Robin was incredulous. 'How did you get into Oxford with such appalling results?'

'I probably interviewed very well!'

'Why is St Anne's taking rubbish like you then?'

'They gave me an Exhibition. . . .' I smiled in the face of Sir Robin's apoplexy.

'What?! Did you have to sit for it? You mean you got in on sexist reasons. They just wanted to have a man!'

'But I get everywhere on sexist reasons', I answered. Sir Robin had the last line. 'Well, darling, St Anne's has gone down in the world!'

Lady Day left, and I picked up Sir Robin's mention of Richard Ingrams. 'I know your remarks were in jest, but don't you feel there is a similarity between you? You both highlight controversial aspects of politics.'

Sir Robin thought not. 'He's made a great success of his particular thing; he's made a national name for himself and has never had to be beholden to anybody. *Private Eye* is something totally new, and Richard Ingrams is one of the remarkable figures of the time, but I personally don't happen to like what he does.'

'Why not? If it's good professional journalism, surely. . . .' I was cut off.

'I didn't say it was "good professional journalism". I don't think good professional journalism consists in telling lies about people who may not be able to afford to correct them.'

'Don't all newspapers tell lies?'

'If a newspaper tells a lie about me which is damaging to me, they will deal with the matter properly and according to law without fighting it out and dragging it out. They don't make a business of libelling people in the hope that most people won't sue them. I know a lot of ordinary people who have been damaged by *Private Eye*. I'm not talking about the big shots who can look after themselves, I'm talking about ordinary people, young journalists for example, who have had *Private Eye* saying, "This lady is only in her job because of this, that and the other." A total, total lie.'

'Going back to where we were before tea, I wanted to ask you about your role within British television. You once applied for the job of Director General.'

'Yes, when a successor to Sir Charles Curran was called for in 1976, I was asked by Sir Michael Swann, the Chairman of the Board of Governors, to put my name forward, which I did, and I went onto the short list. When I went for the interview, one of the Governors said, "What experience have you had, Mr Day, of organising an organisation of 28,000 staff with a turnover of £300 million?" And I had to say, "None at all." I then said, feeling that this was my most plausible defence, "This is precisely why I'm applying, because I think the BBC should not be looking for an administrator but an editorial leader. In my submission the Director General's first job should be editorial."

'For very good reasons Ian Trethowan was chosen. I am confident that if I'd been on the Board of Governors, I would have chosen him too.'

'What do you regard as your responsibility within the BBC now?'

'I regard my responsibility as helping to ensure that television contributes to the understanding of difficult problems.

Sir Robin Day as cox in the Oxford Union *v* Cambridge Union Boat Race, 1950

'The process over the last twenty-five years of having intelligent and relevant interviewing as opposed to the flunkey interviews which used to exist before (which you wouldn't remember) is absolutely fundamental. This has been very good for politicians because they've begun to communicate with people in a grown-up way instead of talking a lot of nonsense. I'm not saying that television interviews always get near the truth or anything like it, of course they don't, but a good television interview should cause a public figure to talk a little more clearly and meaningfully about his responsibilities.'

Sir Robin is almost unique among television interviewers for refusing to be fobbed off. He asks the basic sort of questions which many politicians may wish to have taken for granted. I compared him with David Frost, who allows the issue of an interview to slide into show business. 'Do you scorn David Frost's style of interviewing?'

'I think he's done a great deal of damage to current affairs television by his introduction of certain techniques, yes.'

'Such as?'

'Well, this idea of the audience. There was a series of interviews where people sat before audiences who would be baying for blood—it was really quite nauseating. And he'd change his technique according to whom he was interviewing. If he thought someone was unpopular, he'd throw muck at them, if he thought they were heroes, he'd lick their feet.

'Basically he's an entertainer, and a successful one, and that's his approach. I thought the interview with Nixon was not very good. It was made to sound tough and probing, but it could have been done very much better.'

'Wasn't Frost chosen because Nixon wanted the best interviewer around?'

'Nixon was interviewed by Frost because he was offered a couple of million dollars for it.'

'You think that was the reason?'

'Well, what else?'

'What about the Shah of Iran, then? He wasn't wanting for any cash.'

'That's a good question. It may be that in his declining years, what the Shah wanted was to get his case across as a figure in history. This could only be done by someone whom they thought would help him.

'My reputation is not necessarily that. Both Nixon and the Shah would want to be interviewed by someone whom they thought was on their side. I would be neither for them nor against them. I would be just a journalist asking them what I thought, in conjunction with my editor, would be the right questions.'

'There is the opportunity to make quite a bit of money in television, isn't there? Do you think you've exploited this to the full?'

'No, I don't think I have. People appearing on television don't make nearly as much money as the executives or entrepreneurial people in television. People like Frost or Alan Whicker have become millionaires by their investments. My income is that of a good professional man, but it doesn't make me rich because of taxation. I couldn't stop work tomorrow.'

'But have you been paid a fair price?'

'Yes.'

'You don't feel under-rated?'

'No, I don't complain about that at all. What I do complain about is that I haven't, owing to our system of taxation, made as much money as I would have done as an individual.

'If I'd set up a coffee shop or a garage on the Great West Road thirty years ago, and had as much luck and success as I've had in television, I would now be a millionare because I would have had something to sell. But I've nothing to sell now. All I do is just go onto a higher income. High capital is freedom. High income is slavery.'

It was typical of Sir Robin that even such a self-deprecatory statement as this sounded like a question. There was, however, one occasion which he told me about as I followed him up the stairs from his basement study to the front door, when he found himself tongue-tied.

'I remember going to interview Marilyn Monroe a long time ago, back in 1956. Unfortunately I wasn't able to ask her any questions.'

'Why not?'

'Because she was doing a "silent". It was because of her film contract! So I was told to go and just pretend to be talking with her! I gave her a red rose. She was utterly gorgeous.'

I shook hands with Sir Robin outside the front door and staggered off around the corner. It had been an exhausting morning. It crossed my mind that perhaps Marilyn Monroe hadn't been such a dumb blonde after all.

Michael Heseltine

PEMBROKE, 1951–54

One of my father's friends who remembered Michael Heseltine from school had insisted on telling me some story about how Heseltine ('Goldilocks', the lads called him), had made quite a name for himself by selling old beer bottles from a nearby pub to the boys, who then used them as hot-water bottles. 'With those old-fashioned wire tops, d'you know, they were just the ticket.'

Why, I asked, didn't the other boys go directly to the pub themselves? 'Ah!' he mumbled, pulling at his walrus moustache, 'ah!' He didn't know the answer to that one.

So the first thing I said to the Secretary of State for Defence was:

'I understand you used to sell old beer bottles for the boys at school to use as hot-water bottles.'

Lord Greystoke, who had been draped behind his desk as though for a Dunhill still life, jack-knifed upright.

'Um ... er ... the....'

His brain must have been spinning back like a fruit machine. At last his eyes clocked in line. 'No, I ran a refreshment service where I brought lemonade and various other forms of beverage into the house and sold that. It was nothing to do with selling beer bottles. It was a very practical entrepreneurial manifestation at an early age. I sold it for thrupence a glass if I remember correctly.'

The Secretary of State looked justifiably pleased with himself for dealing with that one.

'So you didn't sell them for hot-water bottles?' I asked, disappointed.

143

'No,' Mr Heseltine looked contemptuous, 'there was never any water given to it one way or another. There is no foundation whatsoever for this extravagant exaggeration. I simply sold lemonade—proper lemonade.'

Cursing the old colonel from Shropshire, I hurried on to Oxford. Mr Heseltine, in control once more, swept his goldilocks back in shooting-brake style and looked at me warily.

'What did you expect to find when you went up to Oxford?'

'What did I expect to find???' he screeched; raw, terrified, enormous, incomprehending incredulity quivering all over him.

'Yes,' I hesitated, double-checking that it wasn't such an outrageous question—it didn't seem to be. Mr Heseltine, alarm scrawled all over his face, rushed in with his answer.

'Well, I went to do a degree. I went to do all the things you do at the age of eighteen when you go to University—very exciting. Joined the Union, joined the Conservatives, got a degree, made a lot of friends—very exciting formative period of my life. The most exciting thing about the whole,' he scrabbled for a word which apparently didn't come, '*thing*, is actually growing up in that environment, that stretching intellectual environment. People of very different backgrounds, very different opinions. Um ... very affectionate memories I have of those three years.'

'So you were interested in politics right from the start?'

The mention of politics acted as a banana to an orang-outang. 'Oh yes,' he murmured. 'I was a member of the Conservative Party before I went to Oxford, and I joined the Union the day I got there.'

'And you went on to become President—did that teach you a lot?'

'Yes. Not only do you learn to speak in a rather formal environment at an early age, but you meet and listen to some of the best speakers of the day. And because I became an officer, I got very considerable administrative experience at an early age of virtually running large parts of the Oxford Union. That was very satisfactory, and we had a lot of success: we got the membership up, we solved the financial crisis for a few years.'

'So it was a good training for being a politician?' He munched another mouthful.

'I would say the best, at that age. As good as there is. And of course particularly because you meet a lot of people, from all political parties, who are also going into politics. So you're learning the lessons which are going to stay with you for the rest of your life in the political world. It's not so much a replica but an anticipatory form of existence to what you find in politics at the House of Commons.'

'What attracted you to politics in the first place?'

Mr Heseltine was finding this too easy. 'I think that's a very difficult question to answer. It all happened at an early age: I found myself in the school debating society, I was interested in issues, interested in the art of communication, the challenge of debate. But now, politics is for me the area where the opportunities are the greatest for the particular interests I have.

'I'm interested in achieving results, I'm interested in influencing the direction in which our society moves (both internally and externally), and there is no other career which I am aware of where you get such an opportunity to play such a role in the issues of the day. I have spent a lot of time with the private sector in the publishing business, but there's a much wider dimension in the job that one does in politics. The pace of it is very fast. . . .'

The pace of the monologue was hotting up too, so I ducked in with: 'But what if you'd been out of power for the last six years?'

'Well, I was, I was out of power when we lost the election in 1974, and it wasn't until five years later that we came back in. So one did one's best to help the Party in opposition as well as actually having a role in the publishing world. You can't be both in opposition and Government at the same time.'

I nodded wisely. Mr Heseltine ran his hand luxuriantly through his hair. 'Government is much better, I can tell you that! But if we went into opposition again, I suppose I would spend what time I could helping the Party.'

He made it sound a remote possibility.

'Why did you choose defence?'

'I've never chosen a job in politics yet. They've always been offered to me by various leaders of our Party, and I've always been amazed how stimulating they all are—transport, environment, defence. I wouldn't have predicted that I would have gone into any of these fields, but I've been completely absorbed by them when I got there. I think that's true of most political jobs: there is just such an opportunity and wide spectrum of challenge, that whichever job you're in, you find bits of it which interest you most.'

I glanced around Mr Heseltine's Whitehall office. Large enough for a game of croquet, there were a few pieces of government mahogany, an old globe to one side and, taking up most of the wall behind him, the sort of electronic map of the world that a James Bond villain might produce from behind a revolving Canaletto. The Soviet Union, bright red, seemed more than ever hugely poised to gobble up Europe—so big, it seemed Europe might disappear just by its shifting its weight. I asked what I imagined some of its inhabitants would be interested in.

'What is the exact process which has to be gone through before a nuclear weapon is fired?'

'Huh!' said Mr Heseltine and was quiet for a moment. Outside the birds twittered away, time bombs ticking.

'To keep the peace is the short answer to that. I mean, all I would be prepared to say is that the control of these weapon systems is under the tightest political decision-making—both on this side of the Iron Curtain and the other. But nobody will be prepared to go into any detail with you on the precise mechanism of the system.'

'Under what circumstances do you envisage. . . .?'

Mr Heseltine held up a senatorial paw. 'I don't have any way of discussing that with you in public. The whole purpose is to maintain the peace, and nobody can get involved in detailed discussions as to what happens if the peace breaks down. We believe our policies of defence are sufficient to stop that happening. We've worked at it for nearly four decades with total success.'

'But what about the world in fifteen years' time when lots of other people will have nuclear weapons?'

Mr Heseltine was sublime: 'It's very difficult to know. I think that I would believe that peace in the Western world would be preserved, and I don't believe that there will be a confrontation between the Superpowers because the risks are too high, the stakes are so well known. There is no credible thought process that can persuade either side that it is worth doing. So whilst I would believe that the doctrinal conflict will remain, and that from time to time there will be individual isolated political skirmishes, I don't believe that it will lead to the destruction of the peace.

'If you say, "What about the Third World?" well, that's much harder to predict and that's one of the reasons why we signed the Non-Proliferation Treaty. I attach importance to that. My hope would be. . . .'

In front of me, Mr Heseltine was beginning gently to sway in time to his own plausibility. He reminded me of *The Jungle Book*, and Kaa swinging in front of Mowgli:

'. . . that as governments of the Third World mature, by that I mean simply have been around, that they will themselves learn to produce continuity in government, which would therefore not be revolutionary, and I think that once you have a continuity of government, under whatever system, a rational process develops, and that rational process will be as appalled at the concept of nuclear weaponry as we are in those countries which now possess such powers.

'Ideally it would be better to stop the proliferation, but in politics it's always a mistake to try and analyse tomorrow's problem in terms of the exact replication of today's. It never is like that. What we have to work to is a situation where there is a much more stable political decision-making process in the world of tomorrow; where individual countries have a maturity of judgment and a rational approach to judgment which will lead them to the same views about the course of military capability as we have in the West.'

'But all the same,' I said, struggling to shake off Kaa's hypnosis, 'you must have analysed under which sort of conditions you would be prepared to react with nuclear weapons?'

'Why, why,' crooned Kaa in reply, 'why do you have to pen yourself in to a whole range of hypothetical situations which you cannot in detail foresee? All we occupy ourselves with is the need to maintain deterrents. The purpose of deterrents is to prevent anyone calculating that it is worthwhile to attack us. It is not worthwhile attacking us. There is no victory. That is the policy that we pursue, and you don't need to go further working out in detail what follows if they do attack.'

'You must have a trigger point. . . .'

'We have the ability to inflict unacceptable damage on the aggressor. That is all they need to know. They must not doubt our willingness to do that. They do not need to know what they would have to do to make us do it. Indeed it would be very dangerous if they did know that, because the lower you make the risks, the more attractive those risks become. What you are suggesting I do is define the low risks—I'm not in the business of doing that.'

'I am not suggesting you define them,' I said. 'I was just wondering whether any deadlines were in existence.'

'Perhaps I should spell it out.' We were both getting rather irritated. 'There are lots of things that as a Secretary of Defence you simply wouldn't dream of discussing in public. My task is just to leave one very clear impression and that is the capability to inflict,' I waited for the chorus, 'unacceptable damage on an opponent. I don't find it difficult to explain that.

'But if you say, "Well, show me how, when and why," then it would begin to get involved in that dialogue, and my whole purpose is to stop it happening anyway.

'If I just reflect on a personal basis, I don't believe that anyone can foresee these events anyway, because they would be foreseeing it from a one-sided position, and it never is one-sided—'cos it's always two-sided, and it's unpredictable and all sorts of instances happen which you haven't calculated. So there's no point in making hypothetical judgments on a text-book analysis of what the situation would be like. If you had sat here four years ago and asked, "Where do you think the threat most imminently likely to appear is?" I wouldn't have got many

'Who knows what fifty decades will look like?'

Michael Heseltine

marks for saying, "We're going to invade the Falklands." Who would have thought of the Falklands! So it's not real to try to lay down where your strength lies, and what your talent and capability would turn out to look like in practice.'

Mr Heseltine rolled his eyes so much they practically turned full somersault. 'It's not real.'

'What's it like negotiating with people who have completely different ideological backgrounds?'

'Just the same as negotiating with people of your own ideological background: you're negotiating with people.'

'What about with politicians who have become politicians for different reasons than you?'

'It's not like that. You are dealing with people, and you know that they have to make judgments about power in their own context—human motives are universal.

'You see, "isms" will give you a very false impression of what the structure of power is, of what politics is all about. The disciplines that control those "isms" are fascinating. So within the Soviet Union, say, there is one "ism", but a range of disciplines—whilst their preoccupations are not the same as ours, they use the same skills in trying to make decisions about the allocation of powers. There is a very political process at work which operates through a series of judgments, so there are the questions: "Should more money go into defence? What about economic development?" So with the Soviet Union, the question is: "How do they control the various power structures that go into the make-up of the country? How do they keep each of them satisfied that he's getting a fair share of whatever action there is around?" These are the critical influences of policy. Of course, they don't have a public opinion in the sense that we do, that we have a media, but they do have a series of pressures within their system, and the art of coping with those pressures is a political art.

'So it isn't difficult to talk to people who come from different systems. Governments may be of all sorts of different political persuasion—look at Western Europe in the fields in which I operate! But the people you're dealing with are usually motivated by what one hopes is an enlightened self-interest in their country.'

'Would you measure your success by the fact that there has been political stability?'

Mr Heseltine loved that one. 'I have no doubt that the fact that the governments of Western Europe have pursued policies in alliance with the American and Canadian peoples to deliver peace for the unprecedented period of nearly four decades is one of the supreme political achievements of history. What more can you do for people than give them an environment of peace?' asked Mr Heseltine, disarmingly. 'What higher priority could you pursue? And we've done it. And there's no risk that I see of that breaking down in the foreseeable future. We have to work at it, keep up the capability and determination, keep up the diplomatic skills and energies that make the system work and coalesce.' This was real rousing "play up, play up and play the game" stuff. 'But it is the supreme achievement of the most successful alliance the world has ever seen.'

'But what about looking ahead...?'

'That doesn't really give a very helpful perspective on what we are doing now.'

'What I mean is that, yes, I agree that four decades is a remarkable achievement—but can you see it continuing for another fifty decades?' Mr Heseltine flashed that devil-may-care smile.

'Who knows what fifty decades will look like?'

'Isn't it part of the responsibility of the job to lay down those sort of foundations?' I countered. Mr Heseltine reverted to Kaa with a sway of the head.

'For fifty decades?!'

'Well, fifty years then.'

Kaa answered to the tune of 'Trust in me...': 'As far as I can see, I cannot see a breakdown of the intellectual basis for deterrents which we have achieved for the maintenance of peace. I can't see how you are going to get that in the Western world. No one has ever put to me a scenario when it did so break down.'

'What about if a Labour Government gets in?' I idly asked. The change in Kaa was galvanic. One moment he had been relaxing in the breadth of his charm, hair smoothed back and eyes all innocence. The next thing I saw was the Spitting Image puppet, hair agog and rabid eyes, erupting out of him like the Alien from John Hurt's stomach and cork-screwing towards me.

'Aaargh! Are you talking about that?!! I thought you were talking about *me*! *My* policies! If you put *them* in, I can think of all sorts of things that would happen....' A spot of phlegm jumped on one lip. 'You would shatter the NATO alliance, cause a great surge of isolationism in America, cause fragmentation within Europe. They haven't begun to understand the implications of their policy!'

'But I can't be expected to answer for that—I spend my time trying to expose it.'

'It seems extraordinary to me,' I flatly said, 'that two parties should have such diametrically opposed policies.'

'Not extraordinary in the context of Labour Party history,' trumpeted the army-jacketed figure in front of me. 'They are going through a very left-wing pacifist phase, much as they went through in the 1930s. Do you know that the slogans of the one-sided disarmers are the slogans of the pacifists of the 1930s? You just look at the demonstrations or the speeches—the arguments are the same! The fact that we have now got nuclear weapons is just an additional dimension to a debate which has always been in the Labour Party, and not as something totally more dangerous. We had it in the 1930s when it had devastating consequences. Hitler made a classic misjudgment on the basis of that sort of argument.'

'You think that a Labour Government would unravel all your policies as quickly as that?' Mr Heseltine ravelled himself back into a more coherent coil and smoothed the rabies from his face.

'Well,' he joked, 'you've got to see a Labour Government in power first, and I don't see that—and if you do, then they've also got to stick to their present policies, and I don't see a Labour Government in power as long as it does stick to its present defence policy.'

'Doesn't the fact that elections are slightly random frighten you? The fact that people can vote for the wrong reasons?'

'Well, it is a free society, but it does seem to balance out. We do have one of the largest majorities in post-war history, and no small element of that is the fact that we have a Labour Party with the defence policies that they have.'

And that was where we left it. With a flash of a smile, Lord Greystoke returned to his native jungle of international arms control. On the wall map all the colours of the world seemed to be flashing warning lights, and this was before anyone had heard of Westland Helicopters.

Bob Hawke

UNIVERSITY, 1953–55

Someone poked their head around the door.

'The Prime Minister is just coming.'

The next thing I heard was a shout from the direction of the stairs. 'Is Hizel out of thet blaady shiwer yit?'

A muffled answer seemed to satisfy him, for a moment later in came Mr Hawke.

'Gudday!'

I stood up to shake hands.

'Mind if I smike?'

'That was just what I was going to ask you.'

'Well then, we're off to a good start!' said Mr Hawke and reached for a box of cigars. We sat down, and I watched him as he began lighting up. He was much smaller and looked more worn-out than I had imagined. With small hands, little feet in polished black slip-ons, light blue socks, open-neck shirt and that wave of hair above his terrier face, he looked less like yer average Aussie from Down Under, rather more, in fact, like some well-to-do hairdresser.

Mr Hawke was a Rhodes Scholar in 1953, and when I asked him what he hoped to find at Oxford, he began: 'I was hoping for ... liberalism. I was hoping for ... the spirit of ... free and untrammelled interchange of ... ideas ... and tolerance of points of ... view. And in ... that ... I was totally ... satisfied.'

I leant forward in astonishment. Mr Hawke seemed to have started an elaborate impersonation of a sleep-walking pilot at the controls of a runaway aeroplane. In slowest motion his hands fumbled for all sorts of switches inches from his face, but each time it looked as if he

'Before I left the University of West Austraalia I had virtually finished and Arse degree majoring in Economics.

Bob Hawke, Rhodes Scholar

could pull it out of its nose dive, the plane would bucket and he would lurch backwards, lose his place and have to start all over again.

In spite of this, he was determined to get to the answer, and, bit by bit, he managed to scratch it out. It was an exhausting performance. That done, he crashed out behind a large puffball of smoke, apparently fast asleep. It was a hard act to follow.

'But wasn't your tutor supposedly. . . .'

'Mmm?'

'Wasn't your tutor supposedly intolerant? Didn't he tell you to go away?'

'Ah yis, but you don't judge a whole great institution by one person, do you? He had a . . .' Mr Hawke screwed up his face in agony as the nightmare returned, '. . . particular set of . . . prejudices, let us say, and . . . indeed . . . you could almost say ideological . . . interests in . . . the institution that I was proposing to investigate, research and . . . to put it in its simplest .. terms . . . he had a vested interest in research not being done.'

Taking his eyes off the ceiling where they had been transfixed, he tipped his neck so they swivelled towards me. They latched onto my shoulder.

'But I haven't spent my life being one that is easily put off by prejudices or stupidity, and I wasn't on that occasion. I was very grateful for the support, unquestioning support, I received from my college and Rhodes House, who saw this posed impediment . . . for what it was.'

'Didn't you ever entertain the idea of reading an Arts degree at Oxford?'

'No, because before I left the University of West Austraalia I had virtually finished an Arse degree majoring in Economics, so at Oxford I felt there was an opportunity to do some research work in some area which combined my interest in Economics with Law (my primary degree). It emerged quite clearly,' he repeated this without a ghost of irony, 'it emerged quite clearly that the thing which combined my interest in Law and Economics was the Austraalian institution, the Conciliation and Arbitration System, and within that the concept of the basic wage which had emerged in the early 1900s. And no one had done any work on it.'

'Really?'

'No, and fortunately Rhodes House had all the basic source material that I needed. In a sense, paradoxically, I was probably better placed to do the work in Oxford than in Austraalia. I mean there wasn't a great stream of people lining up to read that material.'

For the first time, he looked straight at me, and I could clearly see his eyes, black as footprints, pinched deep in his face. He had about him something of the bony stiffness of an old person, but the most extraordinary thing was his tortured speech rhythm, which seemed to hit him on and off. When it hit him, he would pause for some seconds between words, even words which I expected to be part and parcel of each other, like 'points of ... view'. And into these pauses were absorbed intricate hand movements. They started up again when I asked, 'What about your religious life at Oxford? I read that just before Oxford, you had been to India, which reshaped your religious attitude.'

'Well, I suppose that was where the weaning ... process was virtually concluded. I mean weaning process in terms of dissociation from formalised organised religion. I guess that the shock of India, and the irrelevance of the organised ... church, as I saw it, to the needs of its environments and the needs of the people ... it was just a very ... impactive thing for me. I gradually withdrew from regular association and church-going.'

'You have said you're an agnostic, not an atheist—what's the difference?'

Mr Hawke lurched forward in his chair. No longer the pilot, he was now preparing for some form of underwater karate and went through alarming motions of holding his breath and whirling his hands. 'The difference is well ... known and reasonably well established in the ... dictionaries and in my ... mind well established. I ... I ... think it's an act of ... rather heroic intellectual proportions to assert that there is no God or being. I am not in any sense phased or upset by those who are so certain of their intellectual...' he made it sound oddly phallic, '... equipment as to be able to make that assertion. They are satisfied from their own intellectual processes—I am not offended by it, I just tend to ... marvel at the heroism. And in the same sense, the preparedness of the people unqualifiedly to believe the assertions about a God, whether it be in the, you know, Judeo-Christian framework or of the Eastern religions, their preparedness to embrace all the elements of those creeds ... I find ... equally ... heroic.

'So I am also in the position where I know that my own life has been shaped abundantly by the tenets, the fundamental tenets of Christianity. My father and mother have always impressed me not only with the beliefs but the practical applications of those beliefs, and that has really shaped the way I approach life. So one has an indebtedness to those things that I am not prepared in their entirety to embrace and this creates...' there came a sideways underwater karate chop, 'it's not an intellectual problem, it's just that it's the total framework of my thinking and experience. So agnosticism, it's a long answer to your question, Edward, so agnosticism therefore reflects my lack of preparedness to make these heroic assumptions others are prepared to make, and yet acknowledges the enormous indebtedness I have to Christian ethics and ideals.'

'So was it seeing Christianity as being inadequate to cope with the problems of India which started that?'

'I don't think you have really quite got the point. I was not approaching it in terms of thinking that Christianity in Southern India was going to provide the answers to all the problems in India. It's not as simplistic as that. What rather struck me and increasingly offended me was the irrelevance and hypocrisy of the institutionalised church there.

'I remember it sticking in my mind—it was Christmas Eve, and I was walking down the streets of this town, Cottyam, and I heard carols being sung from within these relatively lavish Christian homes. The lines which stuck in my mind were ". . . and the world to Christ we bring", and I thought of what the reciprocal was. I saw here was the world, and there was the Church. And it just seemed to be that it was all pretty silly.

'Let me be fair to the Church in 1985 compared to the Church in 1953—you wouldn't make the same criticisms now.'

'What did you think of the Hindu religion?'

'Well, the thing that I find ultimately tragic about the religions of India is that they are based upon the essential proposition that the condition of life, of the human being in question, is ordained—is part of a succession of existences. And indeed, if the individual accepts that condition and lives in obedience of what has been ordained, he will then gradually move up in his next existence. Now, that is a recipe for complacency and conservatism of the worst kind.'

'Because he's doing nothing about it . . .?'

'Worse than that—its not just doing nothing, but that doing nothing is the very essence of the religion. That you are in a pre-ordained stage of development in an old, ineffable drama, and that to try and rebel or change or improve that is contrary to what life in its succession of stages is all about.

'For one who has a concern about the social condition, for one who believes that ultimately politics is about the creation of happiness for individuals and that you should do all you can to change the conditions to give people the opportunities to develop their talents—which is my basic belief to what life's about—then that religious approach is a barrier to how I think.'

As he said it, I wanted to cheer him for being an angry man who once had this vision of what should be done and who has been living ever since trying to do something about it—and now looks so old.

'If you want to talk in religious terms, I find the concept of reincarnation, of a succession of existences, far more compelling than the concept that one existence, one infinitesimal point on the head of a pin, is all you get in the whole stream of existence. It is more logically attractive, but what is appalling is then accepting that it's wrong to struggle to improve the condition of existence—the only one we know about.

'Any rate, Edward,' surfaced Mr Hawke, 'that is getting into rather esoteric territory.'

'One other thing about religion, though,' I went on, 'is that it must make it easier to govern.' His trowel-shaped mouth turned down.

'History wouldn't sustain that proposition, I wouldn't think.'

'Well, in the sense that if there's religious order, there can be political order....'

' I would simply say that the elements of religion at the present time and in the past with regard to the Irish question, say, wouldn't suggest that government is easier.'

'No, I wasn't talking about conflict between religions, I was just proposing that in a country where there is a well established sense of religion, like the Hindu religion, that it would be easier to govern than in the West, where religion has disintegrated.' By disagreeing with me, Mr Hawke showed the real extent of his instinctive ambition for social reform.

'You know, when you're talking about governments, you must not be simplistic and simply say "religion". I mean, if you're talking about the problems of government in, say, India or China, well, there are so many different elements of historical significance that just to pick out religion is not very revealing. But let's take India and China, for instance: I can't help feeling that it's easier for the Chinese government to achieve their revolution (which they are doing with enormous success now) than it would be in India where all the taboos would get in the way.'

I realised that it was potentially the sort of dingbat argument which wouldn't get anywhere, so I changed the subject. 'Something else which struck me about you, was your involvement in Israel—where does that stem from?'

'I suppose, again, it was a mixture of strains in my experience. I've always had a ...' the pause which fell as Mr Hawke gathered a word was the longest to date. There would have been time to boil a kettle as the silence gathered pace and at last broke with, '... *hatred* of prejudice. I've always disliked seeing people being hurt because they were different. When I went to University, I remember having a sense of ... guilt in thinking back over some of the schoolboy attitudes and expressions one had perhaps easily let pass by. I had gone to University almost exactly when Israel emerged in 1948, and I remember thinking with pride about the emergence of the State of Israel, and how here at last was a home for these people who had suffered so much through the centuries.

'Then, despite the attacks on Israel which were made from the day of its creation, as far as the world community was concerned, Israel was now by itself. And then, through the 1960s as there was a growth of antagonism and hatred for Israel, I began to read and think about it and eventually went there in 1971. I saw that here was a country with people who were literally in fear of their capacity to exist. There was no doubt that it was the intention amongst Arab states, the PLO, to wipe them out—not just to inflict some casualty, but to obliterate the country. The hypocrisy of the world in ignoring this just appalled me, so I just felt that whatever I could do, I would try to argue the right of Israel to exist.'

'Was that just a contemporary political thing, or did it tie in with your early reading of the Bible?'

'Aw! I mean, how can you measure these things? I mean, there's no doubt that, on my first visit, being confronted with these names of places that I'd read about and thought about as a child—how do you measure what impact that has on you? I'm not clever enough to do that, and I don't think anybody else would be.' Mr Hawke punched his cigar towards me: 'I mean, how would you measure it?'

I took the point. Mr Hawke was busy relighting the stub of his cigar, his eyes disappearing as he squinted to avoid the smoke. I went back to another offshoot of his going to Oxford. 'When you went off to Oxford, did you find you grew away from your parents?'

'I didn't grow away from my parents. I never grew away—there's a confusion in what you say; I think in many ways I've grown closer to them.'

'But one does have to grow up.'

'It doesn't mean growing away from your parents.'

'To a certain extent, it must mean standing on your own two. . . .'

'Oh, physically, yea. But I'm talking about the emotional ties which you have. Of course, I left home in 1953 to go to Oxford and I never lived at home again. You grow away in that sense, but I think my appreciation and understanding of my parents has increased over the years.'

'Having been a father yourself, what's it like seeing your own children growing up through that age of twenty to twenty-five?'

'It is a variegated experience . . . I guess one has the experience that so many parents have of, on the one hand, seeing certain things being done which you think are . . . wasteful of talent, and on the other hand having to exercise the self-discipline that I think you must do, and re-alise that it's their life, they've got to make the decisions. Trying to give some indication of what you think, but not pushing that to the point where the actual love which exists between parents and children is going to be alienated by the attempt to impose. Now that's been the di-lemma of the ages for parents, I guess, and ... I have had no special magic for escaping that dilemma.'

'It must be very difficult knowing when to hold back—'

'Yeah, it is. And the great...' Mr Hawke juggled both hands as though trying to gauge the weight of something at the market, '... tragedy is trying, often unsuccessfully, to get their acceptance to the fact that there is one commodity in life which is not replaceable, that you can't go down to the supermarket and buy some more of, and that's time. And it's always disturbing to see young people thinking that they can get away with certain things, that it won't matter too much ... in a sense it may not, but you can never get back that time.

'And so if you see a person down the track, and you know that they could have been a fuller person, have had more opportunity to do more for other people, that's always the most hurtful experience of life.

'Now, Edward, you raised this about my own children, and I'm not necessarily applying all those things I've just said to them, but for them as for others, I think that that is a fact of their existence. Having said all that,' Mr Hawke suddenly cracked a smile like a can of Fosters, 'I have great joy with my children and my grandchildren, one of which has just arrived and I saw just before I came in to see you—my first grand-daughter!'

'That must be marvellous,' I agreed.

'I might say that I must be the most prolific Prime Minister in Austraalia's history. We started off in March '83 with no grandchil-dren, we now have four. When we were waiting for our first one, I was surprised at the number of people who said, "You'll get more fun and joy out of your grandchildren than your own children." I used to say, "Don't be silly!" But it's true in a funny sort of sense: you get all the joy of being with them, but when they get too much trouble you can—shooo!—shunt them off in a way you can't with your own!'

'Did you feel ambitious for your children to succeed? Like your mother felt ambitious for you?'

'Well, she certainly did! But I think it's a mistake to be ambitious for your children. What you want to see, and this is what I want for every-one but I base it on my own children, is the fullest development of the talents that are within that person. The great tragedy of life is to see people with obvious talents not developed—this is why I try, whenever

I'm talking to young people like you, I say: "Make as much of your education as you can. Don't succumb to the temptation to drop out and just get a job. Take every opportunity you've got and don't sacrifice the development of talent now for a little bit of passing satisfaction, because you have to live out the rest of your life over such a long period."'

The man who had looked so tired and old was now beginning to slough off this appearance, to struggle out of it as though it was an old jacket. 'You've struck me,' I said, 'as one of the few world leaders who has a real sense of optimism, a feeling that you can achieve—do you still have it after two years in Government, or does that sort of enthusiasm get strangled?'

'It doesn't get strangled—the hands get a bit tighter there around the optimistic creature at times, but I think if you don't retain some optimism and idealism it would be a very souring existence. I've seen it happen with so many people.

'But it is true, Edward, that being in the centre of things, I do see opportunities missed because of pigheadedness, because of sterile adherence to the fashions of an earlier age and I see things which could be achieved if people would just get rid of the shackles of past assumptions and prejudices—yeah, that's frustrating.

'But you still see good things happening. People around me joke and say, "Awh, there he goes looking for the silver lining again." Well, I do search for the silver lining—I hope in the end it makes you a better leader, but I don't know. . . .'

'Isn't it frustrating to think that maybe in ten years' time, what you've been doing will just be seen as something which was fashionable at the time, but actually misguided?'

'No, I've got no fear about that at all. The paths we've opened up will not be grown over by the . . . foliage of the future.

'Externally for instance, the most important thing I've done as Prime Minister of Australia is in our relationship with China. There is no country in the world which has a better relation with China than us. I have established close personal relationships with the leadership of China that has now flowered into exchanges in the economic field which are irreversible.'

'Do you think China's policy of opening up its markets is irreversible?'

'I don't think it is, I know it is. You've got to ask yourself the question: "Where is the locus of power that would lead to a reversion of the policies?" And there isn't one: the army have a vested interest in having the most economic system to ensure they have the best equipment to deal with the threat of the Soviet Union; the technocrats, the educated classes, have a vested interest in the new system because they were the greatest victims of the previous ... stupidities and their talent is now being rewarded; and the peasantry—if there is one thing which is obvious, that's how *infinitely* better off the peasantry is. There are *no* reasons for this philosophy being changed. They don't exist.

'Without question, it is the most important thing that has happened in the world this century. And one of the reasons why I think it is important, which doesn't seem to have been understood is this,' Mr Hawke put the cigar to one side and got both hands ready, 'you can't have China here,' he clenched one fist, 'the Soviets here,' then the other; 'China having abandoned the ... ludicrous irrelevancies and ... inhibitions of Marxist-Leninist economic doctrine, and now prospering, and still, next to it,' he rattled both fists together like a cocktail shaker, 'have the Soviet Union which imposes upon itself the continuation of all those ludicrous irrelevancies.

'Gorbachov was responsible for agriculture for a long time—he knows what is happening in China, he knows that Chinese agricultural produce is going like that.' One hand zoomed up. 'Now it may be some time, but the influence of China with its abandonment of the ludicrous ... unbelievably pointless ... imposition of ... restraints upon the human spirit will get through to Russia.'

He reached for his cigar, then thought better of it and added, 'It is impossible for Russia to isolate itself from what's happening—with communications today, you can't *sneeze* in the White House without it being known in Moscow. Moscow knows as well as the Chinese leadership what is happening in China—that output is going up, income is going up, and all because, in simple terms, the textbook has been thrown out, and the Chinese have released the ... dynamism of the individual and the families.

'Can you imagine releasing anything more dynamic in the world than one hundred thousand million Chinese families?'

This took me by surprise. 'No', I said, thinking it sounded like some sort of germ warfare. Mr Hawke marvelled on. 'Now, that's producing results, dramatic results, and Gorbachov knows it. It's not because Gorbachov is intellectually inadequate, nor is it because of bad climates that Russia has been such a massive failure in agriculture—it's because of the incredible, counter-productive irrelevancies of Marxist-Leninist doctrine.'

'Right,' I said, beginning to feel the drift of his argument like a strepsil at the back of my throat. 'Have you met Gorbachov?'

'No.'

'Will you?'

'Yeah, I hope so.'

'And will you tell him all this?'

'Yeah, of course—that it's happening in China, and also it's reflec-ted in some of the countries of the Eastern bloc: Hungary is infinitely more successful, particularly in their agricultural production, because they've bent the rules. But that's a bit different to China, who have not merely bent the rules—they've thrown the blaady rule book out!'

'What's it like talking with these different leaders—do you actually communicate and make sense or will there always be mistrust?' Be-neath the initial appearance of grotesque nonsense, Mr Hawke's answer was saying something important.

'I do . . . feel . . . deeply that if we were to, as a rather tortured world community, to . . . delude ourselves that we are going to be able to re-solve our differences by appeal to a . . . moral . . . imperative we would be engaged in the most massive exercise in . . . self-delusion ever known. We will not resolve our differences by appeal to moral imperatives.' This was pretty hard going—it got better. 'The secret of good government is to appeal to that factor which is always operative and that's self-interest. You've got to try, if you like, to ennoble that rather intrinsically unattractive feature we all have by making it *enlight-ened* self-interest.

'Look at Austraalia: it has been the basis of my approach to say that we will all do so much better if we work together. It doesn't mean we have to share every vision, but we should at least put divisiveness as an organised way of life behind us, and recognise that if we work together we can produce more, and that will provide more for everybody. That has to be the better way to do it—and it has worked. It has been out-standingly successful.

'And the same in our international relations, we've simply *got* to understand that if we allow the human capacity for intolerance and de-struction to have a free rein, we'll destroy the world.' Mr Hawke looked so disgusted I thought he really might retch. 'We're now in a world quite different from anything else in history: we can destroy *everything*. That's never been a prospect before.'

What was briefly one of those moments of shattering panic and despair at the idea of nuclear warfare exploding everywhere was saved by Bob Hawke just shrugging his shoulders like one of my flatmates and saying, 'All I'm trying to get people to understand is just that that's a pretty stupid thing to do. We've got to learn to live together, other-wise we'll die together. I know that's trite language, but often trite language is also true language. We've got to really believe that we aren't going to destroy one another.'

Because he had made his thinking about nuclear war so personal, I found it easy to ask him about his own death.

'What do you feel about the thought of dying yourself?'

'I don't even think about it.'

'How do you think you'll feel in forty years' time?'

'In forty years' time.' Mr Hawke smiled as though he suspected a joke.

'Yes,' I said, 'you know—just a natural death.'

'Oh! In forty years' time, I think it will have happened by then.' He laughed as he recognised that I had indeed made a joke. 'I may not look it, but I am fifty-five now' (I was in a bit of a fix over this, not knowing whether he was meant to look older or younger) 'and I can say quite seriously I don't spend any time thinking about it. It's just something which will happen.'

I wanted him to think about it, though. 'Is that because you're an agnostic?'

'I hope it's because I'm intelligent! I would think any intelligent atheist, agnostic or believer would have the same view.'

I smiled, suspecting a joke of his, but he was serious. 'I mean, one of the principal things in my life that I've tried to operate is not to waste time thinking about things about which you can do nothing. I have witnessed so many people destroying themselves, or certainly reducing their effectiveness, by spending so much time thinking or worrying about things that they cannot do anything about. It seems to me to be just about the *ultimate* stupidity—really. It is the ultimate waste of time to think about death.'

'Well, now that we are thinking about it and talking about it, don't you think that if one believes in any form of after-life, then that's some form of reassurance? But if you don't. . . .' Mr Hawke cut me off, his windmilling hands practically propelling him in Australian crawl across the room.

'As soon as you use the word "reassurance" you set the terms of the debate. I mean: who wants reassurance? I mean: here's your life.'

He plonked his imaginary life down in front of him like a schooner of beer.

'Who wants reassurance about whether there's another? Whether there's an after-life? Who wants reassurance whether you're coming back? As soon as you talk about reassurance, that defeats the whole purpose of what I'm. . . .'

During the gesticulating pause which hovered over the next word, I quite clearly heard a woman's voice outside saying, 'Is Bab out of thet blaady indervue yit?'

I glanced back to Mr Hawke, who raised an eyebrow towards the door.

'Watch out—you'll go arse over hip down there!'

Bob Hawke, Kirribilli House

'...saying. I don't find that very attractive, that's all. You'd better come and meet Hizel....'

And we packed up and went outside to find the family on the veran-dah. Kirribilli House faces south over Sydney Harbour. It was a trans-lucent clear day. The harbour below was brilliant blue, flecked with the whites of seahorses and splashed with any number of sails. A drove of big yachts came bearing down past us, their spinnakers running before them; on the far side boats were criss-crossing upwind. Through the trees to the right, I could see the shark's teeth of the Opera House fanned wide. The sunlight bounced all around, effervescent as Perrier water.

I was introduced to Hazel. 'Hizel, this is Edward. He's indervuing me for a book about Oxford graduates who have become famous or otherwise. I giss I'm "otherwise", right, Edward!'

'How long are you over for?' asked Hazel. When I said just the weekend, she laughed: 'Oh, hit and run, is it?'

We took some pictures. I wanted to go down a bank towards the water's edge, but he warned, 'Watch out—you'll go arse over tip down there!' and led me round a path.

When it came to leaving, he walked me up to the gate. We said goodbye, and he put a hand on my forearm.

'All the best, Edward. I hope everything goes well for you, mate.'

Dudley Moore

MAGDALEN, 1954–58

'From the age of six, I always rather fancied the power and splendour of the organ. I must have been twelve, maybe thirteen, when the chaplain allowed me up into the organ loft and let me play in the gaps during the services. Then I discovered all those grand things an organ could do during the hymns, how it could play people up the aisle with great pomp. It was even more'—Dudley Moore deliberated over the word and finally enjoyed his choice—'*exotic* than all that, because my left foot is a club foot.

'To play the organ, you have to do a lot of pedal work, but this foot cannot move laterally to the left very much, or vertically up and down too much. To play the pedals, you need both those movements, so I used to wear an old shoe of my mother's, her right shoe on this left foot, which gave me a spring to the left. I also attached an extra-inch wad of rubber to raise the heel higher, which meant that when my foot was down, the shoe was horizontal; when my foot was horizontal, the shoe stood at a 45-degree angle and gave me that vertical movement. And then to keep the toe up, I filed a little groove across the sole and tied a lace under the groove and around the back of my leg so the foot could be manually pulled up.'

My eyes swivelled to the foot. Perched against the table leg in the London hotel room, it was still no larger than a lady's. Inside the stout suede hush puppy, the flesh bunched up to form a nubbly lump. It moved stiffly back into a fold of trouser rather as a tortoise foot might withdraw into its shell, and I looked up to see Mr Moore beginning to laugh. He has a sort of Brer Rabbit face—black eyes, tomcat ears and battered all over. It was now scribbling up with laughter as

167

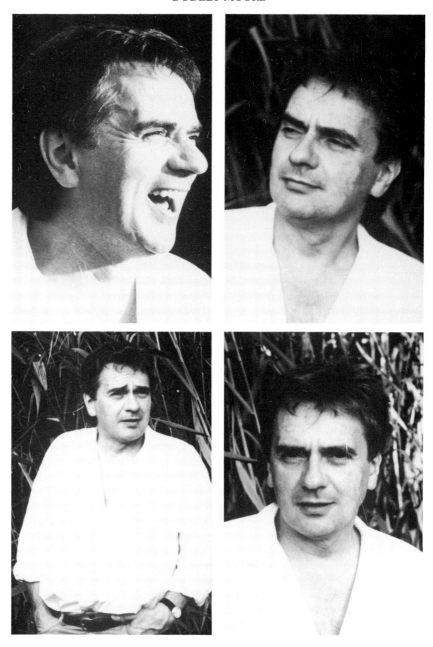

'Do I look like an Oxford graduate to you!'

Dudley Moore, Long Island

he continued the joke. I remember how when Brer Rabbit had been thrown into the briar bush, he had bounced back laughing.

'When I went for my Organ Scholarship at Magdalen College, I had to put on this ridiculous contraption, which really amused the examiners. Perhaps they let me in out of curiosity!

'When I eventually left Oxford, I forgot it in a cupboard in the organ loft. A couple of years ago, Bernard Rose, a tutor of Magdalen, was joking to me about how baffled he'd been to find a strange-looking monster's shoe in this cupboard! I wish he'd known and sent it to me, because it very much facilitated everything, and we had had such struggles to perfect the mechanism.'

'Did you need the shoe to walk?'

'No—just for the organ. It would have been no use for walking, unless of course the streets had been covered with organ pedals, in which case I could have worn it to negotiate my way along to the local Chinese takeaway!' He looked down at the foot. 'Luckily, when you're up in the organ loft, you're not exposed too much. I don't know whether I would have worn that shoe if I'd been playing the piano in a concert hall.'

He had cartooned the picture himself: thirteen years old, dwarfish, club-footed—a Quasimodo of the local Dagenham church. It was hidden up here, out of reach of the school bullies, that he began to explore the nature of music.

'There is something beautifully satisfying about accompanying a choir—it can be so fluid, especially in the presentation of psalms, where the idea is to move with the speech rhythms as much as possible. The organ becomes a delicate sort of breathing accompaniment to the choir.

'And all music which is successful somehow breathes—it breathes emotion to you, even though it cannot have an emotional content itself.'

'Why not?' The dark crinkles about the corners of his black and tan eyes deepened with concentration.

'I remember having a mild argument with Anthony Hopkins during some music programme on television: he was saying that music has no emotion, and I was scoffing heartily. On reflection, I now think he was right. It doesn't really, you see, because although it may have had a particular emotion when it was composed, a piece of music will induce different feelings in different people, and what might seem sad to me might seem joyful to you.

'It's like the tree in the quad.' The crinkles creased into smiles at this simile. 'It needs to be actually heard to inspire emotion. There's certain music which makes me feel extraordinarily happy, or sad, or nostalgic or hopeful—all sorts of feelings so I can't pick anything up or put anything down.'

'What sort of emotion does your music inspire?' I watched his eyes as he thought over his music. They opened towards me wide and violet as sea anemones.

'In the music I write, I try to reflect a sort of nostalgia for a peace which I am always looking for and yearning for. What do I yearn for? Well, the feeling of peace of, if you like, an unconditional love which is so hard to come by, which we all really have a right to as children, but then rarely, often never get. It is a yearning for that sort of gentleness and tenderness which my music tries to express.'

He broke off on the discovery that there was no Coca Cola in the fridge and nothing to eat. He called Room Service with a wink: 'Excuse me, do you, personally, have any ... NUTS?!' An ear-splitting grin and a crackle of laughter as he listened to the puzzled Italian at the other end making puzzled noises: 'We'll have 'em all—salted, dry roasted, cashew nuts, pistachio, almonds, and don't forget the Coke!' They duly came, and scrunching our way through greedy handfulls, we moved to the nature of his clowning.

'I remember playing Enobarbus when a friend of mine, Richard Selig, sat in the front row and laughed [munch] all the way through my performance—whenever I came on stage [munch]! I could not believe he was actually doing this, laughing [munch] loudly [gulp of Coke] at me in my death scene [gulp, munch]! He died of cancer two years later, so I guess he got punished for it [burp]!'

Again the crackle of laughter, but this time the eyes above remained bullet black. I wondered who the laughing Richard Selig had been. Without pause, Mr Moore lifted up the clown's mask as though it was a crab's shell and showed me some of the raw-pink nerve ends.

'I turned to clowning to survive at school. Although I wanted to read and work hard, it was an unpopular thing to do. I realised that if I looked as uninterested in work as the rest of them, and concentrated on amusing my class instead of trying to please the teachers, they might not bully me so badly.

'It was a way of surviving when I knew that, if I attacked, they would beat me up. I would feel like a hornet sometimes, but have to disguise it with humour and just hope it would make someone laugh.

'Most comedians are very enraged people. They become comics because they have never had the nerve to show how they feel. It is important to learn how to exhibit anger in a straightforward, in an honest way. Clowning ultimately just becomes aggravating.'

'Do you feel that those scars have healed?'

'There are always things one should still be chary of, but this is an area of myself and my past which I've tried to address. It is important not to side-step one's anger or hide it away, but most people do—they suppress it, until it eventually erupts and harms either them or someone close to them.'

He remembered Oxford as a period of argument between himself and his Siamese twinned comic half—the ventriloquous puppet who played for all the laughs.

'There was a time at Oxford when I refused to be funny. I resented having to hide myself behind a funny mask—I felt such an idiot, so *ingratiating* all the time, that I tried to fly to the other pole, which is just as useless really, and I walked around being sullen.

'I guess it was just a desperation to be taken seriously. I also think it was having to go through all those adjustments which I had to make coming from Dagenham High School, which had not prepared me for the Oxford social life at all. Everybody else seemed so comfortable and at ease, but for me it was like being plunged into an exotic battlefield.'

This second ironic use of 'exotic' had little of the humour of the first.

'All their experience of public school was totally remote for me. I felt very ill at ease and out of my depth, and also frightened, sometimes very frightened, by the place. I guess Oxford was just a time of my life that was unhappy. With hindsight, it represents a part of my early dark tunnel days. Those early years of growing up were horrendous.'

By the time this story had ground to its halt, we were both staring owlishly into the space between us.

I asked where the loo was. It turned out to be a splendid affair with brass pipes and a wooden seat, but with one strange quirk: after a while of propping the seat up, only for it to guillotine down a few seconds later, my double-taking was interrupted.

'You have to hold the seat up with your other hand!'

Raucous as a crow, the voice had come straight from the film character Arthur. Back in the room, Dudley Moore had refilled the glasses and had balanced his on the arm of his chair. To prevent the glass from slipping, he was keeping one hand on the stem and having to sit up straight to reach it. Pinned to the chair in this fashion, he had only to wobble his head slightly, to look like a Thunderbirds' puppet at the joystick of some galactic starship. I returned to my question about *Arthur*:

'For my money that film worked because it was about a man who was unconventional in that he wanted to have a good time—he really wanted to communicate with people, he wanted to be close to them.'

'What about the morality of letting Arthur get away with both the girl and the money?'

'Well, I'm very bad on morality—morals are man-invented and

need investigating at every turn, but what did strike me about the film was how honest it was. It proposed this fairly unpleasant but honest notion that he was going to turn down the girl whom he loved because he couldn't turn down $700 million. He wasn't a perfect person and there was something morally dangerous but actually highly courageous about him saying, "I want the money." I mean—would you turn it down?' More raucous laughter. 'It had nothing to do with morality, he was just being outrageously honest. But then of course he can't stand the thought of it, and decides he's going to have the girl. I love that part—it has great life. And then he wheedles himself back into the money!!'

Mr Moore disagreed with my stiffened-upper-lip suggestion that such happy-go-lucky endings were the necessary evil of Hollywood.

'No, no, no—it's so easy to reflect life, it's so easy to write something which goes the same dismal damn way that everything else goes. Okay, so you read a Chekhov short story and see a reflection of the difficulty of life and of living, but Christ!—we know all about that, we're bloody well down here living it! And I'm not sure that it necessarily gives one the feeling of sadness or knowledge about how difficult life is.

'I admire people who manage to put a rocket-like finish to their films—it's more difficult to make people happy. I don't care if my films try to end optimistically, I don't care whether people find them conventional, or over optimistic or "Pollyanna-ish", I don't care—so long as they are funny.'

He shrugged his shoulders and seemed to shrink a size or two.

'I just feel that a lot of anything I do is going to get dumped on—the critics want to tear me apart, which is fine—I've got sort of used to it. I'm used to Alexander Walker not liking anything I do, I'm used to film critics despising me. It's hard to take it, it's hard to accept it and it's very upsetting, but I've finally learnt that when someone appears on television and says, "We are now going to review the new Dudley Moore film," I turn off. I don't want to hear what they say, I tell my friends just to let me know the good bits and not to come and say, "Wasn't it awful what he said?" It's too hard, because, God knows, people can lose their hearts very easily in the motion picture industry.'

'How do you keep your heart?'

'I just trust myself—I don't trust God or believe in any gods, so I have to believe in myself. I did wrestle with all that until maybe six years ago when I finally felt that I wouldn't find a solution and it wasn't helping me, so I decided to look into myself for answers.'

'What were you looking for when you were looking for a god?'

'I suppose for a meaning to my life. When we're looking for meanings to our lives, it is usually because we're not enjoying them. If you're enjoying life, then all the answers are there, but if you're suppressing a lot of things, then life can become rather grey because you're not really being yourself. To my mind, this can happen because you're putting responsibility out there somewhere rather than accepting it yourself.

'It is not a comforting thing to know that I have to look to myself for the answers, because it means that it's up to me whether I enjoy life or not.'

'So is it frightening not having any god?' The intervening moments passed as though my hand was on his wrist and waiting to feel the first pulse.

'No, I just know for myself that when I die, then I don't exist. It makes me feel very alive to know that it will be like that, although it doesn't make life any easier.

'It is hard to admit one's mortality—death is not exactly a subject which I'm good at facing, but what I do admit is that in life I should give myself a chance to live. I should not run myself down in comparison with other people—I should allow myself the knowledge that I am who I am. Once you lose the notion of comparison, then you can get on with your life and work and expression of yourself. To be aware of where one is and who one is is painful, but it's not as painful as that neurotic pain of being always submerged in a mist of not understanding why.

'So, curiously, there are no props anymore. The prop to one's life becomes one's own feeling of self—that becomes the nourishing element. Knowing who you are, and that to express yourself honestly and courageously in your life is the only, the only real way, to feel alive. In fact, what I have really been working towards all my life is reaching out to other people in a more and more honest and vulnerable way.'

The last moments of the interview seemed to fall into the sort of time-warp which might happen at two o'clock in the morning when, too tired to recognise conventional barriers of pretence, words cut to the marrow:

'What you want—that is the most important thing. Of course, it's very unfashionable to look for what you want—after all, it's selfish, so we are told. But actually it isn't, because saying what you want is the only real path towards the real validation of other people, if you'll pardon that Californian expression. Because if you really want something, if you really desire another person for instance, that is the best thing in the world that you could give them: to really want them, rather than just wanting to do something for them, is actually much more giving. I'm not talking about rape, I'm talking about taking something from another person in the sense of wanting their love. It should be a very flattering thing for them to know that they are actually, authentically, a *wanted* person.'

'But they may be happy enough without you—'

'You want me to *kiss* her!'

Dudley Moore with Tracey, Long Island

'Then they will just say no.'

'Doesn't that hurt you?'

'Well, that's life, isn't it? Life is full of abrasions of that nature. You know—you might desire this, but you're told no, you can't have me, and so you move on. Unless you make it the project of your life to wrestle with that for four or five years—' He broke off and I wondered whether the beamish boy of Hollywood would allow himself a happy-go-lucky ending—he didn't: 'Until you realise that it's not what you want, or you still can't have it, or it can't give you the emotional nurturing that you need.'

The telephone rang and broke the spell. It was suddenly time to go. As we said goodbye, he looked up with concern. 'Was any of that of any use? We've come a long way from Oxford.'

Peter Jay

CHRIST CHURCH, 1957–60

'My own overwhelming memory of Oxford life was that there was an absolutely clear demarcation point which came two thirds of the way through my second Michaelmas term; indeed it was on 28th November 1958.'

This was Peter Jay, sometime Economics Editor of *The Times*, sometime Ambassador to Washington, sometime Chairman of TV-AM.

'Before that date, my conception of life was that scholastic academic work was what one was basically there for, that it should occupy twelve hours a day, and that you only broke, interrupted or suspended it in order to take exercise.

'This was roughly how I lived, and is the origin of the perfectly true story about how I discovered a recording of the Brandenburg Concertos which played for exactly thirty minutes a side and, on one of those old-fashioned gramophones which could play a stack of records, I would tie back the arm to make it play the same side over and over and over again, in fact twelve times to make six hours, and then I would stop for sport and do it all over again.'

It seemed about time I got a word in edgeways. 'So this was how you worked?'

'That was basically how I worked. I had been to a school which had put tremendous emphasis on collectivism rather than privacy in that there were no studies or individual bedrooms, so everything you did was in a mob. I found then, and have found ever since, that that was what I liked. I detest being on my own: I detest privacy, I detest silence. I detest all those things one was supposed to like.'

'I met a girl. . . .'

Peter Jay on 28th November, 1958

He remembered his punch-line.

'Beyond 28th November 1958, everything was totally different.'

'Don't tell me—the record player broke.'

'No. I met a girl. . . .'

'Well?'

'. . . Whom I liked. This was something which had never happened before. Having come from a monastic boarding school and a monastic prep school and the Navy, I had never encountered women before and I found the discovery very exciting and preoccupying, and my impression is that ninety-five percent of my energy and time thereafter was taken up with that pursuit.'

Mr Jay apparently did not think much of my questions, so he asked the next one himself.

'So if somebody asks how, in five percent of your time and energy, can you be President of the Oxford Union and do Finals at the same time? The answer is: "I don't know, except that I did!" I suppose I didn't sleep very much!'

Mr Jay took First Class Honours in Politics, Philosophy and Economics. 'What did you think of the course?'

'As far as I was concerned, PPE was a course of philosophy. During the two long vacations you get at Oxford, I read one book—working eight hours a day.'

I didn't suppose it had been an Agatha Christie . . .

'The book was Immanuel Kant's *Critique of Pure Reason*. If you read five pages an hour you are doing well. It takes two long vacations to read it properly and understand it.'

'Why did you specialise so much in philosophy? Your later life seems to have drawn more on politics and economics.'

'It was about the things that I wanted to think and learn about. I concentrated on philosophy for the same reason that other people go skiing or learn Greek—it fascinated me. Philosophy is something which interrelates with every other subject there is in the sense that philosophy is about conceptual analysis, and the analysis and manipulation of concepts is a precondition of and a part of a study of almost anything.

'As far as politics was concerned, I felt very guilty. There was no politics in my first year unless you count de Tocqueville as politics (which I counted as French and French is something I have neither then nor since been able to handle at all), so all the politics came post-28th November and was totally neglected.

'I remember reading my Politics Papers in Finals with a growing sense of despair. There were twenty-six questions in the paper, and I had got to and read question twenty-five without discovering a single question which I could begin to answer. Question twenty-six in June of 1960 said: "Explain the dominance of the Conservative Party since 1951." Since I had lived in a political family, and my father's entire political life had been taken up with the dominance of the Conservative Party since 1951, and he had told me a lot about it, I seized on this question and wrote non-stop for two hours fifty-five minutes (the first five minutes having been taken up with reading the questions), and, on the strength of that single anecdote, I was given a First. Nowadays, I daresay that wouldn't be acceptable.'

Mr Jay has the gift of the gab. In fact, so gifted is he that he generally seems able to be speaking three or four different gabs at once, all intact with their own parentheses and occasional red herrings. A rhetorical habit of his which further confuses these gabs is his love of three or four words when one will do.

I went back to something he had said. 'You mentioned the French, and, although this is something of a tangent, what do you think about their role in world politics?' Mr Jay had first looked pleased at my mention of the word 'tangent', but when he heard the question he gave me the full frontal smile of someone who has just read question twenty-six.

'I am a strong believer that the community which is primarily and really important in the conduct of Britain's relationship with the rest of the world is not the Common Market but America. America is basically the forum within which (a) we will or won't successfully conduct our East/West relations with the Soviet Union, (b) we will or won't successfully conduct our North/South relations with the Third World, and (c) it is the community within which we either will or won't succeed in making the world economy and its monetary system work.'

Having managed to get in the ABC of international politics, he moved down to France.

'My essential view of the French role in international affairs is that it is frivolous. It is systematically and necessarily frivolous because it draws its inspiration and motivation, whether in monetary affairs or defence affairs, from a desire to oppose or to appear to oppose whatever the Americans are currently proposing—even if it is the same thing the French themselves had previously been proposing!

'Not only does it derive from that, which is in itself a frivolous motive, but it does so in a context in which they are only able to and only wish to take this attitude because they know there is no risk of this attitude actually prevailing. As I once said, which I think sums it up very nicely, "The French win all the press conferences and lose all the negotiations." It is their confident knowledge that they will lose all the negotiations which enables them to win all the press conferences by adopting frivolous postures just to make their role appear more important than it inherently is.

'Fundamentally, France is incurably a Western country. It has no affinity whatever with the Soviet Union and it has as much interest as everybody else in being protected from that threat. France has the same kind of mixed capitalist economy as the rest of the Western world, and the logic of its geography and its political commitments are basically the same as the rest of the West. This makes it regrettable, and a matter for legitimate criticism, that successive French governments have not reflected these basic facts in their politics, but have rather reflected the free-rider phenomenon of taking it for granted that these interests will be looked after by the Alliance whilst indulging in the luxury of pretending to oppose them.'

It had been a pretty good PPE answer. I moved him to the next question. 'Has your optimism in America's role in world politics been dimmed by President Reagan?' The sometime Ambassador to Washington sharpened his pencil.

'No, my optimism has not been jolted in the sense that some fundamental change has taken place in the nature of America or its role in the world—still less of its attractiveness as a place to be and to work.

'Obviously there are many policies which President Reagan seeks to implement which I find to be out of tune with the needs of the times. This flows logically and inevitably from the fact that I believe in terms of'—I braced myself for the buzz-words—'fundamental strategic vision, purposes and policies. President Carter did understand those things.' I thought Carter must indeed have been a remarkable man to get to grips with that lot. 'He did have a very long-sighted approach and he was trying to shift, which was a massive task, the basis of American domestic and foreign policy onto new ground which is, was and would have continued to be relevant to the last part of this century and the early part of the next.

'I naturally regret what to me is an atavistic knee-jerk regression into the standard and sloganised policies of that rather superficial nature of the nineteenth century which the Reagan Administration consistently represents.'

'What was it you admired about President Carter so much?'

'On the occasions when I talked with Jimmy Carter at the War Office or sat around the Cabinet table discussing policy issues I found the impressive thing was his vision, and his understanding for the need for the United States to shift away from the old sterile basis of American foreign policy. This basis had been, in my opinion, definitively analysed and condemned by Henry Kissinger in the 1968 publication *Agenda for the Nation*. Kissinger analysed that if you defined the central problem of American foreign policy simply as the containment of Communism, and if you reacted by supporting every government that said it was threatened by Communism, you would be drawn into increasingly untenable positions. Also, neither within the United States nor outside would you be building a policy which would win the hearts and minds of other people. They would see this as negative and knee-jerk and, in some cases, not just negative and knee-jerk, but shocking and offensive in its methods and in the people it was supporting.

'The need to shift America's foreign policy onto some more positive and enlightened basis which would win spontaneous support in many parts of the world was recognised by Carter and that is what he attempted to do. Kissinger had tried to do it, but, as he himself recognised, he failed because in his first term of office he was preoccupied with ending the Vietnam War and sorting out a détente with Russia and China, and in his second term, Watergate blew everything off course. But Carter *was* seeking to do this.'

'So why did Carter fail?'

'What Carter lacked, which is a fatal flaw in a politician, is communication. He didn't appear to the world at large to be the person I have just described. He didn't appear to be decisive or long-sighted. That was partly because he was a weak communicator, and this was because he was too fastidious. He would constantly strike out pieces of his speech which anybody else had written in any remotely colourful or vivid expression on the grounds that "That's not me—I don't talk that sort of language. That's not engineering in my aseptic and clinical and precise way".

'Also because he was the victim. He was attacked by the Press and the public because he was an outsider, because he was anti-Washington and a Southerner and a Baptist. He became the victim of a degree of malice and misrepresentation and hostility from American media, from long-term Congressmen, from civil servants and from the Diplomatic Corps which made it very hard to be a democratic leader.'

'This is not just hindsight?' I interrupted. 'You saw all this happening?' Mr Jay smiled through me.

'Yes, I wrote it all in despatches.'

'What do you think of the way the Reagan/Thatcher governments are now handling these global issues?'

'Obviously I believe in the global necessity for what I think of as the more enlightened approach—not merely in a soft-headed sentimental sense, but in a practical, long-sighted strategic sense, of combining arms control with appropriate amounts of military strength; of refashioning in a more enlightened and effective way our relationships with the Third World; and of giving a proper emphasis to human rights. I think these policies bore considerable fruit under Carter. They would have borne more fruit if they had not been aborted.

'Rhodesia was an example of this. It was finished off by Peter Carrington, but it was Jimmy Carter who, on 23rd July 1977, actually mapped out the policies. I was actually sitting there around the Cabinet table as he did it—totally spontaneously, he mapped out the basic political strategy which in the end cracked Rhodesia. And credit to Henry Kissinger, who made the initial breakthrough by getting Ian Smith to concede that White Rule would not last.

'So naturally I regret that that sort of global and enlightened vision, which I believe gives the West a better chance of security and survival, and prosperity with the rest of the world than these current policies, has been displaced.'

'In what ways were you qualified to be the Ambassador to Washington? I remember there was some furore about "a job for Callaghan's son-in-law"?'

'Well, the first thing was that I wanted to be quite sure that this was David Owen's idea. It was only when his wife told me how he suddenly sat up in bed one night and said, "I've got it!" that I was satisfied.

'I discovered in retrospect that it was far more like my previous life than I had imagined. I had been a civil servant for the first six years of my working life, so the processes of government and administration were familiar to me. My background in public speaking as President of the Oxford Union was invaluable, and my journalism was important— more important than either of those two. The most important function of any ambassador is reporting what is going on accurately to your own Government. Then, of course, it was vitally important that you were seen to have a direct relationship with your own Head of Government.'

I brought back the Oxford context. 'How had being President of the Oxford Union helped?'

'It was a tremendous asset. In a sense, the greatest problem is the time factor. I suppose during my two years, I must have made about two thousand speeches—if I had had to take time to prepare those speeches, or indeed think about them, I couldn't possibly have done them. It was the fact that it was in my blood and bones—it was like answering the Politics paper!

'There was a lovely occasion when I remember I was told to "make a set of remarks" at some meeting. As we were driving to the hall, I rehearsed in my mind that I would cover the same sort of themes as I had spoken about at my lunchtime appointment. We got to the hall where I was shown up onto the stage where I saw an audience of about three thousand and, as I listened to the man introducing me, I heard him say that I would deliver this year's somebody or other's Memorial Lecture. A Memorial Lecture should last fifty-nine and a half minutes and be about a serious subject! When I got up to speak, I noticed that all the important people who had been at my lunchtime speech were sitting along the front row!

'Then being President of the Union began to help—during the course of my usual light introductory remarks, I thought of a new subject altogether and then did manage to lecture on it for fifty-nine and a half minutes—the first thirty seconds having been taken up with the introductory remarks.'

'Weren't you furious with whoever hadn't told you what it was? If someone set me up in front of three thousand people without a script, I'd go bananas!'

'Well, I'm not the sort of person who gets very annoyed. It's one of my weaknesses—if I did, I think I would be less ill-served.'

Mr Jay was about to say something else, but changed his mind. 'No—by the time I had done the speech, I was so pleased with myself just for having done it that I wasn't cross with anyone!'

'Having worked on *The Times*, having been Ambassador, having worked with breakfast television, what would you say your career has been?'

'I have never envisaged anything as concrete as a "career". One's career is just the sum of all the things you have done and there is no theme, apart from in a very broad sense I suppose, going back to Oxford days, the fascination I have for how a society governs itself. Not just the formal process of government, but the whole process of how it communicates with itself, how it develops certain ideas and principles and preconceptions and prejudices and sets the opinion parameters within which Governments actually try to make and implement policies. I have always been fascinated by that.'

Mr Jay gave a small half-embarrassed laugh.

'I am not sure how far I have articulated it and made it explicit in precisely that way before.'

'Why, when you have moved so closely in the fringes of politics, have you never become a politician?' Mr Jay's answer was surprisingly fierce.

'Because in this country we treat politicians in an absolutely disgraceful way. Public opinion holds them in low esteem—regards them as self-seeking, power-crazed, corrupt and promise-breaking. It is more or less required by the law of the land that if anybody puts forward their ideas on television, somebody else has got to stand up immediately to say that exactly the reverse is true.

'Whilst I understand why all these things have to happen, and whilst it is healthy in a genuine democracy that the public shouldn't hero-worship politicians to an exaggerated extent and should be capable of scepticism and rejection of their leaders, I personally think, as a compulsive and cynical reaction, that the whole process is unjust and revolting. I would not be prepared to play the game under those rules. If the public wants politicians and then treats them like that, they can't have me.'

'But you have been looked to as a possible leader—indeed, *Time* magazine named you as one of the potential world leaders of the next century, which interested me as you are not a politician.'

'Yes, but it would not occur to any American, asked that question, to look exclusively at elected politicians. The leaders of America do not come from the ranks of their politicians. Indeed, one of the attractions of the American political system is that the Presidents and most people in their administration normally come from a background of some kind of expertise in business or management or perhaps economics or commercial banking.'

'Or peanut farming or movies!' I added.

'You see, I don't think that "being a politician" should be a profession in itself. I think that the way the Government here junkets portfolios around between ministers whose only expertise is in getting elected is not the best way of getting policies well thought out. It also has the effect of throwing the thinking about policies back onto either the traditional clapped-out ideological party reflexes, or onto the permanent civil servants. Permanent civil servants have a lot to be praised for, but their experience is constrained within Whitehall in a rather artificial way so they will provide little more than traditional responses to problems which are increasingly less traditional in their nature.'

'What sort of education would be more appropriate for government? Oxford?'

'Nothing would be worse, in my opinion, than for Oxford to be self-consciously preparing people for government.

'On the other hand, it seems to me to be perfectly legitimate to ask the question: "As a matter of fact, did the teaching you had at Oxford, or Cambridge or Brixton Jail or wherever actually contribute to your qualification for government?" Now, it would be very hard to give an affirmative answer to that question. Government is not something for which you can be prepared. I think what is needed is knowledge of and intelligence about some subject—maybe a very broad subject, but at least something which you could draw on when you are in government.

'There is another broader point, perhaps particularly a PPE point, which is that I think the whole of British education, particularly Oxbridge education, puts an overwhelming emphasis on analysis. You are taught how to make distinctions, how to take concepts and arguments and hypotheses and reduce them to their essential elements. And when you have done that with great precision and elegance, you have achieved an academic goal and, if you show sufficient skill in the eyes of the examiner, you may achieve an academic honour. Now, there is nothing like that in the rest of your life (except becoming an examiner). Everything else you do, if it is about any practical question, has the purpose of saying at the end "...and therefore we should be doing this".

'I remember this striking me very forcibly in a rather concrete moment. On my first day in the Treasury, I was handed a file and told: "Here is a problem—send me a minute on it with a recommendation for a course of action." I remember doing the analytical part with some facility and confidence, but then I came to the "...and so what?" part—there was no procedure! The reasons for that are very clear, which is that there are no Aristotelian, watertight, logical moves by which this can be done, so it cannot be taught. The analytical moves can be guaranteed by Aristotelian, categorical, watertight, rigid logic, but the synthetic moves cannot. That is precisely why they are referred to as "synthetic".

'It seems to me that the trouble is that the whole of one's life subsequent to University is engaged in precisely this. It does not exclude analysis, but in the end we face the question—what do you think? Do we buy or sell? Not merely are you not equipped with any tools to work this out, but Oxbridge more or less brings you up to believe that there is something disreputable about doing it at all. The sort of person who gets a First Class degree wouldn't do it.'

I was getting slightly muddled by all this, so I went back to the question: 'So what is your answer?'

'I am now doing precisely what I was complaining about! Having analysed properly, I am not at all sure how I would change the design of the educational institutions.'

Thinking of his somewhat Laputan involvement with TV-AM, I asked whether he preferred analysis or decision-making?

'I like making decisions. I am somebody who very much thinks of themselves as a doer, an actor rather than a commentator.'

'So what went wrong with TV-AM?' The man who had introduced the idea of breakfast television to this country, who had raised a second mortgage on his house to pay for a share of the first breakfast-time television company, fell silent. After a few months as Chairman of TV-AM, Mr Jay had been sacked, and had watched his idea turn

'If the public wants politicians and then treats them like that, they can't have me.'

Peter Jay

into a success without him.

'I have kept silent about TV-AM because, either at Oxford or at Winchester, I was taught that it is unethical to comment about these sort of things after you have handed on that kind of role to your successors—whatever the circumstances. While this is clearly an ethic which is not universally acknowledged or practised, it is mine. I would only say that it is absolutely clear to me that the basic aims and objectives which TV-AM had for breakfast-time television were soundly based, were eminently achievable and indeed have been achieved.

'I have no doubt whatsoever that the experiences of both BBC and TV-AM have proved that the beliefs upon which the thing was founded were strategically correct and fulfillable. Unfortunately, at the beginning, TV-AM had tactical problems which were specific to it and not fundamental flaws in the idea.'

He lamely concluded, 'I have no doubt that the idea has come to stay.'

When I met Mr Jay, he was busying himself with freelance journalism. It seemed that this was just a stop-gap before he moved his career into another dimension. Having achieved notable success as a young man in three different fields, I reflected that the potential was still all there for Mr Jay to go a long way—either way.

Richard Ingrams

UNIVERSITY, 1958–61

Soho by daylight is a knotting of streets where video-nasty shops, peep-shows, arcades and Chinese restaurants stand deserted amidst last night's garbage. The red and gold trappings of Greek Street shone bleary and dulled in Monday-morning grey, and the Coach and Horses, where we met for lunch, hung heavy with yellowed smoke. After steak and kidney pie with boiled potatoes, Mr Ingrams crossed the road to Number 34 and led the way up and around steep staircases to the *Private Eye* offices. Piled high with newspapers, *Who's Whos* and all sorts of press-cuttings sent by all sorts of people, the offices looked more like a lopsided Dickensian filmset than the premises of an influential magazine. We squeezed past a coffee machine and the photocopier to get into Mr Ingrams' office—the same mess. Here though, was a difference. Amongst all the paper, a few well defined trophies stood out: a lifesize cut-out of Sir James Goldsmith marched across one corner, a photograph of Jeremy Thorpe smiled from a silver frame near the telephone and a picture of Sir Anthony Blunt hung on a wall. Surrounded by this human menagerie, Mr Ingrams recounted his version of 'Oxford and beyond'.

'One had had the idea of Oxford being a very glamorous place. Full of eccentrics and aesthetes and witty people. But when I got there, there were just a lot of men in duffle coats. I remember a slight feeling of disappointment to find all those duffle-coated men wandering up and down the High Street in the place of the strange homosexuals and men in flamboyant clothes I had expected.

'One of the jokes *Parson's Pleasure* coined—the magazine I set up there—based on all this duffle coat business, was the phenomenon of

Richard Ingrams playing one of the caged kings in *Tamberlaine*, 1960

the "Grey Man". We would describe all the other people at Oxford as "Grey Men", for which we got some stick from people who said we were snobbish. In one issue we had a photographic feature of Wells dressed up playing the part of a "Grey Man", who was someone who went to Oxford and spent his entire day in the library. Wells occupied a window in The Broad and sat there all day writing out his essay and picking his nose.'

John Wells had written to me describing that campaign: 'Ingrams had decided that the Grey Men were taking over, so we all obediently abused them. They usually appeared in drawings by Rushton, clumping along in baggy flannels and a duffle coat. Occasionally I impersonated him in photographs with my trousers tucked in socks beside a bicycle outside the library, creating havoc by mismanaging a punt on the river and even sitting in a shop window, hamster-like at his weekly essay, blind to the merry pageant of life.

'Ingrams was also worried by Beatniks, and once wrote a memorable description of a kitchen sink/Beatniks hero's morning routine in *Parson's Pleasure*, during which he shaved with the jagged edge of a half-opened can of baked beans.'

Mr Ingrams went on: '*Parson's Pleasure* had been started by Adrian Berry. It was exclusively about people in Christ Church, so it was full of gossip items about these men who nobody else in Oxford knew. In a sense, it prefigured *Private Eye*, because it brought home to me that you don't have to know who the people are to enjoy reading about them. We filled it with gossip about unknown names, and *Private Eye* has worked on the same idea. In fact, people like reading about people they don't know anything about. The only joke of Berry's I remember was his advertisement in *Parson's Pleasure* saying that anyone found in Peckwater Quad without cavalry twill trousers would be fined. It ended up saying, "Harry Finers for Harry Non-Twillers", which was the sort of ridiculous jargon used by Christ Church people.

'I was very lucky to be at University College with Paul Foot, and we did a lot of things together as well as *Parson's Pleasure*. There seemed to be a perpetual party in his rooms where we wrote sketches, and we went to auditions together.'

He rested his chin heavily in both hands and looked woebegone. 'I had expected to find Oxford full of very funny, witty people who would all be wanting to do the kind of things that I wanted to do, but there were only five of us. It was strange to realise that I was one of them. And I had exactly the same feeling when I went into the outside world. I thought there would be masses of people trying to do what I wanted to do, but there weren't any at all. The difficulty to find a cartoonist, for example. In the whole of Oxford, there was nobody who could do cartoons, so we had to import Rushton to draw for us. I find that very interesting.'

He pondered for a moment, then pronounced, 'It boils down to the fact that there are very few people who can make jokes.'

He left Oxford with his band of merry men and his sense of humour intact. He still fosters the élitist nature of *Private Eye*. 'Although *Private Eye* has expanded a little, the original nucleus was a small group of people who had been at school together. It is very important to keep up this little gang, this little clique of people with all their in-jokes.

'This may be so if only because nobody else will publish what I want to write. Nobody at Oxford would, when I was writing purely humorous articles, rather in the style of Paul Jennings, who used to write a slightly whimsical column in the *Observer*. I could never get anything into *Punch* either. I wouldn't think of sending things to *Punch* now, because Rushton used to send them drawings which they rejected. *Punch* has gone rapidly downhill for a long, long time. In a way, *Private Eye* was started as an alternative.'

I wondered if he saw himself primarily as a humorist or as an investigative journalist.

'A bit of both. I would just put "journalist" on my passport. I'm not quite sure what a humorist is. I do have a number of heroes, but I shouldn't think I have much in common with them—people like Beachcomber, who invented the certain style of *Private Eye*, which is one of parody-journalism. Peter Simple is the same kind of thing—both these styles involve inventing a cast of comic characters who crop up with joke names like "Glenda Slagg" or "Lunchtime O'Booze". All that is common to the style of Beachcomber or Simple; the stuff we actually write isn't so much.'

The day-to-day stuff of *Private Eye* sits happily on the fence between satire and slander, and blithely swings its boots in both directions. Whilst Mr Ingrams enjoys the cavalier nature of that humour, it is the identification and stalking of individual prey which really captures his imagination.

'If satire is to be good, it should be informative and helpful. I always think that, if pressed about my own activities, I could compare them with putting weed-killer out in the garden.'

He glanced fondly at the noticeboard, where the caption of a *Radio Times* front cover announced: 'The Thorpes: A Family At Peace.' 'This is a helpful activity as long as you put it on the right plants. It involves quite a lot of care and attention not to put it on the wrong ones—what I mean by this is that I don't go around blasting away indiscriminately. Unfortunately this activity has become more and more of a responsibility of late. The trouble with *Private Eye* is that it has been very successful, it now has an enormous circulation and is known to make money. It thus makes one's position more difficult.' He reminisced: 'In the good old days, *Private Eye* was smaller. So long as we were known to be a worthless, penniless newspaper with no assets of any kind, people could say, "Oh well, people take no notice of that kind of thing." So we could get away with a great deal more. Now the position has grown more complicated.' He ruefully shook his head and looked persecuted. 'Now *Private Eye* is reduced to doing all sorts of things like checking stories.'

He saw my eyebrows rise.

'I've never known what "checking stories" actually means. It was under great discussion in a libel case last week. What it seems to involve doing is ringing up the person you're attacking and saying, "We're going to attack you, what's your comment?" Well, most people I've rung up slam down the phone or tell me a pack of lies. I was criticised for not talking to Esther Rantzen, but the very few times I've talked to that woman, I've just had to listen to a lot of absolute rubbish. It's not worth listening to. So when people said, "Why didn't you ring her up and ask her what her view was?" I answered that I regarded it as pointless. That is not to say, though, that quite a lot of material in *Private Eye* could not have quite a lot more work devoted to it—I would agree about that.'

When I suggested that the number of court cases must indicate that *Private Eye* should feel obliged to verify its material, Mr Ingrams was unrepentant.

'I try very hard to keep out of court. To get into court is to be involved in a terrible nightmare, which in my view bears no relation to the real world. I think the libel laws are very much weighted against the defendant. I am often involved in making apologies for things I know to be true, because that is the easy way out, and we cannot afford to fight a libel action. We have just fought and lost a libel action of £90,000. When that sort of money is involved, you obviously think twice about it.

'In its history, *Private Eye* has only been in court about half a dozen times, which proves that we have been very, very choosy about going to court. Pretty well always, we settle libel actions out of court—mind you, a lot of libel actions are also settled by the other side who have issued the writs, but then decide to drop them. I have absolutely no faith in the legal system as far as libel is concerned. *Private Eye* has never won a libel action, and as I have obviously been convinced of my own rightness in the matter in all the cases which I have taken to court, I have a very low opinion of the courts.'

His flinty eyes met those of Sir James Goldsmith in the corner. 'I don't regard going to court and winning as a necessary vindication.'

The attempts of both Jeremy Thorpe and Sir Anthony Blunt to use the law as camouflage provoked *Private Eye*'s sustained interest in their affairs. Mr Ingrams feels particularly gratified that they were both hoist by their own legal petard.

'*Private Eye* was given a lot of stick from the rest of the Press over the Thorpe case. Most of the Press supported him when he first came under fire and criticised us very strongly for intruding into his private life, which I never really thought was the issue—whether Thorpe was a homosexual or not was not really the story; the story was attempted murder. It was a crime which had nothing to do with'—he lingered for a savoury moment—'Thorpe's private practices.

'One of the ironies of the case was that his lawyers only embarked on this attempted murder story to protect him from the Press. In fact, I don't think the Press was ever a real threat to Thorpe—everyone in Fleet Street knew all about the Scott story long ago but they didn't see the point of dragging it up. Thorpe, however, was convinced that he was being hounded by the Press, and that any minute the *News of the World* would splash out his story. But everything only came out when this bizarre murder story was launched. The moral of that case is that *Private Eye* was not remorselessly probing into people's lives—that often, by resorting to law, people simply draw attention to themselves.

'This happened with Sir Anthony Blunt as well. When that book came out—which didn't even name his as "the fourth man"—Blunt got wind of it and got hold of a libel lawyer to write to the publishers saying, could they please send him a copy of the book? This begged the question: why should Sir Anthony Blunt want to read this book? What is his interest? Once he had made that move, he gave *Private Eye* a story to write about, because we could say, "Lawyers acting on behalf of Sir Anthony Blunt have contacted these publishers wanting to see the book: what is it all about?" Immediately he did that, he put his head above the parapet—by going to lawyers and trying to legally hush things up, he committed himself. All I was doing was looking for a story. There was no Blunt story until he made it possible. Everybody knew that the book was about Blunt—it was perfectly obvious—but what could you say? You couldn't come out and say, "Blunt is the man in this book who is described as Maurice (or whoever it was) because that would invite a writ and you had no proof. Nobody could prove it— the British Secret Service couldn't prove Blunt was a traitor—it was only on the basis of his confession.'

He qualified my criticism that he and the magazine often did probe into private lives unnecessarily. 'We don't want to know about people's private lives, unless there is an element of humbug involved. Although

'I always think that, if pressed about my own activities, I could compare them with putting weed-killer out in the garden.'

Richard Ingrams, 34 Greek Street

actually, as a general rule, if you are in public life (and this applies to me, too) I suppose your private life is constantly subject to investigation. I don't see anything wrong in writing about private lives—it's not unjustified, and it's certainly interesting.'

When I quoted the Albert Schweitzer edition, in which *Private Eye* had contrived to attack Schweitzer for no reason, Mr Ingrams leant back and couldn't suppress a broad grin. 'Oh, that story about Schweitzer! That was all to do with Claud Cockburn, who once came in as a temporary guest editor. His principle was that there is no one whom you cannot find a bad word for, and he came in and clapped his hands and said, "Right, who are we going to attack?" It was decided that Schweitzer looked too good to be true, so he was our man. I cannot remember what he wrote, but funnily enough, after the article, a lot of anti-Schweitzer material did come out—his leper colony was very inefficiently run, he refused to use any of the sponsored equipment, and so on. There was a case against him.

'What Claud meant is that there are always sacred cows around. Even today there are some sacred cows. Winston Churchill of course was absolutely the sacred cow. Mountbatten was a sacred cow— *Private Eye* gets a lot of stick for saying that Mountbatten was a homosexual, because he was the kind of person you shouldn't say that about now that he is dead. Lord Goodman is another one, although he is less of one than he used to be. At one point, Goodman was regarded as probably the greatest man in Britain—it's hard to believe! I used to collect quotations about Goodman. Michael Foot said that he was a "Dr Johnson in his command of English" which was absolute rubbish, and Bernard Levin said he was "a saintly man". All of which is completely wide of the mark! I knew Goodman as a libel lawyer and I regarded him as an enemy. The only people I really go after are people who sue and their lawyers.'

The last interchange was the most revealing. 'Do you see yourself as a moralist?' I asked.

'No. Well, I suppose I do condemn quite a lot, but I try not to be censorious.'

'Isn't Dr Johnson one of your heroes?'

'Very much so.'

'Didn't he say, "We are all perpetual moralists"?'

'I think Dr Johnson had a right to moralise. I wouldn't regard myself as anywhere near that.'

As the tape switched off, he looked cryptically at the machine and said, 'Will you doctor my words?'

He presumably knew what he meant.

David Dimbleby

CHRIST CHURCH, 1958–61

'My father hated it when I brought Oxford friends home. By two in the morning we would be discussing the nature of God, or Berkeley's Proof of Existence, by when we would all be shouting at once and showing off our latest piece of philosophy (probably picked up at 2 a.m. the previous day) as though we had known it all for years!'

Mr Dimbleby smiled dimples at the memory. 'We must have been insufferably arrogant! That old ontological proof of the existence of God: how did it go?

'"God is magnificent, mightiest, all-powerful, all-present, all-seeing."

'"Fine, does he then exist?"

'"I don't know."

'"Well, if he didn't exist, he would be that much less so than if he did, thus he has to because you have already qualified him as magnificent, mightiest ... (see above)."'

Mr Dimbleby picked out the loose thread in this logician's cat's cradle. 'Of course, the flaw is that the word "exist" does not represent a quality. It is a pre-supposition of the idea of God. If you are talking about God being x, y or z, you must already be talking about him existing. You cannot give him the attribute of existence without him existing first. So it was gibberish really—high-ranking gibberish, but gibberish. It doesn't help with your faith in religion.'

Leaving my brain clunking round like a demented Rubik's Cube, he dodged back into the cradle of academia.

'But there were those wonderful moments in the excitement, in the intellectual fervour, of discovering the process of thought when I did feel that answers were possible for everything, that everything could be

'Logical, rhetorical argument and thought processes: they have always been the core of an Oxford education.'

David Dimbleby on a Bullingdon Club outing

worked out by thought, that one could discover'—the words tripped fast upon each other's heels—'the Truth with a capital T about man's moral make-up, a true system of ethics, a foolproof answer to God's existence'—one side of the Rubik's Cube reckoned to have that one sorted—'but I pretty soon discovered that this was not so, that there were intractable problems which would not submit themselves to pure reason, and so logic became only one weapon in the armoury. Of the weapons which the University offers, it must be the best.'

He defined the value of argument for argument's sake.

'Logic, rhetorical argument and thought processes: they have always been the core of an Oxford education, and the beauty of this education is that it teaches you not to be seduced into believing verbatim what purports to be an intellectual argument when you later come across it in the business or political arenas.

'I read philosophy, which was a "clever-stick" sort of thing to read. Everybody at Oxford thinks they are cleverer than the next man, but if you read philosophy you feel you know you're cleverer than everybody else! It's a style of thinking which is very intoxicating, and it was the only time in my life when I saw what real thinking was in a world where people generally don't think very much. My life is now spent amongst journalists and politicians, where argument is not an intellectual matter at all—it is just a matter of assembling a few prejudices and instinctive feelings and wrapping them up as a "clever" argument.'

He paused, carefully touched his fingertips together, the thumbs under his chin, the forefingers on his lips, and listened as I asked how philosophy reflected the world, especially a world where people don't tend to think.

'Philosophy is what everybody, in some form or another, uses to define reality. Anything to do with ways of making a form out of impressions, making an intellectual shape out of your observations or your senses or whatever it is, is a valuable philosophical process at whatever level it's conducted.'

'But,' I struggled to ask, 'once these forms have been made, can the process still be described as "philosophy"? Or don't people rather just know what they think and think it?' Mr Dimbleby allowed a short pause, in which he contrived a respectable three-point turn.

'Yes, I suppose that's true. People love frameworks—it means they're safe. How wonderful: learn a few catch-phrases, a few definitions, fit them to things and then you need never think again. You can spend the rest of your life being snotty!'

Mr Dimbleby himself, however, as demonstrated above, draws away from catechisms of any kind. A big book entitled *Structuralism* caught my eye on the bookshelf. 'Are you a Structuralist?'

'I've never read that book! I don't think I would be. I'm against any political dogma in literature.'

'How do you read literature?'

'For the words. It's like your question about whether it's worth spending three years at Oxford learning thought processes which don't apply; I think the idea of reading books in a non-verbal way, in a way not obsessed with the way words are used, how they are made to mean things, is a gloomy way of reading. What I distrust about Structuralism is the overtone of disapproval which goes along with it: "This author is not worth reading because he is typical of upper-class life in the eighteenth century." Structuralists make certain writers important for political reasons even if they write badly, and other good writers don't matter because of their background. This attitude becomes dangerous, not least because it closes people's minds. It becomes a one-way way of looking at things.'

Mr Dimbleby's chariness of framing patterns of response suits him for his job. He is a political journalist who presents the rights and lefts of British politics. He distrusts cast-iron frames of interpretation not least because he has had an insight into live politics and seen that even the most cast-iron ideals become bent beyond recognition in the process of forging a policy.

'I don't have any sort of political ambition in me, and I don't think I would find the political process very satisfying. In the end, it is a mixture of combinations of pressures of such different kinds, that what politics is thought to be about by ordinary people is lost, and politicians become engaged in a quite different game of reconciling and balancing off pressures that nobody outside Westminster knows anything about. And politicians can never publicly reveal these things, because to reveal them would make the politics of policies and ideals seem almost irrelevant.

'If you were a Minister of Education, you would have to cope with political pressures from your colleagues, from the Opposition, from what had been done before, from the civil servants and the National Union of Teachers ... until in the end the course you would be forced to set to accommodate all their interests would bear little resemblance to your original view. But despite all these modifications necessary to get anything done, you would still have to defend your policy as consistently and as vehemently as though it was your first chosen ideal route.'

Consistency of opinion is not a chore Mr Dimbleby would wish to be saddled with for long—he rather more prides himself on his philosophical contrariety. 'I reckon I actually have more of a barrister's mind than a politician's. That is why I liked logic at Oxford the best—I

have such a short attention span that I like picking up a subject, working hard at it, and then totally forgetting it. That would be my ideal
life.'

Indeed, his political convictions are so lacklustre that even the implications of interviewing a Prime Minister fail to hold his attention for
long. 'I forget the most extraordinary things. If I'm interviewing the
Prime Minister, I always have to put the name of the Prime Minister at
the top of my piece of paper so that I can remember it.'

Being so careful not to remember the Prime Minister's name is
symbolic of his general care not to remember a consistent package of
policies in the danger that he might be branded as a political goat—or
sheep. Maintaining that he has not been 'remotely tarred by any political brush', he prefers just to present the show and then disengage himself from the act whilst Punch and Judy battle it out—an occupation,
he remarked, which has long been a source of entertainment.

'The language of politics has always been the same—you only have
to read Trollope's accounts of the House of Commons in the nineteenth century to see that it was equally adversarial and full of factions.
People always complain: "Why is there so much faction?" But politicians will always cluster around each other and attack everybody else.

'Nowadays most politics that matters in terms of election is conducted on television, and television tends towards confrontation because
it needs entertainment and confrontation is entertainment.'

'Isn't it dangerous that television fuels that?'

'Oh, extremely dangerous.'

Here was a quick glimpse of an actual Dimbleby opinion through a
gap in the hedges which he habitually builds around his bets; but no,
shears were promptly produced, and the offending statement
trimmed. 'Well, it is dangerous, but I mean there are dangers everywhere. If television decided not to fuel it, but to bend over backwards
and avoid confrontation so that politics became very dull, you would
have a lot of people turning off or falling asleep which would be just as
dangerous.'

Now that he was firmly wedged back on the fence, he delivered a
quick harangue at the should and shouldn't-dos of television.

'I don't think television has got politics right, and what is increasingly happening is that we get frivolous, badly done politics at popular
times, which discredits it; and you get severe, long-winded, doom-
laded politics at unpopular times to clear our consciences: "We're
doing serious stuff, but we aren't wrecking the ratings."'

'This is the most dangerous of all abdications of responsibility. The
whole point of the BBC, if you're a true Reithian, is that if you're
receiving public money, you have a sacred responsibility not to fritter it

'I longed to be Spencer Tracey.'
David Dimbleby on Wimbledon Common

away, but to attempt to enliven and interest and, if I can dare use the word'—he swallowed before putting his neck somewhere on the line—'*educate* people. I'm certainly in need of educating about politics and world affairs, and to turn our back on all that for the sake of popular programmes with big audience ratings is wrong and it's got to change.'

'Why were you loth to use the word "educate"?'

'Did I? Oh yes, I did use it. Well, I don't want to give the impression that I mean education *de haut en bas*. I mean education in a proper sense, you know ... revealing. I don't mean that I've got things to teach people (because I'm sure I haven't), but I think programmes should have things to teach. That is why the BBC is there, and if it is seduced into behaving like commercial television, then it will have no further purpose and we will have lost a remarkable visionary use of a popular medium.'

A strand of hair came adrift and interrupted the indignation. Mr Dimbleby patted it back into shape. In fact, it had been his hair which had been troubling me all along for, almost too good to be true, there it sat plumped up like a snug bird's nest and offering an almost irresistible provocation to pull it off. Perhaps Mr Dimbleby sensed this, because he watched warily as I produced a camera, and dived outside for a hairbrush. 'Do you think I ought to brush my hair? It always looks untidy and I don't want to look bad. I'll just go and check.'

As I focused in and out on the freshly immaculate head of hair, he talked of his family and home. 'Almost all the pictures are done by my wife's family who were painters in the 1930s. We never spend much money on furniture, so it's all rather tatty and shambolic and comfortable.

'My own family has always been rather exuberant and lively, but we lived in a remote part of the country, where there weren't many people.'

Whereabouts, I wondered, expecting North Uist at least. He tried to dodge and weave around the difficult fact that it was actually Surrey. 'Oh, in the depths of west, east, north, south, north-west Sussex— actually south-west Surrey. Not at all like living in London anyway.'

It was one of the few facts he had given away. Another one came as we went outside and he was keeping a close eye on the wind. 'I'm a hopeless actor. I always longed to be one; I longed to be Spencer Tracey. To be Spencer Tracey is my only real ambition! Somebody once told me I looked like him, so I wanted to be in movies, but I could never find my Katy Hepburn!'

I tried to recall that old ontological proof of the existence of Katy Hepburn.

Auberon Waugh

CHRIST CHURCH, 1959–60

I had visited Auberon Waugh with Marcia, one of my house-mates, and sent him a first draft of the article. He returned it with the following comments:

Dear Mr Whitley,
I must make it absolutely plain that this piece is not to appear as if it were an article written by me. This may sound pompous, but as a professional writer I am simply not prepared to let material appear under my by-line as if I had written it, when in fact it is culled from some random, half-drunken and besotted remarks made staring into the golden face of your beautiful companion.

Apart from anything else, if I were to write you such a long article as that, I would charge you about £20 million for it.

Otherwise, I think it is quite a jolly little piece.

Yours sincerely,
Auberon Waugh

The piece in question had gone something like this.
'I never went up with any serious intention of working, because that wasn't part of my idea of the Oxford myth. The myth I knew was very much my father's ideal—one sees it in a rather coarse, crude form nowadays, that myth of lotus-eating and champagne-drinking.'

Clutching his Pimm's with his three-fingered hand, Auberon Waugh shifted his bottom and warmed his rhetoric. We were sitting near some French windows, hot and lethargic, admiring the view of Somerset which hung motionless in the middle distance.

'There was bloody little sex and there weren't any orgies, but I do remember scenes of tremendous drunkenness.'

Auberon Waugh

'There was a small minority who were anxious, as part of the classi-cal myth, to get Firsts and Blues. They would spend time discussing who was "First" material and who wasn't. But none of my friends did any work. I did jolly little work—so little that I was thrown out, so I really lived up to it.' Both eyes beamed with evident satisfaction in disconcertingly different directions: 'That was my sister's fault; she told me that you only had to do three hours' work a day, but I even failed that—my work probably amounted to less than three hours a month. Everybody used to deny furiously that they were working, when actually they were shutting themselves up to pass the exams. I wrote only one essay, which was about something called "The Hook" in logic, and the tiny amount of work I did on that convinced me that the whole thing was total rubbish—a complete waste of time.'

Mr Waugh fidgeted; at odds with the rest of the landscape, he seemed wickedly awake. His voice, sharp-pitched, was punctuated by a metallic chuckle.

'Memories of ostentatiously and self-consciously punting out to picnic with champagne, though we could never find anybody who was good enough at punting. Dimbleby could punt, but then he was a suc-cess story. Both the Oxford Union and *Isis* (the University magazine) were going through the Dimbleby Days. As a kind of anti-Dimbleby (general king) and anti-Jay (intellectual king) movement, I founded a ghastly club called the Carlton Club, which was full of right-wing Tories and was a very dismal affair indeed. All we did was have huge dinners like any Oxford club. None of the friends I moved with were very interested in it.'

'Had you attracted a hard core of followers by then?'

'I don't think you could describe them as "followers", because most of them were much grander than I was. There was a recognisable circle of people who spent most of their time eating and drinking. They were consciously the "Christ Church Hoorays" group, but a bit better than the crowd one sees today; they were rich and euphemistic and interested in aesthetics and also, slightly pseudishly, in things like Victorian art and architecture! When one sees young people still doing all that now, one thinks they are frightful bores.'

Whilst he feigned to swig some Pimms, one eye flitted a suspicious look at us as if we might be furtively passing a Victorian artefact under the table. We weren't.

'Were you sad to leave that homemade world?'

'By the time I was thrown out I was getting rather bored of Oxford. What I saw in the future was only going to be a continuation of what I had been doing, and I didn't see many surprises coming. Actually, whilst we were all pretending to be terribly rich, we really weren't rich enough, and the truth is that we drank plonk.' Then his baby face puckered like John McEnroe's at a bad line call. 'But I hadn't got into the Gridiron Club, which was a source of great bitterness to me. It was a really terrible blow—if I had stayed another year, I would have got in. It was playing a bit fast to get in that first year, but as my year moved up to become the second generation, they would have elected me.

'There had also been bloody little sex. We had all had to really work at it, and that might have softened up by my third year. There were three or four token girls—"groupies", I suppose, but compared with today, there was jolly little.

'My daughter is at Durham now, and it seems that there, as elsewhere, everybody shacks up with a "steady" and sticks to them throughout their time. This seems very pathetic. They never go anywhere without them—they even go on bloody holiday together. So, there wasn't much sex, there weren't any orgies, but'—he produced two wonderful after-dinner tales—'I do remember scenes of tremendous drunkenness. I remember a party in a room in Canterbury Quad, where the ceiling was almost as high as this one. One of my friends was sick, but he didn't vomit downwards, he stood up and leant back and vomited upwards. He produced this remarkable column of vomit which hit the ceiling and left a deep stain, before, of course, coming down!

'The other occasion, I remember, was the great scandal caused when a fellow called Aubrey Bowden nearly raped or raped Sarah Quennell outside the Bodleian Library. His excuse to the Proctors was that he mistook her for a telephone box. They seemed to sympathise with that. God knows what they do with telephone boxes!'

He was now on to caricaturing the types of people who inhabit Oxford. In his downstairs lavatory, framed cartoons depict him scribbling away with sulphuric acid, his forehead bulging with venom, but this thumbnail sketch of Oxford was more bemused.

'I wouldn't satirise anybody, because there aren't any power figures. One isn't up against anybody in the way one is at school, or in the Army, or in later life. There is nobody who threatens.

'It attracts those Masonic style of people, who really enjoy idiotic rituals. I think there is more of than around than one realises, but one sees it throughout Oxford. Unless people come from public school or the Army, they cannot understand what is happening. They cannot understand the rituals of why one should propose a toast to a chair or to a chamberpot! All this survives very much amongst the dons. It is even stronger in the Law Courts, where they insist on endless half-baked rituals and have the same mystique about port and claret.

'And everybody will be a little odd. Certainly, all my friends were distinctly odd. It was somewhat cultivated then, but they have sub-sequently stuck to the persona they then adopted. You see, everybody is experiencing their first taste of freedom at Oxford, so any sort of oddities which were kept down at school or home suddenly emerge. On the whole, they are very much capable of pretending to take things seriously and then, when they hit a particular note, they'll collapse and you'll realise the whole thing has been a total joke. None of them will be the sort of hard-edged, pompous person you find at Cambridge—they are less ambitious. There was a genuine contempt for ambition in my time.

'That lovely story about Lord Curzon when he was envoy in Paris. . . . He was all dolled up in his medals and robes and whatnots, waiting in the Great Hall of the Embassy for a banquet to start. He thought that nobody was looking, so he started doing a little dance in front of the fireplace, when in fact a child was watching him—which seems to me to be a typical Oxford story.

'A lot of this happens in *Private Eye*, which is what I mean by people laughing at themselves. We all go to *Private Eye* lunches and tend to cultivate the more anarchistic sides of our natures, which Cambridge people won't do so much. None of my diary sets out to be serious or to provoke people; a couple of feminists generally write to complain, but I set out to amuse people purely by my posturing act. I started it up when I was sacked from the *Spectator* in embarrassing circumstances. It started as a take-off of Alan Brien's diary in *The Times*, and I even grew a beard to mock him. His diary was packed in after six months, whereas mine has been going for ten years.'

Mrs Waugh came in to announce lunch. A bottle of Californian wine called 'Stag's Leap' was produced, which a shipper had hoped might feature in Crispin de St Crispian's wine column:

'It's got a huge arse—something you can really get into!'

'Bron! Behave yourself!'

During lunch there was much discussion of the game of croquet we would play before leaving. Mr Waugh has invented his own notorious rules, which he explained to us in the teeth of loud and derisive oppo-sition from the rest of the family.

The rules provide that the two teams of two play each hoop for itself, the first team with both balls through wins that hoop, and play continues to the next. The game is started by a long shot across the lawn to the first hoop, the closest ball then having the opening shot. In between each hoop, you can croquet everybody as often as you wish.

So it was that, well tanked-up with Stag's Leap, we climbed up a pathway between rhododendron bushes to the croquet lawn. Mr Waugh played a Ballesteros to the first hoop, and he and Marcia went

Auberon Waugh poised to do battle on the croquet lawn, Combe Florey

on to take the first three hoops, with Mr Waugh instructing Marcia and assisting her with her swing, like something of a cross between the Red Queen and Aubrey Bowden. At one point his son Alexander tried to help Marcia aim up a shot. He stood astride the hoop, a foot on each side, and said:

'Aim between my legs, and you should come up with something interesting.'

'Are you trying to imply something about your genitalia, Alexander?' Mr Waugh asked idly.

Her shot sliced drastically wide, and gave us the hoop. All even up to the winning post, with Mr Waugh snapping, 'Do shut up!' every time we abused him or Marcia. She surprised us all by hitting the post first. Alexander clocked in second, leaving Mr Waugh and me. He croqueted me, put the balls together and took careful aim. I saw my ball inevitably hurtle towards the undergrowth, and turned to watch Mr Waugh. Like the croqueted balls, each eye seemed to be turned outwards—one following mine, whilst the other tracked his own on its whistle-stop run towards the post, which it hit by a whisker.

Hot and out of breath, we sat down and drank tea as the heat went out of the afternoon.

The following edition of 'Auberon Waugh's Diary' contained his version of the day.

Thursday

'For nearly a month I have been drinking nothing but Californian wine as part of a fact-finding enquiry for *Tatler* magazine: does it promote incoherence, psycho-babble, moral collapse and even homosexualism among its devotees? I rather fear it might.

'Another problem is whether one can seriously urge the impressionable rich to spend their money on wine called things like Stag's Leap, Inglenook and Napa Valley Zinfandel, however nice it seems to taste. This is not just a question of snobbery, but represents a serious moral dilemma, like "modernising" the Prayer Book.

'At lunchtime two Oxford undergraduates arrive, saying they want to write a book about me. I do not catch the girl's surname, but she seems quite exceptionally graceful, intelligent and pleasing. This is most unlike the usual Oxford undergraduate nowadays, but even so I shoo them away after tea, having to write some rubbish for the *Daily Mail* about snooker.

'Some time later, I learn she comes from a famous ducal family, is the daughter of a proper earl and a first cousin once removed of the Queen. Damn, *damn*, DAMN! It proves my point that one should never approach a bottle of wine without carefully studying what is written on the label.'

Michael Palin

BRASENOSE, 1962–65

It had all started rather well—a grin for the camera outside, a jolly caper around the coffee machine. 'Water in, coffee in, all systems ready to go. Oh no! Cleaning lady has taken the plug out. Put it back in, whoops, switch on ... and hey presto!' Then the contrived sense of hysteria was switched off and with a complacent, Maxwell House smile, Michael Palin composed himself for my questions.

'Oxford was a wonderfully liberating experience, because I suddenly found myself being able to choose what I wanted to do, rather than being forced to read Latin and French all day. It was also the first time that I mixed with boys from a non-public school background. Since the time I left my Sheffield prep school, from the age of fourteen to nineteen, I had only met the same sort of person as myself— tentative public schoolboys. Oxford was an introduction to lots of grammar school boys, where things like background, parents, parents' cars, and money no longer mattered. At Shrewsbury School, everyone had been so conscious of the ritual of being at a place of tradition, that a horrible sense of privilege dominated the school. This I didn't see at Oxford. I was aware that places like Christ Church might operate like that, but Brasenose had a genuinely wide social mixture—bottles of Merrydown on the lawn at Magdalen was the closest we got to Evelyn Waugh's Oxford!'

Michael Palin was at Oxford at the crest of the Sixties. It was a time of infectious optimism when, alongside the thrill of sex and drugs and rock and roll, there arose a feeling of confidence which carried people towards their instincts.

'There was a feeling that good times were ahead, that you were

'You cannot say: "You must not do more than three plays a year about Polish lesbian babysitters."'

Michael Palin

lucky to be there and that we were all very much in control of things.

'I worked on the fringe of the art world in that very unspecific area between comedy and cabaret. Whereas at Cambridge there was the Footlights Club, which was a rallying point for undergraduates who wanted to do revues and cabaret, there was nothing like that at Oxford. We were just a disparate group of people who bumped into each other at the King's Arms.

'I never had the feeling that comedy or carbaret was definitely what I wanted to do, it was a nice process of discovery. I just went along and met up with somebody who had a similar sense of humour. He was more ambitious than I was, and he said, "Listen, don't let's just talk about these jokes and sketches, let's actually go and perform them. It can make us money." So we went to the Union cellars and earned thirty shillings a night. One of our sketches involved us miming things happening with a bucket of water—stepping in it, spilling it, throwing it. A clever sort of idea. After a year and a half, we were reasonably well known, and we were asked to go up to the Edinburgh Festival. It was only after that, when agents from London discussed my shows, that it became apparent that I might earn my living from acting.'

'Should there be some formal institution at Oxford, like the Cambridge Footlights Club?'

Mr Palin thought not. 'Too much power should never be given within any sort of area, whether it is the revue establishment, the acting establishment, or the musical establishment. People should be free to write or act whatever they want.' He cast around for an example. Rather like watching a roulette wheel, I wondered what he would alight on—dead parrots, fish-slapping housewives, Polish lesbians...? It was Polish lesbians. 'Even if that means élitist plays about Polish lesbians smashing up babies in prams. But I hope people don't go, and that those sort of plays don't work, which will make people tend towards more commercial ideas. It is impossible to enforce artistic standards. You cannot say, "You must not do more than three plays a year about Polish lesbian babysitters."

'There is such a thin line between what is constructive and destructive about the freedom of Oxford that it is difficult to make the distinction between those who are élitist, dabbling dilettantes and those who are genuinely trying to experience something. Some of them are going to fail hopelessly, and some will appear awfully arrogant and pretentious, but by the same token, others, and I feel I was one, will benefit from being able to do what was probably awful pretentious nonsense in the Union cellars for thirty bob a night.'

'Pretentious nonsense' is a tag Michael Palin and Monty Python have dutifully avoided ever since. Their humour is a curious hybrid between chaotic farce and disgust, and Mr Palin pared away some of the flesh to show me the bones.

'Monty Python does try to involve our own sort of ideas, whether they're political, social or whatever, into the sketches that we write. It doesn't always have to be that way—we can do something totally ridiculous and silly like'—he cast around for an example. The wheel stopped—'the fish-slapping skit, which even the wittiest Marxist couldn't say had a political context.

'But there are attitudes behind what we write, and it is very important that they show through. There is a reluctance to accept authority unquestioningly, which is an extremely loose definition of saying what we comment about, but I prefer to say that than say it's anti-authority. Pythons are not anarchists by any means, but when we get together and start assembling material, the most fertile ground for our comedy is the follies of the people we see around us, and it is even worse when we feel that those people are in a superior position over most people and are still more stupid. That is where our area goes, and that can go through from merchant bankers to doctors or actors—wherever we see any sort of pomposity or pretension. If we feel that somebody in authority is telling people to do something whilst being totally unsuitable to that position, it is gratifying to be able to deflate them by humour.'

He further defined that area by showing where their humour went wrong.

'In *The Meaning of Life*, we had a long session where we were trying to write about the end of the world and life in four hundred years' time. That was an area which never worked itself out. I couldn't quite see why at the time, but I now think it was too general. We are much better on specifics—in *The Meaning of Life*, there was something about a hospital where a baby is born. Instead of there just being the mother and the doctor and then the baby, there are all these machines. All this technical equipment is brought in, which is a good comment on what nowadays tends to happen in hospitals. It worked better because it wasn't so woolly.'

The Life of Brian exploited the edge of farce which the Bible balances on, but Mr Palin maintains, never overstepped into blasphemy. 'We were using the story of the life of Christ in order to have a go at the Church establishment. Python's primary criterion is that whatever we do should be funny, and I think that if you do something which is blasphemous, it would be shocking, and you would have failed to make people laugh.'

'Do you believe in Christ?'

'I was brought up to go to Church; I'm now saying that I am an agnostic with doubts. If Jesus did come to earth, I would love to discuss the film with him.'

Under cross-examination about how careful he should be to avoid slander, Mr Palin faltered and could only muster up a couple of one-legged sentences.

'We are a comedy group—we tend to make people laugh. Satire and slander aren't terms we would use—they are society's terms. They evolve from a law which is not made by us, but by somebody who's written down in some dusty journal what satire and slander is. We just observe and comment on human behaviour, and I feel that there is very, very little that we shouldn't say or couldn't say about anybody at any time. My selection process is purely what I think is funny.'

The process of contriving humour is necessarily esoteric, and Michael Palin took me through the portals of Python, into the workshop.

'It is an entirely anarchistic commune. Having established whether it's a book or a film, we split up into the traditional groups in which we operate. The groups are Graham Chapman and John Cleese, Terry Jones and myself, and Eric Idle and Terry Gillan writing on their own. We split up for ten days or a fortnight, and then all meet up for a massive reading session, where all the material that has been assembled over those two weeks gets read out aloud. From that group, little categories of material will take shape. There might be 5 percent to 10 percent which is just perfect, and we all think is marvellous, so that's left on a pile and not touched. There will be 20 percent which is nearly there, but perhaps needs a bit of work, so those who wrote it will go back to work it out again; this leaves a large area, perhaps 50 percent to work on. About 20 percent is binned. What's left is the stuff that those who wrote don't feel they can take any further, so they give it to somebody else—Graham and John will take away something that Terry and I have started and so on. Then we split up for another two weeks, before another discussion, which lasts intensively for two or three weeks, by which time most of the material has probably been written—in a sense by all of us both indirectly or directly in group contribution.'

'John Cleese stands out from this group as surely as Mick Jagger stands out from The Rolling Stones.' I pointed out. 'Doesn't this frustrate you?'

'Not any more. It maybe did at one stage, but I've always found that it's completely understandable that John should stand out from the rest of us. For a start, physically he stands out in any circumstance. For instance, John would be the first to admit that he's not the world's greatest character actor because he can never submerge himself and disappear inside a role. He tends to play John visually, so the public always has a very clear view of him. John tends to be fairly dominant, but that all goes with his height and size and imperial bearing. In fact, it is not something which worries me any more. In the early stages, it worried me more—after we had done two or three series, John said that he was going to leave. That was when I slightly felt that perhaps he did over-dominate it. Then we did a series of six shows in which he wasn't involved, and I think we got even bigger viewing figures. Although a vital element was missing, I would have felt a vital element was missing if either Graham, Eric or Terry had left.' He blinked a couple of times. 'I really do.' His voice continued petulantly: 'Monty Python is by no means John's show. Although he came up very strongly in terms of the influence he had on us, it is really a genuinely combined effort.'

'You have been amongst the rudest of people I've ever had to talk to.'
Michael Palin to EW

The Missionary was Michael Palin's first solo film made outside the umbrella of Monty Python. I hadn't enjoyed it, and these are the last few minutes of the interview:

'Did you feel that *The Missionary* had the same quality of humour as *The Life of Brian?*'

'*The Life of Brian* was a bit harder than *The Missionary*, which had a rather more gentle quality to it which was just telling a story. *Brian* was a series of sketches and observations about life now as well as life then; I don't think *The Missionary* had quite that aim.'

'Because it had struck me that the style of humour was out-of-date and rather slapstick.'

'I'm sorry you found it thus.'

'That scene, for example, when you explain to your wife what a "fallen woman" is, and she asks if it's somebody who's broken their ankle. "No, my dear." Somebody who's broken their leg? (With eyes rounded) "No, my dear." How could you put that into the film?'

'Oh dear! I'm sorry. It's just that I've got to go.' Mr Palin stood up and turned away. He suddenly wheeled back to me, shouting, 'I mean, how can you ask a thing like that? What do you mean: how can I put it into the film? ... Because I happened to think it was funny, I thought it worked. You didn't, fair enough, but don't come here and ask me, how can I dare put something like that in a film? Honestly, that's the most pissing awful thing I've ever heard.... If you didn't like the film, you didn't like the film, but don't say, "How can you put it in there?"' He stuck his face right up to mine, so I could clearly see the veins jumping in his forehead. 'Because I'm an imbecile, BECAUSE I'M NO GOOD AT WRITING FUCKING COMEDY—that's why I put it in there.

'Right, I'm off. Cheerio. I hope your thing comes out really well.'

He ran down the stairs, and I realised that this was not one of his skits. Footsteps came bounding back again. I tried to make it up: 'Mr Palin....'

Still shouting at me and shaking with rage, he stumbled across the room and found his house keys. 'Don't "Mister Palin" me. I'm not a man who gets angry very often, but I find that you have been amongst the rudest of people I've ever had to talk to. You've just got your own boorish ideas ... I'm prepared to discuss things in a reasonable attitude, and I think there are lots of criticisms I would make, but to say to me, "*How can you put something like that in?*" What do you mean, how can I put it in? I don't know what you mean. I've got to go, so I'll just have to say goodbye.'

Two sobs down the stairs, the front door slammed, and I was left sitting in his house amongst the satirist's memorabilia. Mr Palin, it seemed, was exempt from his own dictum: 'I feel that there is very, very little that we shouldn't say or couldn't say about anybody at any time.'

Diana Quick

LADY MARGARET HALL, 1964–67

'Do I look awfully smudged? I feel as though there are just black smudges where my eyes should be.' Diana Quick sipped coffee and smiled. 'We didn't get to bed until six this morning.'

I had been listening for the first splashes of rain from a low, ominous sky, when Miss Quick silently materialised down the stairs. With raggled hair and bare feet, Indian jewellery and wide-lipped eyes, she injected a feline and lethal element into the Chelsea lounge.

The actress in her is close to the surface and provides alternating voice patterns and vocabulary which turn between the sensual lilt of the chenille-trimmed Julia Flyte to haggling Cockney with a raucous word like 'wank'.

'I hadn't formed these ideas about Oxford being a wank, at its crudest level, in terms of professional experience, until I became President of the Dramatic Society. I had enormous unformed yearnings to do it better, to act better, but the gap between my professional aspirations and the actual shabby, dilatory, dilettantish productions we were putting on suddenly became clearly focused when I returned from my Christmas holiday at the BBC. People constantly frustrated me by not turning up to rehearsals—that would have been fine if they were just acting for fun, but then they would talk a lot of hot air about their play being a springboard into the profession. It started to really irritate me.'

She was determined to try to shake her contemporaries out of the other-worldliness of Oxford dreams and hash.

'I said, "Listen, let's make a choice—either we can just have fun, or we can make this into a stamping ground before pursuing our careers

'Nobody ever said, "I like this!" or, "This is garbage!" We weren't allowed to express a personal opinion—it was all received wisdom.'

Diana Quick

(Yeah, let's do that, they said) in which case let's take it seriously (Yeah) and try to develop technical skills."

'I would organise movement classes, voice classes, directors from London to take workshops—two people might turn up. It was hopeless. I got very disappointed and angry, but I suppose you cannot impose any kind of formal organisation on something which should be organic by its very nature.'

The academic side of her Oxford life was a disappointment for exactly the opposite reasons: she felt her tutors were trying to impose patterns of response on her. Her eventual repulsion of this indicates how close she felt to the organic spirit she herself had tried to formalise in the theatre.

'Nobody ever taught me to think. Nobody ever encouraged me to have an opinion about anything—all they had ever said was, "What does Bradley say about Shakespeare's tragedies?" "Have you read Eliot on Jacobean drama?" Nobody ever said, "I like this!" or "This is garbage!" We weren't allowed to express a personal opinion—it was all received wisdom. Having to write essays on a different author each week made reading become a kind of duty which more or less destroyed my love of words. One of the consequences of this was my reaction against it. I didn't open a book for five years, I became a hippy, took a lot of drugs, and I didn't want anything to do with people who talked that kind of language. It took me those five years to be able to open a book and think, if I don't like this, I don't have to get an angle on it. I don't even have to start on page one.'

The academic study of drama was not, ironically, to help her when it came to interpreting and enacting a script. She does not believe acting can be academically analysed.

'Actors and actresses talking about acting are hopeless. They can never tell you how they actually do it, because they don't know. When Sir Larry discusses his acting, he talks absolute drivel—that's not what he does or how he does it. There is no method. What you use is yourself, your personality, your experience, what's happened to you that day. Basically I would look at a play in more or less the same way whether I had gone to Oxford or not; in fact I was probably disadvantaged by having an academic mind, because it encourages you to make too many decisions too early in the rehearsal process. Acting should be a co-operative thing—you do a lot of finding out as to what happens between you and the rest of the cast, so it is a mistake to read the part and say, "Oh yes, I'll do it like this."'

She gave an example to demonstrate how the academic mind can divorce the words from the play:

'I don't know if you are involved in acting, but imagine a rehearsal.'

She leant towards me intently, her eyes never leaving mine whilst she quietly mouthed, 'Imagine we're doing Romeo and Juliet.

'We both know the story and we may have some ideas, but what happens in the rehearsal is that we have to have the texts in front of us because I don't know the words, neither do you. What we're trying to do is play lovers, young lovers, in love for the first time; we don't know each other, you and I, so we have to deal with that, feeling shy and: "Will he think I'm any good?" But despite all this, your primary relationship during this very crucial time, the first three weeks, is with this book in your hand. What we're trying to play is this tempestuous and passionate, intimate relationship, but what we're actually doing is reading out words written in black and white which say: "Thou knowest the mask of night is on my face." It should be to *you*—I've just said: "Look, you've heard me say how much I really, really love you and I'm really embarrassed and feel vulnerable about this, but the thing is, if I possibly could, I would show you how I feel and its a jolly good thing that its dark, otherwise you would see me blushing...." What comes trotting out instead is: "Thou knowest the mask of night is on my face, else would a maiden blush bepaint my cheek." It's a terrible thing! Look at us now—we're talking and neither of us is sitting with a book trying to put it through print. The academic mind is dangerous—it is too drawn to the words and tends to keep the rehearsal too cerebral and conceptual, instead of letting it be something that happens between two people.'

Having sat as still as a rabbit in front of a weasel, I shifted and reached for a cigarette as she turned away. I wondered how aware she was of her ability to spellbind, but instead heard myself asking an inane question about how she came to be a theatre actress in London.

'I came up to London in the late Sixties and spent a lot of time hanging around the Royal Court, which was exciting with writers like Joe Orton and Edward Bond. I was just part of the great tide of people who were mainly out to have fun, and it was the greatest fun! At home with lots of people coming by, going to concerts, making great food to eat, seeing what would happen next ... the thing about acting is that it is by definition an erratic job. What would happen is that I might get a job, which meant I could pay the rent for that month, but then it would end and maybe I couldn't work for another month, so I would just hang out. Within our circle of friends, our house was a nice place to be—there was always a floating population and what would happen would be that whoever worked bought the food, the records and the movie tickets and the dope, and whoever wasn't working looked after the house and had a good time, then the roles would change over.'

Since that time, she has established herself as a leading lady of the theatre, and has also diversified into film. With her performances in *The Duellists* and *Brideshead Revisited*, Miss Quick successfully bridged the gap. She analysed the different excitements of the different occasions.

'The adrenalin produced by performing live when you know that once the curtain goes up, that's it, you're on a roller coaster and you can't stop, is just fantastic. You can't interrupt and do another take—if you miss a line or a step, you have to forget about it, and go for the next one. When it works well, it's the best drug I know. It must be to do with manipulating people.

'The thing about film is that it is altogether a much more private activity. It's more intimate—it's like working in miniature. You may do a master shot, but alongside that you will have all those different shots, close-ups, which will require detailed work—this has nothing to do with the very essence of theatre which is projection, which aims to get to the back of the hall whether it's Covent Garden or some housing estate. Film is entirely to do with making the camera come to you—it's the opposite technique and experience. Instead of making yourself open and covering large distances, you have to make people come to you—not by demonstrating, not by explaining, just by doing it.'

She highlighted one of the difficulties of theatre. 'Acting in a theatre is so difficult; it is so difficult to actually get up and do it in front of an audience, and the other thing is having to reproduce it. If I have to do it night after night, it's hopeless. I crack after three months. I get to the point where I cannot remember whether I've said the line or if it was the night before. The best system is the repertory system where, as a working actor, you have a variety of parts. That works well; it is refreshing and stimulating to use different theatrical muscles for each one.'

Looking across the index of West End plays, she is saddened by the inability of London theatre to catch the imagination of the public and arrest the increasing flow of people towards the cinemas.

'I can't bear going up Shaftesbury Avenue and seeing all the theatres either sitting in the dark, or playing old trash for tourists. The reason why they put on this trash is money: the demand to get a return means they have to go for the lowest common denominator. It is very hard to know where the really good new work is. People who can really write tend to be seduced into movie writing because there are much better pickings there—you can make tons of money—but theatre is important.'

She sees theatre as a more direct and powerful confrontation between artist and audience than the cinema.

'It is a safety valve, a mirror if you like, for society. Sometimes it has periods of neglect, when it seems quaint and irrelevant, as now, but sometimes it seems more timely. This last happened in the 1960s, starting with Osborne and Arden. Then it was working-class theatre, social realism—it only lasted ten years, it was brief, but everybody was surprised at what was happening; they were surprised at this tremendous energy being articulated in the form of theatre.'

She described David Hare's play which she picked out as an exception amongst clichéd box office bonanzas. 'I'm now in a play called *A Map of the World*, which is rather contentious. It is a bold and big step forward for David Hare, where he takes on much wider, more epic subjects than he has ever done before. It's about what makes people believe what they've chosen to believe. At one point somebody says, "Everything that suits us, we place upon our map." The play describes how people appropriate the past and tailor it to confirm their opinions. It is a debate between right and left, and I stand in the middle. I offer my body as a prize to the winner of the political debate.'

Although she is an actress who has spoken on feminist issues, indeed, who has formed 'Women's Playhouse Project' ('Women in theatre have a raw deal. Traditionally, leading parts are male, so there are very few meaty parts for actresses.') she enjoys the controversy surrounding her part, but is genuinely committed to trying to redress the traditional imbalance between heroes and heroines, which gives the hero 'all the plum lines'. This chauvinism is often exacerbated in love scenes, where the audience is explicitly invited to the side of the male predator. Miss Quick gave me an example of this traditional approach to filmed sex.

'There was a scene in *The Duellists*, where I was supposed to have just made love with Keith Carradine, and we were having a post-coital chat. Ridley, the director, came up and said, "I don't think you should have any clothes on." "What's Keith wearing?" I said. "He'll have his breeches on." "If Keith takes his clothes off, I'll take off mine." So we went to Keith: "Would you mind taking your breeches off?" "Fuck off!" was his reaction. So why should I be the one who everyone is staring at, not listening to the dialogue? It would have been nothing to do with the scene—it would just have been a case of: "Oh, she's got big tits."

'I'm not cynical about this. There is a book called *The White Hotel* which I think is terrific, and I'm very keen to play the woman in the film. This may or may not happen (currently Barbara Streisand hopes to play it), but if I was to play it, it is one of the most sensual things I've ever read, and it would require very, very explicit and hopefully extremely erotic love-making. I'd do that, because that is what the story is about.'

As Julia Flyte in *Brideshead Revisited*, Miss Quick played a love scene with Jeremy Irons. Sitting cross-legged on her haunches, she threw her head back and laughed at the memory.

'Let me tell you about Jeremy. He'll murder me, he hates it when I talk about it, but I was so pissed off with him that I talk about it whenever possible.

'It is the only bit of sex in the whole book, so it is tremendously loaded. Actually, it is supposed to be a very perfunctory fuck, when he just stakes his claim in the ship, so if we had followed our brief, it would just have been a quick one two, but we decided that it was one of the few moments to show real tenderness and peace between these two very troubled spirits. We decided not to make it as Waugh had written, but somehow softer.

'At last the day arrived when we were going to do the sex. We closed the set, which means getting rid of all the gaffers and sparks and extras, and decided how to shoot it, where to put the camera, who'll be on top and then we start to rehearse. It was the funniest thing you've ever seen! I took my trousers off, leaving just my cotton briefs and a silk shirt, and Jeremy climbed on top of me wearing hairy Harris tweed trousers! I said, "Jeremy, will you take your trousers off, please?" "No darling, I'll take them off for the take." "Fucking right you will, but listen, the whole point of this rehearsal is for us to get over feeling shy, and get used to each other's bodies."

'So he reluctantly took his trousers off, and we writhed around and gasped a bit, whilst Charlie figured out how to track the camera, and worked out some shots of my fingers stroking his back, and what would happen after the climax ... but it is *deeply* embarrassing to do something so private in such a matter of fact and public way. When we had broken the ice, the unit came back, and we prepared for the take. At this moment, Jeremy announced that he's going to keep his underpants on: "Why?" said Charlie. "Because nothing looks more ridiculous than a male arse pumping up and down, so I'm keeping my pants on, which is what Brando did in *Last Tango in Paris*—and he also wore Wellington boots to make sure they didn't photograph him below the waist." "Well, I hope you'll take off those boots, Jeremy."

'So we got into bed, but the sheets were satin, and they kept slipping off Jeremy's bottom, so Charlie had to get a wardrobe lady to pin the sheets to his knickers! We did the first take, puffing and panting away, and afterwards Charlie came over, and I could see he didn't know what on earth to say! Later, he told me how he was so inhibited, because he had never seen another man making love before, and he suddenly felt that any note he gave Jeremy was not a director directing an actor, but one male criticising another male's sexual technique. He felt terribly cautious, and all he said was, "I think you should be a little more ecstatic." "Yes, darling," said Jeremy. "And Diana," he said to me, "you can put your legs up over his back, but not so early!"'

'So on the next take, Jeremy was banging away and I was writhing away, when Jeremy suddenly yelled out, "Ohohohohaaargh!" I lay there and thought, What on earth is that? and started to roar with laughter, but suddenly remembered the camera, and quickly pretended to be in ecstasy too, so I went, "Ooooh." That's the one they used for the film!'

'What is it like pretending to make love with somebody you find yourself attracted to?'

'It's great to play a love scene with somebody you really fancy. It makes life a lot easier, and it's no accident that actors are always falling in love with each other, because they play these intimate relationships all the time.

'If it's an attractive person, which it often is, it's very hard for it not to carry over; when 5.30 comes up, you can hardly put your clothes back on and say, "Goodbye, I'm going home to the wife." But it is the weirdest thing—it is odd, because actors never talk about it. They never talk about how they have a life and feelings and problems and relationships outside their work. How many stable relationships have you ever heard of between actors? Acting, by definition, is a promiscuous profession. You work intensively with a group of people, and then everybody moves on to work with other people. Sometimes you may not like whom you're acting with, so there is no chemistry and it becomes purely an acting job, but occasionally you do fall in love, and it is very odd because it is hard to remember what's real and what's the part. It is marvellous on the scene itself, where the question of what is your real life and what is the life of the film becomes irrelevant for the purpose of work. It is afterwards that it becomes confusing, especially when you find the person you fall in love with happens to be married with six children.'

Fresh from New York, Miss Quick produced bagels and jam. She enjoys the vantage point of an international actress, who can afford to wait for the good roles to come knocking at her door, and from this freelance independence she looked at the two major institutions of English theatre.

'I have a strong feeling that theatre should be about doing plays and it shouldn't really matter where they are—it could be in the street. Theatre is the art of imagination, anything is possible—it's just whether you can conceive it or not. It's magic. It should not be about buildings, or salary structures or bureaucracies, which is why both the National and the RSC can be terrible places. Under Trevor Nunn's influence, Stratford has preserved more of a company feeling, but I am terribly disappointed that they've gone down the same road as the

National, which is to institutionalise themselves with a huge operation, a huge building, and huge financial pressures which makes it such an unwieldy monster.'

It is the atmosphere of an institution which can, in due course, kill the spirit of spontaneity, as Miss Quick has seen.

'In an ideal world, you would go to the National and be offered three parts, which is what the repertory system is all about. What very often happens, however, is actors go in on just one play and then they are asked if, as a favour, as they are there anyway, they would take a small part in something else. This seems to happen a lot to the middle-range, solid, decent, able character actors, who find themselves seduced into staying there and letting the institution close over their heads. They settle for this extra £20 a performance, and think they probably wouldn't get work elsewhere. These people who could be so much more talented settle for that, because it's a steady job inside a steady institution, which in my opinion is settling for less than they deserve.'

She added further insight to the problems inside the National. 'When you're backstage, it's like working in the most anonymous, Kafkaesque place: it's just corridors, doors off and tiny dressing rooms, which all face each other over a glass quadrangle like rats' cages.

'The whole thing was designed by committees, and it falls through every possible stool in that it doesn't satisfy any basic requirement. There is a sensible reason why traditional theatres are as they are. From the Restoration period to the First War, theatres were built to a pattern, usually with curved backs and steep galleries, so that the audience was all contained rather than sent away. They made it as easy as possible for the performer to establish a relationship with the house. You have to be able to embrace the house and from this point of view all the theatres at the National are a nightmare: the Lyttelton is so wide that it is like acting in cinemascope—in order for the audience to have any sense of the scale of the proceedings, when you are on stage, you have to stand half as far away again from your scene partner as you would in real life otherwise you look like tiny matchsticks. It is stupid to have to worry about that. The Olivier is so big that the space is too huge to command. There are only certain, very few, key points on stage where you can stand and command everybody's attention. This is so stupid. Here is the National Theatre, which has been a dream for so long, and they have fucked it up in every way.'

Diana Quick retains much of the angry ambition of the dramatists of the Sixties. She recognises that she will not become a screen idol of the Eighties. 'I don't look how a leading lady should look—that is the

'Imagine we're doing Romeo and Juliet.'

Diana Quick

hard truth of the matter. There is a certain received idea about conventional English beauty, with which my face does not comply.' But she would not accept any of those roles anyway, because they take traditional femininity for granted. She fiercely questions the mould of English theatre, and is concerned to establish women as alternative directors and producers. 'There is not a single woman director of the National—it's absurd.'

We finished the tape, and scuttled through the thunder storm to Park Walk, where we had lunch. She chatted to the flower shop proprietor on the way who said, 'Just look after this for me love,' and gave her a carnation.

Martin Amis

EXETER, 1968–71

'I still have nightmares about it. They say to me, "You have to do your Finals again. You did quite well the first time, but not well enough." And of course I'm late and drunk and nude. But I think, well, I can probably talk my way through Shakespeare, bluff through the seventeenth, eighteenth, nineteenth-century papers—but what about the Latin? And most of all, *what about the Old English?*'

Martin Amis clenched his teeth as though for a dentist's drill.

'Ouch! Christ! Shit!'

He rocked backwards and forwards. He might even have moaned a little. 'I enjoyed Old English,' I said. He shivered. 'I burnt my copy of *Beowulf*. No, actually I didn't mind slogging through it—it was quite relaxing after all that wretched nine-to-five sensitivity you had to display everywhere else—you just thumped through the translation. The most hateful thing about it, as either my father or Philip Larkin said, was having to pretend it was good. That was what was so exhausting. All that shabby fiction the dons go through of insisting "it's all good stuff" . . . It's *terrible!*'

Mr Amis retreated deeper into his armchair, a small figure curdled up with rage.

'What was your interview like?' I asked. 'Was it anything like *The Rachel Papers?*'

'No, it was very genial. I was terribly nervous—I had my hair slicked back over my ears. It was long then.'

'How long?'

'Semi-hippy length. Over my shoulders. And I had this hideous suit. I had two interviews, the first at St John's with John Carey. He

'Wouldn't you know it looks good? How like it! The one thing that will fuck up everything, the worst thing ever, and it's gorgeous!'
Martin Amis

read out sentences from D. H. Lawrence and asked what the key word was. I didn't seem to pick it. Then one at Exeter College with Jonathan Wordsworth, who was terrifically droll.'

'My house-mates were taught by Wordsworth,' I chipped in. 'They used to call him "The Scrotum".'

'Why?'

'Because his face was all puckered, and creased like one.' Mr Amis seemed disappointed it was just metaphor.

'Maybe it's more puckered now. I always thought he was a very handsome chap.'

'What about his teaching?'

'I got on very well with him. Of course, he is totally without theory about English literature. I now think perhaps I could have done with a bit more theory, because literature was still taught just via a value judgment—you would be sent away to read Keats' *Odes*, and the burden of your essay was how you got on with them, whether you liked them or not.'

'What, just emotional value?' I tried out.

'Yeah, whether you thought they were any good, whether you thought they were too much this or not enough that. I don't really know how fruitful it is to have nineteen-year-olds being snooty about Keats. We were still living a bit in the shadow of Leavis in that we were looking to detect high moral seriousness rather than just learn something about it. I think it should have been weighted more towards knowledge than just to response.'

'So you didn't have any strict literary theory?' This was all getting a bit flash.

'Well, literary theory was considered a different paper really—it was dealt with as a subject, and not something which would inform your view of literature. I mean it would have been terrible to be taught by a deconstructionist or structuralist, but I could have done with some serious thinking about genre, you know—*what is a tragedy?*'

Bottling down a frenzy of panic in my stomach as I thought he expected me to answer, I shrugged, coughed, flicked some ash, fumbled with my nose and said, 'Yeah, but Carey doesn't do all that, does he?' Mr Amis reached for the tobacco on the table between us.

'No, Carey is more of a Leavisite than I think he admits.'

Yea, I thought, if only he knew....

By this time he had lifted a clump of tobacco from the tin, draped it along a Rizla and, apparently using only finger and thumb, conjured up a roll-up. I thought perhaps I should bite the filter off my Silk Cut, gob it into the ashtray and lean forward muttering: Ouch! Christ! Shit! However, the moment passed and I sat back pretending I wasn't

231

wearing a City suit. Lighting up without pause, Mr Amis went on.

'But intelligence is not what you necessarily get from a writer. You're getting a vision of the world which isn't always sane or reasonable or consistent—it's generally more frenetic than that.'

I doubted it could be as frenetic as me gibbering for something intelligent to answer. '. . . Being a good critic,' I slowly began. I had another go. 'Being a good critic wouldn't be much help to a writer, would it?'

'I think so,' said Mr Amis.

'But would it, though?' I asked, head to one side. Of course it would, imbecile! I screeched to myself.

'Of course it would—I think all good writers should be able to do criticism, it's known as "writing left-handed". I'm always very shocked when a writer who I have some respect for starts writing discursive essays and he can't do them, he turns out to be hopeless with concepts. Just as you would expect a surrealist painter to be able to draw a hand or a face. A bit suspect if you're completely at sea with rational writing.'

'I was really thinking,' I said, thinking along the lines of changing the bloody subject, 'thinking along the lines of something Iris Murdoch said, which was how literary criticism has made young writers so self-conscious, that they distrust telling a story, and start telling a story about telling a story.'

'And form and motif and so on,' yawned Mr Amis where I had lurched off. 'We should be aware that we are using literary criticism very loosely, but I think academic literary criticism probably does have a bad effect on writers. It's easy to see this in America, where novels are almost written to be taught—you see all the topic sentences being written into the prose. Yes, that is one way of making literature moribund.'

'What do you think of Iris Murdoch? She hasn't been affected by, you know, all that, has she?'

'She's certainly not modern. Although actually there is a bit of ambiguity about who is the narrator, there are invisible narrators like in *The Philosopher's Pupil*, and she does have ironic narrators and semi-unreliable narrators which are all modernist tricks. But the illusion is very powerful in her writing—that is what it is mainly about: she is a passionate writer. I find that the belief she gives to her characters and situations is almost frightening.'

'I suppose she is probably so. . . .' At this point I think I dropped into a post-structuralist accent to let on that this was something I really knew something about: '*sincere*, because she thinks that people would start distrusting the written word if it all became very self-referential.

People would no longer believe it could actually *describe* anything. Do you see what I mean?'

'Yeah, well … yeah. I don't know. I think it's just the way she writes.'

'Uh-huh,' I agreed with a lugubrious nod, 'I see what you mean.'

We were both beginning to enjoy this. Mr Amis smiled. I had noticed earlier how his teeth were darkly brown like old bananas, or the teeth on some piece of jawbone you come across in a field or wired up in a museum. I wondered if this was from smoking as he folded another squashy cigarette into the ashtray.

'Looking at your writing,' I said, 'it struck me that instead of being as heartless as everyone says, some of it is actually quite soft, quite sentimental.'

'Whereabouts were you thinking of?'

I described the episode in *Money* when John Self picks up a prostitute, and then finds she's pregnant so just talks to her at the bedside—it didn't seem much to do with John Self.

'Oh, but it is—he admits he's talking crap to her. But even then he wonders if he could wangle a hand job out of her, pregnant or not.' Mr Amis wolf-whistled admiringly. 'As he sobers up, he's got the cheek to wonder about a hand job!'

'What about the ending of *The Rachel Papers*? That was quite soft.'

'No.' Mr Amis looked indignant as though I had wrongly accused him of shop-lifting. 'There's no sentimentality there. That's the most vicious ending I've ever written.' He dropped me a hint. 'I mean, I am known as a writer without a drop of sentimentality in him.'

'But after a while I find it quite nicely sentimental when you go back to describing all the puke and phlegm and pus—it's reassuring.'

'Yeah, you do get an odd sentimentality from concentrating on unpleasant aspects of experience. There is a sort of falsifying sentimentality in that, that perhaps I could be accused of, but there's not much puke and phlegm in my stuff. People think there is, but there isn't much.'

'Do you enjoy writing set scenes, like the sort of situations you contrive, more than telling a narrative?'

'I suppose I do. It's nice when a plot works out, but the importance of plot rises as the level of fiction goes down. I thought it was ridiculous when Ian McEwan was accused of plagiarising a plot from Julian Gloag—in serious writing you can't plagiarise a plot. You could only do it from thrillers, because all they are is plot. The nearer you get to *Ulysses* or even Dickens, the plots disappear in importance. Springs to action and motivation are important, but plot, shuffling people around, deceptions, letters, death mysteries—it's so crude! Look at Dickens—his plots are a total wreck. Did you know that the plot of *Little Dorrit* rests on someone leaving money to their nephew's lover's guardian's brother's younger daughter?' Mr Amis flashed me that dry-rot smile. 'Who cares? You can't get, wow! steamed up about that, can you? And that's because the plot takes him so far away from what really interests him, which is writing about London and prisons.'

'The same is rather true of you, isn't it? I found I couldn't understand the story of *Money* at all. I could never see how the story worked, or what Fielding Goodney did.'

'I think I failed to make a point about the fact that it was totally motiveless. Up to a point it had a motive, but then beyond that Fielding was just caught up with it and let it go on. He got too interested in it and wanted to see how it would turn out.'

'You mean, Fielding was. . . .'

'Yeah. There's that moment when John Self is about to walk out of the hotel when he's just had the impossible script handed in. If he had walked out, then Fielding's little conspiracy would have worked. He would have sued the stars for non-completion of contract and he would have made his money from the deal. But he doesn't, and from then on his motivation is totally opaque. We just don't know why he went on with it. But that is in some ways the theme. The theme point is that money is a conspiracy, that it's something we all just go along with. We don't question it because we're hooked—it's an addiction. It's also like fiction in that you just want to go on turning the pages and you never stop and think about it. Most people's lives are devoted to the accumulation of money without any inspection of why this should be the case, or of what money really is.

'So I originally wanted the book to be motiveless, but then I needed some spring, so the first half is triggered by Fielding. The second half is completely motiveless—it is just money which sweeps everybody along.'

What with the 1970s armless black leather armchair, the guitar propped against the wall, and the stereo, Mr Amis' otherwise empty room could have been a film set for *The Rachel Papers*. What was even more pertinent was the scattering of 'casual' books over the coffee table. 'What are these?' I asked. Mr. Amis moved so he could poke them about. His pale, childlike face swam out from the black leather, much as Charles Highway might have staged it as, with a hushed voice and a deadly-nightshade frown blackening his eyes, he threw away some peroxide lines about his everyday reading.

'A mixture . . . I'm doing a piece about darts later on in the year; I've been reading a lot of nuke stuff recently. I'm also looking into a fascinating subject called non-fiction, which is something I've neglected. It turns out to be quite an interesting field, you know.'

'What sort of writing is it?' Mr Amis could have been checking off a shopping list—milk, eggs, bread, loo roll. 'Modern science, astronomy, nuclear physics, that sort of thing—study of man, basically. For instance, I realised I didn't really understand Darwin. It's also a great field for imagery—science has a beautiful conceptual world. Do you remember C. P. Snow's great Cambridge lecture, "The Two Cultures"? He was absolutely right in saying they are potentially one culture, and that the scientific culture is as beautiful as the artistic or literary one. Beautiful in a completely different way and serving different needs, certainly a much more enclosed model of beauty than the great spawning, quintillion literary one.'

I thought of something to say, then thought better of it. This was Mr Amis' set piece, and he delivered it with style: a sort of listless child-Hamlet lying hunched and spastic on the edges of philiosphism.

'You can even guess at the beauty of maths too—even extraordinary subjects like the philosophy of maths, or the philosophy of sub-atomic electro-dynamics.'

'What is the philosophy of sub-atomic electro-dynamics?'

'Well, you know, the most pumping obvious question in sub-atomic spheres is that as you can't watch an experiment without participating in it (because you have to do all sorts of things to be able to see it—least of all shine a light on it), all sorts of uncertainty principles get going.'

'What if you don't look at it?' I smart-asked.

'If you don't look at it, you won't see anything, right? But if you do look at something, you yourself are setting up the answer you're going to get. All sorts of things like that—things that don't happen in the Newtonian world of the usual forces of inertia, friction and gravity. What you are doing is predicting a probability that you, as part of the experiment, will see something—philosophers have a field day with that!'

I tried to echo his cheese-grating laugh over that one. He went on. 'Funnily enough, whilst it seems that right up to Einstein, scientists were very interested in the philosophy of science, now they're not at all: right now, they're just cowboys out on their own. Epistemology is not a part of what they're up to, they're just doing their stuff. In physics they feel they are so close to the tremendous unification, they're so close to physics being over as a science, that they're not waiting for the philosophers to help guide them through.'

'Guide them through to exactly what?'

'The unified field theory, as it's called. There are four forces: the strong force, the weak force, the electro-magnetic force and gravity. They have now unified the electro-magnetic and weak force. The weak force is what makes particles decay, and they've unified it into what they call the "electro-weak force". They think they can now go for one force, that they can make them mathematically all assimilable to each other.'

'Surely it's the philosophers who are doing that?' School circuit-boards, crossed my mind. 'They can't still be doing physical experiments?'

'No, it's not philosophers at all. It's the mathematicians and the physicists.'

'Aren't they just experimenting with the philosophers' theories?'

'Theory is nothing to do with philosophy. Philosophy is just getting it all straight afterwards. You know: "What do we know? How can we know it?" All that sort of thing. But I gather that what will happen when they've got all the four forces together, is that they'll have a model for the beginning of the universe. They will have cracked that, and they'll know in what state all these things can live together. How it was pre-big bang, which will be pretty interesting.'

'What the hell sort of a model could that be?' I said, beginning to feel a bit left out.

'Oh, just a mathematical model. I imagine what the line is, is that the four forces were only separated by the big bang. Anyway,' shrugged Mr Amis, 'we digress.'

'How are you going to use all this in your writing?' This was the 'my-next-novel' question for Mr Amis.

'Well, my next novel will have quite a lot of nuke stuff in it. It's odd, because I always knew I'was going to call it *London Fields*. I've been doing it for a year or so, two years maybe, and only the other day did I realise why it was called *London Fields*—there is actually this place on the outskirts of London called London Fields which is where I would have my characters thinking of and harking back to in contrast with London itself, where the idea of a field and London is now such an impossible notion. Then the other day I realised about fields of all the other kinds—force fields, nuclear force fields, magnetic fields.'

'It's a lovely title.'

'Nice, isn't it?'

'You know,' I said, 'something which struck me about your writing is that in three hundred years' time, I think people might look back to you in the same way as we now look back to, say, Thomas Nashe, as someone who had an extraordinary vocabulary, but who was actually quite limited in terms of locality, and locality of time.'

Mr Amis busied himself with some tobacco before answering.

'That may be true of what I've done so far. But I think there's an attempt in my writing to see the present time in the context of other times, not by expiating it, but some attempt to see what we have reached. Yes, I'm interested in the present, but not the random present. I do deal in things that are very peculiar to our time, but that's probably what all writers think they're doing—trying to get the measure of their time. It's frivolous to try and do this without knowing anything about what came before, or having any sort of spiritual projection of what is to come.'

He blew out a cloud of blue smoke which rose and turned Coca-Cola brown as it passed through the sunlight.

'But . . . I think I'm on to it, you know. I mean, otherwise I wouldn't continue. I think I am saying something about the state of the health of the planet. It's seen only from my limited point of view, but I'm trying to do that. So I don't think it's parochial really, or parochial in time. It may look that way, but I don't think it is.'

'Does your next novel seem very different to you?'

'Not that different, although other people may think so.'

'What about all the nuclear force fields you were mentioning?'

'Ah! This nuke business. . . .' Mr Amis curled up his lips like a Swiss roll. He looked as full of loathing and dread as he had about his Old English paper.

'I think the whole trouble with the nuke business is that nobody has actually seen that we are now at a sort of evolutionary climax. This is absolutely the most testing time for the species that there has ever been. The planet is really unrecognisable now in all sorts of moral and imaginative ways from forty years ago. It is absolutely the failure of people to realise that, that we have gone on living so equably with it.'

'Isn't it because they've realised that, that they've managed not to fire the missiles?'

'They haven't had a crisis in the last twenty years, but does anyone think there isn't going to be a crisis?'

'Did you see *Atomic Café* last week?' I asked. Mr Amis nodded up and down. 'Do you remember the bit when the US Colonel is telling his men that they are going to be stationed close to a test explosion? And he says, "You'll see this mushroom cloud, and you'll think it's the most beautiful thing you've ever seen. . . ." Then of course they all get the most appalling radiation.'

'That is the most amazing thing about nukes, that they are an absolutely beautiful sight.' Mr Amis' voice came as thick as fur. 'An atomic explosion is incredibly beautiful. I mean—wouldn't you know it looks good? How like it! The one thing that will fuck up everything, the worst thing ever, and it's gorgeous!

'But do you remember the pigs on that programme? They were the worst thing. Uurrh! Christ! To see those pigs going up in flames, squealing, was enough reason for the planet to disarm. And then you cut to some guy, some real arsehole idiot, with a picture book showing a pig, a red marker pen in his hand, and he's wondering how to start. Then the camera pans down to show you this pig lying panting in agony with its bottom half just turned to bacon. It was the most appalling thing I've ever seen.'

'I suppose it will be more frightening when lots more people have these bombs, won't it?'

'Well, that's frightening, but even just the superpower possibility is frightening. I know it's the least likely, but I think that to talk in degrees of likelihood when the whole idea of the species is at risk, when all those unborn people are at risk, and all the past is at risk, is absurd. People haven't understood the nature of the risk. To gamble when the stakes are infinity....' Mr Amis threw away the rest of the sentence. 'I don't see how we can go on thinking about them as military things. They are clearly not military items—they are this planet's cyanide pills. Boy! Does that stuff hate our life! There are dozens of ways that stuff hates human beings—you see, apart from the blast, the heat, the shock, the weather, the plants, the food chains, the diseases, you then get nothing but syllogisms, which is that when two bad things happen, usually a third bad thing emerges which they don't know about yet.

'Did you see those shots of salmon eggs that they had exposed to radiation?'

'No,' I said. Mr Amis made a contracting noise in his throat as though gargling Dettol.

'Instead of turning into fish, there was just this pool of shit with the occasional, completely deformed fish with no eyes, or no tail. You've got to understand, Edward, that stuff really doesn't like us. It's very anti-life, that stuff. Everything about it.'

'So what do you think will happen?'

'The next phase is going to be the first superpower deep conflict. It's very hard to imagine how people are going to react to it. Because when there was Cuba, we didn't really know quite how much this stuff had got in for us. *London Fields* is going to be set against a deep crisis— what effects will it have? What effects on just the normal running of a city? Mortal fear is going to be very strange. I think the leaders are going to look very different on television—they are going to look really crazy or ill when they don't stop the first crisis. But if we survive, then people will come out with such wet pants that maybe there will be a new impetus to do something about it.'

Mr Amis shrivelled himself into one side of the chair so that he looked like one of the salmon eggs he had described. 'They have done a rather attractive and gloomy calculation—they worked out mathematically that there should be intelligent life within eighty or one hundred light years of Earth, and the astrophysicists are rather surprised that we've had no contact of any kind with this. Just perhaps radio contact of some kind, which travels at the speed of light, or TV for instance, which is very visible throughout space—you know, *The Two Ronnies* are floating around somewhere in the biosphere. The theory is that there is a cut-off point in the evolution of planets, that they get so far, they invent nuclear bombs, and then they don't make it, they blast themselves back into the Bronze Age. There should be these super-advanced societies emerging all over the universe, but they never get beyond this crux.'

'Well, we have—provisionally.'

'We've gone for forty years with it—not very long. Perhaps nobody survives. Perhaps it's just too tempting having the stuff there. Physicists have imagined this huge model—if you could see all the stars through a wide-eyed camera lens, you would see planets exploding everywhere.'

'Like popcorn?'

'Fireworks,' said Mr Amis with a dead mushroom grin.

'Does that make you more or less religious?' Mr Amis was back deep in the shade of his chair. Only his eyes were clearly visible; they glistened and protruded heavy on his face, lumps of sweet and sour pork.

'I am totally godless,' he said in a voice which said that God was the deadest baby around. 'But I do believe in the human soul, not in its immortality, but in the potentiality of it being there.'

'Wasn't it always there?' Mr Amis thought not. It seemed ordinary people too were just born dead babies:

'I don't think the privilege of being human is automatically dispensed to every citizen in the globe. Not everyone is human. This is amply demonstrated by opening any tabloid newspaper—you see there are a lot of sub-human people around. They just didn't make it; they didn't get to be human.

'I am religious to the extent that I believe in something as vague and as trivial and banal as collective good intention—or collective absence of bad intention.'

'What do you model that on?'

'On literature. If you expose yourself to thousands of tremendous achievements from the human soul and brain and pen, I don't see how you can avoid some notion of continuity and collectivity.' It sounded like the same predicament as the baconised pig. 'I find that sort of exploded nineteenth-century idea of the religion of literature rather gratifying, because what the fuck is the definition of religion anyway? Having some sort of emotional relationship with your creator? I don't go for that at all, although I can see that spiritual struggle is clearly a part of what the planet is engaged in, and not doing terribly well at either.

'You mustn't underestimate the solace of religion—it gives you all these sombre allegories of things working out all right in the end. Don't despair. *We'll fix you up later.*'

'Where do you get your solace from?'

He may not have meant it to come out this way.

'Oh; shit, literature and, you know, family life and all that.'

But I think he probably did.

Charles Sturridge

UNIVERSITY, 1969–72

Anthony Andrews reconstructed this telephone conversation he had with Derek Granger, the producer of *Brideshead Revisited*:

> '*There is a possibility that we may get going again ... we may have found a director.*'
> *I was absolutely convinced that if anybody was going to take it on, they would have to be somebody steeped in experience of production, certainly production of film for television, so I was agog.*
> '*Well, don't keep me in suspense. Who is it?*'
> '*Charles Sturridge.*'
> *The name meant nothing.* '*Who's he?*'
> '*He's a good friend of mine.*'
> *(Pause.)*
> '*I'm thrilled, Derek*' *(thinking he'd finally gone off his rocker).* '*What's he done to recommend him for the job?*' *(The biggest television production ever mounted.)*
> *(Long pause.)*
> '*One or two rather interesting documentaries.*'
> '*Uhhuh.... Good.... Anything else?*'
> '*One or two* Coronation Streets.'
> '*Well, Derek, we both love* Coronation Street, *but is this sufficient?*'
> *I thought Derek had really gone round the bend and I frantically phoned up all my chums asking if they had heard of Charles Sturridge. The only one was Diana Quick, who had known him at Oxford, and liked him too. Filled with horror and thinking that everything was going for a burton, I flew back to London and agreed to meet this Charles Sturridge*

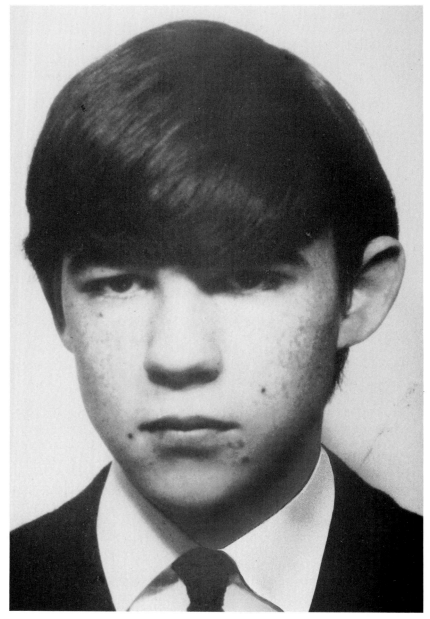

'I would argue very strongly that the opportunity to take an initiative, even a stupid one, is what is valuable about Oxford.'

Charles Sturridge

for lunch at Wheelers, in Old Compton Street. I walked in to see a bottle of Dom Perignon, which showed some style, two glasses, and what appeared to be a somewhat nervous ten-year-old, with scruffy hair and a funny tie, sitting behind them. He looked just like Just William! Charlie has always looked about ten, but on this particular occasion he looked worse. Over lunch, I was beginning to give him a hard time.

'What on earth makes you think that you can bring this book to the screen?'

But when he began to describe his plans, I realised that he not only knew the book inside out, but he had a vision of it which was extremely clear. It was the clearest piece of information of the whole production. What he was saying made absolute visual sense. I could see it, I could understand it and I was terribly impressed by it.

For all my talk about Sebastian Flyte, I could never have had the inspiration or the facility to portray him without the help of one Charles Sturridge. It was his overall conception, without doubt, which made Brideshead Revisited *the success that it became.*

Diana Quick put in another piece of the jigsaw.

'During the strike, he used to visit me in Manchester and sit around saying, "I should be directing this. I am the best person to do it, why don't they give it to me?" Perched on my make-up table, looking about eight years old!

'It is scary to have your wildest dream suddenly come true. A couple of weeks later, Charlie found himself directing Laurence Olivier.'

Perched up in an armchair, having dished out vodka and cigarettes, Charles Sturridge, still looking fresh from prep school, gave his own version of what it was like being in the right place at the right time.

'There is no doubt that, had I been put up as a candidate in normal life, nobody would have taken the chance. The fact that there was no director never emerged until the Thursday the strike stopped. Suddenly, they had twenty-four hours to find one. I got a phone call on Friday afternoon and saw all the rushes, from the make-up tests to the final shooting, on Saturday. Derek met me in a Manchester hotel on Sunday, where we walked up and down the corridors and discussed some ideas. It was November 1979 and time was very, very short. Derek rang up at midnight, and asked me if I would do it. In the way when one thinks incredibly fast in those bizarre moments, I thought I should be brave. We started shooting nine days later.'

The wildest dreams of the *Coronation Street* director had landed plumb in his lap. Only twenty-eight, he was directing the most ambitious film production in the history of television. The beginning of the story goes back to Oxford, when Mr Sturridge first found the opportunity to realise his potential.

'At school, I had been taught to think that my life would be operated by various influences out of my control. When I got to Oxford, I found I was barely manoeuvred at all. To begin with, that makes you very passive, but then you begin to find out that something will only work if you manufacture it yourself.

'It is very difficult not to get some advantage from having three years to enjoy doing what you want with your time without a great deal of risk. Quite what you decide to do is entirely up to you, but in my case I wanted to work in theatre, and the ability to do play after play after play was extremely useful. Until Oxford, I had led a financially precarious life, so to be able to lead a life of financial safety was very welcome. I could stage a completely insane production of *Henry V* and not be stung for it.'

Mr Sturridge half-stubbed out his cigarette, leaving it broken and smoking in the ashtray, and reached for another.

'I'll tell you another genuinely remarkable thing about Oxford—you have an enormous pool of people you can draw on. You can do what the National Theatre does, which is pull on an extraordinary and varied selection of people to help you, which gives you a huge amount of power and potential ability.

'So if you have the capability, you can do anything. Because I was interested in theatre, I did little else apart from act or direct. It actually doesn't matter what you choose—it can be work, sex, alcohol or drugs! What is important is that you are undergoing this peculiar, formative period of your life where you can do what you like with very little risk. You can operate over a safety net.'

'You mentioned drugs—were there a lot of drugs around in Oxford during the late Sixties and early Seventies?'

'We were on the edge of the more obvious aspects of student radicalism. It was that rather murky tail-end of the hippies, and there was a large amount of people who took them very seriously.'

'Did you?'

'I was a much less serious drug-taker than a lot of my contemporaries because I was rehearsing and working all the time. I took drugs in a much less passionate way than other people—if you are obsessive about one thing, you are less obsessive about something else. For working, any kind of drug is a complete waste of time.'

'What about your academic work?'

Mr Sturridge blew a large and contemptuous cloud of smoke towards the ceiling.

'Academic work? I found I was never really asked to use my own mind in academic work. We were just supposed to cover a wide spectrum of other people's opinions and present them in an articulate précis.'

'So your theatre work was different?'

'Yes. In the theatre, you are using your mind in a much more inventive, powerful, useful, interesting way, because you are being asked to rivet an audience's attention, and it could be onto some old, familiar, flabby drama, but you have to do it or they won't come. In academic work, your tutorials are all lined up, and you just go along and collate then regurgitate these historical or fashionable opinions about a series of works.

'The only essay I got an alpha for was when I wrote a long piece on the yet unpublished *Jumpers*. I quoted extensively and built a long thesis around the play, feeling quite confident that nobody else would have read it, so nobody could check up that what I was saying was true!'

'There's quite a lot of pressure at the moment,' I said, 'on universities to justify their grants—don't you think there should be some sort of stricter supervision on undergraduates to ensure they're not wasting their money? You mentioned sex, alcohol and drugs....'

'No, I don't think the way the University is run should try to lead to some maximisation of the tax-payers' investment in the undergraduate—if that is what you're asking. If you want education to be a paid-for process to provide the correct amount of qualified workers, that is a capitalist ideal and is like saying that the point of making a film is to create the best possible return on the money invested.

'I would argue that in those three years, you should be free to do anything you want. That is the value of the education. There is the risk that you might use that opportunity to drink yourself stupid, but none the less I would be very suspicious of any regulation which stopped you drinking, for example.

'When I was at Oxford, the people I thought were completely misusing their opportunity were those who saw their goals as solely what the University saw them as—the kind of people who recreated their school existence and worked steadily for a good Second. I would argue very strongly that the opportunity to take an initiative, even a stupid initiative, is what is valuable about Oxford. I would advocate that the academic influence should be completely arbitrary.

'I admired that very unvigorous attitude to supervision which Oxford has, because it allowed me to breathe—to think, to experiment, to do productions all the time. The way I work hasn't changed—I still do productions all the time!'

'What about Oxford and *Brideshead Revisited*—how did they overlap?'

'If you want to talk about Oxford and *Brideshead* it is quite interesting. A lot of rubbish was talked about what *Brideshead* said about Oxford—firstly people think that three quarters of the book is set in Oxford, when in fact they leave Oxford on page sixty of a three hundred and thirty-page book. Almost anybody will be surprised by that.

'What Waugh writes about are three or four things—he writes about the depression of someone arriving in a society and clinging to his obscure half-friend from school and a mad relation. In other words someone whose only social protection is the flotsam and jetsam he happens to have ended up with. He then goes through his first summer term, which is incredibly short but everyone remembers it, when for the first time he finds friends. That lasts for about fifteen pages. Then, after that first summer, he falls into a period of depression, of immediate loss of all these friends and a drunken existence of the most charmless type.

'I think it is the most detailedly accurate account of life at Oxford which has ever been written. One of the odd effects of the book is that people remember it like memory, not as they actually read it. What they imagine is that the book is largely about Oxford luncheon parties; they tend to forget that there is a ship in the book.'

Mr Sturridge looked across to the two racks of video cassettes labelled *Brideshead Revisited*, and the dimensions of his inspiration impressed me again, just as they had Anthony Andrews.

'What the book deals with is love, God: love for a man, love for a woman, love for a God. There are few more archetypal emotional human feelings or pivots. The whole of life could be there. To argue that it is a social joke on rich, pretty people enjoying Oxford in the Twenties is to succumb to the sort of journalistic prejudice which surrounds the book.'

'Diana Quick told me that you felt you were the best person to direct it—why did you feel that particularly about *Brideshead*?'

'You use yourself in everything. Bits of yourself are dragged out at different times, but when it came to *Brideshead*, I felt I knew the areas Waugh was talking about: I had been educated a Catholic, I had been to Oxford, I had come from a large family, so I understood family machinations, and I recognised that things like Sebastian's comment—"I'm not going to have you get mixed up with my family. They're so madly charming. If they once got hold of you with their charm, they'd make you *their* friend not mine, and I wouldn't let them"—was an absolutely accurate remark and emotional response.

From those bits I could correlate, I felt I could trust the other bits I didn't know so much about like the Army.'

He offered me another cigarette and hopped over the arm of the chair to find some more vodka. From the other end of the high-ceilinged room of his flat off the Brompton Road, his voice came with surprising authority from the impish figure who might well have been refused drinks at a pub.

'There is a curious sympathy now for a number of books, of which *Brideshead* is the most interesting, which were written about 1942. At that point in England, there was a genuine sense that the European War had been lost, that it was the end of the world and that the world would never be the same again. It looked certain that Hitler was going to win the war.

'It seems to me that *Brideshead* is in a sense rather like a suicide note written by somebody who then wakes up the next morning and is rather embarrassed to find it is still on his desk. He has written all these things out which he assumed would only be read after he had gone into a different world. But the world didn't change that much, he didn't die, and so he is rather shy of some of the things he wrote and the ways he expressed them.

'I think there is a close connection between the world of Evelyn Waugh when he wrote *Brideshead*, and our world now. Both verge on nihilistic depression. *Brideshead* is a book about sentiment and memory, about looking back with fondness. In times of confusion and fear, people prefer to go back to the simple old myths like *Brideshead* or like winning a race in *Chariots of Fire*.'

'Then what about the actual directing of it? How did you feel about directing people like Laurence Olivier?'

'Well, the business about awe and nemesis is that you have it the night before, and I didn't sleep because I was terrified that everybody would laugh at me, and you still have it the minute before, but the minute you actually start work, it isn't an issue. You just get stuck in and concentrate on directing actors.'

'But what about Laurence Olivier—did you just bracket him as another actor?'

'I was obviously aware of his history, and in his case it is, arguably, the history of the theatre of this century, but it is like asking a journalist, "Aren't you nervous of asking Mrs Thatcher a question?" If you didn't do it, you wouldn't be a journalist. You shouldn't be cowed into obsequiousness. If you don't direct, you're not a director.'

Diana Quick had been there too: 'Charlie was petrified by the idea of directing Olivier. How could he not be? But Olivier was wonderful, he was so kind and he smoothed his path so much that, day by day through those first five days, Charlie's confidence soared. They had a very, very good working relationship. They rather fell in love with each other over that deathbed! Olivier was quite frail (he was taking strong medicine which slightly wiped him out), and we had to spend a lot of time sitting around the bed, but they made each take mesmeric. It was incredibly moving.'

Mr Sturridge remembered the first week of directing Olivier. 'There were two particularly extraordinary things about Olivier.

'One is that physically and technically he is the most fantastic instrument. If you have an idea, his physical ability to translate it is huge. One tiny example was the death of Marchmain. There is the scene where he is lying in bed, and he does this speech about ancestry: "Aunt Julia knew the tombs, cross-legged knight and doubleted earl, marquis like a Roman senator, limestone, alabaster, and Italian marble. . . ."

'It is a very curious speech. Waugh is an extraordinary prose-writer, and this is an unusual piece of English prose—very dense, very like verse. As it happens, it has a Shakespearean rhythm to it.

'I didn't know how to do it! Was it a conversation? Was it verse? It is not pentameters, but it has an extraordinary rhythm to it. Waugh is writing what could loosely be called "drama", using words which physically reverberate.

'It was the end of a long day which had started at dawn, and before we shot it, I asked him just to do it, because that might help. Olivier was lying on the bed, and was very, very tired. At the end of a day of filming, the set is chaotic—nothing stops the march of people packing up and wrapping up to go to supper. The other actors were hanging around, not sure if they were needed, but not sure if they could go, so they came and sat on the edge of the bed to get out of the way of the film crew coiling up cables, and to try to hear what he was saying. Eventually, the cable-coiling got slower and quieter, and people vaguely began to realise that something remarkable was happening. Miraculously, everybody stood stiller and stiller, and this incredible scene took place when Olivier did his speech and he did it almost in-audibly, so we had to strain to catch it.

'When we recorded it, the sound operator discovered that Olivier's voice has, at a whisper, a range of an octave and a half. Most people's voices go completely flat.

'The point is that I could never have been as magically inspired as that. His translation of my basic idea of him lying on the bed enriched the speech a hundredfold. Not surprisingly, that was how it was eventually done. What you have got is an unbelievably rich technical performance. It is crude to talk about it like that, but practical.

'If you have an idea, [Olivier's] physical ability to translate it is huge.'
Charles Sturridge

'The other thing which we found we had in common, was our interest in verse. The basis of his thinking has concerned Shakespearean verse, and we both share the obsession that people never actually listen to verse. The problem with verse is that audiences react to it as music and let it drift over them without ever fixing on it as argument. "To be, or not to be" rolls over their heads and is treated as melody, not as sense.

'To some extent, Olivier's historic contribution to drama has been his extraordinary ability to find an unlikely stress to a sentence. He takes not a stupid, but a surprising word on which to hit the emphasis of the line. This jolts the audience out of their trance—they have to listen to the line to comprehend it. We were both curious about the idea of the actor's job of communication, of making people listen. He had to tackle these quite long speeches, so we were concerned with trying to work out a way of how to do a monologue on television which people would actually listen to.'

Mr Sturridge concluded with a simple epitaph.

'One cannot compare his talent in a quantifiable way with others. He doesn't fit easily into any kind of equation. After all the work you do, the treat that you have finally got is that he is the history of the twentieth-century theatre.'

The adaptation of *Brideshead Revisited* broke new ground in television productions by refusing to compromise the book into the traditionally glib terms of the media. Anthony Andrews had isolated that as a vital aspect:

'It created television history, in that we found the facility to actually photograph a novel in all its detail. It was the first time that a novel had been put on the screen in its entirety, and we all knew that that commitment was unique. Everything gets bastardised, type-scripted, compromised in some way, but this didn't.'

Mr Sturridge went back to the text.

'The whole subject of the text is a long, complicated story. We learnt how to translate it as we went along. The main thing which became incredibly clear was that the urge to logicalise, to tighten, to merge, to crystallise—to make this dinner party contain this line, or add this scene to that, was misguided. The more we tried to make it logically coherent, the less sense it made. It became a banal story about a boy who became a drunk. Although it was quite frightening to do it that way, it would absolutely not work any other way.

'People are never amazed after something has been done, but I would say with little fear of contradiction, that if we had presented to someone what we finally ended up with right at the beginning and said, "This is what we are doing. There will be eleven episodes taking up twelve hours..." they would have said, "Get lost!"'

Mr Sturridge explained why most other television adaptations make such sorry viewing. 'If you look at Dickens, who is the most adapted novelist, the mistake is so unerringly simple that you wonder why it happens time and again. Where they go wrong is that they pull out the only thing which is interesting in Dickens—which is Dickens, and leave you with some vaguely melodramatic plot which has nothing in it of what you read Dickens for. They take out all that frightening savage sense of outrage and passion, and they don't understand that you cannot take all the power out of the work and then just photograph the people going through the doors and expect it to be the same thing.

'The thing about *Brideshead* was that if you didn't try and do it for what it was, it wouldn't be anything else. You couldn't make it into a neat television package.'

Mr Sturridge paused to light another cigarette. The light in the room had dulled to a smoky grey, and when he struck the match his leprechaun's face shone orange and black in the flare. I remembered something Derek Granger had told me about the making of *Brideshead*.

'I was very reluctant to have so much voice-over. I thought it was a distortion, and I felt it was pasting together the bits, so I wanted it severely edited, but Charles said, "No, no. You're wrong. I will prove to you that you are absolutely wrong. If you edit Ryder's voice, it will seem intrusive, but if you saturate the picture with it, it will become part of the whole. People will not only get used to it, but they will feel that they have to have it." And he went in and proved it. He created this very powerful and moving device.'

Mr Sturridge showed me some of the photographs of the production. All around stood the huge sets of the interior of Castle Howard or the QE2, with actors as recognisable as Jeremy Irons, John Gielgud, Anthony Andrews, Claire Bloom and of course Laurence Olivier all listening to the small scruffy figure in the centre who was holding a script and a cigarette and commanding their absolute attention.

'*Brideshead* is always difficult to make generalisations about,' Mr Sturridge said. 'It was, if you like, not a little an act of bravado to do it that way.'

I got back to Oxford late that evening. When I stopped off to pick up my mail at college, the college library lights were still on. I peered in to see a handful of people forlornly bent over their books.

An hour previously I had left Mr Sturridge, who had been saying, 'Most people in the world are unbelievably stupid—they will, given half a chance, let institutions dictate their whole way of living to them.'

I felt like crashing into the library, shaking people by the scruffs of their necks and saying, 'Wake up! Let's see more *bravado*!'

Instead, of course, I remembered my unfinished essay for tomorrow and slunk away to regurgitate the Casebook series of essays on Jane Austen.

Tina Brown

ST ANNE'S, 1971–75

I flew to New York the day after I had seen Martin Amis. He had shown me out, saying, 'I once thought of living in New York, but absolutely not now.'

'Why not?'

'It's too money-mad. You get these horrible identifications like money and health which I think destroy the morale of a nation. It's a great place to hang around if you're single, but going there with my wife and tiny child, we found it terrifically inimical. It was just disaster everywhere.'

I had taken a few steps down the stairs, when his door opened again. He leant over the banisters.

'New York—it's okay. Yeah, it's all right!'

New York was anything but all right. For starters, the size of it was just Brobdingnagian beyond belief. The Cadillac which took me downtown seemed to have about six or eight doors armed with black reflector windows like some modern single-storey office block. In fact, I noticed, it was just like all the other cars in the jam. Then of course there was the Lego skyline with the Empire State Building lined with orange and red lights like a Rocket ice lolly, but it was just doing normal things, like going into a supermarket, when everything got badly out of hand. All I wanted was something munchy and a pint of milk, but as I reeled around the shelves loaded with trunk-sized packets of Persil, eight-packs of loo-roll, dustbins of biscuits, I realised that was not the game. The smallest carton of milk packed half a gallon, so I eventually staggered off with that and a rucksack of crisps over my shoulder.

I left that night to spend the weekend in East Hampton on Long Island, which was where I photographed Dudley Moore. When I told him about this problem of size, he agreed. 'I can't understand it—the cars, the pizzas, even the ice-creams: and then look at me! When are they going to do something about *me*?'

Back to New York to see Tina Brown, the editor of *Vanity Fair* magazine who had just announced that she was expecting a baby. Walking up Fifth Avenue, I realised there was a sort of underworld life going on around me. It is all to do with the two cents refunded on each can. The first one almost knocked me over—tall, black, on roller skates, wired up with headphones and a large sack over one shoulder, I watched him Torville and Dean his way through the crowd backwards, sideways, forwards, swoop to a litter bin and top up his sack. Running across from Madison came the next one—a white-haired tramp with a yellow bandana head band, pushing a supermarket trolley and picking the cans out of each bin as though shopping in a fearful rush. The 'Walk' sign flashed, and he darted off across the street at a diagonal, disappearing behind a burst of steam from one of the metal caps over the subway. It could have been a production of *King Lear*. I turned into the Condé Nast building.

'What did you most enjoy reading at Oxford?' Tina Brown sat alert, beaky and sleek as a news reader or a penguin. She blinked out the answer as quick and sure as morse code.

'Jane Austen, George Eliot. I enjoyed the Victorian novelists the best, because my tutor, Mrs Bednarowska, made me understand how modern they were in their themes, and I don't think I would have ever taken that time and attention necessary to really get into them if she hadn't shown me how. In fact, I have just written a piece for *Vanity Fair* about the Princess of Wales, and I found myself drawing on *Middlemarch*.'

'Which character?' I asked, guessing obviously not Dorothea; Celia, perhaps.

'Rosamond Vincy, the blonde with the swan's neck. She always gets her own way.'

'And at the end is pictured as a basil plant,' I added.

'I don't know what she becomes at the end, but she gives Dr Lydgate a very bad time.'

'Yes—he says she's a basil plant, and when she asks him what that is, he answers, "A plant which lives off dead men's brains!"' Miss Brown's clearasol eyes widened, as though she had made some awful mistake reading the news.

'Good God! Well, yes, I had forgotten that line. It's wonderful! Well, certainly—the very same Princess Di!'

She went back to the script.

'And I felt as I wrote it how strange it is that what you learn at Oxford, the books you study, just become indelibly part of your whole sensibility. They crop up time and again—much more so than any of the books I have read since.'

'What sort of social life did you lead?' My eyes wandered to the framed front covers of *Vanity Fair* on the wall behind her. One of them pictured Ronald and Nancy Reagan waltzing. 'Was it all very Zuleika Dobson?'

'That would have been pretty difficult in my room at St Anne's, which was like a kind of Bauhaus telephone box—horrible! The whole college was like a multi-storey car park! Well, I suppose my first year was rather *Horse and Hound* in that I had been to this up-market tutorial which flung me in with all the Hooray Henrys. In my second year, I managed to shed all these freaks, and mixed with actors and writers, which was low-key but amusing.'

'... And a hat, a big straw hat.'

Tina Brown

'How did you dress?'

'Oh God! Annabelinda! I had these "principal boy" shirts made at Annabelinda which were my great extravagance. When I think about it, I feel full of horror. They had large bell-shaped sleeves like that' (she indicated a scoop on her arm) 'very long, and I wore them over trousers ... and a hat, a big straw hat. A total cliché!'

It didn't sound as though she had been as porcelain then as she now seemed with her polka-dot navy blue dress, pearls and pale nail varnish. I noticed her white tights and wondered whether they might in fact be stockings. Rounding off this idle scrutiny with her shoes, I was surprised to see how the tops of her big and second toe, plumped up by the shoe, formed a small cleavage.

'Did you have any particular boyfriend?'

'Well, I suppose there were Simon and Stephen who I used to go everywhere with.' Miss Brown smiled. 'I could never decide between them. Simon was the artistic, writing, frothy, acting one, and Stephen was the sort of Anthony Powell type, dark and thoughtful. He had a sports car and lots of money, and Simon was always broke. So Stephen and Simon and I all went around together—punting, *crème de volaille* at the Elizabeth and dinner outside Oxford at places like Minster Lovell.'

'Did you have any funny adventures?'

'Me?'

'Yes.'

'Simon had all the adventures. I don't think I had any by myself— that's terribly boring isn't it?'

I told her about Auberon Waugh's vomit-on-the-ceiling story— nothing like that?

'No, I'm sorry. I don't have any vomit stories. If you're interested, I was the lead in a pantomime called *Retropilgrim's Progress*. I was Retropilgrim and wore satin boxer shorts and fishnet tights.'

This was a bit more like it. 'Was that fun?'

'No! It was terrible. The whole thing was ruined for me when the John Evelyn column, which was the Nigel Dempster column of the University paper, came and wrote a satirical piece about my thighs.'

'Who could be satirical about them?' I flourished, Sir Walter Raleigh. She brushed this aside.

'Well, he was, which was the end of it as far as I was concerned. I spent the rest of my time creeping around the stage trying to hide them!'

I went back to something she'd said earlier about the books she'd studied becoming part of her sensibility. Thinking of the angry beehive of New York life outside, I asked in what way she felt they helped her in the context of New York.

'Just by being an influence on my mind. My whole outlook and sensibilities are formed by those writers, they live on with me; and when I feel I need support, I turn back to those writers that I studied at

Oxford. Funnily enough, the other thing is that I now enjoy a lot of writers who I didn't like then. I didn't enjoy the Augustan stuff like Dryden, Pope and Swift, but now, living in New York, I find I keep thinking about them.'

'Why?'

'I suppose because they are so tremendously English, and when I am homesick, I think of those very English things. To my amazement, I found myself buying the complete works of Pope, which I have been reading all through the summer and getting an enormous amount out of it—I felt such an affinity with something which is all about English values, English houses.'

'I've never read much Pope,' I said, 'but I suppose I've always taken his Englishness for granted.'

'But it suddenly seemed to have a relevance here which I hadn't felt before. America is a society so much in flux, it is so much money in motion, that when Pope writes about Augustan values, solidity, traditions and the meaning of heritage in his satirical way (which is so unlike the world I'm living in now), he suddenly seems understandable. Does that make any sense or not?'

'Yes, it does. But you must read modern American novelists too, you can't hide from . . .'

'Yes, I read them all the time now. I wish I'd done an American literature course, because I miss not having the grounding that I have in English literature, I don't have so many reference points, but I am getting a pretty good idea of what is being written at the moment.'

'Do you incorporate that into *Vanity Fair*?'

'Yes, I try to. Whenever I read a good novel, I try and get them to write an article. I've just commissioned a guy called Bret Easton Ellis, who's twenty-two, and has written a novel called *Less Than Zero*. I sent him to LA to hang out with rising movie stars, and he's done a fabulous piece.'

'Have you thought of writing stories?'

'Have I? Myself? Well, I have, but I think that I am first and foremost a non-fiction writer. I've tried plays, but not fiction. I don't know whether I have the courage to try.'

'What were your plays like?'

'Very good dialogue, actually. I have a good idea of dialogue, and the structure is something you get better at as you go along.'

'Were they like anyone else's?'

'They were very influenced by T. S. Eliot's plays—*The Cocktail Party* and all that. They were quite funny, sharp, social satires.'

'What would you want to write about New York?'

'I'm saving that up for my book!'

'How have you found living here?' I told her about all the freaks I had seen, about going into a night club where everyone was dressed in Star Wars bright and glittered costume, epaulettes, hair and collars rising like fins. 'It looked like an aquarium of tropical fish,' I said, 'it was so bizarre.'

'New York is a bizarre place. I can tell you, it really is strange! God! When I arrived, I didn't even have anywhere to live. But it was enormously exciting, because one thing about America is that they really back you up in terms of giving you a machine to function—they gave me everything I needed to make a success of it—it was just up to me whether I could or not.'

'So tell me what it was like arriving here.' Miss Brown smoothed her skirt and smiled, pearls and dimes.

'I felt so beleaguered at the beginning that I stopped going out. I couldn't cope with going out to dinner and have all these people aggress me. New York is such an aggressive place, and people would come up to me the whole time, stab me in the chest with their horny finger and tell me what I should be doing, why what I was doing wouldn't work, and who was I anyway? This Brit who didn't know anything about America. It was all pretty hideous. You see, when I came here, the magazine was down the tube, it had bombed out, and nobody believed it could resurrect itself. And America, particularly New York, has this Broadway philosophy of success—you either get it right immediately and you're a success, or you're ignored and you're a flop. There is nothing in between, and nothing else counts. And don't expect to have any respect for being a creditable failure because they won't give it to you—you'll be invisible. You see, they don't like the concept of working on something to make it a success, so they were very rude and gave me a lot of flak.'

It didn't seem to have been anything Miss Brown couldn't handle. She sat there as composed as the Princess of Wales, with those large blue eyes which come from short-sight, her blonde hair tossed like a salad and her hands calmly on her lap. 'What else would you like to write about New York? What else is being saved for your book?' Miss Brown's answer could have come from the sharp end of one of her plays.

'Well, I find the snobberies of New York very funny. Everything is about money, and about status, and about label—what are you *doing*? Just watching the turn-around in the way people treat me now that the magazine is a success is very funny—they fawn around me because they think it's working!'

She lifted up another New York stone and poked about underneath. 'I'm also very amused at how English taste has taken over New

York. Everywhere I go, it's all chintz, fake library veneers and people pretending to be the Duke of Beaufort. The whole interior design boom is English, which I find quite funny because that is what I left behind me.'

'After *Tatler*, you must be something of an expert at it.'

'Exactly! I thought *Tatler* would be the last I would see of it. I fled from it, and the last thing I wanted to do was find that every house in New York was done up as some kind of phoney stately home.'

Her impression of New York was so different from Martin Amis' that I asked her if she had read *Money*.

'Yes.'

'Did you like it?'

'No, I didn't actually. I thought it was unrealistic.'

'In what way?'

'Well, I thought it revealed his lack of having lived in New York. It was totally inauthentic, and it rather irritated me as a result. I mean, he should have spent more than three or four days in New York to think he was able to write about it.'

'But it wasn't so much about New York itself, was it, wasn't it more to do with John Self in New York?' Miss Brown had no time for this sort of inside-out argument.

'I think he has done that trick too many times. Well, it was okay. Yes, it was *all right*, but I think there are much better American novels being written.'

'Let's move to what you are doing with *Vanity Fair*,' I said, and we dropped Martin Amis like a piece of fall-out. 'Have you just superimposed the *Tatler* formula onto the magazine?'

'It has a lot in common with *Tatler*, but the problems are completely different. You see, for starters everything in England is so cosy and identifiable and familiar. There are class codes, class speech, class education—there is a secure audience. If you are doing something like *Private Eye*, you know you're talking to a group who all understand the jokes. In America, everything is much more eclectic—everything is so enormous that it's impossible to get a handle on it in the way you can in England. You have to come up with a formula which is more communicable.

'You also can't make it as insular in outlook, because the fact is that people in Washington aren't interested in the people in California, and people in Chicago won't be interested in what's happening in Texas, whereas everybody in England is interested to know what's happening in London. I had to find a common denominator which wasn't as narrow as social understanding.'

'What did you come up with?'

'Well, it's a flashy, modern magazine, if you like, of culture and style in which I try to mix up the literary with the popular. Have you seen this issue?'

She pushed over a copy of *Vanity Fair* with Dustin Hoffman sitting on the cover looking flashy and modern.

'I've got a big piece about the American writer Paul Golds, and then there's a piece about a crazy socialite called Princess TNT of Bavaria. It's a question of juxtaposing the serious with the frivolous, which is something the Americans have been nervous about.'

'Why's that?'

'Because they are much more intellectually insecure than the English. They tend to think that if something is serious, it has to be only in serious company—otherwise it can't be serious. What I've been doing is to explain to them that this is not the case.'

'And having the scope of the whole of America to exploit must be quite something.'

'It's fabulous. There are all these places to draw on. I haven't even run the really big Miami pieces yet, and there's so much going on there. I've just appointed a Texas editor, I have a Dallas correspondent, one in Chicago. I think that being English is an advantage, because I retain a certain romance about America that a lot of New Yorkers don't have. New Yorkers are very provincial—they only ever think that New York is interesting. I scream at my staff and say to them, "What about Texas? What about Florida? What about the South? New York is *not* the only place where things happen."'

'Then there is the other English advantage, which is the fact that the English sense of humour is much more sophisticated. Intellectually we are much more ready to take risks than the Americans.'

'If you ally those two things with American money and marketing, you get a pretty strong combination.'

Miss Brown gave the merry laugh of a cash till ringing up. 'I think it is anyway!'

The potential success of *Vanity Fair* had had a pretty good run for its money, and I turned to my last topic, headed 'Harold Evans'. 'I read *Good Times Bad Times* on the plane,' I said. 'What did you think of it?'

'What did I think of it? Well, I think it's a brilliant book. What do you think of it?'

'I don't think he should have written it—he should have kicked Murdoch out.' Miss Brown looked at me as though I had said something incredibly intelligent.

'Well, of course that would have been a very good thing to have done, but I think rather unrealistic. He did make that point in the book—why he didn't do it. When you are trying to edit a paper and the management want you to leave, there is a death by a million small things every day. You can't continue.

'More important, he *would* have been able to continue had it not been for Charlie Douglas-Home. Harry could have fobbed off Murdoch if Douglas-Home had been solid. What he couldn't do was fight off Murdoch with his own deputy editor being Murdoch's tool.'

We argued backwards and forwards over this for a while, with me saying it was crying over spilt milk, and her saying there was nothing he could have done, he was the meat in the sandwich; until I eventually concluded: 'Well, it was such a wretched pity considering it was *The Times*.' Miss Brown, crab-like, nipped in the last word.

'It was tragic. I mean—if only Harry had fired Douglas-Home straight away. That was his big mistake. We all make mistakes. I can tell you, I fired all the people on this staff as soon as I arrived.'

'Why did you do that?'

'Because they were people who couldn't do the job. The magazine was a disaster. My brief was to save the magazine, and I couldn't muck around. I was keenly aware of what my husband had been through, and how you have to have a very loyal staff. You can't achieve any kind of creative success unless you have people on your side who respect you and support you. You want to be able to concentrate on being creative, you don't want to worry about office parties and who's scheming with who. That's a total bore.'

'How much do you and your husband influence each other's approach to journalism?'

'He influences me more than I influence him, I think. He's taught me an enormous amount about photographs and layout. I've adopted all his principles of design. He believes in strong layouts, white space, something which looks clean and legible, and he's really hammered that home to me.'

'What about your family—you won't mind bringing up your children in America?'

'No, not at all, because we have a house which we bought on Long Island which is by the sea. Do you know it there?'

'I know East Hampton.'

'It's very near there, near West Hampton. The American summer is one of the nicest rituals I have found in my life here. I just love it. Every weekend, we go to our lovely old shingled house on the beach, it's like the Riviera. I've always wanted to live on the seaside, but in England the houses on the sea are awful and the weather's terrible.'

'Will you bring up your children in New York?'

'I wouldn't hesitate to have a child in New York—if you've got a place to go to at the weekends, it's fine. When it gets to the age of ten, I

'The mouse that roared.'
　　　　　　Tina Brown describing the Princess of Wales

might start to think ... you know, New York can be a bit frightening.'

'Will you educate it in America or England?'

'I've decided it would be nice to have a mixed education—the best of both. It would be nice to go to school in America and then university in England, something like that.'

I could see that at least one person in New York was going to have a well laid-out, clean, legible future, whilst the rest of the city was left to get on with its own life.

I left the hair-conditioned coolness of Miss Brown's office where money and health sat blooming around the mother-to-be. On the other side of Madison Avenue, a beggar stood in the middle of the pavement. The passing crowd widely side-stepped him, allowing me a clear view—sunglasses, a billboard and a billy-can silently held out by the stumps where his arms stopped short. Next to him, the crowd had found something more interesting. I crossed over and jostled in to see what it was. Another beggar had a blanket spread out in front of him, covered with battery-operated, wriggling plastic hands. 'C'mon New York!' he was shouting. 'Check it out! Check it out!'

William Boyd

ST HILDA'S, 1980–83

'They're called loss adjusters. They say, "It'll take years to grind through the courts and get the money—why not settle for cash now? Waive the £2 million, sign here and get £500 grand today." I'm told a lot of them are ex-servicemen. They're called loss adjusters because they adjust the loss in favour of the insurance company.

'Anyway, I just thought it was such a good title: "The Loss Adjusters." It's so wonderfully grim and black. Eerie.'

'It's funny,' I said, 'all your titles are somehow off the wall—they always intrigue me.'

'Well, I take a lot of trouble over them, and work very hard trying to get them. Often when I hear a good title, I write it down and hope that one day a story will come along to fit it.'

'That's like writing pop songs to videos!'

'That's right! But no, I mean it took me ages to find the title for *Stars and Bars*. I'd almost finished it before I finally came up with what I think is the perfect title.'

'I couldn't work out why it had worked so well.'

'I think quite simply because it rhymes! There aren't many rhyming titles, in fact I can't think of any others. Also it sounds like stars and stripes, stars in your eyes, stars and sky, there are lots of resonances. People think of the stars in the sky that the prisoner seeks to see through the bars of his cage, which makes for a nice weighty metaphor about the human condition, or of dreams and ideals—you know, it's anything.'

William Boyd toyed with it once more. '*Stars and Bars*—I was really pleased with it. It's got that funny ring to it; not many novel titles have that jingle.'

'What was the original title?'

'Appalling! I was going to call it "Twenty-Two Roads", or "Road to Luxora Beach", "Life in Luxora Beach". Terrible, terrible titles! It was the same with *An Ice Cream War*. It was originally called "Betrayals" and umpteen other titles until I came across the phrase and I knew *An Ice Cream War* was absolutely bang on.'

Stars and Bars had just come out in paperback, and William Boyd and David Puttnam were working on the film script when I saw him. For all the runaway bestseller success surrounding him, Mr Boyd was as relaxed as if giving a tutorial. He told me how the film was getting on.

'Henderson is the real problem because he's the star and he's going to be on screen for 99 percent of the time. He's got to be ace in order for the film to work. If he's not quite right or funny enough, the whole thing will fall flat. It may collapse anyway—we're having a fight with Warner Brothers about the actor.'

'Who do they want?'

'None of the obvious choices are acceptable to us, i.e. Hollywood choices like Michael Caine, Dudley Moore, Jeremy Irons....'

'Wouldn't Dudley Moore be good?'

'He's too small! I also think he's very mannered and sort of odd. And we don't want it to be a "Dudley Moore film", we want to find somebody like an English Dustin Hoffman as he was discovered in *The Graduate*.'

'It would be good, though,' I persisted, 'if Dudley Moore played Henderson, and you made sure he played him straight—not as Dudley Moore. I think he's better than his films.'

'And he does make me laugh, Dudley Moore, that's true. But I think he's changed since he became a star. You know, he has to have it off with at least one actress, and there has to be a drunk scene.'

'But there is that wonderful drunk scene at Gage's dinner party' ... Mr Boyd wasn't going to let a Dudley Moore foot get in the door.

'That's not in the script any more! We don't have Henderson getting smashed in the same way. Anyway, we have a big audition tomorrow, so we might know our fate then.'

We moved back from tomorrow's meeting, back from *Stars and Bars*, right back to his childhood in Africa, and his education. Mr Boyd went out to find a bottle of wine, and the interview began in earnest. 'What sort of life did you lead in Africa?' I asked.

'It was a very pleasant colonial existence. I lived on university campuses most of the time, which are vast, forty square miles to cycle around in, big bungalows, the social life centred around the staff club with the swimming pool, tennis courts, bars. When I was on holiday I just seemed to go to parties and barbecues the whole time. Although life was sometimes a bit difficult with the Biafran War and military coups, it didn't impinge on the holiday spirit I always associated with life out there. As a callow, unreflecting youth, I really enjoyed it—it may have been harder for my parents, but to be a teenager there was great.'

'Did they feel comfortable?'

'They grew to like it less as they grew older and times got more diffi-cult. Things began to bother them—they found it hard to take their money out, lots of goods were hard to come by, you know, spare parts for cars, basic things like tomato sauce—mayonnaise became impossible!'

'What about you?'

'I never thought about it then. I was very uncurious, and I just accepted the experiences as part of my home. I was last there in 1974, and it was only then that I saw it with some sort of objectivity.

'But as a child, I accepted everything—even during the Biafran War, when the place was swarming with armed troops and you were constantly being searched and stopped at road blocks and guns being pointed at you, it didn't unsettle me in the way it would now. The minibus I used to go into town in would be stopped, we'd be ordered out and searched. I was usually the only white boy there. I remember one military coup, when masked students with guns flagged us down and ordered us off the bus. We were herded off for a while and searched and then they let us back on again. I felt no sense of danger at all—it just seemed part of the delightfully bizarre side of living in Africa, and your journey being interrupted was just one of the minor irritations.

'I also remember standing with my father at the bottom of the garden when there was a full-scale riot going on at the university. We could hear guns firing and saw tear gas drifting through the trees at the bottom of the garden. A lot of the rioting in *Good Man in Africa* comes from that experience. And my father, who was a doctor, had to get in his car and drive through the rioting to get to his clinic which was full of students with their heads broken by the riot police. He didn't seem worried by it.'

'Did you feel at home there?'

'No, I don't have any sense of my roots being there. I just recognise that for twenty-one years that was my home, and since then home has been various other places.'

I told him how my upbringing had been deeply rooted in Shrop-shire, which was something important I would never lose.

'I don't have that feeling. You see, I knew I was a white man in a black African country, and so obviously just in transit there. Actually I'm a Scot; both my parents are from Fife, and my mother has a house near Peebles in the Borders. I love that part of Scotland and I have a vague sentimental attachment to it, but even there I don't have what you described. I feel as at home in London as I did in Oxford, as in Nice or West Africa. I'm wary about making anything grandiloquent or grandiose about a sense of exile or rootlessness, but there isn't anywhere that I think: Come sixty-five, this is where I'll go back to to touch base with.'

I said that I found Scotland a strange place—completely foreign from England.

'Oh, it is, it's strange in lots of ways. Scotland reminds me of Chekhov's Russia—it's got this strong sense of identity. There is also the same sort of decaying genteel class as the Russian landowners, melancholic, drinking too much.'

Typically Mr Boyd's imagination had rumbled Scotland as a potential idea. 'I'm getting increasingly interested in it as a phenomenon. Did you know it's the only country in the world to voluntarily surrender its independence? Which it flogged to the English.'

'How do you mean?'

'The aristocrats flogged the country to the English for a great deal of money and some titles—that's how the Act of Union came about. England simply bought Scotland lock, stock and barrel.'

'Was that James VI of Scotland selling out to become King of England?'

'I'm not absolutely sure of my details, but it's a fact that the Scottish aristocrats, who were the powers that be, sold their claim to independence to the Court of England for a sum of something like £700,000. There was a price tag on Scotland. Actually I don't think it was James—who was the king before James?'

'Elizabeth was Queen before James I.'

'Maybe it was after James. I'm not absolutely sure—but it is a fact that money changed hands.'

'And you were educated in Scotland,' I said. 'I've read some of what you've written about school—what was Glasgow University like?'

'I enjoyed it immensely. Glasgow is a big, vibrant, warm-hearted place. It was very good for me just to live in a city for the first time, where there are ordinary people going about their business, and you're not a special case, you weren't segregated on a campus.'

'What was the teaching like?'

'Oh, very liberal compared with Oxford. We had a take-home paper for our Finals. Our Shakespeare paper, for example, we had three days to do it so we could look up everything and turn in a fantastic-ally polished essay, but there was a limit of, say, two thousand words.'

'What sort of things were you saying about Shakespeare?' Mr Boyd may have been faintly embarrassed. He shuffled his hair around a bit.

'I remember being particularly pleased with my essay on *King Lear*. What I did was to actually count the number of times "nature" and "nurture" appear in the text, and I produced this with a flourish at the end of my essay to make some wonderful point about how to interpret the play!' He laughed as he flourished: 'That the play balances on the poles of nature versus nurture. . . .'

'And let's hear it for Nature,' I yelled, 'who wins by 300 versus 270!'

'Yes,' Mr Boyd rounded off. 'A truly great metaphor sequence!'

'What sort of critic were you?'

'I became a sort of old-fashioned New Critic, if you know what I mean. I was a close reader, very much concerned with the nuts and bolts of the text, the mechanics of it. How you can take some prose and strip it down like an engine and put it back together so you can see how it actually works. I was a critic in the mould of I. A. Richards and Empson. I actually think that everything that they thought has just been mimicked by structuralism and post-structuralism, and dressed up in jargon.

'I taught for five years at Oxford, and I only realised in the last three that in order to prepare undergraduates for their Finals, I had to make sure they knew how to recognise a question which was to do with modernism, post-structuralism, deconstructionism or any other of those isms.'

'I don't think I ever really latched on to those.'

'It's really simple once you penetrate the fog of pretension and jargon. They're simple ideas that can be traced back to I. A. Richards and the Russian formalists of the early twentieth century, which was where he got it all from. Once you've realised that, you can carve your way through Derrida and see that he is actually making a very banal point. It's a dead end.'

'What exactly is the point?'

'It's all to do with the subjective versus the objective. Can you make literary criticism a science? And if you do, what are the criteria you use? It's an attempt to make literary criticism, which had hitherto always been thought of as a matter of taste and evaluation, something precise. But the only way you can make it precise is by saying that everything is completely imprecise and that one reading is as good as another. This is where a philosophical background is useful, because you see similar kinds of exercises have been tried out in philosophy in the eighteenth century, and they led to dead ends. You realise that nobody actually reads books like that.'

'What was happening in eighteenth-century philosophy?' I realised about Mr Boyd that I instinctively felt comfortable asking him all the sorts of questions I should have known the answers to. And he was generous enough to give me serious answers.

'Well, the debate was started by philosophers like Hume and Locke, who were trying to find out, you know: "Does that table exist? What are we?" Questions of personal identity. Hume ended up saying that there's no way you can prove cause and effect, so therefore you can't know or be sure of anything. The fact that the sun has risen the last few millennia doesn't prove that it will necessarily rise tomorrow. You don't know when you bite into an apple that it won't taste of roast beef—it might do!

'Somebody asked Hume, "How do you live day to day?" And he said, "I only think like that in my study. When I go outside, I'm a naïve realist like everybody else. I know that you exist, that the world exists and that the world of solid objects exists."'

Mr Boyd showed me the knuckle of his argument.

'And I think the same thing has happened with literary theory—that it is, as it were, trapped in Hume's study. Although there is no way you can defeat those post-structuralist arguments, because they do have a kind of logical consistency, the fact is that nobody ever reads a book like that apart from academics. When we read books we do bring into it all our tastes and prejudices, and we do evaluate and judge them.'

'And your writing, more so than most of your generation, stands out by not being afraid to tell a story.' I mentioned Anthony Powell and Iris Murdoch, traditional story tellers.

'I think that's true. Having studied and taught literary theory, I have no interest in writing a post-modernist work. It seems to me to be completely futile and self-regarding and navel-gazing. It's the Hume's study paradox again—there is a world of readers out there, common readers, and they're the people you should be interested in. I very much agree with what Iris Murdoch has written about it, about litera- ture and truth. People do look for and find truths in novels. We all know it's just one man's invention, but people want to be seduced by books, they want to pretend it's real—therefore it seems silly to me to keep reminding people that it's not real, that it's just a text invented by some guy living in Fulham. Everybody who opens a book is aware of that, but they want to imagine it's about a real world and they will judge it as if it were.

'There are other delights to be got from literature as well, I mean, purely aesthetic, to do with style: the book as a work of art. One of my favourite writers is Nabokov, who is the least realistic writer, so I'm not a zealot about realism, it's just that I don't see it as a profitable road for me to go down. There is a tremendous basic human urge to have a story told, and it's one which I struggle to fulfil: "What happened next?" You know: "Once upon a time...." Story-telling is such a basic thing.

'I hope my novels are as sophisticated as any novel in terms of construction, in terms of consistency of their point of view, and buried within them are all sorts of ideas and metaphors and image sequences, but essentially I want to tell a story about these people, and I want you, the reader, to believe that they actually exist. I want you to suspend your disbelief and enter into the book. And all successful story-telling, whether it's theatre, or television or film, if it's popular in the best sense of the word, meaning that people get pleasure and education from it, is successful precisely because of that.'

'But even though you said that, a lot of what interests me in your writing is not to do with plot—it's to do with everything else which gives it context.'

'I suppose the plot is the spine and I put a lot of flesh on to do with characters and humour, but the first thing I have to satisfy is what happens. Once that is clear, once there is a drive to read on, it can be as rambling as I feel.

'I think novelists are divided into stylists and story-tellers. A lot of the writers I like are stylists like Nabokov and Martin Amis, but style isn't the prime element in my writing which draws people to read it.'

'Why do you think people do read you?'

'I think it is ... they may read it because of the humour, or the diversity or the difference, or it's the tale which provides the satisfaction.'

'Well, it seems to me a lot of your language is as rich as Martin Amis'.'

'I'm pleased to hear you say that, because it's something I work on and I think it gets better with each novel. But my style isn't, to use a modish literary term, as fore-grounded—it doesn't leap out and grab your attention in the way Nabokov's or J. G. Ballard's does. Their styles are so potent that it's almost all you need—it's intoxicating.

'Ballard's plots are completely unimportant, they're just an excuse for his style to take flight which it does in sustained passages of quite astonishing idiosyncracy and virtuosty. Then you get somebody like Graham Greene who is almost entirely plot. His style is deadpan, there are very few flourishes, sparing use of simile and metaphor. But it doesn't matter, that's fine—the house of fiction has many windows!

But this is where you get to another division within the novel—the idea that either the novel is just the document of the individual, or it tells you what it's like to be living at any one time.'

'But all too often the lazy tutor hasn't read enough, isn't quite sure if he's right, can't quite remember that quote and you've won. You've lived a little dangerously, but you've won.'

William Boyd

'Tell me about that.'

'Well,' began Mr Boyd, 'if you want to understand the history of the human race, then the place to look for it is in the novel. The novel of the story-teller is a sort of repository of truths and aspirations of the times of the author. But a stylist is somebody who's more interested in creating a work of art, an aesthetic object like a Fabergé egg which is beautiful to look at, and you admire and appreciate but from a completely different point of view—not because it can sharpen your pencil, or tells you something about what it was like to be alive in nineteenth-century Russia. It's a division in art which is going to exist for a long time.'

Up to this point, the tutorial, as it so seemed, had rambled along fairly broad-brush lines. It now focused on the more specific as I asked Mr Boyd about his Oxford thesis, which he had written about Shelley.

'More specifically, it was on the intellectual background to Shelley's prose and verse. It was three quarters written, I had done the interesting bits, and I was meant to get down to the solid scholarship of collating texts and diligently getting a bibliography in shape. That's when I knew I wasn't a scholar.'

'It sounds completely exhausting.'

'It is. The last six months of writing a thesis are basically clerking and it's absolutely as boring as hell. It has to be meticulous at Oxford, and you get referred if there are too many errors; you know, they write, "Mr Boyd, We found seven errors in your first transcribed passages. May we suggest you go back and check all your transcriptions?" Slightly pedantic.'

'Who are these people? Are they great teachers themselves or literary boffins?'

'They are the experts in that field. If you're writing a thesis on Shelley, the person who is examining you will probably have written two or three books, have edited Shelley and generally know a hell of a lot about him. And then as my thesis was quite broad and dealt with a lot of philosophers like Kant and Plato, I might have had an examiner who was a philosopher, who might have said, "I'm sorry, but your reading of Kant is completely wrong, mate." And so I would have to rework all that.'

'How does all that philosophy fit into Shelley?'

'Shelley read a hell of a lot of philosophy, possibly second only to Coleridge in the scope and scale of his reading. He was very influenced by what he read, and one can trace the influences in his verse and his prose, but people who have attempted to do so have usually got it lamentably wrong.'

'Perhaps I have Shelley all wrong, too,' I said. 'I'd imagined that he was a wishy-washy lyricist.'

'Not at all. You see, what happened was that he was reinstated by the Victorians after his death. They delighted in him as a writer of dreamy love songs and wistful landscapes. Not a bit of it—he was very left-wing, vegetarian, political. "Ode to the West Wind" is a political tract. That image of him in an open-necked shirt with long hair is absurd. He was a pamphleteer, into Home Rule for Ireland, took up all the trendy causes. He married a girl of sixteen who later committed suicide in the Serpentine. He went to Italy with Godwin's daughter, Mary, whom he married and who wrote *Frankenstein*. It's an amazing life story.'

'What about you? Do you write poetry?'

'I wrote some very bad poetry when I was at university, but that only lasted three months.'

'Poetry now seems so fragmented and difficult.'

'Again, I think it's an acquired taste. You've got to persevere, and the rewards from it are completely different from reading a novel. It's all to do with a delight in language. The trouble with poetry now is that it is all so tributary. If you think how Tennyson and Byron sold tens of thousands of copies—the only serious poet who has done that since was Betjeman. Look at popular poets now: Pam Ayres! My God, what a terrible state it's in.'

'What about issues, then?' I asked, wondering if Mr Boyd would confess that his next book was vegetarian propaganda.

'No, I'm not interested in preaching or engaging myself politically. Martin Amis put it very succinctly when he said, "Anyone can write a committed novel. Commitment flows as hugely as the sea." That is absolutely true—we're all against racism, famine or nuclear war; it's much better to write as good a novel as you can. I don't want to write a campaigning novel about the appalling state of housing like Dickens, but there is no doubt that there is a point of view in my books which is politically left of centre—most novelists are on the side of the unlucky and the unfortunate. I think it would be very hard to write a good fascist novel.'

I asked Mr Boyd about his time as a teacher at Oxford and his view of that generation of undergraduates. How brilliant were they? How much had they impressed him? His answer was typically blunt.

'I've taught at a good half-dozen Oxford colleges, and the fact of the matter is that most undergraduates are pretty average. They are not passionately interested in their subject—only one or two argue the toss about anything. As a teacher, most of the time you're just correcting or commenting on dutiful, worthy, Beta-standard essays. When I went there, I thought everybody would be as fired up about things as I was, but it wasn't true. There are a lot of very average undergraduates at Oxford.'

'How were the few above-average ones different?'

'They were much more interesting, because you had to have done your homework as well in order to be able to argue wth them. One of the people I taught was very very clever. I mean, you keep hearing that phrase bandied around, but I think I've only met one person I would consider very very clever in the sense of intelligence—you know, darting around and picking on things. We had two great terms sparring away and she ended up getting a First, which I had seen coming all along.'

'What were you sparring over?'

'She was clever enough to try and bluff her way through you. She would use her intelligence as a kind of goad and be deliberately provocative or deliberately abstruse and thereby be testing and challenging her tutor. You see, she had already bested a couple of tutors who didn't want to teach her because they knew she thought they were useless, and so her attitude to me was: "Okay, you claim you can be my tutor and cleverer than me—let's see how good you really are." And so I had to pick up the gauntlet which she threw down. It was far and away the most stimulating teaching of my career as a college lecturer.'

'How did this challenge to you manifest itself?' I said, beginning to get drawn into the story.

'She would say to me, "I'm going to write an essay in an hour—give me the most difficult title you can." So I would think up a real, real bastard title, and she would go away to the college library, come back in an hour and there would be her essay. You know, sometimes they were terrible and she was lying and trying to hoodwink, but then you only knew that after you had engaged her intelligence with your own and called her bluff.'

Mr Boyd moved to a tangent from this highly charged tutor/pupil relationship. 'But getting Alphas is just a game anyway. If you know the rules of it, you can get an Alpha any time you want, which is the key to passing exams—nothing to do with your fervour or your love for literature. And not many undergraduates crack it. If you've cracked it yourself, you can then see somebody else who's cracked it, who knows how to write an essay that looks like they're incredibly clever and know a hell of a lot, and you have to give them an Alpha for it—even if you recognise the bluff! Academic life is, on the whole, bluff and double bluff, and one bluffer can recognise another and they'll both have Firsts whereas the worthy, intense student who says, "But I love Keats! But I love Shelley!" will only get a Beta.'

'What's the trick?' I asked (thinking of my younger brother, sitting Oxbridge that term).

'The trick is just a kind of fluency—there is an essay technique you can learn which is to do with, put simply, quotation, reference and a kind of sophistication which can be sometimes a bit shocking. It is like writing a story—the first line has got to be really punchy, and that first paragraph has got to get that bored tutor sitting up in his seat saying, "Hang on a minute," but by then you have slammed in these references, and sometimes the more obscure the better. And you must have an argument. Your essay must have a swing to it, be provocative—hence the nurture/nature count-up, it should be something of a *coup de théâtre*. Sometimes people are too clever for their own good, and if you're a little bit cleverer than them, you can catch them out.' Mr Boyd suddenly turned gamekeeper and accused the imaginary student: '"But have you read *The Brothers Karamazov*?" And then, ha ha! the bluffer has been caught out in his bluff and it's a fair cop. But all too often the lazy tutor hasn't read enough, isn't quite sure if he's right, can't quite remember that quote and you've won. You've lived a little dangerously, but you've won.'